SEVEN SECONDS

THE GABRIEL WOLFE THRILLERS
BOOK 14

ANDY MASLEN

TYTON PRESS

For Jo

It is not good for man to be alone.
Genesis 2:18

1

ESSEX

Corporal John Richards woke, as he always did, at 5:59 a.m.

His wife rolled over and flung out a hand, catching his in a sleep-weakened grip.

'Morn',' she mumbled.

'Morning, gorgeous,' he said with a smile, bending to kiss her. She smelled warm and sexy. 'See you later.' He was due on duty at MOD Rothford at 7:00 a.m., guarding the gate.

She rubbed at her nose, smiled and then rolled over. She was snoring quietly as he went for his shower. Ten minutes later, exactly, he dressed in his uniform and went downstairs to put some toast on and make tea.

He glanced out the kitchen window, to see whether anybody was about on Gladstone Road. Sometimes he saw their neighbour, Roy, a large man with a small dog. Roy's bearing suggested he found the contrast embarrassing, as if he'd been spotted wearing high heels and a skirt in the centre of the village.

Of Roy, there was no sign. But John frowned anyway. Someone had parked a big black car right outside his house, blocking his drive. He pulled the net curtain aside for a better look.

This was no ordinary car. It was a Camaro. One of the new ones. A jacked bodybuilder among the weedy family saloons and hatchbacks that populated the rest of the street. Captain Wolfe had one. It was a standing joke between them whenever he or that gorgeous Israeli fiancée of his, Eli, dropped in at the base.

If you ever need someone to look after it for you while you're away, just let me know. You can drop the keys through my letterbox!

Haha!

Captain Wolfe would smile and say, 'Maybe next time.' Or Eli would wink at him and say, 'Why, John, fancy giving me a ride?'

And John would blush, pleasurably, as she grinned at him before gunning the huge V8 engine and rattling the muscle car's fat black tyres over the traffic restrictors.

Of course, that was *before*.

Before some nutjob terrorist had blown the admin block to shit with a truck bomb.

Before another member of his gang – or the same one, for all John knew – carried out a hit on Colonel Webster.

Before the outfit Colonel Webster ran – whatever it was (they all had ideas, but as no word, not even a mouse-fart, ever escaped, it was all speculation) – was shut down. Orders from on high.

He'd seen neither of them since. Didn't really expect to. That was the way with Special Ops types. For a moment, though, he wondered whether Captain Wolfe had come to say hello. Bit bloody early in the morning, though. John peered at the side windows. Blacked-out. Illegal. He rolled his eyes. Yeah, because *that* would be a problem. But he couldn't see whether anyone was sitting behind the wheel.

Shrugging, and realising it was more likely to have been joyriders, he went to the front door, intending to take a look inside the Camaro. One way or another he needed it moved or he wasn't going to be able to get to work.

A white padded envelope lay on the doormat. John flashed on a course they'd all undertaken on the risks of IEDs and chemical/biological weapons in the post. Uprated security in the wake of the attack a year earlier.

'Nah,' he said to himself. 'Who'd go to the trouble of sending anthrax to a bloody corporal?'

He bent and prodded the envelope. It was lumpy. Not deadly white powder then. Maybe Sarah had ordered something online. But their regular delivery guy never appeared before seven at the earliest. He picked it up and turned it over.

He frowned. No address label with a QR code. Just his name.

John Richards.

And a slightly smeared image stamped in black ink.

A wolf's head.

He took the envelope back to the kitchen and slit the non-opening end with a boning knife from the block. Spread the sides apart with two fingers and peered inside.

With a growing sense of puzzlement, mixed with excitement, he upended the envelope and tipped the contents into the palm of his left hand. The black plastic key fob had the usual white symbols: lock, unlock, bootlid, plus a red speaker with jagged red lines. He flipped it over. A gold cross: the Chevrolet logo.

Possessed of a sudden insight, his heartrate speeding up like he'd just mainlined a quad espresso, he aimed it at the car through the kitchen window and depressed the open padlock icon. The indicators flashed orange. He pressed the closed padlock. Another flash.

He reached into the envelope and pulled out the sheet of paper that had enclosed the key. Opened it out and started to read the handwritten letter.

Dear John,

You always admired 'the Beast'.

She's been in storage since I bought the Jag. That's not fair on her, or you.

I'm leaving, and I want you to have her. Before you protest (not that I am there to hear it), I have already transferred the ownership to you. You should be getting the new V5 in the next couple of weeks. The rest of the documentation and the other keys are in the glovebox.

I hope she brings you pleasure.

One request. She has a name: Lucille. It was given to her by a friend. Please keep it.

Yours,

Gabriel Wolfe

He read it a second time. Nothing changed. More for form's sake than out of any genuine belief he was still asleep, he slapped himself. Hard. He was still standing at the kitchen counter. The key was still in his hand. The car – *his* car – was still outside.

The toaster and the kettle switched off simultaneously with a double clack, making him jump. Ignoring both, he went outside, blipped the fob a third time and pulled open the driver's door.

After lowering himself into the fatly padded seat, he inhaled deeply, drawing in the rich smell of leather, underlaid with a delicious tang of petrol. Or was that just his imagination? Didn't matter. Smiling, he reached across and lifted the catch on the glovebox. Inside, just as the letter promised, lay a black leather folder that, when he checked, contained the service handbook and half a dozen documents, plus two more keys.

As he sat there, caressing the perforated leather steering wheel, he wondered about that phrase in Captain Wolfe's letter.

I am leaving.

Leaving for where? And who just gave away a superb sportscar like that? They nodded hello to each other. Swapped a bit of banter. But that was all. Hardly the basis for a gift like this.

He shook his head.

'Not my problem, is it?' he said aloud in the empty cabin, then patted the steering wheel. 'Well, Lucille, this could be the start of a beautiful friendship.'

He twisted the key in the ignition and grinned as the

deliriously loud engine roared into life, shattering the peace on Gladstone Road.

2

ALDEBURGH

Suicide notes were harder to write than Gabriel Wolfe had imagined.

The ex-Para, SAS member and government assassin stared at the sheet of pale-blue notepaper through his tears.

The ache in his heart was a constant physical presence. There right up to the moment he fell into an alcohol-induced sleep around midnight, maybe later. At 3:00 a.m. when he invariably woke up from a nightmare. And waiting for him as soon as his eyes clicked open at 5:00 a.m. every day.

His life had reduced to a single word. A condition that demarcated the line between living and dying.

If.

If Eli had survived the gunshot wound to her stomach...

If his lengthy delusion that he'd saved her life on Scalpay had been reality...

If he'd chosen a different career...

Then she'd be alive. They'd still be married. And their unborn child would be growing in Eli's womb.

It was time to end it all. To disappear.

He picked up his fountain pen. A gift from his father. Swirling sea-blue lacquer and gold. His name minutely engraved on the shining band around the fattest part of the barrel.

And he began to write.

I always wondered what sort of a father I'd make. Meeting and then falling in love with Eli, I began to imagine a future for myself – for us – where I would be permitted to find out.

Marrying her was the happiest day of my life. Yet even as we strove to enjoy that simple series of small events together, evil people were plotting our destruction.

We tried our best to ignore them. We travelled to Israel, Eli's birthplace, and still her homeland, for a blessing. It was there, in the Judaean Hills, that she first revealed to me that we were going to be parents. It was also there that our enemies launched their first attack, killing my friend, mentor and commander.

Neither was our honeymoon sacrosanct. They kidnapped Eli and took her to an island, where, in the fullness of time, they murdered her and attempted to murder me, also.

Now I have nothing. I have lost the woman with whom I imagined I would spend the rest of my life. I have lost the child who would have given new meaning to those years we would have spent together.

Life has ceased to hold any value to me, or any purpose. I always saw myself as a man of honour. Yet what has my honour bought me, but pain, sadness and loss?

There was a time when I would have taken this loss as the launchpad for yet another mission. I would have pursued the guilty parties to the ends of the Earth. Hunted them down and killed them.

But what good would that do? Would it bring Eli back to me? Restore her, in all her glorious, life-giving, fierce, argumentative, beautiful spirit? Or would it merely result in more spilled blood?

So, like the Roman general of old who has fought and lost one too many battles, I have decided to leave this life at a time, and in a manner of, my own choosing.

To my remaining friends, and my sister, I can only say I am sorry for the grief I will cause you by this final action.

Goodbye.

Gabriel Wolfe

When he was done, he folded the sheet of paper neatly into three. Stropped the creases with the back of his fingernail until they were as sharp as blades. He inserted it into a mismatched envelope and propped it against a small white vase containing a fresh bunch of yellow freesias. They were Eli's favourite flowers, their honeyed fragrance bringing more tears to his reddened eyes.

That task ticked off on his mental checklist, he hefted two 20kg bags of ammonium nitrate fertilizer onto the kitchen table, keeping them well away from the vase. He'd picked them up cheap. The farmer he'd bought them from was moving to Spain. He'd sold up to one of the agri-combines flexing their financial muscle across the Suffolk landscape.

The diesel fuel oil – a really quite *substantial* quantity of diesel fuel oil – was already aboard *Lin*. He'd inherited the boat from his father, who'd named it for his wife. Ironic, really. Given they'd both died aboard her.

The previous week, he'd bought the few other parts he needed right here in town. That was the wonderful thing about IEDs. They were improvised. A battery here, some bell wire there. A half-dozen parts scavenged from innocuous household appliances, and bingo!

He looked around him. So many little traces of her remained. The bunches of dried herbs tied with string that hung near the cooker. The jars of fragrant spice mixes she loved to cook with: za'atar, ras el hanout, hawaij. A strip of photo-booth pictures stuck to the fridge beneath an Israeli flag magnet. The two of them crammed in together, pulling faces – tongues poked out, eyes crossed – like lovestruck teenagers.

9

He shook his head. The curse of the Wolfe family had struck again. Hamas couldn't manage it. German neo-Nazis couldn't manage it. Corrupt multinationals hadn't managed it. Evil regimes from Latin America to the Middle East hadn't managed it. Terrorists, gangsters and mercenaries hadn't managed it. But where the national, corporate and individual death-dealers had all failed, he, Gabriel Wolfe, had succeeded.

Eli Schochat, who'd survived rocket attacks on her neighbourhood as a child. Who'd served tours of duty with the IDF, Kidon and Mossad. Completed missions for the Department without so much as a scratch. This amazing, combat-hardened, beautiful woman had not survived marriage to him.

It was time he was gone.

3

Two hours after finishing his note, Gabriel was motoring out from Aldeburgh beach into deeper waters. The sun was warm on his skin. A cool breeze, hardly more than a whisper, was swinging around from east to north-east and back again. Not really much good for sailing. But then, sailing wasn't what he'd come out here to do.

Behind him, the boatyard owner raised a hand in farewell. Gabriel waved back. Then he turned the boat, keeping the petrol-blue waters of the North Sea to starboard, and opened up the throttle.

He motored south for a couple of minutes until he had a good view of the Brudenell Hotel. On sunny May mornings like this one, tourists and residents enjoyed breakfast on the hotel's sea-facing terrace beneath a blue-and-white striped awning. He and Eli had done the same, many times, smiling at each other over coffee and croissants, simply and uncomplicatedly in love.

Two blonde children, a boy and a girl, were playing on the beach in matching purple sun suits. They'd found a patch of sand among the stones but paused in their digging to wave at him, spades held aloft like swords. He waved back. Though he didn't smile at them.

Eli had been pregnant when she died. She—

He shook his head violently. No. Not died. When she'd been *murdered*.

He'd imagined a future where his only activity on a given day might be scrambling about on the pebbles with his son or daughter. Teaching them to sail. Eli and he living on the money he'd salted away, rather than the proceeds of state-sanctioned assassinations.

The mercs who'd murdered Eli had murdered their baby, too. It was too much to bear. He blinked away tears.

He hoped John would enjoy the Camaro. It really was too big for English country roads, but that was his problem now.

Gabriel had found a good home for the Jaguar, too. His friend, an artist named Bev Watchett, had protested volubly as he pressed the keys into her paint-spattered palm. But he'd said, 'where I'm going, a car won't be much good to me'.

Bev had looked him in the eye, hawk-like and said, 'You're not going to do anything silly, are you, Gabriel?'

And he'd forced himself to laugh and said, 'If you count moving abroad for work, then yes. Otherwise, I wish you'd stop looking this gift horse in the mouth and just take the bloody keys!'

He hove to directly in front of the Brudenell. He felt bad about spoiling everyone's breakfast, but he didn't want his final act to go unwitnessed. He set the timer.

With seven seconds to go, he leaned back, took a deep breath and closed his eyes.

4

Kit and Molly Sherborne smiled at each other. They'd decided to call this holiday – their first since the lockdown – their honeymoon. Married for five years, and with four-year-old twins, they'd never got round to having a proper holiday after their wedding day. Then the pandemic had put everyone's lives on hold.

Sophie and James were playing happily on the beach while their parents enjoyed their hotel breakfast on the terrace. The sun was bright, giving the North Sea the kind of sparkle they'd always associated with the Mediterranean.

Molly put her cutlery down and pointed at the children.

'Look, Kit, they're waving at the guy on the boat. It looks so cute, like one of those paintings we saw in that gallery. Get a picture.'

Smiling, Kit raised his iPhone and squared up the shot. The children, spades upraised, in the foreground, the yacht in the middle-ground with white clouds on the horizon. Beautiful. He tapped to bring the lens flare effect into play. Transparent purple, yellow and pink hexagons lanced diagonally across the composition.

Perhaps sensing what their father was doing, the two children turned in unison towards the camera. He'd always found it slightly uncanny, the way they seemed to be two halves of one person. As babies, they'd often start crying at exactly the same moment. Or, if one was poorly, the other would start fussing.

'Hi, Daddy,' they shrieked out, two high-pitched voices turned into one.

Kit frowned as his perfect image vanished before his eyes. But the kids looked so happy, he decided to shoot a video instead. He looked down to reset the camera and raised it up a second time.

The boat exploded.

In that single, terrifying moment, Kit's overstressed brain couldn't process what was happening. A blinding white flash followed by a rolling fireball. The crack-boom reached his ears a split-second later. As the phone fell from his hand, he was up on his feet and heading towards the wooden plank barrier separating the terrace from the beach.

The fireball boiled up and out, changing from rose pink to brick-red. The boat itself had been completely obliterated, blackened shards of the hull and superstructure flailing outward in a ragged sphere away from the point of detonation. Narrow plumes of black smoke starred the sky like the spines of a sea urchin.

The children were screaming, paralysed, faces masks of naked terror. He vaulted the barrier, unaware of his wife just seconds behind.

A second explosion threw even more debris upwards, but it was smaller than the first and Kit even had time to think *fuel tank* as he reached his children and scooped them, weeping, into his arms.

Burning metal, wood and plastic rained back down into the sea, splashing like gannets diving onto a shoal of surface-feeding fish.

Beside Kit, Molly grabbed Sophie from him and together they ran back to the hotel. Ahead of them, the other guests were watching, mouths agape or holding phones up to capture the scene. An older woman wearing paint-spattered overalls was weeping.

'Christ!' Kit said as he slumped into a chair, James weeping inconsolably in his lap. 'What the fuck just happened?'

It was a mark of the shock the entire family was suffering from that neither Molly nor the two children pulled a face and admonished Daddy for 'naughty words'.

On the surface of the water, a few patches of oil burned, emitting sinuous tendrils of charcoal-grey smoke. The pall thrown up by the blast was already coming apart, drifting ashore, bringing with it a sickening stench of burnt plastic and an evil, greasy smell that would haunt Kit's dreams for weeks to come.

'Oh God, the sailor,' Molly said, clapping her hand to her mouth. 'Do you think he's all right?'

Kit looked at her. But what he saw was the dark-haired man on the boat, his hand raised in an answering wave to the children's, seconds before his boat turned into a fireball with him at the centre of the destruction.

'Is he, Daddy?' James and Sophie asked in a single, trembling voice. 'Is the sailor man all right?'

What could he say? Kit wasn't experienced in these things. He didn't know about explosives or boats, or emergency medicine for that matter. He worked for a firm of accountants in Cambridge. But he had a shrewd idea of what might happen to a human being sitting on a boat that blew up like someone had put a bomb on board.

He tried to smile and had to stop when he felt his lower jaw start to wobble.

'I'm sure he was fine, kids,' he said, staring into his wife's red-rimmed eyes and pleading wordlessly for her to support him.

'Yes,' she said, in a voice hardly less steady than Kit's. 'I'm sure the sailor man's fine. Now.' She inhaled sharply. 'Who wants an ice cream?'

It was too early for ice cream. They all knew it.

In the police investigation that followed, Kit's video became one of the central pieces of evidence. Enlarged, enhanced, colour-balanced, manipulated along dozens of parameters by digital forensics officers, 'the Sherborne video', as it became known on social media, led directly to the Suffolk coroner's eventual verdict: accidental death.

Owing to the explosion having occurred on the water, it was impossible to examine the wreckage forensically. The pieces of debris, which, from the video, appeared to have had a maximum size of no more than ten or twenty centimetres, had been swept out to sea on the outgoing tide. The explosion's chemical signature was therefore impossible to determine.

Demolition experts consulted by the detective leading the investigation couldn't give her a definitive answer. It might have been any one of several explosives, from C4 to ANFO – ammonium nitrate/fuel oil.

Nothing remained of the man onboard at all. Divers were sent down to scour the sea bed but bobbed to the surface shaking their heads, like disappointed seals.

'What were you expecting?' the detective's bagman asked as they stood, hands in pockets, on the beach. 'You saw the video. He would have been vaporised.'

'I know,' she said with a sigh. 'I just thought maybe one of the larger bones would have turned up.'

He shrugged. 'Even if by some miracle he did just come apart in chunks, there was a strong tide running. His skull's probably halfway to Rotterdam by now.'

'Anyway, it's not like we need it,' she said resignedly. 'The boatyard guy ID-ed him for us. Gabriel Wolfe.'

'Local?'

'Lived over there,' she said, pointing to the house at the very end of Slaughden Road.

'Poor sod,' he said.

'You don't know the half of it.'

'What do you mean?'

'Three years ago, right? He was taking a leisurely stroll right here on the beach, with his fiancée and an ex-girlfriend,' she said. 'And the ex was murdered right in front of them. Shot. Some sort of contract killer. Wolfe took a bullet in his shoulder, too. I handled the investigation.'

'Did you catch the guy? I mean, I assume it was a man, right?'

'We didn't need to. Gabriel's fiancée shot him dead. Her name was Eli Schochat. Hard to forget. Really beautiful girl. She was carrying a pistol. A Jericho something or other.'

Her bagman was into his firearms, even though as a British cop he didn't carry one.

'A Jericho? That's Israeli.'

'As was his fiancée,' she said dryly.

His eyes widened. 'Wait. She's Israeli and she's carrying? She wasn't Mossad, was she? Oh, my God, she was! She was Mossad, wasn't she?'

'Funny thing, Pete,' she said, unimpressed by her bagman's puppyish enthusiasm. 'I got about six hours into the investigation and the whole thing was shut down on grounds of national security.'

He whistled. Then his face fell.

'Shit. That makes her Wolfe's next of kin. I mean, they'd be married by now, right?'

'Yep. So I need to find a Mrs Eli Wolfe and give her the bad news.'

After three days of trying, DS Amelia Roper was forced to admit that tracking down the widow was going to be harder than she'd thought. Then, for only the second time in her police career, she was informed by her boss that an investigation she was running was being taken over by a 'different agency'. Something about the look in his eye told her protesting would be a waste of breath.

Four weeks after that, all trace of the Sherborne Video disappeared from social media.

5

CHEQUERS, COUNTRY HOME OF THE BRITISH PRIME MINISTER, BUCKINGHAMSHIRE

Gemma Dowding scowled. Scalpay had been a massacre.

But with the wrong people lying shredded by bullets, grenades and mines at the end of it.

Oh, they'd killed the woman. She'd seen the photos. A lake of blood so bright it looked unreal. She'd felt sick, even viewing the death on a piece of paper.

So what? Eli was only there as bait to lure Wolfe to his execution. But the mission had failed. And now she wanted answers.

While she waited for her attack dog to arrive for their meeting, she stared out at the expanse of parkland beyond the window. It was a pretty view, no doubt. But she was in no mood to enjoy it.

Being prime minister brought its share of pressure, to put it mildly. But she was good at delegating, she told herself. There were cabinet ministers there to do her bidding, just as she'd done when she'd been home secretary, and at Justice before that. But *they* hadn't overseen a programme to eradicate undesirable elements from British society by way of Russian-funded death squads.

Death squads. None of them had ever used that particular two-word phrase to describe their criminal justice system innovation. That would have been far too crude. Or, what did the trendy media commentators call it nowadays? On the nose. Her social team were always bandying it about. Idiots.

Occasionally, in an unguarded moment after too much brandy, someone might have said 'DS' aloud. But even that small transgression was enough to earn them a bollocking that left vastly experienced politicians in tears.

No. The approved phrase, if it was ever deemed necessary to refer to them at all, was 'containment units'.

But then that damned judge had taken things too far. Ramage made an unsanctioned containment. Killed a cop's husband and her baby daughter. After that little escapade the shit, it was fair to say, had well and truly hit the fan. And Dowding had been standing right behind its whirling blades.

Ramage had paid with his life, as had the others in the operational command structure. Only one member had escaped the mad bitch's retribution. A member so many layers removed from the containment units and their deeds that 'clean hands' didn't even begin to cover it.

And for a while it had seemed as though the whole thing was going to stay buried. A team had been brought in from an outfit she'd not even been aware existed. 'Mopping up': that was the phrase their commander, a grizzled old warhorse named Webster, had called it. An operative, Wolfe, had been assigned, and soon it was done.

But as Dowding's political rise had continued, its angle of ascent steepening, she'd realised that the highest office in the land was truly within her grasp. And with it, the kind of scrutiny that would eventually, she was sure, link her to those dark days and even darker deeds. Her legacy, never mind her post-Number Ten earnings potential, would be in the shitter. Christ, she might even end up in prison.

The link needed to be severed. Anyone who knew about that hideous clean-up operation, anyone without leverage, anyway, had to disappear. Permanently.

And then, like a gift from the gods, that batshit operative from the same outfit had popped up like a bad penny. His mind twisted by the Taliban into a pretzel. Hot for revenge on the men he thought had betrayed him. When the report had been brought to her, she'd seen her chance.

Via her attack dog, money, materiel and intelligence had been funnelled his way. He'd attacked in Jerusalem and taken out Webster. But something had gone monumentally wrong on the remote Scottish island where it was all, finally, supposed to be contained.

The mercenaries she'd paid for had killed his wife but let Wolfe escape. The fact that they were all dead did not quell her anger. Heads had rolled – not, as on Scalpay, literally – and her wrath had been exacting.

The only one not asked to resign or summarily sacked was her attack dog. Margot McDonnell. She'd been charged with overseeing the operation. Running Bakker. Locating a trustworthy team to support him. Shutting down the Department.

Dowding checked her watch. Where the hell was she? Yes, she could delegate to the cabinet. But the job she needed to discuss with Margot was the one thing she could never entrust to anyone with even a shred of regard for the democratic process or the rule of law.

In that, Margot was perfect.

Behind her, someone knocked at the door.

'Yes!' she barked, irritably.

The door opened and in walked her principal private secretary, Sir Rodney Speer. A career civil servant from the mirror-shined toecaps of his handmade English brogues to the arrow-straight parting in his silver hair. He had it barbered at an establishment on Savile Row that had been old when George the Sixth had been on the throne.

'Ms McDonnell is here to see you, Prime Minister,' he intoned.

'About bloody time!'

He lowered his head a fraction before returning his ice-blue gaze to hers.

'Apparently the traffic was heavy.'

'Well get her in here, then!'

'Very good, Prime Minister.'

He withdrew with the silence and discretion of a butler. She hated him. Hated all of them. Those establishment men with their sneering attitudes. Just because she'd come up the hard way. Comprehensive school and a scholarship to one of the less-fashionable Oxford colleges instead of a private school and the college some seventeenth-century ancestor had endowed.

Two minutes later, the door opened a second time – no knock, she noticed – and in came Margot McDonnell. Somehow, even in a pale-grey suit and white blouse, Margot managed to radiate a dark, almost satanic energy. Her raven-black hair, held up in a bun so tight it looked like a snooker ball, caught the sun coming in through the window. That same light glinted off the edge of the gold wire frames of her spectacles.

'Good morning, Prime Minister,' Margot said, offering a thin-lipped smile.

Dowding felt the air in the sumptuously furnished drawing room chill by a couple of degrees. Well, she'd soon heat it up.

'You cunt. You inefficient, self-regarding, jumped-up, lying, bullshitting little cunt.'

Margot raised one eyebrow so it peeped above the top edge of her golden spectacle frame.

'You're talking about Scalpay, I take it.'

'Oh, you *take* it, do you?' Dowding said, feeling her heart thrashing inside her chest and allowing the adrenaline to further fuel her rage. 'You fucking *take* it, do you? What else do you *take*, Margot? Do you take a bunch of quote-unquote, combat-hardened fighting men to the Outer Hebrides and have them slaughtered by a couple of newlyweds?'

'Wolfe and his bride were hardly just newlyweds, Prime Minister,' Margot said, perhaps unwisely. 'As you know—'

'Oh, yes, Margot. Please tell me what I know. Because I would so like to find out what I know!' she roared. 'Oh, wait. I gave you a blank cheque to fund this little operation of yours. And all your pet jihadi Bakker managed to do was blow himself up with a scimitar—'

Margot smiled. 'Actually, they're called Claymores. He had quite the stash.'

Dowding felt her throat swell as if someone were inflating a blood-filled balloon in her neck.

'Don't you *dare* interrupt me!'

'I didn't mean to be rude. Merely to point out the correct name for the explosive device he used. In the interests of accuracy, nothing more.'

Dowding stared. The woman was unbelievable. There had been times during their brief but intense association when she'd wondered if Margot was all right in the head. She displayed not a shred of emotion, even when asked whether Eli Schochat's pregnancy – for they'd known, of *course* they'd known; the idea that medical records were private was a convenient fiction they fed the public – changed anything. Margot's one-word conclusion had been chilling. '*No.*'

'It's a shame your mercenaries weren't a little more accurate with their guns, then, isn't it?' Gemma held up a hand, fingers stiff. 'And if you tell me they weren't guns, they were rifles or machineguns or whatever, I will personally rip you a new one.'

'They did kill the woman.'

'But not him. Not Wolfe.'

'And Kevin personally killed Webster in Jerusalem. That's a sixty-six-point-six-recurring percent success rate.'

'That's what you think, is it, Margot?'

'Well, it's true.'

'You see, *I* think it's a thirty-three-point-three-recurring percent *failure* rate.'

Margot smiled again. It was like watching a scalpel slicing open a taut piece of skin.

'Technically, they're the same thing.'

'Technically, you left Wolfe alive. Against my orders.'

Margot smiled for the third time. And this time, Dowding thought she detected mirth. It was unsettling. She imagined this might be how a mouse felt if a cat bared its teeth at it.

'Wolfe's dead.'

'I beg your pardon?'

'He killed himself on Monday. Off the coast in Aldeburgh.' She inspected a fingernail. 'It's a town on the Suffolk coast.'

'Why didn't you tell me this straightaway?'

'You seemed to have a few things you needed to get off your chest. I thought it could wait until you'd finished.'

Dowding frowned. Margot was a cool one.

'You're sure he's dead?'

'He left a beautifully written suicide note on his kitchen table then blew himself up on his yacht in full view of twenty-three witnesses, twenty-one if you don't count children. It was even caught on video.'

'You've seen the body?'

The smile widened. Was it her imagination, or were the woman's canine teeth sharper than normal?

'Body? Our explosives experts have examined the video. They estimate he used seventy to eighty kilos of ANFO. There's—'

'Plain English, please.'

'Ammonium nitrate/fuel oil. It's a type of explosive commonly used in—'

'I said Plain English, not a Wikipedia entry. What does that mean?'

'It means Wolfe was turned into atoms. Gas, essentially. Which burned up in the blast. There *is* no body.'

'How can you be sure he's dead, then?'

'He is clearly visible on the video. Waving.' She paused. 'But not drowning.'

Dowding frowned. 'What?'

'It doesn't matter.'

Dowding said nothing; she was thinking. So this was it. After all the years fighting to keep the truth from coming out, the last loose end connecting her to the conspiracy was tied off.

She'd exiled the Cole woman to Sweden, the threat of violence against her remaining family enough to ensure her silence. But with Wolfe she'd had no such leverage. The man had no family. Nobody she could use as a lever. So he'd had to die along with Webster.

Her pulse dropped from its racehorse gallop and she found she was able to bestow a smile on her attack dog that felt at least halfway genuine.

'Thank you, Margot,' she said.

'Will there be anything else?'

'No, there won't. You can go.'

Margot nodded, spun on her dagger-sharp heel and crossed the thick-piled carpet to the panelled cherrywood door.

As she reached out her hand to seize the knob, Dowding called out to her.

'Actually, there was one last thing, Margot.'

She turned.

'Yes, Prime Minister?'

'You're fired. Disavowed, in fact. Speak to Sir Rodney. He'll fill you in. It's a generous package.'

For the first time in the meeting, and, Dowding reflected, possibly in their entire relationship, Margot looked unsure of herself. Brow furrowed, biting her lower lip.

'Disavowed? But you need me.'

'Incorrect. I *needed* you. Past tense. Like your career. Now get out.'

But Margot stayed put. Eyes narrowed, she spoke in an even tone.

'Am I a loose end too, Prime Minister?'

'What?'

'Are you going to send someone after me? Because I strongly advise against it.'

'Is that a threat, Margot? Because *I* strongly advise against *that*.'

Dowding frowned as her former subordinate glanced up at the ornately plastered ceiling. Was she seriously considering her answer? As if there were two possible ones? What the hell was wrong with her? Any normal person would simply say something noncommittal, like, *Of course not, I was merely suggesting blah blah blah*. But then, as she admitted to herself that she'd known all along, Margot McDonnell might be many things, but a normal person wasn't one of them. At last, her attack dog gave a final bark. Or maybe it was more of a growl.

'No. It's not a threat.'

She left, closing the door quietly behind her.

Heart pounding, yet with a feeling of profound relief, Gemma strode to the window and looked out at the swaying trees, the ornamental lake with its splashing fountains, a couple of gardeners pushing wheelbarrows, hoeing weeds. Nodded to herself.

Free at last.

6

HONDURAS, CARIBBEAN COAST

Taking a roundabout route involving five countries, the same number of false identities, and thousands of US dollars paid out in bribes, it took Gabriel a month to make his way from England to Honduras.

His phones, departmental and personal, were now mere fragments of plastic and rare metals at the bottom of the Atlantic. He avoided using computers completely. And he'd grown a beard and let his hair grow out until it was long enough to tie back in a ponytail.

Fetching up in Santa Rosa, a small village on the tiny central American country's Caribbean coast, he didn't so much adopt as fall into a routine. Long walks down the beach, a bottle swinging from one hand. Or using his machete to hack random paths through the jungle that began a few metres on the other side of the coast road.

When his energy ran out, he simply sat down with his back to a tree and slept.

His dreams were never pleasant.

The best he'd learned to hope for were tableaux of dead and dismembered bodies on that remote Hebridean island. The worst he'd come to dread was fear so bone-numbingly real he awoke screaming, sometimes having wet himself, scrabbling for a weapon with which to defend himself against the gibbering khaki-clad monsters with bloody faces and long yellow fangs where their teeth should be.

In those early days, he harboured fantasies of retribution so lurid they'd be rejected by every horror film director on the planet. Deaths prolonged, painful and punishing to those behind Eli's murder. Drugs to keep them hydrated, conscious and fully aware of what was happening to them.

Margot McDonnell, naturally. But also her staff, her remaining operatives, her paymasters. Anyone and everyone who'd so much as signed off on a purchase order for a single hollow-point round was in the crosshairs.

But his grief overwhelmed him completely. How could a man incapable of dressing himself muster the energy, the resources and the will to execute a plan as complex as that needed to take out whatever black ops outfit McDonnell was running?

He didn't cry at all for three weeks. He tried conjuring pictures of Eli in his mind's eye. Dressing her in her wedding outfit, or one of her brightly coloured bikinis, or just a pair of her favourite jeans and a T-shirt. Replaying conversations, dances in the pub when a DJ spun a few records, quiet dinners at the Brudenell or the fish shack further down the High Street.

Nothing worked. He lay on his back under the creaking and largely useless fan, staring dry-eyed at the ceiling, lacking even the energy to aim an imaginary pistol at the antenna-waving blue beetles that seemed to regard themselves as tenants in common with the new human.

Then, one day, everything changed.

He was queuing at the food stall on the main road to buy a

glass of horchata and a baleada of refried beans, cheese and sour cream. New to Honduras, his accent still wasn't great, and he made a mess of ordering. The young girl behind the aluminium counter smiled at him and leaned forward.

'*Puede repetir eso?*' she asked.

He started to repeat it, but then he caught a whisper of her smell. Lemon. And sandalwood.

Eli's signature scent hadn't come from anything expensive. No high-end perfume or designer eau de toilette. Just her favourite brand of soap and shampoo. A mixture of aromas common enough to find its way to remote coastal villages on the Honduran coast, of course.

But for Gabriel, it was too much. It unmanned him in a second. He choked out an answer but then had to turn away as the floodgates opened. Making it to the fat trunk of a felled tree by the roadside that served as a bench for those who wanted to sit while they ate, he hung his head between his knees and sobbed. Then howled, much to the consternation of the other customers for the tortillas, tacos and cold drinks.

A young woman hurried over, even as the others hung back, clutching their cans of pop and foil-wrapped treats and unsure how or even whether to help this clearly deranged gringo.

She'd been behind him in the queue. He noticed her because her T-shirt bore a black and white image of Jimi Hendrix and a quote. 'Music is my religion.' He thought it noteworthy in a Catholic country, doubly so given that Hendrix had always been one of his musical heroes. They'd exchanged brief smiles and then he'd turned his back to focus on the menu. Hand-painted in bright colours on a piece of planking hung beside the serving hatch.

'*Señor, señor, qué pasa?*' she crooned now, kneeling in front of him and unselfconsciously placing a hand on his heaving shoulder.

He raised his head, which felt as though someone had hung rocks about it, and looked at her through tear-bleared eyes. How could he possibly explain what had happened? What did she know of mercenaries, black ops teams, covert insertions, and murderous civil servants with the dead-eyed gaze of sharks?

The look in her eyes, patient, sympathetic, forced on him a realisation. What did it *matter* what she understood? At the heart of his grief was a simple enough story. One comprehensible to every living being on the planet.

He swallowed.

'*Mi esposa murió.*'

She frowned and switched to English.

'I am sorry. What was your wife's name?'

'Eli.'

'Pretty. You loved her very much.' A statement, not a question. 'Tell me, how did she die?'

As interest in them waned, and the everyday concerns of eating, drinking and conversing with neighbours reasserted their grip on the other people around them, Gabriel started to explain to the woman who introduced herself as Esperanza.

Six months passed.

He made progress.

For one thing, and especially since meeting Esperanza, he cut down on the drinking. Not to the levels he'd previously considered one of the hallmarks of a civilised life. No doctor back in the UK would take his honest answer of how many units of alcohol he consumed in a week and smile indulgently. But enough to function.

She told him to call her Pera. '*Only my mum calls me Esperanza.*' He gave her his real first name. He didn't want to start off with a lie. It was a small risk, but nobody was looking for him and even if they were, he'd covered his tracks sufficiently well that they'd never find him in Santa Rosa. If they did, it was simple enough. He'd kill them.

Slowly, they grew more trusting of each other as their friendship deepened. He told her more about Eli and his dreams of the life they had planned. She told him about *her* dream of owning her own food cart.

And he discovered, if not a purpose, then at least a reason for living. Pera's fourteen-year-old son, Santiago, was at an age where without a guiding hand on his life's tiller, from a man he could look up to, the temptations of easy money from the gangs or the cartels would eventually lure him into a life of crime, and, quite, possibly, an early grave.

They fished together, either from the boat Gabriel had bought and renovated, or from the beach. They'd sling out their lines and haul in snappers, groupers, even the occasional marlin, an all-morning battle that left them both sweating and laughing as the huge, sword-billed fish flapped and scythed around in the belly of the boat.

Progress, yes. Of a kind. But his PTSD, dormant for so long thanks to his psychiatrist Fariyah Crace's ministrations, had reared its shaggy, monstrous head once more. Fariyah would no doubt have sympathetic words and be able to provide a rational explanation for the recurrence of his symptoms. But quite honestly, did he really need her to? After all, it wasn't exactly much of a puzzle.

To lose his bride just weeks after getting married, in a firefight. Then to blank it out so completely that he believed her alive and well. Right up to the point his old friend Bev Watchett discovered him gabbling away to Eli's ghost in his garden. Well, it wasn't exactly the *Times* crossword, now was it?

Possessed by his demons, and the ghosts of the past, who had taken up residence inside his head, and occasionally in his house, Gabriel turned his rage outwards. He'd heard of a place in the capital city where a man could be paid to fight and fight hard.

If he couldn't hurt those who'd murdered Eli, Margot McDonnell chief among them, then he'd just have to find a substitute.

7

LONDON

After her brutal sacking at the hands of the woman who'd originally tasked her with eliminating Wolfe and his wife, Margot McDonnell had been consumed by fury. A week passed in a haze of half-formed plans of bloody revenge.

Not only revenge, though.

When she'd asked Dowding whether she was now a loose end herself, the prime minister had been evasive. It didn't matter. Of *course* she was a loose end. And that meant she needed to take immediate steps to protect herself.

Lesser beings would go to enormous trouble compiling a dossier with dates, times, names: enough detail to incriminate Dowding of the most heinous crimes. Margot considered herself smarter. The threat itself was what mattered. It just had to be credible. She called Dowding and in very few words, gave her to understand that should Margot die in any way other than as a very old lady, certain documents would be released onto the internet.

But time in her part of the intelligence community rarely passed purposelessly for long. And grapevines existed there, just as they did in every other sphere of human endeavour.

The day after her final conversation with her former employer, her phone rang as she ran through Regent's Park placing invisible crosshairs on the foreheads of every person she saw. She answered without breaking stride.

'Margot McDonnell?' the caller asked.

American accent. Midwestern. Blue collar origins, softened by decades of mixing with more middle-class types and tempered with the unmistakable edge of hard-won authority. She pictured a silver-haired corporate executive. Not banking or tech. The boss of a state-wide plumbing supplies business, maybe. Or long-distance trucking. A saw mill, or a meat-packing plant.

'Who is this?'

'Ma'am, this is General Copeland D Tookey, US Army Intelligence. I hear you're currently at a loose end. I thought I'd reach out in the hopes I could help you reattach it.'

'Call me back in one hour exactly, General.'

She finished her 10K run thirty minutes later. Back at her flat overlooking Piccadilly Circus, she showered and changed into working clothes: black tailored trousers, white shirt, black leather loafers. She opened her laptop, launched some specialised search software and had the general's army records onscreen when her phone rang again.

'Hello, General. Or should I call you Tomahawk?'

He grunted out an affable laugh.

'The media dubbed me "Tomahawk Tookey". I never liked it myself. You decapitate one insurgent in combat and you get stuck with it. My men called me Six-Foot.'

'For your height?'

'For the depth of hole it was advisable to dig when my boys and me were coming through,' he said. 'So what did they call *you*?'

'Mostly, they called me Margot. Or ma'am.'

34

'No nickname?'

'I believe some of my South African hires liked to refer to me as the "huff poose".'

'What the hell does that mean?'

'Poison pussy.'

'Goddamn disrespectful.' He cleared his throat. 'Let's cut the small-talk. I hear you're out of work. I have a slot in a programme I run. You'd be perfect. Can you come out to DC? Tomorrow?'

'Sounds urgent.'

She heard the shrug in his voice as he said, 'My work is never anything *but* urgent. So you'll come?'

'I will.'

'Great, I'll—'

'On Thursday. I have some matters to attend to first. Until then —' she tapped a nail on her desk, '— Six-Foot.'

The next day, while Margot was out shopping for travel-sized toiletries, a smartly dressed businesswoman bumped into her in the haircare aisle. After apologising profusely, she left. Margot felt around in her pockets and found a folded sheet of notepaper inside her jacket.

Following the instructions written there, she made her way, by a pre-paid first-class air ticket, to a hotel in Washington, DC on a smart but out-of-the-way street. Tree-lined, free of all but the most sober and unthreatening-looking people. In their Brooks Brothers suits, chinos and polo shirts, or upscale running gear, they looked like executives, politicians, aides, lobbyists, lawyers. The noise of their muted conversations intermittently overridden by the murmur of expensive European sedans and SUVs.

She'd gone to meet the general the next day at an office block downtown. Which, she felt, was odd. No obvious military security. No military paraphernalia of any kind, in fact.

After exchanging the usual pleasantries about her journey, hotel and jetlag – fine, perfectly adequate, non-existent – the general got down to it.

'Margot, I run a programme under the auspices, just, of the

Department of Defense. We eradicate America's enemies at home and abroad.'

'So far, so Jason Bourne.'

He smiled, a wolfish expression that revealed yellow canines. A stark contrast to the Americans she'd met so far with their gleaming white teeth like fine porcelain.

'You think we have an elite cadre of assassins targeting terrorists, bombers, insurgents, that type of thing?' he asked.

She crossed her legs, admiring the general for the way his eyes never left her face.

'Are you telling me you don't?'

'Not at all. Our assassins are the best in the world. They're as happy administering a double-tap to a haji as the next guy.'

'Then forgive me, but what's your special sauce?'

The general repeated his lupine grin, wider this time so the tips of those long yellow teeth came into view.

'Our targets. Other outfits go for middle-management. We aim for the board of directors.'

'Aren't the heads of terrorist groups rather hard to identify, let alone eliminate?'

'You misunderstand me, Margot. I'm talking about the hide-in-plain-sight guys. The politicians, the bankers, the religious leaders. The guys who create the frameworks that allow these murdering sons-of-bitches to operate.'

Margot nodded her head, recalling a newspaper article she'd read online a month or two earlier.

'So, purely as an example, when I read recently that President Ali Abdul Khoraman of Western Congo was killed in an unexplained fire at his beachfront villa in Cannes…'

'That was us.'

'I see. And what would my job be?'

'Case officer. You'd be running operations from soups to nuts. Picking targets, assembling teams, planning, monitoring, remote command,' he paused, 'or on the ground if you prefer. Contingency planning, extraction, reporting, assessment. The whole nine yards.'

She frowned. 'Tell me, General, why isn't the CIA already doing this?'

He shrugged. 'Protocols? Over-deference to the regs? Political feeblemindedness? Some lingering sense of propriety? I don't know, Margot, and to be honest, I don't care. In any case, their security is pitiful. In comparison, we make the Agency look like WikiLeaks.'

'Does it have a name, this programme of yours?'

'Evergreen. Want to know why? This country's history is one of men, and, lately, women, carrying guns. Not legal briefcases, not presidential seals: guns. Every four years we elect a new guy to run the show. And just lately, some of us have been growing increasingly dissatisfied with their lack of military experience. Time was, you could expect the American president to have carried a rifle into combat. Now they boast about dodging the draft for 'Nam. The public are no better. It's "thanks for your service and spare us the details. We'll take the rich guy."

'But when the chips are down, who do we send into battle to defend this country's values? Ivy League-educated lawyers? Community activists? Businessmen? No! It's back to the grunts. The men and women in green. As it ever was.'

Margot smiled thinly. 'Cute.'

The general's colour rose a couple of shades from a healthy tan to something with a cherry-ish tinge behind it. He swallowed visibly, his Adam's apple bobbing up and down beneath a turkey wattle neck.

'I've read your file, Margot,' he said in a dangerously quiet voice. 'Page one right through to the addendum. Your psych profile was particularly interesting. Know what they said about you in your deep vetting?'

'I have a shrewd idea, but I've never seen it. Enlighten me, would you?'

'Sure. They said you have a borderline personality disorder with narcissistic personality traits.'

'I'm disappointed.'

His eyebrows elevated a couple of millimetres.

'Disappointed?'

'I wouldn't consider myself a narcissist. I take it you also read my case reports, annual assessments, personal kill records.'

'I did, and that's why I am offering you a job. You're a rare bird, Margot. A stone killer with a flair for admin. We could use you.'

* * *

That had been six months ago. Now she was fully embedded in Evergreen and thoroughly enjoying her work. She'd bought an apartment. And a cat. She called it Hollowpoint.

She still bore a grudge against Gemma Dowding, and followed her premiership for any signs of weakness. When she perceived one, she created a new record in the file she was compiling. Who knew? Perhaps one day Gemma might become a person of interest at Evergreen. And then Margot would consider very strongly moving back into the field.

8

HONDURAS

Gabriel had driven a great many vehicles in his life. An array of beautiful sportscars including the midnight-blue Maserati GT he'd bought after his parents died on board the yacht. Military machinery from jeeps to Humvees, bristling with hi-tech weaponry. Indestructible Toyota Hiluxes, fitted out with Vickers machineguns bolted to rudimentary mounts in their load bays. Motorbikes, eighteen-wheeler trucks, snowmobiles, armoured limos and every type of SUV and 4x4.

But as he drove home from Bonito, the nearest town with a *supermercado*, Wolfe decided he preferred the battered sky-blue 1953 Ford F100 pickup to them all. It was anonymous, for one thing. Just another rust-scabbed American antique among many.

It was reliable, too, not something he could say for the Maserati. Kali was exhilarating to drive. But she suffered from the besetting sin of pedigree creatures everywhere. A high-strung temperament and a requirement for frequent, and expensive, attentions from highly qualified professionals.

But what most endeared the Ford to him was its simplicity. When the Ford *did* grumble, the tools and techniques required to fix it were as simple as they had been when it was new. No diagnostic software needed, no under-dash multi-pin plug to insert before he could take a wrench to the carburettor or replace a leaky fuel hose.

Probably just as well, given that Santa Rosa was not blessed with much in the way of technology. The tiny coastal settlement he'd made his home boasted a few satellite dishes, and most people had smart phones. But folk tended to mend their own kit, just like he and the boys had done in the Regiment.

The Ford's top speed was somewhere around the fifty mark. Soon after buying it, and more from a residual sense of duty than a genuine desire to go fast, he'd pushed it to its limit on an empty stretch of road.

As the needle of ancient speedometer in the dented steel dashboard vibrated its way to forty-nine, he had to clamp his teeth together to avoid having them shattered. He finally backed off the throttle when the steering went eerily light and the Ford drifted towards the cliff-edge.

Today he had no such need. Thirty would see him safely back to Santa Rosa and allow him to juggle the bottle of guifiti as well as the dog-leg gear stick that swung around in the gate like a straw in a Cuba libre.

He took a swig, hissing as the booze coursed down his throat, then steadied the bottle between his thighs while he one-handedly screwed the cap back on.

Every town, sometimes every family, had their own recipe for guifiti. But at its heart was a dozen or so herbs and roots soaked in rum and left in the sun. The particular bottle Gabriel was working his way down tasted strongly of aniseed and ginger.

He waved to a couple of old, chestnut-skinned Indian women walking by the side of the road, woven straw baskets slung over their shoulders piled high with mangos and papayas.

They waved back, grinning to reveal more gaps than teeth in their pink gums.

With the guifiti warming him inside, just as the sun was performing the same role on his exposed skin, he eased the pickup around a long, sweeping curve in the road. The radius decreased halfway around, and for the unwary or the inattentive, this change in curvature could lead to them taking an unplanned detour into the scrub that lined the outside edge of the bend.

Balancing the centrifugal force against the steering rack, the way he used to steer Lin into the wind, he locked out his elbow and leaned into the curve.

So it was at this slight angle that he first laid eyes on the men blocking the road with their off-white, dust-caked Hilux. Four in total. One Kalashnikov between them. Though each had a machete gleaming at his waist. They wore dusty police uniforms. The front of one jacket was dyed maroon by a large bloodstain. He'd met several Honduran cops since arriving in the violent Central American country. As far as he could remember, none had sported profuse facial tattoos.

He slowed, changed down through the ancient gearbox and brought the truck to a halt maybe twenty yards back from the men.

They were engaged in what Gabriel had come to think of as the national sport of Honduras, namely, violent extortion. This particular variety, the unofficial traffic stop, was a speciality of the criminals around Bonito. He'd paid the first couple of times it had happened to him. Then, when one of his new neighbours, an elderly pineapple farmer, had been savagely beaten and had a finger lopped off in lieu of payment, he'd decided enough was enough.

The group's leader, the one with the ageing AK-47 slung over his shoulder, sauntered over, smiling to reveal a mouthful of gold teeth.

'*Buenos días, señor.*' Then, on seeing Gabriel wasn't Honduran. 'Good mornin', buddy. Not of'n we see a gringo on the Bonito Road.'

Behind him, the other three snickered, hands either loose by their sides or caressing the wooden handles of their machetes.

Gabriel smiled back at the man. Noting his stance, relaxed; his musculature, slack; and his eyes, pink with the effects of cannabis. It hardly seemed fair.

'Good morning,' he said. 'Is there a problem? Have you and your friends broken down? Do you need a mechanic?'

The man grinned lazily. 'That your job, is it? Mechanic?'

Gabriel cast his mind back over a great many professional hits. 'In a manner of speaking.'

'Pretty well-paid job.'

'It has its moments.'

'Well in *this* moment, what we need is fif'y dollars from you, my frien'. It gua'ntee you safe passage. Lot of bandits on the Bonito Road. We give you one a these,' he held up a roll of self-adhesive red stars on a strip of shiny backing paper, 'for your win'screen, and you get home safe as a newborn kitt'n.'

Given that unwanted litters rarely survived longer than a day or two in the countryside, this felt less of a warranty and more of a threat. It didn't matter. Gabriel had no intention of paying up.

He looked over the man's shoulder. Standing in the bed of the pickup, leaning on the cab with her arms folded, Eli smiled down at him. The blood soaking her midriff was as bright and as red as it had been that day on Scalpay, but now it didn't bother her. And him only a little. Gabriel smiled back.

'Hey! Gringo!' the man shouted. 'What you laughin' at? Di'n' you hear me? Fif'y dollars US or you goin' to be the one brok'n down.'

He unslung his AK and swung it around until the muzzle was pointing at Gabriel's face.

His *compadres* nudged each other. Used, presumably, to their boss's performances, and assuming they knew what came next.

'I only carry Lempiras,' Gabriel said. 'So you want, what, twelve hundred and fifty?'

The man spat into the dirt.

'Don' bullshit me, man. Ev'ry gringo carry dollars. Only now? 'Cause you tryin' my patience? The toll just wen' up to seven'y five.'

He yanked back on the AK's charging lever for effect, producing a gritty rasp in which Gabriel detected a lack of cleaning of the venerable weapon. Kalashnikovs were renowned for working despite what you did to them, but only a fool would allow dirt to creep inside the moving parts.

He sighed. 'No need for that. I just came back from the bank. Agente Atlantida on Calle de Santalucia, you know it?'

''Course I know it, gringo! Now get me my money and we can issue your travel pass.'

'Sure,' Gabriel said, holding up his hands. 'It's in the glove box.'

The man took his right hand off the trigger to snap his fingers. 'Just get a move on, OK?'

Gabriel leaned over to his right and flipped the rusty metal catch down to release the hinged door of the glove box. In fact, he *had* just been to the bank, but only to withdraw some Lempira. Enough for a month and hardly likely to satisfy the bandido currently looking back over his shoulder and smirking at his accomplices.

From her vantage point in the back of the Hilux, Eli watched him with an amused smile. She was so beautiful. Even covered in blood.

Gabriel reached into the narrow little cubby, past the bundle of greasy pink, purple and green Honduran banknotes. Closed his fingers around the battered but serviceable Vietnam-era Colt 1911 pistol and pulled it out.

The man's eyes widened in panic.

Then a third eye, black with a red rim, opened up dead-centre between them. The report as the .45 ACP round shattered the skull was loud in Gabriel's ears.

The bandit staggered backwards from the force of the point-blank impact, and toppled into the nearest of his three henchmen, covering him in scarlet arterial blood and brain tissue like pinkish-grey porridge.

While the remaining men screamed and dragged at the machetes at their hips, Gabriel was vaulting from the cab. He could easily have defeated them in hand-to-hand combat, disarming them and turning their *goloks* against them. But really, what was the point?

He glanced up at Eli, who nodded.

Then he shot each man in the face, far enough back that he avoided the worst of the blood-spatter.

The machetes weren't totally useless though. He selected the sharpest one, after testing all four blades on a cactus growing by the roadside, and beheaded each corpse.

He climbed into the Hilux's cab, shouted up to Eli to hold tight, twisted the key, and drove it off the road. He arranged the four heads on the hood and used his right index finger to paint a short message on the metal in front of them in blood.

¡NO HAY PASO SEGURO PARA LOS BANDIDOS!

The threat of no safe passage for bandits wouldn't work for ever. But it might buy the locals a little more toll-free time before the next gang decided to try their luck.

He turned back towards the F100.

Behind him, the windscreen of the Hilux blew out with a crash. A split-second later Gabriel caught the crack-thump of a rifle shot. He ducked down and scurried back to his own truck for cover. So the bandits had a guy on overwatch. Clearly not a sniper, or even a marksman. Otherwise Gabriel's thoughts would currently be emanating from a cloud of vaporised brain tissue drifting a few feet off the dusty, sun-baked ground.

He pulled the pistol from his waistband and fired three shots over the lip of the loadbay. Another shot ricocheted off a rock a yard or two behind the truck. Shit. Now what? He was pinned down. Admittedly by a shooter for whom a barn door would present a stiff challenge, but even the worst shooters sometimes got lucky.

He considered the situation from his enemy's point of view:

I'm a low-grade gangbanger with a long gun but I can't shoot for shit. I've just seen some crazy gringo shoot and behead four of my mates. What do I do? Burn through the rest of my ammunition then risk him coming after me too? I don't think so. Come down from my hide and fight it out mano a mano? *And end up just another hood ornament? Are you crazy? Run without at least trying? What will the boss do to me? Can it be any worse than hacking my head off with my own machete?*

Gabriel made his choice, nodding to himself and praying he'd got a bead on the final bandit's psychology. He got into a crouch, keeping his head beneath the loadbay. Then he inhaled sharply and ran round the truck, grabbing a discarded machete on the way. He filled his lungs and yelled a bloodcurdling war-whoop before sprinting towards the low bluff a hundred yards away from the road.

Whirling the machete round his head and firing the pistol towards what he assumed was the shooter's position, he yelled out in Spanish: 'Wait there, my friend. I'm gonna carve you into chuck steak and eat your brains raw. I'm coming for you, motherfucker so don't you be going anywhere, you hear me?'

No more shots issued from the hillside.

Reaching the cover of a tough little thornbush, Gabriel squatted behind it and issued a handful of increasingly deranged and anatomically impossible threats.

Silence. Not even birdsong. Just his demented yells bouncing off the hard red rock.

For good measure he emptied his magazine into one patch of vegetation that might conceivably harbour a sniper. Nothing came by way of return fire.

'Next time, friend!' he screamed into the emptiness.

That night, as he lay tossing and turning, twisted in a sweat-soaked sheet like a shroud, four beheaded gangbangers sang to him from the hood of the Hilux. A bloody barbershop quartet in boaters with candy-striped bands: except the red was blood, dripping down and staining the yellow straw brims.

'You killin' the wrong people, gringo,' they harmonised in a grating screech.

9

WASHINGTON, DC

Margot peered at the screen, marvelling at how she could be sitting here, in her well-appointed office, watching a targeted assassination happening in real-time deep inside Tadjikistan.

The Predator was overflying the kill zone, out of range and sight of the enemy's weapons. They were primitive for the most part. Chinese AK-47 knockoffs dating back to Vietnam. Norinco pistols from the same source that wouldn't look out of place on the shelves of a toyshop. Wildly inaccurate locally-manufactured submachineguns her on-the-ground team leader rated as only marginally better than flash-bangs for all the good they did.

But they did possess a couple of RPGs, and these *were* deemed a threat.

The sand-coloured figures – her team – advanced on the enemy compound. A second screen provided infra-red pictures of the inside of the mud-brick house where the hostages were being held. Ghostly greenish-white figures, recognisably human but shorn of all detail. Four standing, two sitting.

When the shooting started, the impression she was watching a video game increased. Without sound, or the resolution to see the blood spraying, all she was left with, much to her disappointment, was the cartoonish action, as her men advanced, slaughtering the terrorists where they stood.

One of her team fell backwards. Oh, well. They had calculated the acceptable casualties and one was well within operational parameters.

She flicked her eyes to the infrared. The standing figures were running around in a panic. How silly. They were caught like rats in a trap. Not long now and the government minister – friendly towards America – and his daughter would be free.

Then one of the terrorists turned and levelled a weapon at the hostages. Margot leaned closer to the screen. His arm jerked twice and the seated figures slumped sideways. Lying-down figures. Margot's lipsticked mouth turned down in a frown of irritation.

Seconds later, six members of her team stormed the building. Their green-white avatars swept through the corridors and rooms, meeting every standing figure with a hail of gunfire. Finally they reached the room that, until recently, had held the prize.

The terrorists dropped their weapons and raised their hands.

Margot smiled.

Idiots.

Her orders had been extremely clear. Extremely simple.

'Kill them all.'

Which they did.

Her headset buzzed. The comms operator's voice crackled in her left ear.

'Holly One on the line, ma'am.'

'Put her through.'

The earpiece hissed and then Holly One, the team leader, was on the line, as clear as if she'd been speaking from the next room.

'Targets all eliminated, ma'am. Hostages dead before we could secure them. And we lost Holly Three.'

Typical. Try to escape censure by giving the good news first. It wouldn't work. Not on Margot.

'I can see that. What do you think we have all this expensive hardware for? I gave you a simple enough job, Holly One. How did you manage to screw it up so badly?'

'Sorry, ma'am. We encountered stiffer resistance than expected. Maybe we should investigate the locals for a mole. It felt like they knew we were coming.'

Margot nodded, and smiled, even though Holly One couldn't see it. But then, the smile wasn't meant for her.

Of *course* they'd been expected. Margot had warned the terrorists herself. And now the opposition party funding them, unfriendly to America but with extremely deep pockets, would be sending Margot something she'd been expecting in return. A seven-figure sum sent to a numbered Swiss bank account.

Evergreen was a nice berth for now. Excellent pay and conditions. Plush office. A free hand to conduct her operations as she saw fit. But it was never part of the long-term plan.

'These things happen, Holly One. Proceed to extraction point Omega. The chopper will be waiting for you.' She paused. 'Oh, and burn Holly Three's body. Leave it unrecognisable. No dental either. Holly Pine, out.'

It had been Margot's idea to assign code names based on English evergreen species. And she rather liked the sound of 'Holly Pine'. She pictured herself in a skin-tight black leather catsuit, weapons strapped to her thighs, rocking a pair of wraparound Oakleys. Killing everyone in sight.

On which subject…

She left the building and found a quiet spot in a nearby park.

There, she pulled out an encrypted mobile phone once owned by a cartel boss in Mexico. It was linked to a criminal phone network built to replace one that Interpol had broken a year or two earlier.

She made a call.

'Gyorgi. They're heading to the extraction point. I'm sending you the coordinates. You're looking for a chopper branded Tadjik Air. Sky blue and white livery. Tail code GAF-127.'

'Got it. My money?'

'Check your account. Half's already there. You get the other half when I get pictures of the wreckage. Nobody left alive, understood?'

'Understood. Leave it to me.'

She stowed the phone in her capacious black leather bag and took the scenic route back to the office. Investigate for a mole? Forget it! She'd lay the blame on Holly One for poor operational decision-making on the ground. Demand new resources. Offer to select them herself. In truth, she was getting bored of sitting in an office all day. She fancied a change of scene.

In which, she was about to get her wish.

* * *

Her official phone rang as she reached the carpark.

'Margot, it's Copeland. My office, soon as you can.'

'I'll be there in ten, General. I just need to powder my nose.'

She ended the call, imagining the look of outrage on the ageing general's face at her casual deferral of his deadline. And for nothing more than a dainty trip to the ladies' room.

In fact, she had no need to pee. She just liked to wind up the brass whenever she got the chance. She knew how they viewed her. As just another resource. This one a borderline psychotic psychopath with spreadsheet skills. They'd no more try to save her if she got into trouble than she'd tried to save Holly Team Three down there in the stony desert outside Balichur. It was a dog-eat-dog outfit and she intended to be the biggest bitch in the pack.

So, Six-Foot could damn well wait.

Fifteen minutes after she entered the building and passed through Security, she knocked crisply on the general's office door and went in without waiting for his barked command to 'Come!'. She always did it and it always annoyed him. His face suffused with blood, and with a frown so deep it made his forehead look like a satellite image of a mountain range, he gestured for her to sit.

She crossed one trousered leg over the other and smiled at him. Waiting. People were so weird. Why couldn't he see she was just winding him up and not let it get to him? She knew the answer. She just liked the feel of those rhetorical questions. Emotions. That was the answer. It was what made people such as the general inferior to people like her.

They'd break off from plans to retrieve the body of what they quaintly called 'a fallen comrade'. Why? They were already dead! Only now you'd wasted more soldiers by using them as pallbearers. Or they'd avoid taking action that would secure the objective because civilian casualties would be too high. Who cared? Civilians always got killed in wars. Wasn't that rather the point? Margot shook her head in despair.

'Something bothering you, Margot?' the general growled.

She switched on her special thousand-watt smile and beamed it directly into his face.

'Not at all, Cope. Now, what did you want to see me about?'

A muscle had started to flicker beneath his left eye. She found herself captivated by the little shadow that appeared and disappeared in the light from his desk-lamp every time the tiny bundle of fibres contracted.

'I have a little operation for you. For you *personally*. One of our contacts down in Central America said he's got some people who could be very useful to us. On the operational side. They've been harrying government forces all over the region. Guatemala, Belize, Nicaragua, Honduras. They're looking for a regular gig. We've sustained some losses recently, as you know. Time to do some recruiting.'

'Sounds interesting. What do you want me to do?'

'Get yourself down to Honduras and check them out. They're based in Tegucigalpa. It's a hot zone for foreigners especially from the US of A, so I'm assigning you a bodyguard team for the duration of your trip.'

'That won't be necessary.'

He frowned. 'You're a woman travelling alone, Margot. It's protocol.'

'Sod protocol! This is Evergreen, isn't it? We do things our way. Well, Cope, *my* way is to fly under the radar. You send me out with a squad of jarheads in matching Ken Doll covert ops outfits and we'll attract attention from every cartel kidnap team from the Caribbean Gulf to the Pacific.'

The general sighed. 'As you wish. Just don't get yourself killed, OK?'

She smiled at him. 'I'll do my best. Now: my objective?'

'If they check out and you think they're a good fit, bring them in for induction.'

Margot nodded. It sounded exciting. Tegucigalpa made New York in the 1970s look like London's Knightsbridge. A city where life wasn't so much cheap as on a three-for-a-buck manager's special giveaway offer all day, every day. Her kind of place.

She rose from her chair.

'One last thing, Margot,' he said, as she headed for the door. 'Will you at least allow me to provide you with a personal weapon while you're down there? Or did you want to buy one from a pawnshop?'

'That would be kind, Cope.'

'I'll have someone come to your hotel.'

She nodded to the general.

'I'll go and pack.'

She fully intended to. But first, a trip to the range in the basement. She felt herself becoming aroused at the thought.

10

SANTA ROSA

The ex-soldier in the jungle camo fatigues and brown combat boots slowed the hired Jeep to a crawl and then stopped altogether. He climbed out, easing his back muscles and laying a palm across his belly. The pain was still there, and a four-hour drive on the country's terrible roads had done nothing to diminish it.

He stared at the display on the pickup's hood and shook his head. What a sight.

Four decapitated male corpses dumped in the ditch beside the road. Blood all over the dusty surface. Brain tissue and skull fragments littered the rutted tarmac, though the vultures circling high overhead would soon be down to make short work of this extravagant feast.

As he drew closer, a swarm of black and emerald-green blowflies rose from the bodies. Their sound was like a distant forest being buzz-sawed down to clear the way for cattle-farming.

But it wasn't the bodies that had caused him to stop and climb out.

That would be the heads. Arrayed like some medieval warning sign at the entrance to a warrior-king's land.

He walked over to the Hilux, wrinkling his nose at the rotting-meat stench. He glanced at the blackish-purple message finger-painted in front of those tattooed, stubbled and bloody chins.

Beyond the words needed to order a beer or a hire car, he didn't speak Spanish. But he recognised a couple of the words. *BANDIDOS*, obviously. Didn't need to be a Harvard-educated linguist to decode that one. And, from watching a popular ballroom dancing show on TV, he had a fairly good idea that *PASO* meant 'step'. *SEGURO* might be a kissing cousin of 'security'.

So, then, *No something steps security something something bandits.*

Pleased with himself for making the effort, but now having exhausted his translation abilities, he pulled out his phone.

'No safe passage for bandits,' he said aloud, looking up at the circling vultures. 'Not for this sorry quartet, at any rate.'

He'd read up on Honduras before making the trip. Jesus, the place made Somalia look like a holiday camp. A colleague had been stationed in Tegucigalpa for a while in the nineties and had told him her son used to go to his private school carrying a Glock 17 under his blazer. Apparently it was a more popular accessory than the latest iPhone. Illegal, yes. But like every other transgression in Honduras, easily erased with the right amount of cash.

So far, he hadn't met any of the country's criminal fraternity. Nonetheless, he'd been grateful for the reassuring weight of the pistol tucked under his own jacket, though this was Honduran army surplus rather than a tailored English-style school blazer.

The advice from seasoned in-country operatives was simple. You had two choices if confronted by an armed assailant. Hand over your valuables when asked. Or shoot first. Negotiating would get you killed. Running would get you killed. Fighting without a gun would get you killed.

Were the police a problem? He'd asked his colleague.

Inasmuch as it was entirely possible that the *bandido* aiming a large-calibre automatic at your belly was an off- or even on-duty cop, that would be a yes. Wages were low, so corruption was rife. Which had an upside. If you *did* need to kill a mugger or hijacker, as little as a hundred bucks to the first cop to come calling would be your Get Out of Jail Free card. It worked for gun-toting private school students; it worked for foreigners as well, though the price would probably be marked-up accordingly.

He patted the bulge under his jacket. Checked and oiled that morning. Test-fired twenty cliks out of town. Fit for purpose.

But why had Wolfe chosen such a goddamned difficult-to-reach hiding place? Surely with his resources, financial and otherwise, he could simply have holed up in a gated compound like an oligarch or a cartel boss. Monaco, maybe. Or buy a ranch in some remote part of New Zealand, like all the tech billionaires were rumoured to do.

No matter. They'd be meeting soon, and then he could ask him in person.

11

On the last stretch of the beach road before his place, Gabriel passed the simple wooden house Pera and Santiago shared.

Santiago's motorbike was gone from its usual spot in the shade of the mango tree in the yard. He'd be off with his friends somewhere, smoking weed probably, or shooting tin cans off the wreck further down the beach.

Gabriel pulled in at his own place, just another basic three-room wooden house on one floor. Sailboat pulled up onto the beach at the back, a little vegetable garden, somewhat neglected, backing onto the house.

He pushed through the screen door, went into the kitchen and put the chicken in the fridge. His glanced at the table. Pera had left him a note, in her sloping handwriting.

Hey Gabe,
  I got the evening off tonight. Want to come round and hang out?
  Pera x

. . .

She'd said more than once that it would be a lot easier if he bought himself a phone. And he'd said, simply, 'Why?'

Pera had laughed. 'You can get the internet. Send emails. Text me.'

'You live fifty metres down the road. If I want to talk to you I just come round.'

'Yes, OK, Mr Obvious. But what if, I don't know, you have a change of plan and you need to tell me?'

He'd wanted to say that he was through with planning full-stop. Let alone having plans that needed to change. Instead he said, 'They won't.' Though he'd glanced at the floorboards as he answered. Picturing what lay beneath the scuffed and sand-strewn wood.

He looked outside. The sun was high in the sky. Almost directly overhead, so the palm trees fringing the beach cast their broad-leaved shadows almost straight down onto the white sand.

From a cupboard in the kitchen he retrieved a bottle of Cacique-brand guaro, with its red label bearing a golden-headed Mayan priest. He cracked the top and took a swig of the distilled sugar cane spirit. Patriotic Hondurans swore it was as good as Cuban rum. Given they also swore that steaks cut from the bony-arsed creatures grazing the scrubby pastures were as good as Argentinian beef, he felt on safe ground ignoring their opinions.

Guaro was hooch, pure and simple. Not so strong you wouldn't be able to function the next day when you finished another bottle from your stash in a single evening. But strong enough to immobilise you and, eventually chase the ghosts away long enough for you to sleep.

From a residual sense of decorum, he pulled a scratched and cloudy tumbler from a cupboard and half-filled it. He took his drink into the main room. No pictures, but he'd hung a couple of locally woven rugs on the walls. Their zig-zagged patterns in earth tones and muted blues and greens added a splash of colour.

The sunlight, normally so bright he had to screw his eyes against it, was filtered through a white cotton curtain he'd nailed above the window soon after moving in. The flimsy fabric, almost transparent with age, bellied into the room as the sea-breeze wafted across the beach.

But where to sit? The room was crowded. Smudge Smith, his old comrade-in-arms, sprawled across the sagging, rust-and-cream cowhide sofa, staring at the wall where a TV might be, had Gabriel owned one. Britta Falskog, his first fiancée, sat cross-legged on the green, yellow and red rug reading a paperback, *The Girl With the Dragon Tattoo*. Don Webster, his old CO in the SAS and then at the Department, had taken one of the two hard chairs by the little wooden table where Gabriel ate, played solitaire and occasionally wrote.

Sitting opposite Don, setting out chess pieces, was Eli. Sweet, beautiful, dangerous Eli, who in the end had succumbed to every soldier's worst nightmare. The stray bullet.

He held his arms out wide.

'How come I own this place and I'm the only one without a seat?'

The others looked up, but nobody said anything.

Eli held out two closed fists towards Don, who tapped the left. She turned the fist over and opened her fingers to reveal a 7.62 rifle round, its brass case gleaming in the filtered sunlight.

Don's smile faded and then his face contorted in a rictus grin of agony as three bloody bullet wounds blossomed on his chest.

Gabriel slapped his cheek, hard. Again. Again.

'Fuck off, all of you!' he screamed into the empty room. 'Why can't you leave me alone?'

He threw his head back and swallowed the remaining guaro in a single gulp, smacking the thick-sided tumbler down on a rickety bamboo bookcase.

Shaking, whether from anger, fear or adrenaline after the encounter with the four bandidos he neither knew nor cared, he whirled round and left the room to the ghosts of his past.

He grabbed a wide-brimmed straw hat from a peg by the back door and strode out into the heat, immediately feeling the prickle as the soft breeze off the sea dried the sweat from his arms and legs.

Walk east or west? The extent of the choice facing him. It made a change after so many years of calculating survival odds, mission parameters and logistics for off-books assassinations. Santiago had told him the previous day that the sea turtles were laying their eggs to the east of the village. He set off in that direction, the bottle of guaro swinging from his left hand.

Smudge joined him after a couple of hundred yards, falling into step on the seaward side. Since Gabriel had retrieved his shattered skull from a mica-flecked riverbed in Mozambique and returned it to his widow, Melody, Smudge's shot-away jaw had healed itself.

'Hey, boss,' he said companionably. 'Going for a walk?'

Gabriel smiled wryly. 'Well, I'm not on a route march, if that's what you mean?'

'Nah, mate, I get it, I do,' Smudge said, turning a little so he could face Gabriel. Although this did mean the sunlight glittering off the breakers shone through his face a little, rendering it translucent. 'Nothing to do, nowhere to go.'

'I've been to the bank,' Gabriel protested. 'And I bought a chicken.'

'Good choice.'

Gabriel stopped, his feet crunching on a patch of delicate white shells.

'What the hell is that supposed to mean?'

'Chicken? What do you think it means? They murdered her, boss. In cold blood. It was a hit, pure and simple. And you're here, wandering about with your head in the clouds...or up your arse, more like. What's the matter? Scared?'

Gabriel's pulse jumped up, and his chest tightened. Smudge was usually a benign presence. He'd accepted the hallucinations of his fallen comrade as part and parcel of the way he had to exist now. But now he was levelling the worst accusation you could ever make to a soldier, whether serving or not. That he was a coward.

'I'm not scared, Smudge. I'm just not ready for it.'

Smudge rolled his eyes, a disconcerting gesture as they

revolved all the way round in their sockets until nothing remained but white.

'Oh, right. Yeah, of course. Not ready. Of *course* you're not ready! You've turned into some kind of poundshop beach bum, haven't you?' The eyes rolled back into their normal position, the brown irises filled with contempt. 'I mean, have you seen yourself in a mirror? My Christ! It's like Keanu Reeves after a week-long guifiti bender.'

Gabriel responded by tipping his head back, squeezing his eyes closed against the dazzling sunlight and taking a long pull on the bottle by his side.

'You know, for a figment of my imagination, you're not a lot of fun, Smudge,' he said, righting his head.

But when he opened his eyes again, Smudge was gone. Gabriel spun round, convinced this time that the ghostly apparition was real. But he had the beach to himself, as always. He looked down at the fragments of white shell around his feet. His stomach turned over as he thought he saw human teeth among the sun-bleached shards of calcium. Then reality asserted itself.

He kicked the white grit away and walked on, distracted by a flight of pelicans gliding low over the surf, their beaks almost half the length of their bodies. Silver fish broke the surface as the birds' shadows spooked the shoals. Kingfish, maybe, or Spanish mackerel. Good eating for man or bird.

As he pictured the succulent white flesh of a barbecued kingfish, hunger struck him. He veered off into the jungle, searching for a tree that might yield a ripe fruit or two. This part of the coast was rich in mango, avocado and papaya, which grew profusely wherever there was a patch of soil.

He found a mango tree leaning drunkenly out over the sand. Selecting a perfectly ripe fruit, its yellow skin yielding to his fingertips, he plucked it and sat with his back to the trunk. He opened his pocket-knife and deftly removed the wide, flat, sawdust-coloured stone. No need for all that fancy hedgehog business, scoring lines and inverting the skin. He pushed his mouth against the soft, warm, scented flesh and scraped off a mouthful with his incisors.

The flavour of the local varieties of mango was a world away from the one-note samba of the supermarket fruit back in England. Here, they emitted aromas so complex it was like tasting wine. Ginger, lime, green apple, hints of pineapple and peach, even a slight fizz reminiscent of sherbet. He wiped juice off his chin with the back of his hand and stared out over the ocean, trying to forget Smudge's caustic verdict on his new lifestyle.

No hallucination this time, but he did hear Fariyah's irritatingly calm voice inside his head.

Since we both know Smudge isn't actually here, it's not really his verdict you find so difficult to accept, is it, Gabriel?

That was the trouble with trick-cyclists. You let them into your head once and they set up camp permanently. Of course it wasn't Smudge who'd called him out for his cowardice. It was himself. The only person inside his head able to offer opinions about his own conduct.

He tilted the bottle to his lips and focused on the pelicans, which had returned and were now dive-bombing fish right in front of his position. Each bird would start off coming into the wind, before rolling over, wings outstretched, and starting their dive. A few feet or so from the surface, they folded their wings back, like a swept-wing fighter. Just before the point of impact, they let them stream behind them in delta-wing format and speared beneath the waves. They'd emerge, throat-pouch sagging with seawater and its freight of fish.

After a while, the display lost its magic and he let his eyes close. Listening to the splashes and the birds' cries as they fought off gannets and boobies for the spoils, he tried to relax, to forget Smudge's accusations.

Despite the midday heat, the wind off the sea was keeping him cool. Even so, a droplet of sweat had begun to crawl down the side of his nose, setting up an itch he was too sleepy to bother scratching.

He licked his dry lips, crusted with salt evaporated off the sea-spray being blown in towards him from the foamy crests of the breakers. He reached for the bottle; it was empty. The pelicans had disappeared. He tuned out the repetitive sound of the waves as they *shushed* their way onto the beach and focused on the sounds of the jungle behind him.

As always, when he performed this simple exercise, it took a minute or so before he could separate out the buzzes, creaks, growls and hoots that belonged to the various creatures that called this tropical green paradise home.

Amidst the sonic chaos, one sound intruded that didn't belong. A simple rhythm – one-two, one-two – being beaten out by the only creature hereabouts that would deliberately set out to cause him harm.

He had his pocket knife. And he could smash the bottle on a rock to improvise a fine stabbing and slashing weapon. He began levering himself to his feet and turned to meet the intruder.

Gabriel sighed. Not here, too, surely?

12

Seeing who had pursued him down the beach, Gabriel sighed and sat back down again, resumed staring out to sea.

He'd accustomed himself to the ghosts inhabiting his house. Britta, Smudge, Don and Eli were like the stray cats that wandered the beach, occasionally taking up residence for a day or a week in one of the houses. He even had one himself, a regular visitor he'd christened *Babera* for the white bib under her chin.

Inhabiting his house, yes, fine, he could live with that. *Had* to, since they'd shown no sign of leaving. But out here, where he came to get away from the past? Even if it meant viewing the present through the bottom of an empty guaro bottle first? That could get very old, very fast.

He spoke to the surf, not looking round at the ghost.

'Smudge already accused me of being a coward, Boss. You've had a wasted journey if you came to deliver the same message.'

'Hello, Gabriel.'

Gabriel started, knocking over the guaro bottle and not even noticing. Of all the ghosts who haunted him, only Smudge spoke. And then only rarely.

But Don had replied. In a tired voice belonging to someone who carried sadness like a fifty-kilo Bergen.

The ghost emerged fully out of the jungle, ambled onto the sand and cautiously lowered itself to the ground, grunting with the effort and wincing its way into a seated posture.

Suddenly Gabriel was angered by the intrusion. Why couldn't the dead stay dead?

'Am I going to have to find an exorcist?' he asked. 'There's an old Garifuna shaman in Limon who'll perform the ritual for twenty-five dollars.'

The ghost rubbed a hand across its bristled cheek. Then it stretched out its other hand and laid it on Gabriel's forearm. The pressure was gentle, but real. Physical. It smiled.

'It's me, Old Sport. The real me, I mean. Seems it takes more than half a dozen rounds from an M4 to finish Dobbin off after all.'

Gabriel scratched his beard. Tears were welling in the corners of his eyes. He twisted round until he was facing Don.

'Boss? Is it really you?'

He stretched out a fingertip and prodded Don in the ribcage on the right side.

Don winced.

'Careful, dear boy. That's not far from where Bakker put one of his rounds in me.'

Gabriel swallowed hard, trying, and failing, to dislodge the lump swelling in his throat like a mouthful of stale bread. He reached out with both hands and took his old CO by the shoulders. Then he leaned over and hugged him tightly, sinking his face into the crook of the older man's neck. Don enfolded him in a fatherly embrace and held him while he wept.

Able once again to breathe, Gabriel sat back.

'I thought you were dead.'

Don grinned, his weathered face grooved with many more lines than Gabriel remembered.

'So did everyone else, Old Sport. I'm not even sure my doctors had a great deal of faith.'

'What happened?'

'I tell you what,' he said, clambering to his feet and making an old man's noises of frustration as his unwilling joints popped and crackled like distant gunfire, 'I've got my Jeep back there in a clearing. Can I drive you home? Then you can make me a coffee or, if God is smiling on this old warhorse, a proper cup of tea, and I'll tell you everything.'

Shaking his head and feeling on the brink of laughter, Gabriel stood up and followed Don off the beach. They walked through the trees to a leaf-strewn clearing surrounded by red-barked palms festooned with lianas leaning at crazy angles. A late-model Jeep Cherokee in black livery sat like a panther amid the emerald foliage.

* * *

Even on the marginal land between the jungle and the sea, Gabriel had maintained one tiny sliver of England in his rough-built timber and corrugated-iron shack. In a cupboard with a sagging door painted the blue of old Dutch china, he had a box of tea. Not the flavourless brown dust the local bodegas sold. This was genuine English breakfast, sold only in a single delicatessen in Tegucigalpa and purchased mainly by staff at the British Embassy. Pound for pound it was as expensive as caviar, which the delicatessen also sold. But it tasted sublime, and Gabriel made a monthly trip in the old Ford pickup to restock.

The tea made and poured, he offered a mug to Don and motioned for him to take it onto the deck. The two men, CO and captain, unit boss and covert operative and now, what – just old friends? – sat beside each other in rattan chairs staring out at the petrol-blue Caribbean, flecked with darker spots where clouds threw sickle-shaped shadows onto the water.

Don sipped his tea and nodded.

'Excellent brew, Old Sport.'

Gabriel found he had no energy for small talk.

'What happened, Boss?'

'To me?'

'To everything?'

The older man shrugged. 'Let's start with the easy bit. The doctors in Jerusalem had me in an induced coma for a month, give or take. And if you were to measure my nationality by blood, I'm now one hundred per cent Israeli several times over. Uri gave me three pints himself. He was ready to bury me, told me he had the third draft of a eulogy all worked out.'

Gabriel smiled. 'But the old warhorse refused to go quietly into that good night?'

'Something like that. They said there was one afternoon where I died for a minute or two. Heart stopped like a clapped-out Land Rover. They got it going again and after that I started making steady progress back from the brink.' He took another sip of tea and grunted with appreciation. 'Must've had some unfinished business.'

'What about Uri's message? He texted me to say you'd died.'

'We both felt it would be better to sow a few seeds to convince anyone else who might be watching that I really was dead.'

'How did you find me?'

'Ha! Well, you didn't make it easy, I can tell you that. Obviously I started in Aldeburgh. Consulted the local plod, watched that rather fortuitous video. Read your suicide note. I was all ready to agree with them that you'd done yourself in but then I saw it.'

'What?'

'It was just after you waved. The police got so excited about cleaning up all the static, they stopped looking at what they *could* see.' Don paused, and finished his tea. 'If there's any more in the pot, Old Sport, I could murder another. Anyway, where was I? Oh, yes. I, on the other hand, noticed how you were leaning back just as you brought your hand down. It seemed an odd change of posture. The video glitched. Then, of course, you blew the boat sky high and that was the end of that. What did you use by the way? *Plastique?*'

'ANFO,' Gabriel said from the kitchen, where he was pouring more tea.

'Hmm, mm-hmm. Anyway, as I said, the way you leaned back reminded me of something. Those SBS boys rolling backwards off a RIB. Perhaps I simply couldn't accept that you were really at the end of the road, but I asked a couple of people I know to see if anyone else had been shooting video that day. Down the beach, along the coast, you know? Even a doorbell cam might've caught something. Guess what? We found you, swimming ashore in a pair of swimming trunks. What did you do then?'

Gabriel took his seat again.

'I'd left some clothes and a go-bag under an old fishing boat. Wig, sunglasses, standard kit. Nobody was looking at me: they'd all rushed up the beach to see what the fuss was all about. I walked to a hotel where I'd booked a room under a false name, and from there made my way out of the country.'

'Nice work, Old Sport. I mean it. The authorities were convinced you'd gone up with the boat,' Don said. 'After that it was just a matter of waiting. I thought maybe you'd go to Hong Kong to see Tara. Or Russia. Pay a call on your friend Tatyana Garin. I called in a few favours, had the old facial-recognition software busying itself searching for you. We eventually saw you in Miami.'

'We?'

'Me and Uri. He's most keen to meet with you, by the way. So, Miami. You could have been heading for Cuba. But I asked myself, now, Dobbin, where would Gabriel go to hide out after faking his own suicide? Somewhere with minimal chance of discovery. Cuba's just another tourist destination these days, isn't it?

'But topping the Foreign Office's list of places to avoid was jolly old Honduras. Home to MS-13, the 18th Street Gang, the Rio Rosso and Zinguizapa cartels and sundry other charming little outfits all focused entirely on violent organised crime. *That's the place*, I said to myself. I mean, it was a gamble, but I flatter myself that I know my men as well as they know themselves.

'From there, it wasn't really very hard at all. Although I have been hanging around here for a month, making a nuisance of myself in every bar, bodega and bordello from Tegucigalpa to San Pedro Sula.'

Gabriel fixated on the last of the trio of alliterative places Don had mentioned. He realised with a glimmer of intuition how Don had found the final piece of the puzzle.

'You went to Frida's, didn't you? Did you speak to Esperanza?'

Don nodded. 'Charming young lady. Don't rush to blame her. I think she was so relieved that all I wanted to do was talk, she couldn't have been happier to help me. I said I was a friend of your father's. Hondurans place great store by family. I said I had been searching for you all over the world. I think she took pity on an old man.'

Gabriel shook his head. He didn't blame Pera. And if Don had reached Santa Rosa, he would have found Gabriel eventually. At least this way it was via a friend.

'Why, though, Boss? Why come looking for me?'

Don's wiry grey eyebrows shot upwards. He twisted round in his chair to look directly into Gabriel's eyes.

'Why? Dear God, Old Sport, I think of you as a son. Of *course* I was going to come looking for you! After they killed Eli, I knew you'd be in a mess. I tried Fariyah, just on the off-chance, but she hadn't heard from you in a while. When I found out you'd killed yourself on your boat I couldn't believe it.'

'But that's not all, is it? Margot McDonnell and her crew shut us down, didn't they? Are you out for revenge?'

'Aren't you?'

Gabriel sighed. 'It's too soon. She's too well protected. I was going to wait a couple of years.'

'I don't think we have that luxury, Old Sport. From what I hear, she's found a new berth Stateside. The longer you wait, the thicker the walls around her are going to get.'

'Sounds like you have a plan.'

Don offered a crooked grin. 'It's not just my plan.'

'Oh, right. You said Uri Ziff is keen to meet me. Let me guess.

Letting Kevin Bakker get within grenade-throwing distance of Saul put a dent in his pride.'

'It's not just that. In fact, it's hardly even that. It was Eli. Remember, he was her mentor at Mossad, and Kidon before that. Through Bakker, McDonnell took her from him. The Israelis don't take kindly to people who kill their soldiers, whoever they eventually end up working for. He wants McDonnell dead. As do I. As, I imagine, do you. Now we have to make it happen.'

'You want to go up against whatever shady outfit's paying her wages now?'

'You've done it before.'

'I had the Department behind me then.'

Don glared at Gabriel.

'Forget the Department! That was just a name. Every op we undertook came down to one or two operatives. Their personal resources, intelligence, courage, stamina and fighting spirit. The Department was a couple of filing cabinets and a handful of phone numbers.'

Gabriel watched as a seabird dived to pluck a silver fish from the surface of the sea.

'I have a date in Tegucigalpa in a couple of nights' time. We can talk properly after that.'

'What sort of a date?'

'A date where you could make some serious money and I can close off a little niggle.'

Gabriel clenched his fists and stared at his knuckles. The scar tissue had built up over the last few months. He'd been careless the previous time he'd been in the city, partly on purpose, but this time round it was all business.

13

Gabriel's house was too small for a guest. Even one who professed himself happy to 'kip on the floor, where I can keep an eye on you'.

Besides, as Gabriel had pointed out, as kindly as possible to his old boss, 'You've reached the age where I think a bed counts as essential kit, Boss.'

After making the introductions, Gabriel had secured Don a room with a neighbour. Señora Cruz was a widow. She'd lost her husband, a successful pineapple farmer, a couple of years back. She had a big house by the standards of Santa Rosa: two storeys, three bedrooms upstairs and a veranda that gave onto a well-tended vegetable garden.

As usual before a bout, Gabriel paused his drinking for the day. He knew he'd lost some of the edge that had allowed him to perform at his peak for Department ops. But for what awaited him, his residual fitness was more than enough. And, to be honest, he'd always found he could bounce back from the effects of alcohol. Something genetic to do with being the son of a diplomat. That or the army training.

He awoke at sunrise and pulled on a pair of running shoes.

Then he was out of the shack and down onto the beach, heading west along the hard, tide-rippled sand. After five minutes he picked up the pace. After another five he upped it again, coming up onto the balls of his feet as he ran, breathing deeply and steadily, allowing oxygen to flow through his lungs, his bloodstream and into his muscles.

He alternated hundred-metre sprints with longer spells of fast running until he reached the wreck of a wooden barge left over from one of the hurricanes whose southern arms occasionally wrought havoc on the Honduran coast. The wreck's pitch-darkened ribs stuck up out of the sand like the bones of a long-dead sea creature.

Between the upcurved timbers, green and blue crabs scuttled out of his way as he jumped in amongst them. He skipped from rib to rib, sure-footed as a mountain goat, before emerging at the bow and sprinting around the wreck twice clockwise, then changing direction and repeating the sprint twice more.

At the tree-line, a pile of sawn logs waited. Each was two metres long and as thick as a man's thigh. Gabriel hoisted one onto his shoulder, ran back to the wreck and tossed it over the ribs. He jogged back, hefted a second log and brought it back to join its fellow. In this way, dripping with sweat and feeling his muscles burn, he transferred thirty of the increasingly heavy logs from the woodpile to the wreck.

With the transfer complete, he took off his running shoes and slung them around his neck then waded out into the water, its surface warm, its depths pleasingly cool. He swam back to his shack, diving beneath the surface and holding his breath for increasing numbers of strokes.

Back at his place, he showered and ate a quick breakfast of tortillas and refried beans, cold from the fridge. Don arrived at 8:05 a.m.

'Do you want to tell me about this date you have in the city, Old Sport?' he asked, as Gabriel made tea.

'You won't approve.'

'Really? Try me. I think I'll be able to cope.'

'It's a fight.'

Don grimaced. 'Something tells me this isn't Queensberry Rules.'

'There's a ring of sorts. And a referee. But after that it gets a little…free-form.'

'People get hurt?'

'Usually.'

'Seriously?'

'Most nights.'

'Permanently?'

'It happens.'

'You?'

Gabriel held his hands wide. 'I appear to still be here.'

'You know what I mean,' Don growled.

Gabriel shrugged. 'Concussed a couple of times. Split lip. Lost a tooth.' He snarled at Don, pulling his top lip back to reveal a hole among his back teeth.

'Why do you do it?'

Gabriel heaved a sigh. He wasn't ready to tell Don the truth. 'At first I just wanted an outlet. I wanted to hurt people. To force my pain into retreat by imposing more pain on others.'

'Did it work?'

Gabriel shook his head. It hadn't worked the first time. Or the time after that. Or the next. But somewhere along the line, it had become a habit.

He didn't need the money the promoter paid him, a greasy-looking gangster in the pay of the MS-13 who ran the fights in a fenced-in enclosure at the back of his bar. But he'd become addicted to the adrenaline rush of facing off against guys twice his size, tattooed from their insteps to their cheekbones, some sporting hideous arrays of prison ink.

When they grinned at him before a fight, they displayed gold and silver grilles where Mother Nature had placed enamel. Dead-eyed expressions that spoke of countless encounters with death, mostly on the dealing-out end. Leering smiles that suggested the final outcome might involve not just defeat at their hands but consumption by the flames.

And each, at some point, maybe seconds after the bell rang for the beginning of the first round, or deep into the belly of the fight when the dust was soaked in blood and sweat, would discover the same uncomfortable truth. The average-looking gringo with the wild black-and-silver beard and the knife and bullet scars decorating his pelt like birthmarks was far, far more dangerous than they could ever have imagined.

Too late.

With the bundles of greasy dollar bills fattening the promoter's fist, Gabriel would go in for the kill. His opponents were good. Skilful, even. Seasoned fighters with many bouts behind them. But they hadn't fought with the SAS. Hadn't executed numerous covert assassination operations for the Department. Or ranged the globe visiting vengeance on those who had destroyed their families more comprehensively than a death squad.

So when Gabriel decided enough was enough, or received a knowing look from the guy with the pawful of much-crumpled tens, twenties, fifties and hundreds, he'd put the hurt on his opponent – and the fight to bed.

Mostly he tried to avoid lethal strikes. He wanted to win, not to kill. But he knew which injuries were survivable, treatable, and which were not.

Big men would go down, their bloodshot eyes popping as their paralysed lungs tried and failed to drag a sip of air down their swelling throats.

Ripped little bantamweights, fast as lightning, eyes glinting like fighting cocks', would keel over sideways, their central nervous systems knocked out like an electricity substation taking a direct hit from an RPG.

And Gabriel would collect his fee, maybe a percentage of the take, depending on the arrangement he'd made with the promoter. Hot, hard hands would slap his back as he made his way out of the humid enclosure and into the bar for a couple of cold ones.

Cheers in the vernacular blend of Honduran Spanish and one or two of the native languages would bounce off the corrugated iron roof and walls. And Gabriel would politely refuse the approaches of the working girls who liked to screw the victors for a discount, since it burnished their credentials.

He realised he'd been silent for a long time. He refocused. Don was leaning on the wooden rail at the edge of the deck, looking out at the sea.

'I can see the temptation, Old Sport,' he said, when Gabriel joined him. 'Just leave it all behind. Barbecue with the lovely Esperanza, go fishing, take the old pickup for a jaunt into town when you need supplies. An easy life. Uncomplicated.'

'And yet you've come all this way, used all that technology to take me away from it, haven't you?'

'Don't you think it's time, Gabriel? You're a man of honour. Same as me. Same as Uri.' He cleared his throat. 'Precious few of us left, in my opinion.'

Gabriel looked down the beach. Santiago, Pera's son, was up early, kicking a football up and down the sand. He saw Gabriel and waved. Gabriel waved back. Was this it, then? Nothing more than a six-month holiday from reality? An ethics-free zone where he fought like a maniac in Tegucigalpa, beheaded the corpses of bandits who tried to bushwhack him, then spent days trekking in the jungle, living off whatever he could catch, pick or kill?

'What's it all for, boss?' he asked.

'That, Old Sport, is the question. Christine, God rest her soul, was a teacher. She educated kids. Taught them to read and write. To appreciate nature. To see that there was a world based on facts, not prejudice, and that with the right information they could achieve miracles. I never had her aptitude, but I discovered I was good at fighting. And at leading. The work we did together? I hope it meant something. I hope we rid the world of more bad people than we let out into it. What's it all for? For what it's worth, I think you try to leave the world a better place than when you found it.'

'Do you think I did that?'

77

Don turned to face Gabriel and gripped him by the biceps, a lot of force in the old man's hard hands even now.

'Yes, I damn well do!'

'Then how come all the people I love are dead, Don? Explain that to me. I tried to have just a fraction of a normal life. Not much. Just a wife. A child. That wasn't too much to ask, was it?'

Don released Gabriel's arms and let his hands drop to his sides.

'No, dear boy, it really wasn't. Do you want me to blame Dame Fate? Or bad luck? Do you think you're cursed? A walking jinx? "Keep away, I'm Death's handmaiden," that sort of thing? Because I could. I just don't think it would do you any good. You want the truth? It's summed up in a very elegant little phrase you may have heard our American cousins using from time to time on our joint ops. Shit happens.'

Gabriel nodded. Then he ran down the beach to help Santiago practice heading the ball. He didn't know exactly when, but soon, shit would be happening for some very bad people indeed.

Until then, he could try to enjoy the life – the temporary life – he'd built for himself in Santa Rosa.

14

TEGUCIGALPA

Tegucigalpa shared its city limits with Comayaguela, its twin on the west bank of the Rio Grande O Choluteca. If the former was generally considered a dangerous place for westerners after dark, the latter didn't bother with anything as mundane as the position of the sun in the sky.

On the night of the bout, Gabriel paid off the taxi that had taken them from a secure car park below a Marriott on the east side of the river and across into the barrios. He and Don emerged from the ageing Chevy's humid, unairconditioned and cigar-smelling interior into Comayaguela's even more soupy evening.

Barrio Concepcion was, even by the low standards of the city, a poor area. Most of the dwellings couldn't lay claim to the term 'house'. Or not with a straight face, anyway. 'Shack' was closer to the mark. Although given that some of the slum's residents had made their homes in shipping containers, or even wooden packing crates nailed together and roofed with sheets of polythene, even that was stretching the common definition of the word.

Cuarta Avenida ran north-south. Gabriel led Don along its western side for half a block. The night air was redolent of grilling chicken, spices and the heady top notes of home-brewed guifiti. Here and there he picked out the sweet smell of cannabis smoke.

The strap of his holdall was digging in painfully over an old bullet wound. Gabriel transferred it to his other shoulder. A shabby blue and black Adidas knockoff, he'd bought it in the market back in Santa Rosa shortly after arriving in Honduras.

'The bar's at the junction with Calle Cinco,' he said. 'Look for the neon sign. It's hard to miss.'

Just then, a small boy, maybe nine or ten stepped out in front of them. Big brown eyes, an unruly mop of jet-black hair and the broad, chestnut-brown face of a *mestizo*, the Indian-European people who accounted for nine in ten Hondurans. He wore faded jeans with the knees out and a baggy red T-shirt, the instantly recognisable face of Che Guevara printed in black above the word 'Freedom!'. He smiled broadly, revealing large, even and very white teeth.

In passable, American-accented English, he said, 'Hello, buddy. You need a guide? I take you to best bar in the barrio. Chupacabra. Ten dollars.'

Gabriel shook his head with a smile and replied in Spanish.

'It's half a block away. A blind man could find it without a stick. But I've got five dollars US if you want to bring us both a Coke.'

The kid scowled. Then, as if practising for a magic show for older relatives at a christening party or a family wedding, he twirled his right hand with a flourish and dipped it into the back of his jeans.

It reappeared wrapped around a battered, snub-nosed revolver. To Gabriel it looked like a .38 Police Special. An *antique* .38 Police Special. This close, he could see an ugly dent in the barrel. The hammer was rusty and the grip from the left side of the handle was missing.

In fact, the whole piece looked less like an antique and more like a gun-shaped piece of scrap metal. But, yes, he could also see the dull grey noses of the rounds slotted into the chambers. If the kid pulled the trigger, the gun would most likely explode in his hand.

'Gimme all your money, *chelito*!' the kid barked, his unbroken voice acquiring a harshness from somewhere.

Gabriel grinned down at him.

'You're calling me "whitey"? That's not very friendly. Look, son. What's your name?'

The kid stuck to English.

'I'm the Grim Reaper, whitey. Now give me all your cash or I drill you right here. I gut-shoot you.' He essayed a leer, though it came off as stagey: a villain in a school play. Not that this tooled-up urchin looked like he spent much time learning his ABC at *la escuela*. 'You die slowly. Lots of pain.'

'OK, so you're the Grim Reaper. I get it. Respect.' Beside him, he caught a movement as Don moved to create a little more space between them. Gabriel shook his head, minutely. He had this. 'But if you pull that trigger, the only thing you're going to be reaping is your own little life. That monster's useless. It'll blow your hand off. Maybe kill you.'

'Liar! Now give me your money. All of it.'

Then the kid made his next mistake. He straightened his arm. Now the barrel was a few inches from Gabriel's breastbone.

Maybe the gambit would have worked on a tourist. Even a local, if they weren't already running, or shooting the kid dead where he stood in his cheap black trainers. But for Gabriel it was barely even a training drill.

He snapped his hand up and seized the revolver and the kid's hand both, jamming his thumb in front of the hammer to prevent it moving. A sharp twist to the left and the kid was disarmed.

He released the cylinder and tipped the six rounds into the palm of his hand. They went into his pocket. While Don restrained the now kicking and swearing would-be robber, Gabriel cocked the now non-lethal.38, placed it in the angle between the kerb and the tarmac, and stamped on it. The ancient, rusted hammer broke clean off with a metallic clink.

The kid broke free of Don's grip, kicked him hard in the shin and sprinted off, throwing a '*Hijo de puta!*' over his shoulder.

Don rolled his eyes then bent to rub his shin.

'No need for your superlative linguistic skills, Old Sport. Even I can translate "son of a whore".'

Gabriel grinned and pulled his boss upright again.

'It's a little saltier in the barrios. He called you a "motherfucker".'

'Is that all? Well, I've had RSMs call me a lot worse in my time so I suppose I can live with that coming from a ten-year-old. Do you get a lot of that?'

'Some,' Gabriel said as they resumed their journey. 'If you're *chele*, that marks you out as a target. If you've smartly dressed, or you've got a camera round your neck, ditto. You can't blame them. They have nothing here and you get rich Yanks, Chinese or Europeans treating it like poverty tourism. Kids like him are just trying to survive.'

'He *was* going to gut-shoot you, Old Sport,' Don said as they resumed walking.

'He didn't, though, did he? And I was telling the truth. That piece of crap would have taken his hand off,' Gabriel said, shrugging. He pointed across the street. 'We're here.'

They crossed the road, dodging taxis whose drivers' hands appeared welded to their horn buttons.

As they reached the relative safety of the far kerb, Don lifted his chin. 'What the hell's that?'

Above the front door, a bi-coloured neon beast see-sawed back and forth, back and forth. A jerky rhythm. Electric blue as it reared, shocking pink as it pounced.

'*Chupacabra.* A mythical creature. Drains its prey of their blood and organs. In Honduras they go in for the half-wolf, half-cat look.'

'Well it looks bloody ugly.'

'It fits the bar. Come on.'

Inside, loud salsa music competed with a noisy blend of conversations, shouting, singing, laughter and occasional curses, all uttered in the rough-edged, tangy dialect of Honduran Spanish spoken in the barrios this side of the river.

The air was blue with smoke, some tobacco, some cannabis. To that pungent aroma was added a noisome mixture of aftershave, perfume, sweat, vomit and spilled beer.

'We're through there,' Gabriel shouted, pointing to a door in the far corner, behind a pool table at which four heavily built men wielded cues like offensive weapons.

As Gabriel made for the gap, with Don bringing up the rear, two of the ogres moved to block his path, crossing their pool cues like the spears of old-time castle guards.

'I'm fighting tonight,' Gabriel said. 'Archangel.'

One of the guards consulted a clipboard. Scrutinised Gabriel, then nodded and stood aside.

'I've got fifty dollars on you leaving in an ambulance, gringo,' he said as Gabriel shouldered his way past. 'That's if one'll bother coming out to the barrio.'

Gabriel whipped round, causing the looming giant to take an involuntary step back.

'That's a shame. I guess you'll be dumpster-diving for your meals for the rest of the week, then.'

Over the grudging laughter of the second man, Gabriel led Don through the door and into the arena.

15

Margot's plane made a bumpy landing on the scarred tarmac at Comayagua International Airport. As she descended the rackety metal stairs the airport staff had wheeled out from the terminal building, the humidity hit her like a truck. She blinked away the sweat that sprang from her skin like bullets and dripped, stinging, into her eyes. Quite the contrast to her chilly office back in Washington.

In all that air-conditioned splendour, her colleagues had formed, rather too quickly in her view, a firm opinion of their new British colleague. And they didn't bother lowering their voices too much, either, so she was able to hear much of what was said about her.

She was 'prissy'. 'Snotty', even. Perhaps suffering from undiagnosed OCD. Less kindly, some wondered if she was a virgin, so sexless did she appear to be. Some ventured the opinion that what she need was a good hard banging. Others opined that they wouldn't, even if she was the last woman alive.

None of this bothered Margot. Though she had created a spreadsheet. In it, she recorded the offenders' names, faces and, as she saw it, weaknesses.

She didn't intend to do anything with this information. But one never knew. Perhaps a terrorist, domestic or imported, might attack their headquarters. She'd seen a TV show where just such an event had happened down the road at Langley.

And then, who knew? Amongst the screaming and the shouting. The dust and flying glass. The flames, flying shrapnel, nails, ball-bearings and assorted metalware. Vengeance might stalk among the ruins. Seeking out targets.

Their ringing ears would hear nothing. Their scorched corneas would see nothing. Their noses, filled with the acrid stink of C4 or just plain old dynamite, would smell nothing.

But their nerves would feel something. Oh my goodness, yes. The nerves that sent messages of pain, of suffering, of scream-and-panic-inducing agony. Yes, they would be firing faster than a mini-gun.

Because what none of her colleagues had realised about Margot Evelyn Rose McDonnell was that she *was* different. Not, in fact, a virgin. Although sex came way, way down her list of priorities. Something altogether rarer. She didn't like to give it a name. That was for those fools in the FBI's Behavioural Science Unit. Or whatever they were calling themselves these days.

No. Margot was content simply to *be*. After all, wasn't that the mantra of all the wellness gurus? Everyone from actresses advising her to steam-clean her vagina to online hucksters promising enlightenment for just one, totally refundable, $99 lifetime subscription to their wellbeing courses. It was page one on all the books. All the social media ads.

Be the best version of yourself! Love yourself! Practice self-care!

It was just, Margot's approach to personal wellbeing sometimes involved removing that quality from others; inflicting a degree of pain, up to and including death. Some whom she was paid to treat that way. Others where it was more of a personal viewpoint.

There had been a Swiss banker, once. Tall, well-formed from skiing and regular games of tennis at his chateau, where he entertained politicians, celebrities, and, unfortunately for him, arms dealers who supplied Islamist terrorist groups.

The hit was her first. She was supposed to take him out with a long-range shot from the snow-covered mountain overlooking his estate. And, to be fair, she had executed the plan to the letter. She'd donned the white camouflage suit, taken the white-painted rifle up to the hide she'd constructed the previous day. Sighted on the banker's left temple and even tightened her finger on the trigger.

Then she'd watched as he slung a proprietary arm around the shoulders of a girl dressed in a short grey skirt, a white blouse with striped tie, white knee socks and a pair of black pumps. The girl couldn't have been more than sixteen, and the way she was dressed she looked even younger.

His two companions were laughing. One sidled over and cupped her left breast through the schoolgirl blouse she was wearing.

And, very calmly, Margot had released the trigger. It took her another day to make her way inside the estate, bypassing the human, canine and electronic security measures using whatever method felt most appropriate.

She slit the throats of the two guests while they slept, waking them just as the knife completed its left-right journey across their necks, opening their carotid arteries like firehoses, clamping a hand over their wide-open mouths and watching as the light dimmed in their eyes.

The banker, naturally, she saved until last.

When he woke up, the effects of the aerosolised fentanyl she'd administered finally wearing off, it was to find himself duct-taped to his four-poster bed. Stark-naked. Being observed by a clearly terrified teenaged girl, who'd confirmed an hour earlier to Margot that she was fourteen and had been flown in from an island in the Caribbean to 'entertain' the banker and his friends.

Before she began working, Margot advised the girl not to scream. It didn't matter from an operational perspective. Anyone who might have heard her and come running, pistol drawn, was long dead. But it would interfere with Margot's enjoyment of the noises the banker was going to be making.

Smiling at the memory, she entered the terminal building and, forty interminable minutes later, retrieved her single suitcase. Transiting through Customs and Immigration took a mere two hours, under the tender care of officials who had obviously never really given up on the whole Latin American fascist look – blinged-up olive-green uniforms, brown jackboots and aviator sunglasses.

Blotting out the dime-store dictators as they bullied and barked at hapless business executives and, God help us, tourists, she listened to a true-crime podcast about an uncaught serial killer until it was her turn. And then she was outside.

On the taxi-ride into the city, she let her eyes drift over the lush jungle bordering the highway. Honduras was one of the original 'banana republics'. Practically owned by a couple of American fruit companies who'd treated the country like a private orchard. Maybe the Hondurans' resentment at their treatment accounted for the ongoing travel advisories issued by the State Department and the Foreign Office at home. They bothered Margot not at all.

She had twenty-four hours or so before her meeting with the general's contact. The venue was a notorious bar-cum-club in Comayaguela. A hangout for cartel bosses, arms dealers, mercs and that species of useful but uncategorisable person who could be found knocking back drinks in the world's hot zones, from South Sudan to Colombia.

So, she had plenty of time to scope out the location and, of course, collect whatever concealable howitzer the general thought a 'woman travelling alone' might need to protect herself.

The following morning, she arose at 7:00 a.m. and ate a room-service breakfast of strong black coffee, a bowl of natural yoghurt with mixed seeds and red-berry compote, a double portion of steak tartare and toasted sourdough bread.

The red light on the phone was blinking, indicating she had a message. In Spanish-accented English, the hotel reception informed Señora Smith that her colleague Señor Wesson would be calling for her at reception at 10 a.m.

The man who dropped off the parcel for her might have been a desk clerk in a stationery store. Or an assistant shift supervisor in a call centre. He was that interesting-looking. Sandy hair, black-rimmed, thirties-style glasses. Features you'd see on a photo-library model tagged with the keywords: 'average guy + boring looks + forgettable face'. He wore a beige cotton windbreaker and tan slacks.

Only the watchful look in the ice-blue eyes behind those retro specs gave a hint of his profession. That and the stance, at once relaxed and ready.

They exchanged a couple of pleasantries including agreed codewords and then he passed her the bulging carrier bag. It dragged on her hand pleasantly, the thin plastic handles digging into her fingers. Just a little.

She took it back to her room and sat on the bed to unwrap her present from the general. First came a grey, blow-moulded plastic case. She unsnapped the catches and swung the lid back.

Nodding with a practised shooter's appreciation, she lifted out the Beretta 92FS 9mm pistol. She dropped out the magazine, an Italian-made Mec-Gar that held 18 Remington Golden Saber hollowpoints. The courier had added a box of fifty spares as well. Cope was so thoughtful.

She reached into the bottom of the bag and withdrew the second part of Six-Foot's load-out. A handsome folding fighting knife in a black nylon sheath. Yes, that would do nicely.

But maybe she could furnish herself with something of her own. A tradition she'd started back in Zermatt, when she'd partially strangled the banker with the twisted silk cord from his own dressing gown. His penis had swollen grotesquely in response, though she'd quickly resolved *that* little display.

She scanned the room and saw what she was looking for. The lower half of the window was screened with a square of textured, translucent fabric. It was attached by spring clips to a metre or so of braided steel wire, strung to a humming tension between two bullet-shaped steel tensioners.

A little work with the multi-tool she'd brought in her suitcase and she had reconfigured the curtain wire into a serviceable garotte. The tensioners worked perfectly as handles. She coiled it in the palm of her left hand and tucked it into her back pocket. Shaking her head, she withdrew it and threaded it around her waist beneath her narrow black leather belt. Perfect.

The meeting was set for 10:00 p.m. Margot dressed down: Levi's, boots, loose black T-shirt. No makeup. Her phone was in her back pocket. If anyone was foolish enough to try to jack it, she'd paste a look of terror onto her face, stammer out 'Please don't hurt me!' in her best tourist *Español – Por favor no me lastimes! –* reach back, and produce the Beretta from her waistband instead.

Then, acting solely in self-defence, she'd put one of those Remington Golden Saber hollow- points between his eyes.

Or maybe she'd explain she'd secreted her iPhone in her boot. She'd bend to retrieve it, giving him plenty of time to check her arse out, then slip the knife from its nylon sheath and drag it all the way up his femoral artery from knee to groin. People tended to forget about robbery when their lifeblood was hosing out all over the road.

So experience told her.

Failing that, she could always enucleate him. Some people used spoons. Margot couldn't be bothered with all that cutlery. After a delicious cold shower, she'd spent a little time filing her fingernails into points.

All in all, she was rather looking forward to her trip into what one guidebook charmingly referred to as 'Tegucigalpa's hyper-violent, dark twin'.

* * *

She tipped the taxi driver generously and stepped out into the humid night air. Not wanting to arrive without first scoping out the venue, she'd asked him to drop her two blocks further down the street.

It was a poor neighbourhood. You didn't need to be a guidebook writer to see that. But, like all such places, it clearly had a life of its own away from drive-bys, street robberies and sexual assaults. She looked up. Laundry was hanging on a white line that swooped in a perfect parabola between two apartment blocks. Blouses, bras and knickers, men's shirts, kid-sized multicoloured T-shirts and shorts. A family, then.

Two women were exchanging gossip five storeys above her. Her Spanish was adequate, but they were speaking in a thick dialect and she could only make out a few words.

'...*Consuela*...'

'...*puta*...'

'...*Maynor*...'

'...*su pobre esposo*...'

What a story. Consuela the whore and Maynor, her poor cuckolded husband.

Margot strode on, flicking her gaze left and right, plus the odd look back over her shoulder. The Beretta rubbed in the small of her back. A not altogether unpleasant sensation.

Ahead, a small child of perhaps eight or ten years was loitering in the shadow of an alleyway entrance.

Their eyes met. He looked away. Too quickly.

Margot began muttering under her breath. '*Por favor no me lastimes!*'

Would the kid have the sense he was born with and stick to his hidey-hole in the alley? To Margot it was of purely academic interest.

He stepped out and turned to face her, a little knife gripped in his right hand.

Oh well.

16

Gabriel felt the familiar kick of adrenaline.

The atmosphere on this side of the door was altogether darker, both in lighting and mood, than the main space.

A few faces turned in their direction. One or two nods. A couple of grins. And from one leather-jacketed thug with a scar bisecting his milky right eye, a prodigious gobbet of phlegm, directed onto the floor at Gabriel's feet.

Ignoring it, he gestured for Don to look over to the wall on the other side of the fight cage. It was taken up with a vast mural.

A more-detailed rendition of the neon beast from the front of the bar, its overall appearance was somewhere between a wolf and a jaguar. Spines like porcupine quills, as long as its legs, stuck up in a row from its back. Its wide-open mouth was filled with long yellow fangs dripping bloody slime. And its eyes were sharp-pointed ellipses, the yellow of mango flesh.

In the vast, sawdust-floored space, *mestizo* peasants mingled with middle-aged men in business suits, their snowy-white shirts open at the throat. Shaven-headed young men, shirtless, their torsos, arms, heads and faces covered entirely in blue-black tattoos, circled constantly, their staring eyes flicking left and right.

Gabriel inclined his head towards Don.

'Security. MS-13,' he murmured. 'Probably best to avoid eye contact. If anyone asks, you're my trainer.'

Don grunted in assent. 'OK, Rocky. I should probably tell you, I brought a shooter. Nice little subcompact. A Springfield Armory Hellcat down the back of the old waistband. Just like the nightclub guns we used to carry back in the day in Belfast.'

'I would have expected nothing less, Boss. Mine's in my holdall. Smith & Wesson Model 629 with the eight-and-three-eighths-inch barrel.'

'Bloody hell! What are you expecting? Rhino?'

'There's a kind of code. It's a bit like dogs, you know? Nobody really wants to start shooting. So people go for the showier pieces. Wave a big, shiny .44 Magnum in someone's face and they back off. Produce that little handbag gun of yours and they'll probably laugh themselves to death.'

'As long as they're dead, I don't really care how they do it. Anyway, it's got fourteen nine-mil rounds in it so I'd say stopping power shouldn't be a problem.'

'We'll be fine. Now, you need to get a bet on. Last time I met this guy, I let him deal out a certain amount of punishment before I took a dive in the fifth. That's how I lost the tooth,' he said with a grimace. 'I made sure everybody knew I was some kind of Special Forces super-soldier. When I went down, a lot of money changed hands. This time, everybody's counting on a repeat performance. Put as much as you can on me winning by a knockout in the first round.'

'You know best, Old Sport. I brought some cash with me. Your little friend back on the street would have won the lottery if you'd let him get away with it.' He paused. 'Not sure I would have had it in me to plug the little sod, to be honest. So, what sort of stakes do these charming sportsmen lay down on a fight? I don't want to look cheap, but I don't want to look flashy, either.'

Gabriel indicated with a jut of his chin a man in an expensive-looking suit: shimmering silver-grey fabric, elegantly cut, white handkerchief protruding from the breast pocket. His hair was lustrous and dark, slicked back from his forehead with gel. He had a ferocious aspect enhanced by bushy black eyebrows above deep-set eyes and a matching moustache. He was deep in conversation with another similarly dressed man, maybe ten years older, with cropped silver hair.

Beside them, sipping a cocktail from a tall glass decorated with flowers, stood a dark-skinned young woman with the haughty air of a princess. The plunging neckline of her sparkling silver sheath dress revealed a great deal of cleavage. As she turned away from her companion, a similarly scooped backline emphasised the swell of her buttocks.

What was interesting was the way none of the other patrons were making any attempt to talk to her or even get within talking distance.

'That guy over by the bar with the supermodel on his arm?' Gabriel murmured. 'His name is Luis-David Casildo. He runs the Zinguizapa cartel. He bets in multiples of ten thousand US. You'll be fine.'

'What's the drill? Do they have helpful young ladies from the Tote taking bets at the tables?'

Gabriel offered Don an ironic grin. 'Actually, that's not far off. Just look for one of the girls wearing Chupacabra bikini tops and sparkly shorts. They handle the bets.'

Just then, amid the press of bodies and the hubbub of excited conversations, a call went up in English.

'Well, if it isn't the little British commando!'

Gabriel turned. He recognised the voice. The shirtless man pushing his way through the crowd to stand a few feet in front of him and Don was six foot seven, and weighed well over 250 pounds. Most of that was muscle. The rest, bone. Like the security guys, his chest was an overlapping tapestry of indigo tattoos. Women's faces. Spanish quotes with a vaguely Biblical air. Gothic crucifixes. Pistols. Clowns. Eagles. Fanned playing cards. Roman numerals: XIII.

His skull was shaved, which threw emphasis onto the bony ridge above his steel-grey eyes. He balled his hands into fists and jammed them into his hips, narrow where his chest was wide, giving him a swimmer's V-shaped torso.

'Who's this? Your papa?' he asked, staring derisively down at Don. 'They call me *Bola de Demolición*, old man. That's Wrecking Ball to you. I'm sorry to tell you this, but I'm going to give a lot of pain to your boy here.'

'I'm his new trainer,' Don said. 'I've been working with him on some new tactics.'

The giant bellowed with laughter, a bull hearing the funniest joke ever.

'Is that so? I hope they're better than the last ones he tried. They didn't work so well for you, huh, commando?'

'In here, I'm the Archangel,' Gabriel said mildly, visualising the ganglia beneath the skin on the left side of the man's neck.

'You were,' Don interrupted. He stared up at Wrecking Ball. 'Tonight he fights under a new name. The Grim Reaper.'

This drew another gust of laughter from the giant and a few appreciative murmurs from the onlookers, who had formed a loose circle around the three men.

In the shadows towards the back of the room, a sudden movement caught Gabriel's eye. A silhouette, nothing more. But there was something about the way the figure moved that set alarm bells clanging deep in his subconscious.

'I hope you've got a pre-paid funeral plan, *Bola*,' he said. 'You won't be fighting anymore after tonight.'

He turned away, Don at his six, leaving a for-once dumbstruck Wrecking Ball gaping after him.

'That should jack the odds nicely against me,' Gabriel said, when they reached the safety of the curtained-off cubicle that served as his dressing room.

He unzipped his holdall and after rummaging around for a few seconds, produced a small brown plastic medicine bottle and shook out four tablets. He ground them into a powder under the base of a glass tumbler and snorted the lot.

'Amphetamine,' he said, in answer to Don's raised eyebrows. 'Worked in combat. Works here. He'll be hitting it, too.'

Don sank into a bow-legged armchair, its vinyl upholstery splitting to reveal its dirty-yellow foam innards. He sighed.

'Why are you doing this, Old Sport? This isn't you.'

'Does there have to be a reason?'

'Yes, there absolutely bloody well does have to be a reason. It's hardly birdwatching, or taking country walks, is it?'

'I like doing it. It's what I do, remember? Fighting?'

'*Combat* is what you do! You did your duty. Fighting for a cause. Not some drug-fuelled, bare-knuckle brawl in a cartel-owned bar.'

Gabriel finished the water. Shrugged. 'It takes my mind off things. When I'm in there,' he nodded towards the curtain and the space beyond, 'I can forget who I was. I can forget what I had. Or what I almost had. I don't really care anymore, Boss. My life doesn't mean anything. Maybe it never did. Maybe all that time I was in uniform, I was just kidding myself. Fighting for Queen and country? Or just putting two fingers up to my dad? And how did that work out? Not too well, if you recall.

'So, yes, after tonight, I'll come with you and we'll deal with Margot McDonnell. But don't expect me to stick around. If you're planning some sort of Department Mark Two with Uri Ziff, or the two of you are going to try to recruit me to the Mossad, you can forget it. I've experienced everything life has to throw at me and you know what? I think I could easily prefer what death has to offer.'

Don leaned forwards. Put his hands on his knees. Glared at Gabriel.

'Where the hell has this defeatist attitude come from? You lost Eli. And in the worst possible way. I understand, Gabriel, believe me, I do. But this?' He swept his arm round to encompass both the smelly little cubicle and the wider club beyond. 'This isn't you. And nor is the downright nihilistic outlook you're affecting. You're a man of principle. A man of honour. Don't try to tell me that's all gone. Because I don't believe it.'

Gabriel didn't reply at once. Arguing with Don was much worse than trading insults with the Wrecking Ball. That was all show. Pre-fight antler-clashing following strictly prescribed rules. Insult, counter-insult. Dismissive, scatological, calling each other's manhood, or parentage, into question. It went on night after night, week after week, and it meant very little.

But the boss? They went way back.

And right now, he felt that meant about as much as the little bit of banter between him and the Wrecking Ball. How could Don sit there and preach at him. Duty? Honour? Principle? Where were they when Eli was fatally wounded by a mercenary's bullet? What use were they to a new husband who cradled his dying wife as her blood flowed from her body and soaked into his clothes? To a man whose chance at fatherhood had died along with Eli in that smoking ruin of a cottage on Scalpay?

All he'd learned out there was that life was cheap and if there was a God, he had a vicious sense of humour.

'You should go and find one of the Chupacabra girls to take your bet,' he said in a low, flat voice. 'Bet everything you brought. You'll make a killing.'

Once Don had left him alone, Gabriel began his preparations. But every now and again, that glimpse of the stealthy figure in the shadows broke through his mental preparations and threw off his concentration.

He shook his head, feeling the speed coursing through his bloodstream and speeding up his reactions. It would have to wait.

Everything would have to wait.

17

Ten minutes before Gabriel's fight was due to start, Don handed a thousand dollars to a slender blonde in tight red shorts and matching bikini top, a black leather pouch over one shoulder.

'The Reaper to win by a knockout in the first round.'

She tapped a tablet she held in her left hand, tapped again, then frowned.

'Are you sure, señor? It's two hundred-fifty-to-one against.'

'So, I'll win a quarter of a million dollars if he does it?'

'Yes, señor, but it won't happen. That's why the odds are so high. To tempt *los tontos y los soñadores*, how do you say in English, fools and dreamers, yes? Why don't you bet on Wrecking Ball? The odds are bad, but you'll win something at least.'

'Thank you, my dear, but I'll stick with my choice, please.'

'I have to check with somebody. This is a big bet. Wait here.'

Don watched her scurry through the crowd. She went up to a man talking to Luis-David Casildo, the guy Gabriel had identified as the cartel boss. She stood on tiptoe to speak into his ear. He turned and looked in Don's direction. Don raised a hand in an ironic salute, smiled. The man turned back to the betting girl, nodded, then spoke a few words before returning to his conversation with Casildo. They laughed and both looked over at Don again.

They had him pegged as an innocent abroad. A tourist about to lose his shirt pursuing some ridiculous colonial idea of loyalty to a fellow Brit.

Back in front of Don, the girl took his money and printed a slip from a handheld device she lifted from her shoulder bag.

While she continued on her circuit of the arena, Don turned as a cheer went up from the other side of the space. That was where the fighters emerged from the dressing rooms.

When Gabriel stepped into the cage, followed by the ogre they'd faced off against earlier, Don wondered whether the club owner and Casildo were right to laugh after all.

The disparity in the two fighters' physiques was so extreme as to be almost comical. Wrecking Ball towered over Gabriel. Stripped to a pair of shorts, the mismatch seemed starker than ever. His musculature was thick, slablike, decorated with the same blue-black tattoos as the wired-looking security guys.

Something else stood out for Don. Gabriel had acquired a tattoo on his chest, on the left side.

אֱלִישֶׁבַע

It was Hebrew, that much he could tell. Beyond that, he was clueless. Gabriel was the linguist, not he. He'd ask him after the fight.

At the thought, a cold tendril of fear wormed its way from the pit of Don's stomach into his chest, where it wrapped itself icily around his heart. The previous fight had ended when the loser had had his neck broken. The snap as the vertebra gave way had been audible even through the shouts. A harsh crack like a gunshot.

Gabriel had explained that this was a brutal business. More

akin to combat than the sanitised version streamed into millions of homes for beer-and-pizza entertainment. If fighters refrained from the more obviously lethal techniques, it was only out of fear of retribution from the opponent's gang, relatives or sponsors than adherence to a notional rulebook.

Don took a sip of his beer and clutched the flimsy slip of paper recording his potential loss of a thousand dollars or his acquisition of a quarter-million. As he took in the man facing off against Gabriel, pushing his brutish face into Gabriel's, he began to wonder whether he shouldn't have gone with the bet-girl's advice after all.

* * *

Months earlier, as a first-timer, seeking an outlet for his pain and rage, Gabriel had been first on the bill. He and his opponent had played to an early-evening crowd, barely into their second beers, more amused than crazed by the thought of two men going at it like pit bulls.

Thanks to his unorthodox and ferocious fighting style, he'd moved swiftly through the ranks and could usually count on fighting somewhere in the top five bouts. On this particular night, he was third from the top – on at 11:00 p.m.

One disadvantage of fighting in the top half of the bill was the condition of the ring. Cleaners entered the cage after each bout with mops and buckets, but by 10:00 p.m. they were fighting a losing battle. The bigger splashes of blood were removed, but the canvas floor remained slick with the stuff, splotched here and there by thicker clots. Mixed with sweat and the drinks thrown into the cage by enthusiastic, disgusted or just drunk punters, it provided an extra challenge to the fighters.

Gabriel stepped through the wire-mesh gate and into the arena. The hubbub from the punters grew louder. On the far side of the cage stood Wrecking Ball. The referee called them together and stood between them, a short, skinny fellow with a drooping Zapata moustache, his black nylon polo shirt drenched in sweat.

Wrecking Ball towered over Gabriel. Nobody cared. Down here in the barrio, weight classes were for pussies. The overriding mantra was, 'The bigger they come, the harder the fall'. That and, 'Call the doctor!'. If you wanted to fight, you fought. If you got your eye knocked out or your spleen ruptured, well, you chose to step into *la caja*. The rest was on you.

'Welcome to the next fight,' the ref bellowed, producing a surprisingly deep and sonorous voice from so narrow a chest. 'Fighting in the blue shorts... Wrrrr-eckingggg Ballll-ahhh!'

The giant stepped forwards, pummelled his barrel chest with his fists like a silverback, then turned to glare at Gabriel.

'The Ball's gonna smash you tonight, gringo. Finish the job I did on you last time.'

'And in the red shorts, a man you've seen before as Archangel, but tonight he's fighting as...The Grrr-immmm-ahhh Rrrr-eaper!'

Hoots, catcalls, whistles and laughter filled the smoky room and from his position inside the cage, Gabriel saw fistfuls of dollar bills changing hands.

Gabriel ignored Wrecking Ball's pinned pupils as he stuck his face forward. It was tempting to just do it now. A finger jab into the eyes followed by a smash that would shatter his larynx. But they'd call the bets null and void and he didn't want the boss to lose his money. Plus Wrecking Ball had to know why he was going to die.

Many, if not most, of the people currently yelling for blood in the purple-lit arena had committed crimes of one sort or another. Usually violent. Even street robbery usually involved a degree of physicality. It was the tradition in Teguz. The wallet, phone or camera was the prize. The wounding was like a graffiti artists' tag. You had to show you'd been there.

The MS-13 thugs with their zombie-eyes and crown-to-heels tattoos were in a different league. Membership of that elite cadre of foot soldiers was bought with blood. All of it. It was run along similar lines to the Hells Angels. But whereas the Angels might only insist you dealt out a beating, MS-13 went straight for the kill. Literally.

Wrecking Ball was under no obligations to that gang, or any other. He did what he did for purely personal gratification. Gabriel had been planning this act of retribution ever since Esperanza had come home from work one night, weeping, her face a bloody mess, her lip split, her nose a pulpy mess and her left wrist broken.

She'd knocked on his door at midnight. And when he'd led her, gently, to a chair she'd winced as she lowered herself onto its thin cushion. In that instant, he knew what had happened to her. The girls who worked at Frida's had a saying. *Nadar con cocodrilos, espera ser mordida.* If you swam with crocodiles, you could expect to get bitten. A poetic way of saying violent rape was an occupational hazard.

She hadn't wanted to tell him who'd done it, but in the end, although he'd felt bad about asking, she'd told him. He'd started his cage-fighting career out of a sense of hopelessness. He'd end it with revenge.

The bell clanged.

Gabriel stabbed a fast punch into Wrecking Ball's face, opening a cut above his right eye. He danced away as, with an enraged bellow, the bigger man came at him, fists bunched, the scarred and reddened knuckles like the knobs on a bull's spine.

He had to make this look realistic. It wasn't hard. Even as he manoeuvred around his opponent, a glancing blow swung his head around, dizzying him for a second. In a flash, Wrecking Ball was pushing in close, swinging hard punches to Gabriel's belly.

It was a standard attacking style. You winded your opponent with repeated blows driven into the gut. He dropped his guard. You smashed a couple into his face. He went down. You followed him in, attacking mercilessly until either the ref stopped it (if he was lucky) or the man on the ground died (if someone had paid the ref to be a little too patient before stopping the fight).

Or at least, that was what the playbook said.

Gabriel staggered back, then spun round, leaned back and kicked Wrecking Ball hard in the side of the face with the blade of his foot. It was a Tae Kwon Do move he'd built into his personal fighting style, which combined elements of Eastern martial arts, including Kung Fu and the deadly Wing Chun; and his favourite, Krav Maga. Eli had taught him everything she knew about the Israeli fighting style.

The kick jolted Wrecking Ball's head backwards. Gabriel felt something in Wrecking Ball's jaw go beneath his foot. He hoped he'd broken it. But the man appeared undamaged, shaking his head like a horse troubled by a fly.

Blood was running freely from the cut above his eye. And unlike in boxing matches, nobody stopped the fight so he could receive medical attention. He blinked it away and swiped his eye with the back of his right hand, but that just smeared the existing blood over his face and stimulated a faster flow from the cut. He shook his head again, spraying scarlet droplets out in a fan, bright under the floodlights.

Gabriel danced back out of range of those massive fists. This was not playacting in order to drive the odds higher. If Wrecking Ball connected properly then Gabriel would be unconscious and, shortly thereafter, dead.

The crowd's shouts had turned to baying. This was what they came to Chupacabra to see. A genuine no-holds-barred contest with some kind of personal animus between the fighters that went deeper than who got to keep the purse.

Wrecking Ball shuffled closer. Good. He was being cautious. The face-thrusting braggart had been replaced with someone who'd realised here was an opponent who would take some work to put down.

He kicked out at Gabriel's left knee, going for an oblique contact. Regulated fighting leagues banned the move. If one connected, the knee would either break or the anterior cruciate ligament would tear, crippling the fighter. Gabriel deflected the kick with a counter-kick of his own, then closed in and drove his closed fingers into the soft place under Wrecking Ball's jaw.

Fighters like Wrecking Ball studied their chosen martial arts. Practised obsessively, if they were that type of man. But Gabriel had studied human anatomy, too. Not, as a doctor might, so he could understand how to mend, treat and repair it. Quite the opposite. So he could pinpoint the weak points.

He'd identified the least robust joints, such as the hinge where the mandible met the skull. The places where major nerves ran close to the surface, such as the ganglion at the base of the skull. The larger arteries such as the carotid, femoral and brachial. And other, less-obvious, but equally vulnerable elements of the imperfect human body that, if attacked appropriately, would cause their owner excruciating pain, permanent injury and death.

Seconds earlier, Gabriel had delivered a blow to just such a place. It was one of the eight attachments of the tongue. Sometimes, you had to attack what was available, not what the textbooks taught you to target. A man's balls might be protected or out of range. His eyes behind goggles. The back of his skull sheathed in a thickly padded helmet valance. But rare was the enemy who protected the triangle of skin and soft flesh inside the V-shape of his lower jaw.

He closed in on Wrecking Ball, who was hunched over, his face contorted in agony, then, over his shoulder, caught sight of the shadowy figure from earlier. He blinked. It couldn't be.

That split-second of inattention cost him dearly. Out of nowhere a fist as hard and hefty as a frozen leg of lamb connected with his left temple, sending him reeling to the ground.

Above him, Wrecking Ball roared, teeth bared, one gold canine winking in the harsh overhead lighting.

18

Wrecking Ball threw himself down at Gabriel.

To be caught beneath a deadfall of 250 pounds of muscle would be enough to maim or kill him without any of the strikes his opponent was no doubt planning. Gabriel knew, somewhere deep in his brain, that he needed to move. But from nowhere, a quieter, calmer voice, a woman's voice, spoke up.

'Gabe, darling. My soul, my honey. Why not just let him kill you? We could be together.'

Wrecking Ball hung, suspended above him. Teeth bared. Arms outflung like a bear's grasping forelimbs. The blow to Gabriel's skull had put time on pause. It was the only explanation. He remembered an encounter with an enraged American black bear in the woods of New England. Lizzie Maitland had been caught between her and her cubs and been eviscerated by those long black daggers as surely as if someone had come at her with a butcher knife.

He'd shot Lizzie. A mercy killing. He'd shot Sasha Beck, the psychopathic contract killer Lizzie had hired, too. But that was a combat-kill, pure and simple.

'Come to me, my darling.'

Eli stood just behind the immobilised figure of Wrecking Ball, who flickered like a movie frame caught in the projector's gate. Her olive-green IDF fatigues accentuated her figure. A drift of lemon and sandalwood engulfed Gabriel, making him smile. Maybe it would be for the best. He readied himself. Prepared to switch time back on. He could expose his throat, give Wrecking Ball a clear target. One decent punch and it would all be over.

He heard his own hoarse voice, somewhere outside his own head.

'I'm coming, Eli.'

He turned his head aside…and saw the shadow figure for a third time. Only this time, its — her — face was visible in the light of a mobile phone held up by its owner, hoping to catch another Chupacabra cage-kill on video.

In his mind's eye, her features had taken on the quality of a doll's. Now, here in Honduras, he saw nothing had changed. Her face was unlined, expressionless, lips almost invisible thanks to the oddly pale lipstick she wore that matched her complexion. The impression was heightened by the way she wore her black hair pulled back into a bun so severe it appeared to be a coat of shining paint above a high, domed forehead.

Their eyes locked. For a split-second, Gabriel thought she smiled at him.

From nowhere, Smudge yelled at him: *'Boss! Move!'*

Time clicked back on. The animalistic baying of the crowd invaded his ears like an IED going off. He hurled himself sideways, rolling himself into a ball as Wrecking Ball crashed onto the floor, face first. Gabriel heard the crack as one of his incisors snapped clean in two. He pushed himself to his feet, shaking his head to clear his vision, and lashed out a kick into the downed man's already bleeding mouth.

Gabriel felt pain, as hot and bright as a welding torch lancing into his foot, through his ankle and up into his lower leg, as if someone had rammed a sharpened stake into the sole of his foot.

He glanced down. The flesh on the side of his instep was torn and bloody. Wrecking Ball's broken-off tooth stump would have been as sharp as a blade. Now it had opened a deep cut in Gabriel's unprotected flesh.

He hopped back a couple of steps. He needed to end this fast. The tooth had caught a small artery. Blood was jetting out in fast, rhythmic spurts, spraying the punters nearest the cage with scarlet. Not enough to kill him. Not straight away. But it wouldn't stop, and eventually he'd be weakened sufficiently for Wrecking Ball to land a fatal blow or simply get him in a headlock and either choke him to death or break his neck.

Wrecking Ball was on his feet now and shaking his head wildly, spraying his own blood left and right. The cut above his eye was a ragged mess. Strings of slimy-looking red drool swung from his torn lip where the blood from his smashed tooth was mixing with saliva.

He came at Gabriel, fingers curved into talons, but his clouded vision had messed with his depth perception and his aim was off. Gabriel ducked and came up inside his reach, smashing the top of his skull underneath the man's jaw. Gabriel felt rather than heard the teeth clack together and Wrecking Ball staggered, half-stunned by the blow, which had sent his brain slopping back and forth inside his skull: a quart of jelly in a bone bowl.

Bright-neon light flashed on steel, arcing high over the fence and into the cage. Two sounds penetrated his fight-maddened brain simultaneously. A metallic clank and a woman's shout. '*Bola de Demolición! Mátalo!*'

However long she'd been in Honduras, it wasn't long enough to erase either her Irish accent or the cadences of her voice. Margot McDonnell appeared to have taken an active interest in the fight. And she'd just shouted out for Wrecking Ball to kill him.

He looked down. On the far side of the ring lay a broad-bladed machete tipped with a hook: a sugar-cane knife. The wickedly sharp blade would cut through the thick fibrous plants as if they were stalks of wheat.

Yelling in triumph, Wrecking Ball lumbered away from Gabriel, intent on grabbing the weapon Margot had just tossed into the cage. The crowd screamed and jeered. Weapons were frowned upon. The concept of honour among thieves might have disappeared among the barrios of Comayaguela, but inside the cage, some ancient concept of chivalry, or at least fair fighting, still prevailed. Just.

Or maybe they didn't like weapons because they shortened the fight.

Gabriel saw his chance. In a move so simple it might have been perfected by a child at primary school, he tripped his man as he lunged for the cane knife.

Wrecking Ball staggered, then stuck his foot out to prevent himself falling. The sole landed in a slick of blood, whether his own or Gabriel's it was impossible to tell. His legs shot apart, taking him into a painful and unplanned splits.

The next moment, a high-pitched squeal rent the air as Gabriel drove his unhurt foot as hard as he could into Wrecking Ball's groin. He fell sideways, clutching his smashed testicles. Gabriel leapt onto him and dealt a trio of vicious and blindingly fast throat chops with the side of his right hand.

'Die, you bastard!' he screamed as the man's larynx gave way with a sound like bursting bubble wrap. He drove the heel of his hand down against his windpipe. Wrecking Ball thrashed, his face turning first red, then blue. His hands scrabbled against Gabriel's torso, inflicting weakening punches as his brain began to shut down from lack of oxygen.

Finally, he stopped bucking and twisting and lay still.

The crowd went berserk. A lot of people had just lost a lot of money. Shouts. Screams. Insults. Things could get messy. Correction, he thought, rising to his feet and surveying the bloody ruin in which he stood. *Messier.*

Maybe there was one gambit that could prevent all-out war breaking out.

He seized the cane knife and held it above his head.

'*Silencio!*' he shouted in his loudest parade-ground voice.

The noise beyond the mesh stilled. Victors were accorded a few words to celebrate their victory. It was a tradition.

He gestured at the body in front of him.

'*Bola de demolición no era un hombre. Él era un violador.*' Wrecking Ball was not a man. He was a rapist.

'*Lo trato como el animal que era.*' I treat him like the animal he was.

Then he bent, and in a swift movement, removed the dead man's genitals, which he flung to the ground.

He pointed to Margot, who was threading herself through the press of drunk, stoned or just hopped-up-on-adrenaline punters.

'*Detén a esa mujer. Ella le tiró el machete.*' Stop that woman. She threw him the machete.

He dropped the sugar cane knife and wrenched open the gate, slipping in blood and having to grab onto the wire mesh to prevent himself falling, as Wrecking Ball, fatally, had just done.

A wiry man with wild eyes and a shock of sweat-slicked black hair barred his way, a small chromed pistol in his hand.

'You bastard. I lost everything. I'm gonna kill you for that, you English pig.'

Gabriel stepped back and forced his mind to prepare to disarm the man. He couldn't allow Margot to escape.

Then his assailant's head exploded in a welter of blood and brain tissue. The body sagged sideways, the pistol already dropping from the lifeless fist.

Gabriel whirled round.

Striding through the crowd, which parted as the Red Sea had before Moses, was Luis-David Casildo, the Zinguizapa cartel boss. In his right hand, an enormous gold-plated pistol. Gabriel's fight-addled brain refused to immediately provide the make and model. The lights glinting off the yellow metal made it hard to distinguish the outline and shape. Then he had it. A Desert Eagle, that showiest of all showy handguns, fitted with a suppressor as fat and as long as a jumbo hot-dog.

People fell away as he arrived in front of Gabriel, and the noise drained out of the room like water from a shell-holed swimming pool. He pulled the snowy handkerchief from his breast pocket and shook it out. He handed it to Gabriel.

'Tie your foot up or you're going to bleed out,' he said in English.

It wasn't true, but it was a gesture that bespoke peace rather than war. Gabriel accepted the large square of white cotton, flipped it over three times until he had a serviceable bandage, and bound his bleeding foot.

'Thank you,' he said, upright again, realising that he'd already lost Margot. He nodded towards Casildo's pistol. 'Nice gun.'

Casildo turned the monstrous weapon so it caught the light. 'This is my little baby. You know about firearms, my friend?'

Gabriel shook his head. 'Only what I see at the movies. What is it? It looks powerful.'

Casildo's lips curved upwards in a half-smile. Like he only half-believed what he was hearing.

'Desert Eagle. Customised just for me. That's eighteen-karat gold plating you're looking at. She shoots fifty-calibre rounds. They're so big, the mag only holds seven. But believe me, seven is more than you need.'

'I can believe it.'

'Is this right, what you said back then? Wrecking Ball was a rapist?' Casildo asked.

'He was. He attacked a friend of mine in Santa Rosa.'

Casildo shrugged. 'Life is cheap in the barrios, but even so, you did us all a favour. I have daughters myself. You have children?'

Gabriel stared into those deep-set, dark eyes. Did Casildo know? No. How could he?

He shook his head. 'Never had the chance.'

Casildo smiled, revealing expensive-looking dentistry.

'You should, my friend. Children are what make this life of pain worth living.'

'I hope you didn't lose too much money on the fight,' Gabriel said, grimly. Even cartel bosses with gold-plated pistols didn't like losing money on sports betting.

Casildo roared with laughter. Then he shook his head.

'Lose? How could I lose? I was the only man in here who bet on the Reaper.'

'Not quite.'

Don had managed to thrust his way through the crowd and now stood next to Gabriel. A leather bag dangled from his right fist. Its sides bulged.

Casildo turned to Don. 'Did you win, too, old man?'

'I did. I always had faith in my boy.'

Casildo narrowed his eyes so that they reduced to black slits. Around them, MS-13 security were dragging away the punter's headless corpse by its heels, leaving a wide, reddish-grey smear on the concrete floor.

'You're his trainer, yes?'

'Think of me as Burgess Meredith in *Rocky*.'

'Ha! Such crazy movies. I have watched them all many times in my home cinema. So, you are Mickey Goldmill, yes? And this is Rocky Balboa.'

'If you like,' Don said, cautiously, though with a smile on his face.

'I don't think Balboa ever castrated a man with a sugar-cane knife, though.'

Don shrugged. 'Maybe he never fought in the Chupacabra.'

Casildo pursed his lips. Nodded.

'Maybe not. Anyway. Something tells me your boy here isn't quite what he says he is. So, and I say this from a place of respect,' he flattened his left palm against his chest, 'he is no longer welcome to fight here.'

'That suits us,' Don said, then turned to Gabriel. 'Doesn't it, Old Sport.'

Gabriel nodded. 'Fine by me. Are we going to meet any trouble when we leave?'

Casildo raised those dark, bushy eyebrows. 'Trouble? Of course not. You leave under my protection. After all,' he paused, 'who dares, wins, no?'

Then he turned, and, once more, the seas parted for him, closing around his besuited form until he was lost from sight.

Gabriel turned to Don.

'Come on. I need to get dressed then we should get out of here. I saw Margot McDonnell.'

Don's eyes widened.

'You're sure?'

'I'm sure. But she's gone. We need to find her.'

'OK. Get changed. I have a call to make. Won't be long.'

Gabriel pushed his way through the jostling crowd. A couple of guys gave him the evil eye. Perhaps mindful of the fate that befell the first man to challenge Gabriel directly, they limited themselves to glares and pointing fingers. When one got too close, Gabriel feinted a punch, sending his would-be adversary scuttling for shelter behind a trio of bigger men.

The speakers overhead blared, announcing the next bout, and, in a second, all the attention was focused back on the cage.

Gabriel glanced over his shoulder to see one of the strangest sights of the evening, if not of his entire life.

Don Webster, former Commanding Officer of the SAS and boss of the Department, deep in apparently good-natured conversation with Luis-David Casildo, noted murderer of CIA agents and head of the Zinguizapa drug cartel.

19

TEL AVIV – 9:30 A.M.

Uri Ziff looked up from his screen, sighed and rolled his head on his shoulders. An alarming crackle from his cervical vertebrae had him grasping the back of his neck.

Being deputy director of the Mossad undoubtedly had its compensations. But there were days, and this was definitely one of them, when he longed for the simple reality of field operations.

Yes, jihadis would be lurking round every corner, ready to blow your brains out with a Kalashnikov, or themselves – and you – to kingdom come with an explosive belt. But at least they never asked you to appear before special security committees in the Knesset for a five-hour grilling. Or compile hundred-page reports on perceived budgetary pinch-points versus staffing ratios and new Severe Attack Preparedness strategies.

He glanced at the wall of his office that held his treasured photos. Him and the old gang: Yael, Dina, Mike, Elad and Talia. Here, looking down at Jerusalem in their IDF uniforms, arms hung loosely over shoulders or around waists, rifles slung, peace restored. And here, in jeans, leather bomber jackets and T-shirts, Talia in a hijab and long brown abaya. She looked so demure. And the robe did a splendid job of covering her Micro-Tavor assault rifle.

And then his gaze stuttered to a halt on the photo in the centre of the display of black-framed images. Tears sprang from his eyes, as they did every time he allowed them to linger there.

Him and Elisheva Schochat, during her service with Kidon, the tip of the spear. G-d, that girl was a great fighter. Beautiful, too, and with a wicked sense of humour that had the whole squad shrieking with laughter. Eli was staring straight at the camera, the look in her eyes at once inviting and challenging. The Brits had a phrase: '*Come on, then, if you think you're hard enough.*' It had fitted Eli like custom-made body armour.

He fished a tissue out of the packet and dabbed his eyes dry. Sniffed loudly and cleared his throat. Those bastards were all dead on that shitty little island off the north coast of Scotland. But one of them had killed his beloved Eli before he died. Uri shook his head. The woman who'd ordered the attack was still alive. And that could not stand.

The pen he was gripping in his right fist emitted a quiet crack and then broke in two. Vivid-blue ink spurted out, coating his palm. He swore, loudly and hurled the shards of plastic into the bin. While he attempted to clean the ink off his hand, eventually resorting to whiteboard cleaning spray, his phone rang. Another committee meeting? A report deadline moved up to please some minister with too much time and not enough to fill it with?

'Yes?' he barked.

'And a good morning to you, Uri, old boy. How's office life treating you?'

Uri smiled.

'Funny, Don. How do you think it's treating me?'

'Well, speaking as one old warhorse to another, I imagine you've been fantasising about patrolling the border with a rifle in your hands.'

'You're a mindreader. What can I do for you?'

'Gabriel and I are enjoying a little nightlife in Tegucigalpa. And we've caught sight of Tango One. I need you to have a word with the gentleman who wields the power round here. I need him to close off the neighbourhood we're in,' Don said. 'Nobody in or out. But I lack leverage, and he is proving, hmm, mm-hmm, resistant to persuasion. I wonder whether you might oblige.'

At the mention of Tango One, the two men's shared prime target, Uri's mind shifted instantly from administrative to operational modes.

'Put him on,' he said.

He heard the rustle as the phone was transferred and Don's muffled voice saying, 'Uri is an Israeli friend of mine.'

'Who is this?' Uri demanded.

The man on the other end of the line was clearly having a great deal of trouble controlling himself. Uri heard the anger, felt the pounding pulse, as clearly as if he'd been watching an EEG trace.

'My name, Jew, is Luis-David Casildo. I am the boss of the Zinguizapa cartel. Maybe you've heard of us. I have more than a thousand—'

'Luis-David, I need you to shut up and listen very carefully. Or what you'll have is more than a thousand corpses to bury. Did my friend tell you what I do for a living?'

Casildo snorted with derision.

'Run some shitty little gang of ex-soldiers, I am guessing. What do you do, smuggle hummus into Palestine? Control the olive oil trade in Jerusalem?'

Uri had to smile. The cartel guy certainly lived up to the macho image of Latin American organised crime bosses.

'You're actually not that far from the truth, my friend,' he said. 'Many of my staff are indeed ex-military. I am Deputy Director of the Mossad. I take it you have heard of *us*?'

Uri counted off the seconds. He reached five, during which time he looked at Eli's picture once again, before Casildo answered.

'This is Honduras, my Jewish friend. You cannot simply come in here with your men and lay down the law like you do in Palestine. Or will you go crying to your American friends? Send in the CIA? That has been tried before. Only I know where their agents' bodies are buried.'

Uri stood up and walked around his desk. He stood in front of Eli's photograph and, smiling sadly, gently ran a finger across the glass.

'I see. Well, Señor Casildo, now I have to give you a little history lesson. A long time ago, 1960 to be exact, there was a very evil man named Adolf Eichmann. Like you, he did not like Jews. After hiding like a coward in Europe, he fled to Argentina to escape justice. With the help, incidentally, of a Catholic bishop.

'Anyway, our teams of agents tracked him to Buenos Aires and captured him from under the noses of the authorities. We transported him back to Israel to stand trial. He was convicted and hanged two years later. So please believe me when I say that in pursuit of our enemies, we will go wherever we have to. Do whatever we have to. Kill whoever we have to. But no, we will not "lay down the law" like we do in Palestine, Israel or anywhere else. Nor will we ask our American friends for help.

'What we *will* do, on the other hand, is visit hell on your business. We will bomb your plantations, your processing plants, your packaging and distribution facilities. We will kill your dealers, go-betweens, chemists, soldiers, accountants and lawyers. We will destroy your cars, your house, every single one of your possessions.

'And, finally, when only you are left, kneeling with a pistol to your head, whimpering like a dog and begging for mercy, we will execute your wife, your children, your horses, dogs, cats, guinea pigs and hamsters in front of you. When everything is blood and flames and ashes, and you are pleading for us to spare your miserable life, only then will we kill you.

'But that will not be the end of it. I will task a cyber-team with expunging every online record of your operation, its people…and its boss. Señor Casildo, you will not even leave a legacy in cyberspace. The Zinguizapa cartel will be eradicated from the face of the Earth. It will be as if it had never existed. A cheap cigar ground into the dirt beneath a *campesino's* boot heel would leave a bigger trace. Or you could do what my friend wants and close off the neighbourhood.' He straightened the photograph, having knocked it askew. 'Now.'

The pause this time was longer. As it ought to be. A man who'd just been threatened with annihilation needed time to adjust to a new reality that was one hundred and eighty degrees off his previous conception of how things worked.

Uri listened to Casildo's laboured breathing. It would take some organisation to carry out his threat. Probably more resources than his paymasters would sign off. But Uri Ziff, among many other qualities, had always been an excellent poker player. He waited.

His man folded.

'And if I do what you ask?'

'Then the Mossad will focus on Israel's domestic enemies. Of which, believe me, Señor Casildo, she has more than enough to keep the Mossad busy until the end of times.'

'Then I agree.'

'Oh, one last thing you can do for me. I am sending you a photo of a British woman. If one of your men should meet her, I want her detained. Unharmed.'

'Understood.'

The phone clicked. Uri was alone in his office once more. He stared into the kohl-rimmed eyes of the young Kidon operative with the long auburn hair.

He was going to make things right. One way or another.

20

The street outside Chupacabra was as busy as it had been at 9:00 p.m.

Margot looked left and right, cursing her decision to refuse the general's offer of protection. Whores, dealers, pimps and muggers filled the street, their eager eyes flitting among the crowds like hummingbirds in a forest full of flowers. Divining which blossom contained the most nectar, their only real problem.

A kid scurried over, rat-thin, sores on her legs. Her blonde hair was a dirty mess, probably swarming with nits. She held up a wilting white carnation, its petals edged with brown, its broken stem wrapped in soggy newsprint.

'*Una flor, señora? Sólo un dólar.*'

Scowling, Margot dealt the brat a ringing backhand slap to the face.

'Fuck off!'

She turned right and stalked off, the child's stream of invective in broken English rising above the street noise like a piccolo in an orchestra.

What a shit-show! The cartel boss she'd been told would be her go-between was just another swaggering specimen of Latin American masculinity. Far from being able to provide an introduction to a team of combat-hardened paramilitary fighters, he'd patronised her, suggesting she send her boss so they could negotiate man-to-man.

She had seriously toyed with the idea of killing him on the spot. His flashy pistol would be easy enough to turn on its owner. And it might have been fun to see that smug grin fly off, accompanied by the rest of his face.

But in the end prudence had won out. Just. And then, as if confronted by a nightmare, she'd seen Wolfe inside the cage. Bare-chested, tattooed, bearded and bloodied, and staring at her, teeth bared like a feral dog.

He had a sister in Hong Kong. Friends in Israel. Some sort of sugar mummy in Russia. Why had he chosen to go to ground in this Godforsaken shithole? And cage-fighting? Really? Why not just grow a mullet, buy a pickup and start fanboying over NASCAR?

Plus points? At least she knew where he was. And if she knew where he *was*, she could make sure he made the transition to the past tense permanently.

She checked her weapon. The Beretta slid smoothly from her shoulder holster. She dropped out the magazine, although there really was no need: it was hardly likely to have emptied itself without her, now would it? She pressed down on the topmost round and felt the reassuring back-pressure of a spring under full compression. Slotted it home and felt the latch engage with a click.

She did not replace it in its holster. At this time of night, carrying it openly would deter casual muggers from chancing their arms. Which, should they not heed the evidence in front of them, would shortly be mangled by a close-range hollow-point round.

* * *

Back in his cramped dressing room, a length of duct tape closing the cut on his foot, Gabriel grabbed Don by the upper arms.

'She was here, Boss. I saw her. Margot McDonnell is right here in Comayaguela. Or she was. She's probably halfway to the airport by now. We have to go after her.'

'I saw her, too, Old Sport. She won't get far. We need to get you patched up first, or you're going to be no use to anyone.'

Gabriel saw a gleam in Don's eye. He knew that expression of old. It meant that, as usual, Don had something up his sleeve.

'What's going on? What have you done? Did you already kill her?'

'No. But I've had friend Casildo lock down the barrio. She can run, as they say, but she can't hide. Do they have a doctor in this place?'

'No. Your own staff patch up minor injuries. Anything bigger tends to need an undertaker, not a doctor.'

'Very droll. Nearest decent hospital?'

Gabriel shrugged. 'Across the river. But there's a doctor in Comayaguela who looks after the barrio.'

'His number?'

'I don't have it. "His" name is Heleen Schippers.'

'She sounds Dutch.'

'She is. She runs a clinic. We can get a taxi. They all know the address.'

Twenty minutes later, Gabriel was lying back on a battered steel gurney, which, nonetheless, was covered in a spotless white sheet. Heleen was stitching up the laceration in his foot. A temporary blip in her supply chain meant he was enduring the experience without anaesthetic.

A strand of long blonde hair fell over her eye. Tutting, she tucked it behind her ear.

'How did you get this?'

He winced as another stitch went in. 'A fight. At the Chupacabra.'

'Did you win?' she asked, not even looking up.

'By a knockout.'

'Will I be seeing your opponent?'

'Do you ever visit the *Cementerio Municipal*?'

She huffed out a breath, somewhere between a derisive snort and an ironic laugh.

'I see.' She snipped the ends of the last suture. 'There. Keep it clean. Try to avoid stressing it for a week or two.'

'I'm afraid I do need to stress it quite a bit in the next day or so. Could you put some sort of a support bandage around it? Or even some sports tape if you have it?'

Gabriel liked the way this capable Dutchwoman didn't ask questions that would only delay things. Instead, sighing, she went to a cupboard and returned with a crêpe bandage and a fat reel of silver duct tape.

She held them up, one in each hand.

'This is all I have.'

'Perfect. Thank you.'

She set to work and in a few minutes Gabriel felt his foot and ankle could withstand just about anything short of a round from an AK.

'OK, we're done here,' Heleen said. 'If it hurts, take painkillers. Most bodegas in the barrio sell Advil or Tylenol. Look for a packet with the seal still in place. On your way out, please pay my secretary three hundred dollars.'

Don raised his eyebrows. 'Isn't that a bit steep for a barrio doctor?'

Heleen turned to him, eyes flashing. A dangerous expression. Gabriel wondered at his old boss's lack of insight into how things worked in places like Barrio Concepcion.

'Steep? On the contrary. I think it represents extremely good value for money. I mean, I've stitched up a wound acquired during an illegal cage fight. At a club known to be under the protection of MS-13. I'm not going to report your friend here to the cops. And, unlike some of the butchers around here, I haven't given him incipient blood-poisoning, gangrene or Hep C.'

'My dear lady, I'm sorry—'

'I haven't finished! You know how much I charge the residents here? As little as I can. You two have that well-fed look about you, despite your friend's somewhat piratical appearance. I don't know why you were fighting at the dreadful place, maybe some twisted macho *Fight Club* thing. But you can afford the three hundred. Probably more. Pay Alejandra on your way out. I have other patients who need me a lot more than you do.'

Gabriel took Don, who was still apologising, by the arm, thanked Heleen for her help – '*Dank u voor uw hulp*' – earning a brief smile, and went to find the secretary.

Gabriel smiled at the Honduran woman with a frazzled expression on her face and a clipboard tucked under one arm.

Around them children cried or screamed, sullen teenagers slouched, faces sheathed in blood, pale-faced adults clutched their abdomens or groins and babies wailed, adding their own keening to the Babel of noise filling the tiny clinic's dimly-lit waiting room. Posters on the walls warned of the dangers of chlamydia, AIDS and untreated dog bites.

She looked up at him. '*Sí?*' Then, in English. 'You are fixed?'

'*Sí, gracias. La Señora Schippers dijo trescientos dólares.*'

Alejandra nodded, clearly used to tourists being charged what might be called a Robin Hood rate for their treatment.

Don reached into his bag and extracted a bundle of cash. He turned to Gabriel.

'Perhaps you could tell Alejandra we'd like to make a donation. Something of a thank-you for the work Ms Schippers is doing here. Not for us, but for the people of Barrio Concepción.'

Gabriel nodded. The old man hadn't lost it after all. He turned to Alejandra, who was waiting with a puzzled expression on her face as she eyed the fat wad of hundred-dollar bills in Don's hand. He translated the message. Alejandra' eyes widened and then tears formed in the corners, overspilled her lower lids and trickled down her thin cheeks.

Don put the bundle of notes into an inner pocket and handed Alejandra the bag with the remainder of the money.

'Tell her she can use it to build a proper clinic. Maybe pay off any officials or cartel people she needs to get the work done properly.'

Gabriel felt his own eyes welling up as he translated Don's second message.

Alejandra froze, her face paralysed in a shocked expression. She stared at the bag until Don, very gently, took her hand and drew it towards him so he could fold her fingers around the handle of the sagging pouch of money.

Around them, people were staring, caught by the look of surprise mingled with disbelief and growing joy on the secretary's face. Finally she unlocked and called out in a high-pitched, tremulous voice.

'*Señora Schippers, ven rápido! Es un milagro!*'

Heleen strode into the waiting area, a harried look on her face. Presumably being told to come quickly to witness a miracle was the sort of distraction she had little patience for, and even less time.

She looked first at Gabriel, then at Don, then at Alejandra, who was holding out the bag of money.

'What is this?' she demanded.

'Look, look!' Alejandra said, switching back to English. 'They give us all this money. There must be many thousand.'

Heleen took the bag from Alejandra's outstretched hand, spread the mouth and peered inside. She glared at Gabriel.

'Is this a joke? What is that? Counterfeit?'

'I very much hope not,' Don answered. 'I just won it at the Chupacabra betting on my friend here. It's two hundred and forty thousand dollars. Please spend it as you see fit.'

She blinked, long eyelashes sweeping across cornflower-blue eyes at once tired and elated.

'You're not joking, are you?'

Don shook his head. 'I dare say much of the money originated here, or else from wealthy cocaine users. You have far more need of it than I do. And the bag is heavy, it would only slow me down.'

Frowning, Heleen took the bag from Alejandra's unresisting

hand.

'Then, thank you. Thank you, both. You for winning your fight.' She kissed Gabriel on the lips. 'And you for winning the bet.' A more chaste kiss on the cheek for Don.

As they were leaving, she called out. 'Wait! I don't even know your names.'

Gabriel turned and placed his hand on his chest. 'Old Sport.'

Don mirrored the gesture. 'Dobbin.'

Back on the street, Gabriel said, 'That was a magnificent gesture, boss. God knows how many lives you've just saved.'

Don grunted. Gabriel knew how little he cared for praise.

'Tell me something, Old Sport,' he said as they strode back towards the centre of the Barrio. 'That Hebrew tattoo on your chest. What does it mean? Valour? Onwards? Who Dares Wins?'

Gabriel shook his head. What else could he have tattooed over his heart?

'It says, "Elisheva",' he said, unconsciously putting his palm over the ink beneath his shirt. 'Now. We need to track down Margot McDonnell before she finds her way over the river and back to the city.'

They returned to the Chupacabra and started asking around. Someone must have seen *la gringa* leaving.

* * *

Still incensed at the Mossad boss's insolent tone, as if *he* ran Comayaguela, Casildo summoned his second-in-command.

Carlos had once been a promising young officer in the Honduran army. Scion of a middle-class family and graduate of Honduras' elite officer academy. A commando, no less. But when he, along with his men, had finally grown tired of waiting to be paid by the latest in a long line of incompetent governments, he'd told them he was leaving for greener pastures and invited any who fancied a move into the private sector to join him.

Ten had. They now formed the elite kill squad within the Zinguizapa cartel. They undertook to train the Zingus, as the foot soldiers were affectionately known, in better and more effective ways of fighting. Along the way, Carlos Alvarez had risen through the ranks once more. He finally secured his spot at Casildo's right hand after the then-holder of the post committed suicide by knifing himself in the liver, shooting himself twice in the head and then leaping backwards off a tenth-floor balcony.

'What is it, boss?' he asked now.

'I want the barrio locked down, OK? Nobody in or out.'

'What else?'

Casildo loved that about Carlos, a man he had come to see as a son as much as a military commander. He had no time for underlings who would ask dumb questions like: 'Why?' Carlos just listened, said, 'yes', then quietly figured out how to make it happen.

'The woman I was meeting? Margot McDonnell.' He showed Carlos a photo on his phone. 'I want her brought to me. Alive.'

Now Carlos did allow himself one question.

'Do the Americans want her?'

'No. The Israelis. Maybe the British, too. I'm not sure. Either way. If that lot want her, she's worth a lot of money. Maybe we can get some of our people out of prison in the US, too.'

'A three-way deal. I like it.'

Carlos made to move away. Casildo halted his progress with a hand on his arm.

'Wait. That fighter who killed Wrecking Ball.'

'Archangel? Or what did he call himself tonight, The Grim Reaper?'

'I don't care. He's involved, too. And that old guy who claimed to be his trainer. Bring them back, too. Nobody makes a fool of Luis-David Casildo and lives. Not regional governors, not police chiefs, and certainly not a couple of British war dogs.'

Carlos nodded, and this time Casildo let his own *perro de guerra* go.

The cartel boss smiled to himself. Americans. Israelis. Brits. They would all learn what it meant to get on the wrong side of Luis-David Casildo.

21

WASHINGTON, DC – 12:30 A.M.

Dammit, this was one engagement the general would be glad to get out of in one piece.

The rattle of gunfire was a constant, leaving no space in the air that wasn't alive with the barks, roars, chatter and bangs of everything from 5.56s and 7.62s up to .50s and on to the big stuff. The 17.76s and the 9.11s.

The Taliban had gotten hold of some new-fangled ammunition systems that needed no reloading. Each rifle and machinegun fed by an inexhaustible supply of rounds.

His nose burned with the acrid prick of gunsmoke and the metallic tang that only millions of red-hot brass shell casings could supply.

He levelled his M16 then felt a cold wave of panic as the red-hot barrel sagged like silly putty. An advancing insurgent bared ferocious teeth and leapt the barricade, his AK lighting up the few remaining soldiers Six-Foot had to call his own.

The bearded fighter grinned at the general and aimed the smoking muzzle at his midsection. He opened his mouth and emitted a harsh grating sound. Again. Again. Again.

Beside him, his dead gunnery sergeant, the top of his head missing and exposing his brain, nudged him hard in the side.

'Cope, honey, will you answer your damn phone?'

Startled into full wakefulness, the general snatched up his phone, which was buzzing like an enraged yellowjacket on his nightstand.

'Sorry, honey,' he murmured to Jill, his wife of forty-one years. She mumbled something that might have been 'OK', rolled over and went back to sleep.

He got out of bed and left the room, closing the door softly behind him and answering as he entered his study at the end of the hall.

'You OK, Margot?'

'No, I am very much not OK. Your broker turned out to be a weapons-grade arsehole and now I'm stuck in this Honduran slum.'

The general bit back a sharp rejoinder. Casildo was many things but the intel he'd provided had all checked out. Had Margot mishandled him? It was all too easy to imagine. That was a conversation that would have to wait until she was back in DC.

'We can extract you, Margot, no problem. Send me your location.'

'You misunderstand me, Cope. I don't want extracting. I want reinforcements.'

'Reinforcements for what? If the deal was a bust, I want you back here. We need to review the plan and source the new operatives somewhere else.'

'I've identified someone I need terminating with a very great deal of extreme prejudice. I can do the job myself, but just to be on the safe side, I think it would be prudent to send in a kill team. Six should do it. Eight would be better.'

The general rubbed his stubbly chin. Goddammit, this British woman was more demanding than Marylynne when she'd been a one-year-old with six teeth coming through all at once and screaming blue murder at three in the Goddamn a.m. How anyone could be that devoid of normal human emotions and still manage to rile him up with her prissy language was a mystery he was still trying to solve.

Who the hell was scaring Margot so much she wanted a squad to help her out? Because over their time as colleagues, the general had learned to read between the lines of Margot's snotty lingo to the deeper truths she tried to bury. The woman was scared. The offhand remark about taking out the target on her own was just so much BS.

Couldn't be anyone she'd provoked during her tenure at Evergreen. He heard his daddy's Oklahoma drawl in his head. *Maybe they was riled up at first. Then they was dead.*

So it had to be someone from before. In England.

Then he nodded. Of course. Who else could it be? That last operation she'd run had been a snafu of Biblical proportions. Despite sending in another kill team, comprising some of the meanest, orneriest, most battle-hardened killers for hire on Planet Earth, Margot had left Tango One alive. Though she'd managed to have his wife killed. So now he was looking for revenge on his own account and for the cute Israeli chick.

'Just tell me one thing, Margot. This individual you need taking off the board. It's Wolfe, isn't it?'

She paused. So when she spoke, he knew she was lying to him. And for the first time since he'd initialled the form that put her on the Evergreen payroll, General Copeland D. Tookey felt a qualm.

'No, it isn't. It's a Honduran assassin. A solo operator, normally. But he has back-up.'

The general looked up at the ceiling. Noticed a meandering crack in the textured plaster. Like a *wadi* in the Afghan desert. For a split-second he smelled that superheated bone-dry air again.

'It's going to take me a few hours to muster the team,' he said. 'I'll get them down there ASAP. In the meantime, maybe you should lie low.'

'No. I'm going to try to get back to my hotel on the other side of the river,' she said. 'You know, Cope, the locals call Tegucigalpa and Comayaguela the Twin Cities. But I have to say, the resemblance is more Sodom and Gomorrah than Minneapolis-Saint Paul. I have to go. Send the team and have them call me when they get here.'

The line went dead.

The general stared at the black screen in front of him for a count of ten. This was not going to be easy.

He had invested a lot of money, time and men in Margot McDonnell.

22

COMAYAGUELA

Walking on his injured foot, despite the duct-tape strapping, Gabriel could feel a dagger working its way up through the sole into his shin, sliding between the tib and fib towards his knee. Not pleasant.

He nodded at a bodega across the street.

'I need some painkillers. Wait outside?'

Don nodded. Patted his pocket.

The middle-aged woman behind the counter offered him some off-brand opiate painkillers. The pink and yellow box was labelled: 'OxyMega!' He found the exclamation mark less than reassuring. But the woman assured him they were perfectly safe. She herself took them for her arthritis.

He hesitated. It was either the pills or a bottle of guifiti, and although the latter's analgesic properties were unsurpassed, it also brought a swift descent into unconsciousness. On balance, not the best option for a man hunting a deadly adversary through one of the most violent places on Earth. He needed to be able to concentrate, so he bought them despite his misgivings.

Two tablets and five minutes later, all the pain from his foot and the various insults Wrecking Ball had inflicted on his body had vanished – along with a portion of his grip on reality. The people he and Don passed in the narrow streets of the barrio all carried a shimmering cobalt-blue aura around their heads, like gas flames. Their faces appeared to have been drawn by a counterculture cartoonist, grinning mouths filled with oversized square teeth, eyes like vertical ovals with deep black pupils.

'Keep on truckin',' he muttered, then giggled.

Don turned to him.

'Everything all right, Old Sport?'

Don's aura rose into a crest of translucent blue light above his head. It swayed sinuously, like a snake-charmer's cobra. Gabriel was entranced.

'Sorry, what?'

Don peered at him, frowning. Gabriel had to fight down a sudden urge to poke his finger into the black well of Don's right eye.

'Are you high, Gabriel?'

'I think those Oxies might have disagreed with me, boss.'

'Shit. Do you have any of those amphetamines left? We need something to counter the opiates.'

Gabriel shrugged. 'Might have.'

He checked his inside pocket, which felt as if it were lined with fur, and pulled out the brown plastic bottle of little white pills. He popped the cap off and shook four out into his palm. 'Got a couple of coins, boss?'

Don fished around in his pocket and came up with two ten centavo coins.

Gabriel managed to fit the four pills between the two copper-coloured coins and squeezed them together, crushing the amphetamines into powder. He brought it to his nose and snorted it up into his left nostril.

He shook his head.

'Right. That should do it, Let's go.'

As they headed down Calle Cinco towards the Chupacabra, Gabriel was able to monitor the internal cage fight between the amphetamines and the opiates. The stimulants gained the upper hand but the opiates were reluctant to fully relax their grip on his frontal cortex. The result was a strange mental state: sharp-edged, teeth-grinding hyper-alertness mixed with a soft, blurry impression that he was in the middle of a dream.

'Back in the land of the living?' Don asked, as the bar's vivid-neon fascia lighting came into view.

'Yep. Good to go. We need to find someone who saw which way Margot went. Even with the barrio locked down, she could stay hidden for days in here.'

Jaw working as the speed kicked in, Gabriel scanned the crowds, thinning now, but still numerous. A young man reeled out of a doorway and threw up at their feet. The acid stench rose from the sidewalk and acted like a dose of smelling salts on Gabriel. He drew in a second deep breath, voluntary, this time, and looked around.

A couple danced to samba music issuing from a scratched silver boombox that looked as though it had been transported from eighties New York. As they seemed reasonably sober, Gabriel approached them.

He smiled at the man.

'We're looking for a woman,' he began, striving to hit the local dialect of Latin American Spanish.

'Try Mama Argento's on Calle Quatro,' the man said, without breaking rhythm.

'No. I mean a particular woman. A gringa. British. Tall. Pale. Black hair in a bun. Gold-rimmed glasses.'

The man raised his eyebrows at his partner. She, too, kept dancing, smiling seductively at Gabriel as she rotated her hips and sashayed from side to side. She shook her head.

'Sorry, friend,' he said. 'When the music takes you, you know? All you see is the woman you love.'

Gabriel thanked him and walked away. From between the

knees of a couple of pedestrians, a little girl appeared. He couldn't tell how old she was. Five, six? She was small. But there was a look in her eye suggesting she might be older and just undernourished. He'd seen it before. Children in war zones, bombed-out cities, razed villages. Knowing. World-weary. Suspicious. A sharpness, too. Not quite predatory, but a quick-wittedness that could lead to a drawn knife or a picked pocket if you weren't careful.

In a grubby fist she clutched a sad-looking white carnation wrapped in newsprint. The right side of her face was smeared with blood. A recently clotted cut on her cheekbone was still weeping. Around it, a bruise had spread.

'A flower, mister? Only a dollar.'

Gabriel crouched in front of her.

'Who did that to you?' he asked softly in Spanish.

'A gringa bitch.'

'A gringa? Tall? Pale? Dark hair pulled up like this?' He made a fist on the top of his head.

'That's her. Bitch!'

'Which way did she go after she hurt you?'

Her eyes narrowed. There it was. That wiliness in the gaze made a full appearance. She thrust the carnation under his nose.

'Flower more expensive now. Ten dollars.'

Gabriel smiled. Very gently, he took the flower from her hand.

'If you help me, I'll pay you twenty for it.'

She held out a grubby palm, streaked brown with dried blood.

'Money first.'

Gabriel pulled out a few bills and slapped a ten into her hand. She closed her fingers around it and then reached for its companion. He shook his head.

'Tell me first, then you get the rest.'

She turned and extended her free hand, pointing in the opposite direction from the way they'd come.

'Calle Octava.'

'You're not lying to me, are you?'

She shook her head, scowling. 'I hope you find her. I hope you *kill* her.'

Fair enough.

'Thank you.' He handed over two more tens. 'Listen, there's a clinic on Cuarta Avenida. Go there. The doctor's name is Señora Schippers. She will clean up your cut for you.'

The girl snorted derisively as she thrust the fist with the thirty bucks deep into a pocket. 'And take my money.'

Gabriel shook his head. 'Tell her you're a friend of El Dobbin. She'll treat you for nothing.'

The girl giggled, a sharp little sound she almost immediately cut off.

'The fool?'

'Not El Bobo! El Dobbin.'

She pointed at him and shook her head. 'Loco!'

But she was smiling, and she set off in the direction of Heleen's clinic.

Gabriel straightened up. Don was questioning an older man on the far corner of the junction. Gabriel whistled across to him. An old signal. He turned. Gabriel pointed in the direction of Calle Octava. Don nodded and they joined up where the street left the square.

The hunt was on.

23

LONDON – 8:20 A.M.

'Prime Minister, it's Sir Ian Greene to see you.'

Gemma Dowding looked up from the classified document she was struggling to comprehend. Her principal private secretary stood before her. Not quite at attention; his background was Cambridge then Whitehall. Nothing so risky as military service for Sir Rodney Speer.

Even though she hated him, she couldn't help but admire the immaculate cut of his pinstripe suit. Today, he'd paired it with a silk tie in a muted jade-green, with a matching display handkerchief. An uncharacteristic touch of dandyism from the normally staid functionary.

Her pulse kicked into high gear. People always thought being prime minister meant you were the most powerful person in the land. Leaving aside the obvious and grating truth that the billionaires who underwrote half the government's projects, and the foreign sovereign wealth funds who had hoovered up most of

Britain's infrastructure and utilities were the real masters, they clearly had never met the chairman of the 1922 Committee. His word could make or break a prime minister.

She wiped her palms on her thighs.

'Well, you'd better show him in, then. And send in some tea and biscuits.'

Sir Rodney inclined his head with the easy grace of a superior being allowing its inferior to play God.

'I believe Sir Ian is on a diet, Prime Minister. And he prefers coffee before lunchtime.'

She gaped. 'Then get us some coffee! For Christ's sake, just show him in, will you?'

'Of course, Prime Minister.'

He turned and silently crossed the thick Turkey carpet on those mirror-polished shoes. Somehow she doubted his tread would make a sound even if her private office were floored with steel plating. Bloody Dalek.

Sir Ian Greene entered shortly afterwards. She was already on her feet, rounding her desk with as big a smile as she could muster to greet the most powerful man in the Conservative Party.

'Ian, how lovely to see you. Take a pew. I've asked Rodney to send in coffee. I know you prefer it to tea in the mornings.'

She felt a brief thrill at the way his eyelid flickered when she left out his title. These bloody 'knights of the realm' and their letters after their names.

He shook her hand; a warm, dry grip. And he smiled at her. The expression did not calm the butterflies causing her to feel a sudden urge to pee.

They sat in matching red leather Chesterfield armchairs placed either side of an ornate fireplace in high Gothic style. Twisted barley-sugar pilasters, red, cream and navy diamonds inset into black marble. A fluted mantelpiece.

Dowding clamped her lips shut. She was determined not to speak first. Greene caved in. He gestured to the tall windows overlooking the garden.

'Beautiful morning,' he said. 'Though the forecast said it

might rain this afternoon. I hope so. My roses are crisping at the edges. One can't water them either, not with the hosepipe ban.'

'Are you here to ask me to cancel it?'

He laughed. 'Oh, believe me, Gemma, I'd like nothing better.'

He said nothing further. Surely he wasn't going to make her ask him why he'd come to see her. She held her nerve and her breath for another five seconds. Couldn't sustain it.

'You didn't come here to discuss the weather, Ian. Let's have it.'

He twitched at the knee of his suit trousers and crossed his legs.

'I'm afraid it won't do, Gemma. This business with the Russians. You're making us look like a bunch of crooks. Correction, a bigger bunch of crooks. I have the ear of almost three hundred backbenchers and, almost unbelievably, on this issue they are speaking with one voice.'

She felt a surge of anger.

'Those backbenchers you represent' – *like a bloody shop-steward*, she wanted to add, but bit it back – 'owe their jobs to me! *I* delivered our majority. Which, as I'm sure you remember, the *Daily*-bloody-*Telegraph* called, "A political triumph unmatched since Blair's 1997 landslide". *I* won them their seats. And *I* want their loyalty.'

The door opened, and a plump young woman in the black and white uniform of the catering staff delivered a tray on which rested a bone-china coffee jug, a smaller jug of hot milk, a bowl of sugar lumps with a pair of sterling silver tongs, and two matching cups and saucers.

'Thanks, Izzie, love,' Dowding said, favouring the woman with a genuine smile.

When they had the room to themselves again, Sir Ian stirred two sugar lumps into his coffee, before adding milk.

'I thought you were on a diet,' Dowding said.

He shrugged. 'I've cut out biscuits, cakes and puddings, but I refuse to drink my coffee unsweetened.'

'And I refuse to drink hemlock, or whatever you have planned for me.'

He nodded, sipped his coffee, replaced the cup on the saucer with a soft clink.

'You know your Ancient Greek history. I'm impressed.'

'Please don't patronise me, Ian. Believe it or not, there are a few of us comprehensive school kids who graduated from Harry-fucking-Potter.'

He raised his eyebrows. 'Although not, apparently, from the gutter.'

Her fingers tightened on the handle of her coffee cup. She wondered what would happen if she dashed it in his smug, fat-cheeked face. What degree of burns would he sustain? Probably not enough to put him out of action for a few weeks.

'I'm not resigning,' she stated flatly.

'And I'm not asking you to.'

'Then why are you here?'

'To give you an ultimatum. You have a month to strip Dmitri Rublev of his peerage, freeze his assets, make an example of him. Kick him out of the country. This is corruption on a grand scale. It's happened on your watch and the entire country, including your own party, believes you are involved.' He uncrossed his legs and leaned forwards. 'We need a *mea culpa* from you, Gemma. A *mea maxima culpa*. If your knowledge of the Classics doesn't extend to Latin from the Ancient Greeks, that means—'

' – it was through my grievous fault.' Dowding paused. She breathed deeply, trying to quell a wave of nausea that rolled over her like an oil slick making landfall on a hitherto pristine beach.

It had finally happened. The past, from which she'd been running as if her life depended on it, as if it were embodied in a ravening, stinking, feral creature with dripping fangs and grasping, hair-covered hands tipped with yellow claws...the dreadful past, filled with actions she wished she could scrub away like the graffiti in a tube station, had finally caught up with her.

She sighed.

'The trouble is, Sir Ian, I can't.'

'Why not, Gemma. Why can't you?'

She opened her mouth. Then closed it again. The thick black slick was coating the beach, lapping a little higher with each incoming wave, strangling seabirds, polluting nature, ruining EVERYTHING.

Ever since she was a little girl, she'd known she was destined for greatness. While her playmates were dressing their dolls or arranging miniature plastic cups and saucers in front of their cuddly toys, Gemma was speaking sternly to hers. *Teddy, why haven't you done what I told you? I am the Pry Minister, you know. And, Mr Scruff, I said I wanted my picture colouring in by teatime and you went over the lines. This is not good enough.*

She'd clawed and scratched her way through school, passing the Eleven-plus and gaining admission to the county's only grammar school, an hour's bus-ride away. There, she shone academically, enduring the teasing of the rich kids, who mocked her accent and, ironically, also her good grades, which were better than theirs in many cases. Then, university, followed by a stint in industry before beginning her ascent of the greasy pole in Westminster politics.

It had all been going so well. Right up to the point she'd been invited to dinner at a Mayfair club so discreet members of the area's other clubs would have flat-out denied its existence had they been asked. The silver-haired, patrician men who plied her with vintage wines and fine French cuisine had noticed her ascent at the Home Office, they said. She was just what the country needed, they said. Like them, she had robust views on crime and punishment, they said.

And then they explained about Pro Patria Mori. Not a conspiracy, they said, a network. A grouping of like-minded individuals in the law and order branch who felt that the system had got out of balance. There were many contributing factors. Among them, the growth of progressive ideas in society at large. The proliferation of human rights lawyers. And a general brazenness of hardened criminals, especially those who had migrated to the UK from such unholy places as the Balkans, Eastern Europe and the Middle East.

We are here to reset the system, a senior judge said.

To issue a corrective, added a chief constable.

To take back control of the streets, intoned a counter-terrorism chief.

They only needed a political leader to bring the plan to fruition, they said. And Gemma leapt at it, a lion pouncing on a wildebeest. She made it her own. But, as with so many political projects, it required money to sustain its activities.

Of course, we can't pay for this from the public purse, the patrician elders said. *There can be no paper trail. You must make alternative arrangements. Speak to this man. He is sympathetic to our aims.*

And Gemma, drunk on the power that had been conferred on her, and the dazzling prospects they dangled in front of her, had spoken to him. To Dmitri Rublev. An immensely rich Russian. For a few glorious years it had worked, until a human rights lawyer and his daughter had been murdered. The fallout, it was fair to say, had been apocalyptic.

Gemma had escaped with her reputation intact and her secrets buried. But by then, Dmitri had become so much more than merely the banker to the conspiracy, which, after all, was what it had turned out to be. He was a personal friend. A confidant. And a provider of those luxuries that Gemma had come to feel were hers by right. That he also held her secrets gave him an unassailable position.

She found herself rapidly recalculating her life goals. A lucrative post-Number Ten career on the global speaking circuit faded. Not being assassinated in a loose-end-tying-off sort of way came into sharp focus.

She sighed. Overweening pride. The Ancient Greeks had a word for it. *Hubris.* Originally derived from the greatest moral crime in their code of honour. Desecrating the bodies of one's fallen enemies on the battlefield. And, after *hubris,* came *nemesis.* The fall.

She knew herself to be falling now.

It wasn't supposed to end like this. And it had never been about money. Not really. Not at first. She'd needed supporters, backers, for her political project. It was just that, somewhere along the line, the backers had turned into petitioners, asking, gently at first, and then with increasing firmness, for a return on their investment. What could she do but agree?

She looked at Sir Ian.

'Because it's all true,' she murmured, feeling the solid ground on which she'd built her premiership start to loosen beneath the soles of her feet.

'I'm sorry, I didn't quite catch that,' he said in a dangerously calm voice. 'You spoke rather too quietly.'

'I said it's true. Dmitri bought me and Dave the house. The kids' education. He paid for my leadership campaign. He paid for it all. I had to give him what he asked for. He was going to expose me. What else could I do?'

Sir Ian's face turned puce.

'What else…?' He snatched a faltering breath. 'You came in pledging to restore the public's faith, not just in the government, not just in the Tory Party, but in politics as a whole. I recall that pithy phrase of yours at the hustings quite clearly. "I will sweep the Augean Stables clear of the toxic mess infesting this government". Your exact words. You were earning a lot of money as a cabinet minister. Surely you could have paid for your own house like everybody else in the country does. And you were a shoo-in for the leader's job anyway. They all loved you.'

'I had to be sure. Dmitri had success in Brazil, in the Philippines, Africa: all over.'

'Gemma, the man's a criminal! Oh, I know he calls himself an oligarch, like they all do. But Rublev's the genuine article. How could you ever have thought that it was a good idea to get into bed with him?'

She felt herself close to tears. No. She wouldn't give him the satisfaction. She steeled herself.

'If I resign, can you keep it out of the media?'

'What, that you treated the office of prime minister as if you were a tinpot dictator, you mean?'

She felt the blush heating her cheeks as if someone were holding an iron at her face. 'Can you?'

He stood. Brushed at the fronts of his trousers.

'Do it tomorrow,' he said. 'I'll speak to the '22. And *Lord* Rublev of Thetford will remain where he is. Although representations will be made to his office to the effect that he will be *persona non grata* within the British establishment henceforth. Goodbye, Prime Minister.'

Alone in her office once more, Gemma Dowding placed her head in her hands and wept. Not just for her career, but for the days when she had containment units at her disposal.

Sir Ian Greene wouldn't look so smug with a couple of nine-millimetre rounds sharing headspace with his Latin and Greek.

24

COMAYAGUELA 2:00 A.M.

Margot turned off the main street with its milling crowds.

They provided cover, yes, but not just for her. Wolfe and the old fool who'd staged a Lazarus-like comeback from the dead would be out looking for her.

Would they be armed? She chided herself. Of course they'd be armed! That type never went anywhere without at least one weapon tucked away. Mind you, neither did she.

The street she'd turned into, little more than a narrow lane, really, didn't even have a proper name. She despised the Hondurans for their utter lack of imagination. Calling the ninth street in a grid 'Street Nine'. For God's sake! At least it had no streetlighting. She could move more freely in the dark.

A huge black cat ran out in front of her, startling her. Seeing her, it hissed loudly. It arched its back, midnight fur erected into a spiky crest all the way down its spine. Curved white fangs gleamed in the moonlight.

She advanced on it, expecting it to back off or turn tail and scram. It did neither. The arch of its back became so pronounced it appeared to have folded in two. Then it did something extraordinary. It raised itself on its hind legs, front paws outstretched like one of the fighters in the cage back at the bar. She saw a pair of furry balls between its hind legs. Pink-lined mouth wide, it emitted a guttural growl before dropping back onto all fours. It bunched its haunches.

Seriously? The flea-ridden thing was going to attack? She levelled her pistol, extended her arm and tightened her finger on the trigger.

'Piss off, Felix! Last warning.'

Maybe sensing that here was a killer with even less conscience than he had, the vast tomcat took a cautious step back, then slunk off, tail down. Yowling in defiance – but also defeat – it darted between two dustbins from which stinking trash overflowed and vanished down a narrow alley between two shacks.

Margot blew across the top of the barrel, producing a low fluting sound.

'Nice shootin', Tex,' she said.

She walked on. How the hell was she going to get out of this barrio and back to the relative safety of Tegucigalpa? If there were any taxis plying their trade, they certainly weren't doing it around here. She took out her phone. Then frowned. What if Wolfe and Webster were monitoring her comms somehow? Her mouth quirked into a half-grin. Wolfe and Webster. It sounded like a provincial estate agent.

'Ha! You won't find much worth selling round here, boys,' she said to the empty street.

Ahead, two figures emerged out of the gloom. One wore a red tracksuit top over shorts. The other, a white shirt that glowed in the moonlight, above acid-washed jeans.

Margot held her pistol behind her back, clasping her wrist in the other hand. She strolled towards them, a smile on her face. Small-time muggers just going on-shift? Or maybe just a couple of good Catholic boys on their way to some kind of super-early mass.

As long as they left her alone, she'd let them live. But ask for her purse or to talk about Jesus back at their place and she'd send them into the next world without a second's thought.

The man in the white shirt had stopped and was consulting his phone. Its screen cast a pale-blue pall over his features. She saw tattoos. The solid lines, chevrons and stars that indicated at least a passing familiarity with the inside of a Honduran prison. He said something to Red Tracksuit who looked at Margot then back at his friend, nodding.

Then they both looked at her and pulled pistols from the back of their waistbands.

Oh, dear. She'd been rumbled.

She released her gun hand.

The two men, working for Casildo, no doubt, swaggered towards her, splitting apart to present two targets, not one.

White Shirt held his arms wide, and grinned, revealing a white smile.

'*Buenos noches, Señora McDonnell. El Señor Casildo quiere hablar con usted.*'

Margot stopped walking.

In English, she called back, 'Tell Señor Casildo, if he wants to talk to me, he can come out here.'

Her reply drew laughs from both men. She knew the type. Cocky, believing in their own invincibility.

But their confidence was entirely misplaced, based, as it was, on three assumptions. One, that the nines held loosely in their right hands conferred an advantage. Two, that their numerical advantage did the same. And three, the cherry on the cake. Or how would they say it here? *La cereza en el pastel.* And three, that the fact they were facing a woman meant they didn't need to be careful.

They'd never get past the initial selection stage at Evergreen.

She glanced at each man in turn. Range, a very comfortable twenty metres. She wondered whether either man was a decent shot with a pistol. Unlikely. She suspected they mostly either did their victims close up, execution-style, or just fired at random, hoping to intimidate the opposition. She, on the other hand, loved to practise on the range in Evergreen's soundproofed basement, burning through box after box of ammunition and reducing each new target to a tattered red rim around a hole the size of a side plate.

White Shirt levelled his pistol at her, holding it on its side like a movie gangbanger.

By way of a response, she dropped sharply to one knee, raised her pistol gripped in a classic shooter's grip and shot him three times. Twice in the chest and once in the face. He toppled over, blood fountaining from the crater in the back of his skull.

She was lining up her next shot as he fell. Watching a target after you'd eliminated it was for rookies. And Margot was definitely not a rookie.

Sadly for him, it appeared the other gangbanger was. Or at least, he hadn't learned to shed his rookie ways. Gaping, gun-arm dropping to his side, he turned sideways and followed his colleague's downwards trajectory. This unfortunate move led to his receiving a gout of scarlet arterial blood full in the face.

Blinded he swivelled back, raised his pistol and, yes, began shooting at random. The reports were huge in the night-quiet lane, the muzzle flashes bright-orange spears of flame and sparks.

He screamed with each-trigger pull, a stream of invective in some sort of barrio dialect she couldn't translate. Blah, blah...*puta*...blah blah...*coño*. She caught the gist, though. She was a whore and a cunt and, all things considered, he really didn't care for her one little bit.

Had she been capable of experiencing such an emotion, Margot might almost have felt pity for him. Then again, she had a job to do, and if she was better at hers than he was at his, well, whose fault was that?

She stood. No need for a crouch given how fast and how wildly he was burning through his ammunition.

The gangbanger's pistol clicked several times. He stared at it. Then back at Margot, who had closed the distance between them to ten metres.

'*I'm* a cunt?' she asked him in English.

And then she put three rounds into his midsection. He squealed as the hollow point rounds ripped into his intestines, sending a toxic mixture of shit and stomach acid burning through his viscera and into his bloodstream. He collapsed to the ground, writhing, his hands clutched uselessly over his belly, from which blood and other fluids were spurting to create a puddle on the greasy tarmac.

Margot strolled over to him. Stood with her legs akimbo.

'Who sent you?' she asked him, raising her voice to make herself heard over his shrieks.

His eyes rolled wildly in their sockets, white showing brightly in the moonlight all the way round his wine-dark irises.

From between clenched teeth, through which dark blood was now flowing, he hissed out a short phrase in English.

'You're dead, bitch.'

She raised her right foot and brought it down, gently, onto his clasped hands.

'Goodnight, asshole.'

She pushed down. He opened his mouth wide and groaned. A rush of blood issued from his lips, causing Margot to step back smartly to avoid getting her feet wet. His eyes closed and his head lolled to one side.

She put a round into his head. For form's sake.

She walked away. Planning her next move.

—

25

Gabriel scanned the roofline as he and Don hurried down Calle Octava. He wouldn't put it past Margot to have stashed a sniper rifle somewhere. An insurance policy in case whatever she was doing down in Comayaguela went south.

A working streetlamp, a rarity in the barrio, lit the side of the building they were passing. Gabriel crossed the road, back into the shadows.

The houses on the opposite side of the street were typical of the few remaining Spanish-style buildings in the barrio. Peeling stucco, in pale blue, pink, white and apricot; graffitied, pocked with bullet holes and cracked off in places like picked scabs. Wrought iron balconies, still in good shape, though some leaned precariously out from the walls where their bolts had come loose or rusted through.

At the end of the street, a white dome surmounted by a gold cross gleamed in the moonlight. Nothing dilapidated about *this* example of colonial architecture.

They strode on, keeping a few metres between them at all times, guns held ready. Not for the first time in his life, Gabriel wished he had a long gun and not just a pistol.

Just then, a burst of small arms fire had him flattening himself against a wall. Behind him, Don was doing the same. He'd heard three shots, closely spaced, in a distinctive rhythm. A double-tap, then a third. *Two to the chest, adjust aim, one to the head,* he thought. A professional. Or at least someone who knew how to kill efficiently. Then a longer burst accompanied by screaming. Someone was burning through a pistol mag. *Un*professional.

He pictured someone wildly unloading at their target, who probably wasn't even bothering to hide.

The last round exited the muzzle. Silence. He could see the guy, a mugger or maybe one of Casildo's heavies, squeezing the trigger with frustrated rage.

Bang-bang-bang. Three more rounds. A different weapon. More screaming.

He strained to pinpoint the direction the shooting was coming from. But there was nothing he could get a fix on.

Finally, a fourth shot. A coup de grâce. *A professional,* he thought. Then, *a shooter.*

And then, as sure as if she'd been standing right in front of him, brandishing her pistol, he thought, *Margot.*

Don arrived by his side.

'Think it's her?' he asked.

'Has to be. Did you get a fix on the direction? These echoes are making it hell to pinpoint.'

'Sounded like she's a street or two over to our left.'

Gabriel nodded. 'Let's go, then.'

* * *

Gabriel and Don weren't the only people to have heard the gunfire. On the far side of the church, a squad of Casildo's men, led by Carlos Alvarez, was quartering the barrio, looking for the three *descos,* short for *desconocidos* – their word for outsiders, basically, anyone who didn't belong in the barrio.

Carlos held up a clenched fist. His men gathered into a knot behind him.

'Red, Three Fingers, go that way. Come in from Avenue Nineteen.' He pointed to a different street, narrower than the first. 'Detonator, Killshot, take the alley. I want them alive. Anyone who kills one of them, I expect him to put one in his own head. Or else I will. Got it?'

'Got it,' they chorused.

'What about you, Boss?' Three Fingers asked.

He pointed upwards. 'I'm going up there.'

Carlos carried a rifle slung over his back. He'd taken it from his Jeep before starting the search for the three descos. Most of the Zinguizapa soldiers, if they had long guns at all, used Kalashnikovs. Carlos despised the Russian-made machine guns. Not because of their functionality. Everybody knew an AK was unbreakable. No, it was because they were communist guns. Carlos hated communism more than he hated the Morazan Cartel, who operated out of San Pedro Sula.

The Mora boys were just the competition. They fought wars over the business, but they all agreed that free trade was the perfect economic system. The Americans might have fleeced Honduras back in the day; those United Fruit guys with their private armies had plundered the country's wealth like latter-day conquistadores. But one thing they had left behind was *capitalismo*.

Unlike the Soviets.

Those bastards had turned Cuba into a failed state. Nicaragua, Venezuela: they were just as bad. Everybody could see capitalism was the answer. So, no. Maybe the AK-47 *was* indestructible. But he, Carlos Iago Montebello Alvarez, wouldn't be seen dead with one of the ugly plywood and pressed-steel *monstruosidades* in his hands.

So Carlos carried a brand-new Barrett bolt-action rifle with a top-of-the-range night-vision sight mounted onto the picatinny rail. Courtesy of Uncle Sam. Well, an ATF marksman anyway.

He began climbing the rusty iron fire escape up the side of the warehouse. He'd told his men not to kill the descos, and that was set in stone. But they'd need bringing down somehow, and he reckoned a well-aimed shot to the leg would do nicely.

* * *

The two corpses lay ten feet apart in a deserted street. Gabriel checked the rooflines. Too dark to see anyone hiding up there. Margot had shot the men with a pistol, so even if she were up top, she wouldn't be able to hit him.

Both men had been shot centre-mass and then finished off with a shot to the head. He took their pistols and stuck them into his waistband. The combined weight of the two nines and the Smitty was dragging his trousers down over his hip bones. He yanked them up and tightened his belt. Now where?

Don caught up with him. The old man looked…old. He was trying not to show it, but his breathing gave him away. An unpleasant grating lay beneath the whistle of air. His face was pale, too, with two high spots of colour on his cheeks.

'Boss, you look like shit.'

'I love you, too, Old Sport,' he said with a grimace. Then he winced and clutched his midsection. 'I'm going to be slowing you down if we stick together. This damn gunshot wound Bakker gave me in the belly is making its presence felt. The Israeli doctors said I should take it easy from now on. Not sure chasing villains all over a barrio in Honduras was quite what they had in mind.'

'It's OK. I was going to suggest it anyway. It's a shame we don't have a rifle, though. If we could find a kill room, you could be up top somewhere providing cover.'

Don wrinkled his nose and scanned the rooftops.

'Trouble is, Old Sport, in this warren who's to say where we'd end up cornering her?'

'What are you going to do?'

'Head back to the hotel. Call Uri. See if there's anything he can do. I hate to say it, but my urban warfare days are behind me. But I might be able to do some good coordinating things.'

A clatter of a dustbin lid had both men whirling round, but it was just a dog, nosing around in the trash looking for scraps.

'You still got that nightclub gun of yours?' Gabriel asked.

Don pulled it out of his waistband. 'It's good enough to get me back to the relative safety of downtown Tegucigalpa.'

'I'll swap you. Your Hellcat for this.' He proffered the nine that hadn't been emptied. 'Proper stopping power and it looks more impressive too if any wide-boy tries to relieve you of your wallet.'

Unsmiling, Don accepted the trade. He held the pistol at arm's length side-on.

'What d'you think, Old Sport? Your boss is a proper gangbanger now, hmm-mm-hmm?'

Gabriel laughed. The sound felt inappropriate give their situation, but humour found you in all kinds of weird situations.

'If anyone *does* try anything, stick that in his face and say, '*Quemada tus talones, hijo de puta.*'

Don repeated the phrase a couple of times. He grunted. 'Well, I know what the second half means, thanks to you. The first?'

'Honduran slang. Literally, "burn your heels".'

'But, basically, "scram".'

'Basically. With extra chilli.'

'And if they don't?'

'This is Honduras, Boss. Shoot to kill. They will.'

'Noted.' Don looked up the dark street, then back at Gabriel. 'Take care of yourself, Gabriel.'

Gabriel extended a hand, but Don pulled him into a fierce hug, clapping him on the back before releasing him.'

'Call me when it's over. If I have any news from Uri I'll call you.'

And then the old man turned and was gone. He walked away with a measured stride in which Gabriel thought he could detect a certain stiffness, as if he were unwilling to go faster for fear of causing himself pain.

Alone in the street, alone in the barrio, with a target to track down and who knew how many more of Casildo's men on his own tail, he headed into the shadows.

Time to get real. Time to disappear.

26

Gabriel ran through what meagre intel he possessed.

Tango One was in the wind. But she'd encountered two of Casildo's men and they'd clearly tried to take her in, or down. They'd failed. It spoke of overconfidence on the one hand, and Margot's tactical skills on the other.

They'd have underestimated her. Honduran machismo made the regular Latin American variety look like Arthurian chivalry. He pictured their last moments. Swaggering over to her, nines held casually, off-target. All threat-display, no preparation to actually take a shot. Probably bantering with each other, making lewd sexual suggestions.

And then…a look of surprise on their tattooed faces as, from nowhere, she'd produced her own weapon. He recalled the flurry of shooting. Chaotic. No shots aimed. One at least had expended every round in his gun without hitting anything important. Just contributed a few more pockmarks to the ragged, ice cream-coloured stucco on the surrounding buildings.

If Casildo had sent men after Margot, he wouldn't have left it at two. He'd have put out the cartel equivalent of an APB on her. So there'd be more teams. And what of him and Don?

Would Don's threat to annihilate Casildo's entire operation have worked?

Gabriel doubted it. In his experience since fetching up in the country, Honduran organised crime bosses didn't respond well to threats. They tended to up-armour and go in hot and heavy. To the victor the spoils; to the loser, a nice view of the city from the top of a stake on which your head was impaled.

Casildo might have played along while he considered his options. Then his pride, severely wounded, would have kicked in hard. He had three westerners on his turf. One with a quarter-million dollars in his bag. It screamed, 'hostages'.

Or would Casildo feel that the damage to his honour couldn't be repaired with mere cash? If Casildo had turned up at the SAS training base in Hereford, beaten the Regiment's best fighter to death, then threatened the CO, Gabriel felt sure the boys wouldn't have been content with a payoff, however big.

So. Urban warfare it was, then. To the death. Margot McDonnell was going to get what was coming to her. But so would any Zinguizapa soldiers who either got in his way or tried to take him on.

He moved to the spot where the stray dog had been rootling around in the trash. He upturned the bin and emptied it out. Spreading the noisome waste out on the tarmac, he found what he was looking for. A mess of dark, slippery grease someone had scraped off a much-used cooking pot. He scooped some up on the tips of three fingers and applied it to his forehead, cheeks, lips, and neck. His beard did a good job of camouflaging his jawline. The stench was unbelievable.

He carried on walking, watering eyes scanning each new alley entrance and road junction, looking for Margot. Ears pricked for any sound, especially the metallic clicks and scrapes that might indicate a gun being reloaded or a slide being racked.

A shout broke the silence. A man calling out to a partner in the rough dialect they spoke up-country.

'Anything?'

'Nothing. The bitch must be around here somewhere. The boss shut the barrio down tighter than a nun's pussy.'

'How about the two men?'

'Carlos and his team are on them. If he gets them in his nightsights he'll bring 'em down for sure.'

Gabriel's spirits brightened. This was excellent news. At least one of the pursuing force had a rifle. And not just some beat-up AK, either. A rifle with a night-vision scope.

Gabriel turned towards the voices. Around the next corner he came face to face with a man staggering along, an empty bottle of guifiti dangling from the fingers of one hand. It wasn't the alcohol that arrested Gabriel's gaze though. It was the man's coat. A scuzzy dark-grey trench dappled with innumerable stains that turned it into a mottled piece of urban camouflage.

'Hey, man, you wanna watch where y're goin',' the drunk mumbled, attempting to step around Gabriel.

'Hot night for a coat, isn't it?' Gabriel asked. 'You must be roasting in that.'

The drunk blinked and tried to focus bleary eyes on this polite stranger.

'Found it, di'n' I? Pretty stylish, no?' He gave an off-kilter twirl, lost his balance and staggered against Gabriel.

'I'll give you ten dollars for it.'

The drunk narrowed his eyes. A hawkish glint appeared in their unfocused pinkness. He folded his arms, still clutching the empty guifiti bottle.

'Gimme fifty an' it's yours.'

Gabriel stuck the muzzle of his revolver in the drunk's face.

'Or I could blow your head off and take it anyway.'

Eyes popping wide, yellowish whites showing all the way round honey-coloured irises, the drunk backed away, hands held high.

'No, no, man. Ten's cool.'

Gabriel handed over a bill. The drunk shucked off the coat like a snake shedding a particularly unpleasant skin. He held it out.

Gabriel put it on. It reeked of body odour, alcohol and vomit. But at least it distracted from the stink of the cooking grease in which Gabriel had slathered himself. The drunk turned to go, scrunching the bill in his left fist.

'Hey, friend?' Gabriel hissed after him.

He turned. 'What? You want my pants, too? I gotta keep my dign'y, man.'

'Have you seen any strangers round here recently? A woman. Pale, black hair. Maybe carrying a gun?'

The drunk made a dumbshow of putting his finger to his chin, staring up at the night sky, wrinkling his forehead.

'A woman? Yeah, well, y'know, maybe I did. But—'

Gabriel tired suddenly of the playacting. He raised the Smith & Wesson a second time.

'I just gave you ten bucks for a coat you fished out the trash. Consider that a retainer. Now, have you seen her?'

'Yeah, yeah, OK, man, calm down. Mother of God, don't shoot me. I gotta wife an' a kid. No, wait, two kids.' He swiped his hand over his sweating face. 'Pale. A gringa? Yeah I saw her 'bout five minutes ago.'

'Where?'

The drunk turned and pointed towards the church.

'Near Santa Maria de los Dolores. Maybe she was goin' in to pray, y'know?'

Gabriel thanked him, though he felt the money was more use to the man than a gringo's gratitude, and made for the church, the trench coat's filthy skirts flapping around his knees.

Around the next corner, he almost ran into three of Casildo's men. No rifle, thank God, but they each held a pistol. One was clearly in charge, barking orders and sending the other two running off down side streets. He turned and saw Gabriel.

Gabriel slumped to the side, leaning against a wall of peeling wrestling posters, the fighters resplendent in brightly coloured full-body leotards, their faces obscured by cartoonishly decorated masks. Out in the open, no chance of a surprise attack, and with the other two cartel soldiers mere yards away, he opted for a different strategy. Head down, he started singing.

The song was one Pera had taught him on a warm evening about a month after he'd arrived in Santa Rosa. The porch at the back of her house was lit with candles in coloured glass bowls and their light was augmented by the luminous green of fireflies that whirred overhead.

The first few times he'd attempted to sing it, he'd ended up with tears streaming down his cheeks. But gradually, he'd learned to control his emotions and he eventually found a kind of peace in singing its simply-worded refrain.

'My love lies where no pain can reach her,
She is peaceful, sweetness, light.
She stole my heart, and took it with her,
Now I mourn her through the night.'

The cartel guy approached. No pistol in sight. That was good.

'Hey, you! Have you seen a—' He got close enough to smell the sharp stink of the coat. 'Mother of God, what the hell have you got on you? You smell like death. Hey! I'm talking to you!'

Gabriel raised his head and looked into the gangster's eyes. They widened as they registered the hellish visage facing them, streaked and smeared with the revolting grease.

Before he could do, or say, anything further, Gabriel stabbed out his right hand and seized his man by the throat, fingers clawed in tight around his windpipe, also closing off the carotid arteries on each side of his neck. The man struggled to draw his weapon. Gabriel disarmed him with his free hand, the pistol clacking to the ground as it fell from his numbed fingers.

The man's mouth opened, and his tongue protruded. His eyes bulged as he struggled, fruitlessly, to draw in so much as a sip of air. Gabriel hooked the man's left leg out and twisted him over his outstretched knee, lowering him onto the joint, where he jerked his arms together around his neck and broke it with a quiet snap.

He lowered the lifeless body to the ground and commenced a fast and efficient search.

He didn't need the man's gun, but a blade would come in handy. He struck lucky. A chromed butterfly knife in a trouser pocket. He transferred it to his own pocket then dragged the dead man over to a dumpster. He lifted the lid, releasing a swarm of flies that buzzed in an angry cloud around his grease-smeared face. He heaved the corpse over the lip and down into the mounded cardboard, soiled diapers and spilling-open bags of domestic rubbish.

With the Smitty now in the front of his waistband, he went after the two other Zinguizapa soldiers. It would be easier to hunt Margot if he didn't have so many men on the lookout for him.

27

Margot checked her watch. Realistically, it might be morning before the general got anyone into Comayaguela. And that was if he had the right people in the right place. He ran Evergreen on the lean side. It wasn't as if they had squads of operatives lounging around on sofas playing 'Call of Duty', waiting for a call of their own.

She turned left into Avenida Sula. It ran in a straight line all the way to the river and then across into Tegucigalpa. It was a wide boulevard lined with trees, a relic of the days when the Spanish had run Honduras and tried to replicate Madrid in their new homeland. Picturesque, maybe, although the ravages of time had dealt the once-magnificent thoroughfare some telling blows.

Like all the other buildings this side of the river, the ones facing the street had long since given up any pretence at middle-class respectability. Their stucco walls were pitted and pockmarked. Streaked with green stains descending from broken and split gutters, or brown from leaking plumbing.

Wrought-iron balconies from which colonial rulers might once have watched civic parades now played host to feral cats, sprawling collections of overgrown pot plants and laundry. The drying clothes were piled over the railings, festooned on rotary dryers, and slung between apartments on washing lines, white against the indigo sky.

She didn't like it. Too wide. Too little cover. Effortless sightlines for shooters. She diverted into a side street and continued her zig-zagging progress towards the river.

Someone shouted.

Shots rang out. Pistols, she had time to think, as she ducked into an alley reeking with the rank, gooseberry tang of tomcat piss. Her heart racing, she readied herself. Raised her gun.

'I've got her,' someone called out in Spanish. 'Down there.'

Answering shouts. She assessed the threat. Two voices after the shooter's. Three men in total. Boots on the tarmac. Running.

She lay down on her belly, ignoring the suddenly intensified stench from the greasy water now soaking into her clothes. Commando-crawled to the entrance of the alleyway. Poked her head out just enough to see.

Coming straight across the road towards her, guns swinging at their side, were two of Casildo's men. They were focusing on where her head would be if she were dumb enough to stay upright. It made her job a lot easier.

She squeezed off a shot, aiming centre-mass. Took the lead man in the belly. He screamed and folded over around the entry wound. Stumbled sideways.

She left him alive. An old trick. Kill your man, his comrades ran on. Or they ought to, if properly trained. Wound him – badly, painfully, loudly – and they stopped to help him. He was dead anyway, this one. He'd either bleed out or she'd finish him later.

The second man stopped, turned, bent to try to haul his screaming friend to his feet. Big mistake.

This time Margot had the luxury of time to aim. She folded her left arm in front of her and lay the pistol across her forearm. She sighted carefully and squeezed the trigger. The crack of the round exploding from her barrel echoed off the buildings on the far side of the street.

The round entered his head just to the left of his nose, obliterating a star-shaped tattoo in the process. He died without making a sound. The dim sodium streetlights rendered the scene in queasy shades of yellowish-grey. The jets of arterial blood from the ruptured arteries in his brain, spurting six, seven feet high into the night air were purple instead of bright-red.

She was about to get to her feet, then remembered the third man. She waited. The man she'd hit in the stomach had stopped screaming. Either he'd lost so much blood he'd fainted, or he was too weak to make any noise. The original shooter appeared on the far side of the street. She readied herself.

But this one was cunning. He stayed partially hidden in the shadow of a spread-branched tree. She could discern his outline and the change in quality of the darkness indicating his body. But at this range she'd never hit him.

He was going to let his comrade die. Clever bastard. Better trained than his number two, anyway. She looked over her shoulder. The alley was blocked by a tall chain-link barrier at the far end. Scaling it wouldn't be a problem, but those fences made a hell of a racket and he'd come after her in a flash. Shoot her in the back while she was climbing.

'*Puta!*' he yelled at her. Then, in English, 'Come out, bitch. The boss wants to see you.'

He emphasised his point with a burst of automatic fire. Nothing too serious in terms of calibre. It sounded like a submachinegun. An Uzi, maybe. At this range, virtually useless as long as she kept her head down. But he could pin her down until reinforcements arrived. And that, she could not permit to happen.

She looked up. A long, humped grey cloud was sliding towards the moon, borne on a brisk night breeze that had sprung up. Its leading tip cut into the fat, cream-coloured disc, removing a crescent. Margot readied herself for a counterattack.

The cartel man loosed off another burst. How many rounds did the average submachinegun mag hold? Thirty? Forty? He probably had one or two more bursts left before he'd have to reload. She needed to tempt him to burn through the rest of it.

The cloud continued its progress across the face of the moon, now obscuring half of it. She withdrew into the shadows and got to her feet.

'Señor Casildo will cut your balls off when you return empty-handed,' she yelled in English. 'You'll have to get a job as a eunuch in some dollar-a-fuck whorehouse.'

She didn't care if he understood all of it. Or any of it. The provocation was enough. For good measure she twisted her arm over sideways so she could elbow around the slimy brickwork, and sent a couple of rounds his way.

He yelled an oath. So unimaginative. Men everywhere were all the same. Two or three short, brutal, Anglo-Saxon words. Then they were done. He speech marked the abuse with a sustained burst of fire. The bullets smacked into the stucco above and around her position, sending brightly coloured fragments of centuries-old plaster snowing down around her.

The click as the gun dry-fired was audible from her side of the street. She heard him swear under his breath. On her toes, she ran lightly across the street. The moon was now totally obscured by the cloud. The streetlights were revealed as useless, powerful enough only to illuminate the top third of their own supports.

As he fished out another magazine, he kept up a torrent of invective aimed at his weapon. '*Vamos! Vamos, bastardo!*' The metallic clicks and scrapes as he tried, and failed, to seat the magazine in the receiver made her smile. She was only ten metres away now. She took up a crouching shooter's position and called out to him.

'*Oye! Eunoco!*'

Startled into forgetfulness, he whirled round. His head was only in the light for a second. But a second was more than Margot needed. Calmly, she shot him between the eyes. Blood and brain tissue sprayed back, coating the poster-covered wall behind him.

She followed her shot in, crouching by his body to retrieve the submachine gun – not an Uzi, but a Heckler & Koch MP5K, an impressive weapon for a gangbanger. Where he had failed, she succeeded, slotting home the new magazine with a practised movement, snicking it home into the receiver with a quiet click.

She pulled the charging lever back and let it go with a satisfying snap. She nodded with satisfaction.

OK. It felt like the odds had just shifted decidedly in her favour.

28

General Copeland sat by the window in his darkened study, staring down at his neatly mown lawn.

A pair of bandit-masked raccoons were playing on the grass, mown shorter than a grunt's buzzcut. The moonlight heightened their black and white colouration while draining the hues from the rest of the yard, so the whole scene looked as though it had been rendered in monochrome.

He ought to be scrambling an extraction team. Margot was an asset; she'd called for help. Evergreen looked after its people. That was the gold standard. No man – or woman – left behind.

Yet, he hesitated. For shortly after his call with Margot had ended, he'd received an email from a contact in the trade section, AKA the spook department, at the US embassy in Tegucigalpa. Unusual levels of gunfire across the Rio Grande. Was it anything to do with his operative?

Tookey and Ryan went way back. They shared intel, flouting

the rules of both their respective organisations. But once you'd saved a man's life, all that bureaucratic bullshit was worth less than the ancient, immutable elements of the warrior code. Loyalty. Honour. Duty.

'Yes,' the general had said. 'I was about to start putting an extraction team together.'

'Really,' Ryan said, his voice emotionless. 'My advice, Six-Foot? Stay the hell away. This shitshow ain't even halfway over and already social media here's lighting up like the Fourth of July. Believe me, you do not want to get in the middle of this. I've even heard chatter the city's going to send troops in if things don't settle in the next hour. Your guy's going to have to fight his way out or die trying.'

The general didn't bother correcting Ryan on Margot's gender. It wasn't relevant. In any case, he thought of all Evergreen agents as 'guys'. He had no time for any of that PC bullshit. If you had to say 'him or her' or 'his or hers' every time you gave an order, briefings would take twice as long as they needed to.

'We listened in on a call from between an undercover DEA agent inside the Zinguizapa cartel and his handler,' Ryan said. 'Apparently Casildo has pressed the nuclear button. He wants your operative in chains. And not just her. There's two ex-Special Forces Brits running around Tegucigalpa like they're in Mosul. Any idea who they might be?'

The general rubbed his chin, feeling the short bristles sandpapering his palm. Of *course* he knew who they were! Or, one of them, at any rate. Wolfe. Who else would it be? And Margot had lied to him about it. He'd asked her flat out. Was it Wolfe? And she'd denied it.

He scratched his head as he watched the raccoons tumbling and playfighting. Like kids. He sighed. He and Jill had just the one child. Lance. As soon as he was old enough, the boy had signed on with the Marine Corps. He was a natural. Aced Swim, Grass and Firing weeks; a natural at all the disciplines from combat marksmanship to land navigation. Even showed an aptitude for languages, so the Corps had put him through a university course to learn Arabic, Pashtun and Russian.

His career had been like something out of a recruitment brochure. Two tours in Afghanistan. Combat missions *and* hearts and minds. A gifted linguist with a knack for developing relationships with tribal elders and civilians alike.

He'd been sitting in the house of a sheikh, sipping peppermint tea and discussing local security arrangements, when an ISIS suicide bomber had parked an ageing Russian-made truck directly outside the house and blown himself, the truck, the house, the sheikh and his bodyguards, and family – a wife, two sisters-in-law, and six children – and Lance, into atoms. There'd been nothing left to bury.

It had nearly broken Jill. She'd been catatonic with grief for three months. On drugs that turned her into a zombie for another six after that. The general had poured his grief into a deep well and capped it off with a sturdy, iron-bound wooden lid branded with the Corps motto: *Semper Fidelis*. Returned to his office. Carried on working.

If Lance's death was to mean anything, he *had* to. It's why Evergreen had come into being.

And the general wasn't going to waste any more people on a maverick agent from England who disrespected him, and Lance's memory, by lying to his face. It was a dog-eat-dog world. Margot knew that when she signed up.

He pushed the phone away from him on the immaculate desk and went back to the bedroom to dress. He had some work to do.

29

COMAYAGUELA

Keeping to the deeper shadows in the lee of the buildings, Gabriel made his way down Calle Seis.

Sporadic gunfire ahead told him Margot was still in the barrio. Maybe Casildo had thrown up a ring of steel around the slum, preventing her from escaping to the relative safety of Tegucigalpa. It made sense. With the resources the cartel boss had at his disposal, Gabriel would have done the same.

Piercing a brief lull, the unmistakable sound of a rifle. Not an assault rifle: the rapid crack-crack-crack of 7.62 or 5.56 rounds fired on full auto. This was a single shot. A marksman's shot. Considered. The report echoing high off the buildings.

He looked upwards. Hoping the sniper might shoot again and reveal himself with the muzzle-flash. Nothing.

Maybe he had the right idea, though. Casildo's men were all, or all but one, at street level. Gabriel didn't like those odds. If he went up onto the rooftops, it would be one on one. Better. Even if his opponent was carrying a rifle. Besides, if he could sneak up on him, get in close, then high-powered or not, a long-barreled rifle would be little more use than a baseball bat.

He swung himself up onto a dangling fire escape, whose lowest section didn't quite reach the ground. Swearing as a rusted section of the handrail cut into his palm, he climbed up and reached the flat roof a few short seconds later.

The gunshot had come from down the street. Keeping low and running on the balls of his feet, he traversed the roof, running round the hutches and coops where the residents kept pigeons and rabbits, presumably for food.

Ahead, another shot. This time he saw it. The muzzle flash bright against a coal-black sky. Two blocks to go. He ran on, leaping the narrow gap where an alley pierced the solid terrace of houses at ground level.

Once on the same roof as the shooter, Gabriel flattened himself to the bitumen roofing felt, still sticky from the day's heat and smelling strongly of tar. Breathing slow and steady, settling his pulse, he slithered towards his target, his fingers coming away gritty and warm from the roofing felt.

The Smitty was digging into his belly and scraping along the roof. He didn't want the shooter to hear it so he pulled it free and stuck it into the back of his waistband.

Thus unencumbered, he crawled on. With ten metres to go, he spotted the shooter. He'd set up at a corner of the roof looking down at a crossroads. Mobile phone at his side, its screen glowing blue. The rifle looked to be something modern. Not one of the large-calibre, long-range weapons they used in Afghanistan: the Barret M82 or the Accuracy International AX50. No need to make a two-thousand-yard shot in the barrio, where the average distance before your target could dodge behind a building was probably two hundred max. But bolt-action, and sophisticated. Designed for combat, not hunting.

He was lying flat, holding a pair of binoculars to his eyes. Totally focused, as a good sniper should be, on spotting his target. But a good sniper, a *really* good sniper, ought also to be situationally aware. Unless he was well inside his own lines, or completely and verifiably alone in his chosen nest, he ought not to leave himself open to a surprise attack.

Gabriel got up onto his hands and knees. Slowly, he tipped and twisted the butterfly knife so that its swinging handle opened, rotated and closed again, locking the blade in place, all with little more than a soft whisper as the metal parts slid over each other.

He began his final advance on the sniper. His aim was to capture the man and find out exactly what his orders were.

Maybe there was a way to negotiate his and Don's safe passage out of the barrio. Although the desire for vengeance against Margot still burned like an underground fire in Gabriel's breast. So any deal was also going to have to include his killing her first.

Just five yards to go, and a pigeon coop to his right for one final piece of cover.

Somewhere beyond the ramshackle wood and chicken wire structure, he heard a soft sound, then the clicking of claws on the roof. A low growl in the back of a throat that sounded vaguely canine. What the hell? He jerked his head round. Was it a fox? Some grimy-furred doglike animal with a long sharp snout and bright eyes that glinted with predatory focus was approaching the coop.

Maybe the birds inside smelled it. Or they employed some other, purely avian, sense to detect the threat. Either way, from being utterly silent as they slept, the birds within began flapping around and tootling in alarm. The fox growled and leapt at the chicken wire.

The sniper spun round, half on his feet, at the noise.

'*Madre de dios! Que pasa?*'

Gabriel was exposed. The sniper's eyes widened. He swung his gun up.

The fox yipped in frustration and bounded away across the rooftop. Gabriel flung himself sideways, tucking himself into a ball as the sniper fired. The noise was enormous as the round exploded from the muzzle with a foot-long flash of orange flames. Gabriel's left cheek flared white-hot with pain. He clapped a hand to his face. Felt immediately where the round had seared a trench through his beard. It came away wet.

Another centimetre to the left and his jaw would currently be spinning to the street. Another ten, and his head would have exploded into pink mist.

Sparks dancing before his eyes, already disturbed by a pulsing green afterimage, he moved fast. Maybe it was the image of a shot-off jaw, but now he had company: Smudge was with him, a ghostly M16 at his shoulder.

'Gotta move, Boss. He's not going to miss with his second shot.'

The shooter was working the bolt, but in his haste and shock, he'd wrenched it and now it was jammed.

Men going up against Gabriel Wolfe didn't get two chances. Knife clamped in his right hand, Gabriel closed the distance between them with a flying dive. He cannoned into the shooter, knocking the rifle out wide to the right. They fell together, Gabriel on top of his man and immediately bringing his arm up to get the knife to his throat. He still wanted him alive, but survival had to come first. You couldn't do much negotiating if you were dead.

Something told him this was no day-rate cartel heavy. The man had had training. Military training. He twisted out from under Gabriel and brought his right knee up sharply into Gabriel's balls. The pain exploded between his legs and even as he rolled away, he had to fight back the nausea that threatened to engulf him.

The shooter was on his feet now, a hunting knife waving back and forth, leaping effortlessly from hand to hand, its wicked edge glinting in the moonlight. Behind him, the pigeons were hooting and flapping still. Why no pistol? There could only be one reason. He wanted Gabriel alive. And Gabriel didn't want to draw any more cartel men with gunfire.

The shooter feinted then lunged, knifepoint at gut-level. So, his orders were to bring Gabriel in alive, but not necessarily unharmed.

Gabriel put his hands up. Dropped his own knife.

'OK, OK. It's over. I surrender.'

The shooter's brow furrowed. His hand dropped a fraction.

Gabriel kicked the knife out of his hand then sprang at him, fingers clawed into hooks. His left hand missed its target, skidding off his cheekbone, but the right dug deep into the man's left eye socket. Gabriel clenched his fist, feeling the man's eyeball give then burst beneath his fingertips with a liquid pop. He screamed and clamped his hands to his face.

Gabriel stepped back, gave the man's right wrist a jerk and snapped it cleanly. The slender bones of his lower arm broke one after the other in quick succession. The sound like a pump-action shotgun being racked.

It was over. The shooter fell to the roof, groaning and rolling from side to side. Gabriel had no time for the niceties of war. An enemy combatant was down, but Gabriel wanted information. And he wanted it now.

'Is Casildo after me, or just McDonnell?'

The shooter moaned again, turning to spit blood and saliva onto the roofing felt. Gabriel slapped him hard.

'Look at me! Open your eye or you'll lose that one, too.'

The man took his hand away from his face and opened his remaining eye.

'You don't have to die here,' Gabriel said. 'I can let you live. I want to know what Casildo told you.'

'I failed him. I'm dead already. So fuck you and fuck your mother.'

Gabriel lifted the man bodily and hefted him over his head, arms locked out. God, that speed was good stuff. That plus his own body's adrenaline had doubled his strength. He staggered to the edge of the roof.

'Last chance,' he grunted. 'Tell me.'

'You're a dead man. The barrio's on lockdown. See you in hell, gringo.'

Gabriel leaned forwards just enough and tossed the man off the roof. He made no sound as he plummeted to Earth, landing with a wet smack on the road.

Gabriel was already turning. He retrieved his revolver and

picked up the rifle. No Soviet-era AK for the Zinguizapa sniper. This was a Barrett 98B, a sophisticated bolt-action military sniper rifle, chambered for .338 Lapua Magnum rounds. How had a Honduran cartel got hold of one? An awful image flashed across Gabriel's inner eye. A US marksman engaged in anti-drug trafficking ops in Central America. Shot dead or tortured and then relieved of his weapon.

He laid the rifle on the ground. He needed to fix the jammed bolt. At least it was back in the right hands now. Or as close to them as it was likely to be. For Gabriel had lost his illusions somewhere between Scalpay and Santa Rosa. If he'd ever done good, and he clung onto that idea as tenaciously as a dog with a stolen steak, his deeds had been coloured in shades of grey that had got progressively murkier and harder to distinguish from the purest white – or black – as the years went on.

Let's not forget that Mozambican politician you murdered, an inner voice sneered. *He was innocent. But you were just following orders, weren't you?*

'I had no choice!' Gabriel said.

Of course you didn't! Poor little Gabriel Wolfe. Forced to kill Philip Agambe, weren't you? Poor little soldier boy.

'Shut up, shut up!' Gabriel shouted, clapping his hands to his ears.

How about that Russian cook? All he did was make you delicious food and lend you his book on mushroom hunting. And how did you repay him? Slaughtered him like a pig.

'No, no! It's not true.'

The figure loomed over him. A demonic form, clad in blood-red camouflage fatigues, a red beret draped rakishly over one eye.

Of course it's true! it yelled down at him. *Jesus, I thought I was bad. But compared to you, I'm Tinkerbell! A woman only has to get close to you and it's like she just fucked a Claymore. BLAM! Blood and body parts everywhere. Maybe I should message Esperanza and tell her to buy herself some body armour.*

'Please stop,' Gabriel moaned, sinking to his knees, head hanging low on his chest.

Oh, I'll stop, all right. I'll stop when—

The demon, or whatever it was, didn't get to finish its sentence. Smudge's voice cut across its mockery.

'Oi, shithead! Eat this.'

A burst of automatic gunfire. An M16, its aural signature as distinctive as Smudge's south-east London accent.

Gabriel opened his eyes. Smudge was standing there, rifle in hand.

'Come on, Boss,' he said gently. *'You've got work to do. You got to put all that shit behind you. McDonnell's out there laughing at you.'*

Sniffing, Gabriel scrubbed at his eyes and began working on the Barrett's jammed charging lever. It took five minutes, but eventually he managed to free it. A dab of grease from the muck on his face eased it into position and though it resisted a little, it moved smoothly back and forth.

He patted the Model 629. Nodded to himself. Heavily armed would just about cover it. He must be carrying ten kilos of hardware.

The rattle of gunfire snapped him back fully into present reality.

He set off across the roofs.

Heading towards the sound of the shooting.

30

Gabriel knew Margot would be trying to get back across the river. But Casildo had locked down the barrio. That meant men at the bridges and the roads leading out into the neighbouring slums.

She was giving a good account of herself, though. As he checked each new road he came to from the rooftop, he saw a succession of corpses lying sprawled on the tarmac. Stray dogs were already pulling and nipping at their exposed flesh. Huge rats darted forward when the bigger scavengers retired with their booty.

How long would Casildo's men hold the line and not try to kill her? The sniper had said he was already a dead man because he'd failed in his allotted task. So Casildo was a brutal boss. Gabriel shook his head. Of course he was! He ran a drug cartel not a department store.

So would they keep taking losses until either she escaped or they got lucky and winged her? Or would one trigger-happy soldier miscalculate and accidentally kill her? He'd presumably have to disappear himself. But Honduras was a big country, with copious employment opportunities for a man willing to kill without mercy.

He found her fifteen minutes after killing the sniper.

She was backed into a corner, a submachine to her shoulder, firing short bursts as a trio of cartel soldiers advanced on her, taking cover behind parked cars, whose bodywork clanged and clonked as her rounds tore through the side panels and hit the steel and cast-iron beneath.

The final round left her magazine. The cartel men cheered derisively – an incongruous sound after a firefight – and emerged from their hiding places, machetes drawn.

'The boss said to bring you in alive,' one crowed. 'He didn' say nothing about fuckin' you up a little first.' He grabbed his crotch. 'Or maybe just fuckin' you.'

Gabriel shrugged off the trench coat and balled it up on the roof's low parapet. He didn't have time to calculate windage; it was a still night in any case and the range was short enough for it not to matter. With the rifle's fore-end pushed down onto the wadded-up fabric, he sighted through the scope on the crotch-grabber and shot him through the head.

As the skull exploded, filling the air around him with pink mist, the other two gangsters shouted and ran for cover, firing wildly in all directions. Margot, he noticed, looked up at the rooflines of the surrounding buildings. A woman used to working with sniper cover, he had time to think, before shooting the second man in the chest. He fell sideways, clattering into a dumpster that wobbled for a few drunken feet on its unlocked castors.

That left the final man, now ensconced in a doorway and firing short, controlled bursts back at Gabriel. A third shot took him in the head and he died with his mouth stretched in a rictus grin, blood fountaining from the exit wound in the back of his head, painting scarlet arcs all over the white stucco wall behind him.

Margot had a fix on him now. She looked straight at him.

'Evergreen?' she shouted.

That's what it sounded like, anyway. Some sort of codeword to identify friendlies.

She'd recognise his voice if he shouted back. He summoned

up a long-buried memory of Vinnie Calder, whose Camaro had passed through Gabriel's hands and into those of Corporal John Richards. Shaped his mouth to produce his dead friend's Texas drawl.

'Evergreen!' he yelled back. 'Hold your position!'

That was all she was getting until they were face to face.

Margot nodded, slung the submachinegun into the shadows and pulled out a packet of Marlboros, the red-and-white packaging distinctive even in the dim light from the streetlamps. Gabriel remained in position. Positioned the cross-hairs on the glowing tip of the cigarette. He could shoot her dead right now. She wouldn't know what had hit her. Dead before the sound of the bullet reached her.

But that would be the problem, wouldn't it? Dead before she knew who was killing her. And why. She had to understand that decisions always have consequences.

She'd relaxed, now the firefight was over. Now, as she believed, she had a sniper to help her make it out of the barrio in one piece. She leaned back against the wall, one ankle crossed in front of the other. For all the world as if she were an undertaker planning her morning's work in some old-time two-horse town, after the sheriff had despatched the desperadoes with his six-gun.

Gabriel's pulse had settled to a steady sixty beats per minute. Despite the fact he was looking through the rifle's high-quality optics at the woman who'd ordered Eli's execution.

He dropped the cross-hairs and sighted on Margot's left knee. A big artery, the popliteal, ran behind the kneecap. It linked to the bigger, fatter blood vessel, the femoral, in the thigh.

Hit the femoral and she'd bleed out before he reached her. Hit the popliteal and she might survive. Especially if, as now seemed increasingly likely, she knew her battlefield medicine. She'd fashion a tourniquet, probably by ripping up her shirt to stop the bleeding. It wouldn't matter.

He shifted his aim fractionally to one side. Through the scope, her knee was the size of a melon. Shot placement was easy. He breathed out, waited for a heartbeat and squeezed the trigger between that beat and the next.

Margot's knee exploded. She screamed as her leg buckled and she fell sideways, smacking her head against the tarmac. Gabriel was already on the move, racing across the roof and shinning down a drainpipe, the rifle slung over his shoulder. He dropped to the ground in an alley between the building and its neighbour and was running across the deserted street seconds later.

Margot was clutching her shattered knee, and moaning inarticulately. He'd missed the artery, that much was obvious. But her left leg lay in an expanding pool of dark, venous blood. She'd clamped her hands around the leg, just above the knee. As he arrived, she managed, through some huge effort of will, to shuffle backwards until she could lean against the wall behind her.

Her eyes wild, she looked up at him and swore.

'I knew you'd come after me.'

'And here I am,' he said, keeping a couple of yards back, the rifle aimed at her midsection. 'What are you doing down here, Margot?'

'Does it matter?' she hissed through clenched teeth.

'It might.'

'Can I trade intel for my life?'

He shrugged. 'I don't know. What can you tell me?'

She looked down at her ruined flesh, red and pulpy through the blown-out knee of her trousers.

'You need to get a tourniquet on that. I'm going to bleed out otherwise.'

Gabriel unclipped the strap the cartel shooter had added to the rifle. He dropped it onto her lap, drawing forth another yelp.

'Do it yourself.'

With gritted teeth, through which her grunts of pain were almost suppressed, she fed the webbing under her leg. She slid it beneath the knee, moaning once more. Then she pulled it towards her and tied it off, before twisting the free ends around each other until the strap was digging in to the flesh of her thigh.

'Promise me you'll let me live if I tell you why I'm here.'

Although he kept his features neutral, Gabriel couldn't believe what he was hearing. Had she forgotten what she'd done on Scalpay? In Vietnam? In Jerusalem? At Rothford? So much blood on her hands, so many lives extinguished by bullets, blades and bombs.

Did she really think he was willing to deal? Whatever unholy business had brought a British spook, if that's even what she was, to Honduras was of no interest to him. But part of him, the part trained since his late teens to acquire strategic and tactical intelligence, wanted to know. Old habits still died hard.

'Deal,' he said.

'You mean it?'

'I give you my word as a man of honour.'

She sighed. The outbreath morphed into another groan and she clutched the improvised tourniquet tighter with both hands.

'I won't tease you, Gabriel,' she grunted with pain, 'with the intel. Here it is. I work for a US military outfit called Evergreen. Black ops. Covert assassinations. The usual.'

He nodded. Reflecting on the very dark world he inhabited where extra-judicial murders conducted by agents of the state were considered 'the usual'.

'And?'

'The boss is a three-star general. Copeland D Tookey.' She grunted out a low chuckle. It sounded full of pain. 'They call him Six-Foot. I was meeting Casildo to arrange the hire of some new men. We didn't hit it off at all. I was figuring out my exit strategy when I saw you and, well, you know the rest.'

'That's it?'

She shrugged. 'They operate out of 1325 Barbara Ndefu Parkway in DC. Super-discreet. Look for Patton, MacArthur, Sherman, LLP on the name board.'

Her gaze shifted over his shoulder, just for a second. He caught the movement, turned and fired at the oncoming cartel fighter, whose pistol was already raised. At this range, the rifle round blew a hole straight through his chest, bursting his heart and taking a fair amount of flesh and bone fragments out of the exit wound to spatter onto the asphalt. He died without making a sound.

Gabriel turned back to Margot. Her right hand had snaked inside her jacket. She wore a sly expression even on her whitened features.

He shot her through the right shoulder.

'We had a deal!' she screamed as her right hand fell, uselessly, to her side. She clutched her shoulder. Blood issued between her fingers, staining the pale fabric of her jacket a deep red.

'Which you were about to break.'

'I was going to help you! Casildo must've sent his whole gang onto the streets after us. We need each other, Gabriel. Let's team up, at least until we're out of this hellhole.'

Gabriel squatted in front of Margot, and pushed the Barrett's muzzle against her chest, directly over her heart.

'I get Bakker's motivation. He thought Don and I had betrayed him. What I need to know is why you were involved.'

She'd gone into shock. She answered through chattering teeth.

'I had orders from Gemma Dowding. The prime minister,' she added, as if Gabriel had been away from the UK for so long, he might have forgotten such facts.

'Bullshit. You're just trying to save your own skin.'

She shook her head, coughing suddenly.

'Let me make one call and I'll prove it to you.'

Operating on no more than instinct, Gabriel agreed. 'If your hand comes out around anything except a phone, you're a dead woman, Margot.'

She tightened her lips as a spasm of pain wracked her.

'Just let me, OK?'

Slowly, she snaked a hand inside her jacket and drew out a phone. She fiddled with it for a few moments then showed Gabriel that she'd set the call to speaker.

'This is Gemma Dowding. Leave a message.'

Gabriel recognised the prime minister's voice. So far, so convincing, although any number of spooks might have it in their contacts file.

'Gemma, it's Margot. I have some very interesting news about Gabriel Wolfe.' Margot's voice was tight and compressed with the effort of speaking through the pain. 'Believe me you're going to want to hear it. If you're there—'

'What do you want now?'

Compared to the measured tones of the pre-recorded message, this was a woman under stress. No careful modulation of vowel sounds to give her voice a more cultured sound.

'He's alive.'

'What? How do you know? I checked the police reports. He blew himself sky-high just like you said.'

'I'm in Honduras. I have him under observation right now.'

Margot looked up at Gabriel and winked. The expression filled him with wonder, that a woman with two gunshot wounds could find the energy for game-playing.

'Jesus, Margot. I told you to get rid of him and you screwed that up. Now you're telling me he's not dead after all. You need to kill him. Do not lose him again.'

'How can I, Gemma. I'm disavowed, remember? *You* disavowed me.'

'Yes, well, we'll have to reconsider that, won't we. Look, just get it done and come to see me. We'll have a chat, yes?'

'Of course,' she paused to stifle another cough, 'Prime Minister.'

With the phone back in her pocket, she looked up at Gabriel.

'Why did she – does she – want me dead?' he asked, shaking at the revelation that the person who'd ordered his, Don's and Eli's murders was the prime minister herself.

'She'd been running an outfit like Evergreen in the UK. Apparently you know about it. That makes you dangerous.'

In that moment, Gabriel realised how far back the web of lies ran.

'Pro Patria Mori,' he said quietly.

Margot nodded. 'She deported the cop who wiped most of them out. Threatened her family unless she kept quiet. You and

Webster were the last two people in the UK who knew about it. I was using Kevin to take you off the board.'

'Weren't you worried she'd want you off it, too? After all, now you knew about PPM as well.'

'I took out an insurance policy.'

'Wait. You said Don and I were the last. That's not true. I know the cop you're talking about. Her boss was a high-up in the Met. And there was a journalist, too.'

Margot's eyes flicked from side to side. He could see her formulating her next evasion.

'Cop's too high-profile. She's an assistant commissioner now. Too many questions if she died or disappeared. The hack's like me,' she groaned. 'Big fan of insurance.'

'What are you telling me? That Don and I, and Eli, were just easy targets because nobody would ask questions?'

Margot grunted out a sardonic laugh. 'She was never a target. Just collateral damage.'

Gabriel strove to process what Margot had just told him. After all the missions he and Eli had run. All the wars they'd fought in. All the action they'd seen, from the Middle East to Africa, South-East Asia to mainland China. Eli had lost her life because of a murderous conspiracy that had put down its black, twisted roots in the fertile soil of Westminster.

'That has to be worth my life,' Margot said. 'Can you take me to the hospital now? I'm not going to be able to get out of here like this.'

Gabriel stood, and aimed the rifle at her head.

'Goodbye, Margot. This is for Eli.'

'What! No!' Her eyes flashbulbed. 'We had a deal. You gave me your word. As a man of honour.'

'I have no honour left, Margot. What little I'd been conserving, I buried along with my wife and our unborn child.'

He curled his finger around the trigger. A faint tang of lemon and sandalwood caught in his nostril. He thought of a life he'd once had. And of the life he now never would. A faraway voice, *her* voice, whispered, '*Do it now, darling. Do it for me and the baby*'.

Margot McDonnell's head blew out from the left side, her brains splattering the sidewalk for six or seven feet. Shocked, Gabriel jumped back as an artery in her head let go, firehosing scarlet arterial blood high into the air.

But he hadn't fired. Hadn't even got beyond first pressure.

A small, high voice behind him. A voice he recognised.

'*Adios, puta!*'

He whirled around. Standing a few feet back, a Colt .45 pistol looking comically oversized in her small fists, was the little flower-seller. Her face was clean, shockingly bright against the grime of the rest of her skin. The cut Margot had dealt her was closed with bright-white butterfly sutures.

She smiled up at him. In English, she said, 'Señora Schippers is a very nice lady. She gives me a lollipop because I am "a very brave little girl".'

Before he could reply, she skipped away, the gun dangling from her right hand as other girls might swing a doll, and disappeared around the corner.

Gabriel took one last look at Margot McDonnell's body. He'd thought he'd be killing the architect of Eli's death, but she'd fallen back on the oldest, most threadbare excuse of conscienceless killers everywhere.

I was just following orders.

What orders. And from what a source!

So his mission was not over after all. Gemma Dowding was trying to tie off all the loose ends.

She didn't know that, for Gabriel, she'd just become another dangling thread.

31

WASHINGTON, DC

The general arrived at the office on Barbara Ndefu Parkway at 3:15 a.m.

The situation room was manned around the clock, its satellite and drone feeds displayed on tessellated monitors forming a giant information wall that took up an entire side of the rectangular space.

In calm, clear voices, shorn of all inflection, case officers communicated with ops teams from Jordan to Moscow, Phnom Penh to Berlin.

On sending Margot down to Honduras, he'd diverted the nearest surveillance drone to Tegucigalpa. Now he ordered one of the techs looking after the drone feeds to bring it up on screen.

'Switching to infrared,' the tech said, in an emotionless, efficient voice.

'Zoom in on the Chupacabra, then begin a street-by-street sweep,' the general commanded.

It took eighteen minutes and twenty-one seconds for the drone to locate Margot McDonnell's tracker and for its infra-red camera to zoom in on the woman herself. The general followed her as she moved, zig-zagging and always choosing the narrowest roads, in her attempt to reach the river and the safety of her hotel in Tegucigalpa.

He grunted with appreciation for her urban warfare skills as she was confronted by, and systematically took out, a succession of armed kill teams, presumably Casildo's men.

Then, the showdown. One of the cartel soldiers had a rifle and was sniping from a rooftop. The general watched as he shot Margot. Not killed her; that was clear from the way she fell sideways and then clutched her leg. So he'd aimed only to immobilise her.

Casildo wanted her alive. A hostage, then. In some ways that was a blessing for Margot. The general had no illusions about the way Latin American drug cartels operated. A few days, even a couple of weeks, of confinement – however meagre the rations, however rudimentary the accommodations – was preferable to what awaited traitors, spies and government agents captured by the Mexicans, Colombians or Hondurans.

As used in the modern world, the word, 'torture' had lost some of its original terrifying connotations. Partly, the general was forced, reluctantly, to admit, thanks to his own government's activities at various CIA-operated black sites. Not to mention the treatment of captives at Abu Ghraib. But what the spooks inflicted on their prisoners? Waterboarding, beatings, stress positions, sleep deprivation? That was little more than a West Point hazing compared to the Latin Americans. They were like medieval inquisitors, witch-finders and Vlad the Impaler all rolled into one.

An unpleasant image – the aftermath of a mission to support Federal troops in Mexico's notorious Guanajuato state – swam to the front of his mind. A grove of avocado trees festooned with the silvery-purple intestines of five SWAT-team members captured in a firefight by the Jalisco New Generation cartel. He shook his head to dispel the horrific vision.

The general had no intention of sending more men in to extract Margot. Ryan's advice had sealed the question. But he thought he could probably pay for her release when the inevitable ransom demand came in. He owed her that much, at least.

As he watched the feed, he ran numbers in his head, estimating what sort of ransom the cartel would demand for Margot's safe return. Then a small figure, a dwarf, he thought initially, crossed the street, raised its arm and shot her dead right in front of the sniper.

Jesus! They said life came cheap in the barrios of Comayaguela. They weren't kidding.

The sniper exchanged a few words with the…not dwarf, it moved like a…child. Then it skipped, it literally *skipped* off.

The general shook his head.

'Kill the feed,' he instructed the tech.

The screen flipped back to some other city, some other mission.

And the general's mind flipped back to his earlier thoughts. He needed a new case officer.

32

COMAYAGUELA

The city Gabriel had happily entered less than twelve hours earlier now felt like a prison.

His target was down, but in her dying breath she'd implicated another woman, so powerful as to make Margot McDonnell look like a kindergarten teacher.

Yet prime ministers held no special fear for Gabriel. The first he'd tangled with, Barbara Sutherland, had been forced into obscurity so complete even Twitter had given up speculating on her whereabouts. The second, Joe Tamerlane, was rotting in an unmarked grave deep in an inaccessible valley somewhere in the north of England.

Perhaps there were some MPs who still genuinely believed they were doing good for the people who elected them. But on the extremely rare occasions when Gabriel caught the news before decamping to Honduras' Caribbean coast, all he'd seen were the corrupt, the venal and the downright criminal shouldering each other aside to get their snouts in the trough. A trough filled with public money.

Gemma Dowding had ordered his and Don's executions. She was also responsible for Eli's death. It seemed once she'd got the taste for removing enemies of the state with a bullet, she'd never lost it.

But he had one advantage over her.

He was dead.

* * *

Three blocks west of Gabriel's position, Casildo was speaking to one of his squad commanders, a burly former police captain named Raúl da Silva.

'Where is Carlos?' Casildo demanded, hands on hips.

'We can't find him, boss. We've been trying him on the radio but he's not answering. I think maybe one of the gringos took him out.'

Casildo ground his teeth, expensively restored from their former poverty-stricken ruin to fine, American-style dentistry. Carlos was a good man. A son to him. More loyal than a Goddamn dog. And this English commando or whatever the hell he was had murdered him.

'New orders,' he said in a low voice his men had learned to fear. 'Kill him on sight.'

'You don't want to capture him? We could bring him in and you could take your time with him, boss.'

Slowly, Casildo turned so that he was face to face with da Silva. He glared down at him. Was pleased to see the way the man quailed before him.

'Questioning my orders, Raúl?'

'No, boss. Of course not. I just thought—'

'Carlos was my best man. A military sniper. Now he's dead at the gringo's hands. How long have you and your men been out there after him?' He held up a hand to forestall the inevitable excuses. 'Shut up! I don't care. My point is, from what I hear, a lot of my men are dead, and this Englishman is alive. So I'm thinking, it's time to end it. Fuck the ransom, fuck the Israelis, fuck the Americans and, most especially of all, fuck that Englishman. I want him dead, you understand me?'

'Yes, boss. Yes, I do. Absolutely. I'll relay your orders.'

'Do that.' He checked his watch, a hundred-and-twenty-thousand-dollar platinum and diamond Patek Philippe. 'It's 4:05 a.m. now. I'll give the man who brings me his head before 5:00 a.m. a fifty-thousand-dollar bonus. Before 6:00 a.m., a twenty-five thousand dollar bonus. If he's still alive after that, I'll come after *your* head myself.'

Da Silva swallowed, nodded tersely, spun on his heel and left at a run, already shouting into his radio.

* * *

From his vantage point in an abandoned apartment on the second floor of a broken-down block, Gabriel watched as more cartel soldiers swarmed onto the streets. They bristled with automatic weapons, everything from submachine guns to assault rifles. He'd even seen one man swaggering down the street with a sand-coloured M250 belt-fed light machinegun over his shoulder.

He'd never lost faith in the benefits of SAS training, but they'd always relied on superiority of numbers, the element of surprise, or both. At the moment, he had neither.

He called Don.

'Did you make it back over the river OK? I'm in a bit of a tight spot,' he said when Don answered.

'I did. Not without a spot of bother of my own, but let's say the old warhorse hasn't completely forgotten the pull of the harness, eh? What's the situation?'

'Casildo's mobilised his whole force. That's what it looks like, anyway. Dozens of men, all heavily armed.'

Don started to answer but then the line crackled, sputtered and died. Gabriel looked at his phone. He had plenty of charge left. Was it Don's phone that had run out? Or worse? He had no time to ponder such matters. He pocketed his phone and prepared to exfiltrate on his own.

His main problem was lack of numbers. But it was also lack of transport. Making it out of the barrio on foot was going to be time-consuming, and it would leave him vulnerable. He wanted a set of wheels. Getting mobile would restore to him at least one of the elements for a successful exfil: the element of surprise. Casildo's men were all hunting a man on foot.

But where would he find a suitable vehicle? The streets of Barrio Concepción were mostly free of cars. Anyone rich enough to own one had it parked out of sight or locked behind tall gates. Those that remained were beaten-up and rusting, more likely to break down just as he drove towards a cartel roadblock as power him through it.

The answer, when it arrived, was as obvious as it was frightening. The vehicle he'd steal was back at the Chupacabra. Casildo didn't live in the barrio. He'd have a fortified estate somewhere out in the countryside. He and his men would have driven in. Probably in a convoy of SUVs, minivans and trucks.

The boss's vehicle would be the pick of the bunch. Gabriel visualised something black and gleaming. A Cadillac Escalade or a Lincoln Navigator. If he preferred European iron, an Audi Q7 or that stand-by for global elites from Hollywood A-listers to organised crime bosses, the Range Rover.

Casildo's would be armoured. Perfect for protecting its occupant from the attentions of rival cartels, Honduran government forces, or foreign agencies like the DEA or ATF. Perfect, also, for busting out of a barrio currently under virtual lockdown thanks to Casildo's men.

Keeping to the rooftops, Gabriel began his journey southwest, back to the club where his night in Comayaguela had started.

33

The ground-floor lights at Chupacabra were all out. Even the flashing neon sign above the door had been turned off.

From his vantage point on the roof of a warehouse across the street, Gabriel surveyed the vehicles parked in the vacant lot on its eastern side. Four all-black SUVs: a Chevy Suburban, two Escalades and in the centre of the lot, the colony queen surrounded by its soldiers, a Mercedes G-Class SUV. Gleaming in the moonlight, its mirror-polished paintwork looked wet.

The Merc had to be Casildo's personal transport. It sat on raised suspension and the way the glass reflected the moonlight told Gabriel it was bulletproof. That meant the bulky, squared-off bodywork would be too. That kind of tuning could easily add a ton or more to a standard spec vehicle, so he would have upgraded the engine, too. No point sitting in a tank if the weight of the armour meant your performance was scarcely better than a family sedan.

Leaning against the Merc's rectilinear flank, smoking, a single cartel soldier. Casildo's driver, Gabriel assumed. A short, scrawny fellow, clearly chosen for his driving chops rather than his *cojones* in

ANDY MASLEN

a firefight, else why leave him behind? Yet he still had an AK-47 slung over his shoulder.

Gabriel spent a further ten minutes watching the parking lot, just in case the driver had a backup who'd left him to take a leak. But no. Clearly everyone Casildo could rely on to shoot straight was out in the barrio, looking for Gabriel.

He still had the Barrett, but it had no suppressor. A rifle shot in the dead silence of this part of the barrio would bring more heat than Gabriel wanted. It would have to be a close-quarters kill.

He descended from the roof, with the rifle slung over his shoulder. Reaching ground-level, he silently unfolded the butterfly knife and locked the blade into position as he watched the driver from a deep pool of shadow.

The driver turned aside and flicked his cigarette into a black puddle, the red tip spiralling crazily as the butt flipped from his fingers before sizzling out in the water.

He pulled out a pack and while he busied himself extracting a new smoke, Gabriel slipped from his hiding place and darted across the road. He picked up a golfball-sized stone from the gutter. Perfect for the job he had in mind.

When the driver's back was turned, Gabriel stepped out onto the sidewalk and threw the stone in a high arc that ended with a loud clang as it bounced off the Merc's vast black roof.

'*Hijo de puta!*' the driver shouted, whirling round and scanning the empty roadway. '*Malditas ratas callejeras!*'

Gabriel had witnessed for himself how dangerous the 'fucking street rats' were around this neighbourhood. One had just killed a highly trained spook-cum-assassin with a purloined pistol. Probably lifted from the corpse of one of the driver's compadres. There were plenty of them lying in the streets of the barrio. But Gabriel was an altogether different class of rat.

Still swearing at the imaginary child-vandals, the driver strode away from the G-Class, off the lot and into the street proper, drawing his pistol. He rounded the corner and came face to face with Gabriel, who now held the rifle over his right shoulder, right hand gripping the stock lightly. His left, which concealed the knife, hung loosely by his side.

'What's the matter? Street rats key the boss's Merc?' he asked in the rough barrio accent he'd been studying since arriving.

The driver eyed the long gun, then squinted up at Gabriel.

'Who the hell're you? And what's with the shit on your face?'

Gabriel grinned and rolled his eyes.

'Reinforcements. Camouflage. Any sign of the Englishman?'

'No. He'd hardly come around here, though, would he?'

'I don't know. Maybe he's got his eye on the G-Class.' Gabriel dropped his voice and injected a little steel into it, mixed with one of the almost musical tones Master Zhao had taught him as part of his Yinshen Fangshi training. 'It'd make the perfect getaway vehicle. Just look at it.'

The driver did what he'd been told to before he'd even realised he was complying with a total stranger.

Gabriel stepped towards him and drove the butt of the rifle into the side of his head, directly over the temple. The crack as the fragile sheet of bone fractured like an eggshell was crisp and clear in the depths of the still night air. The driver staggered sideways, raising his left hand to the smashed-in section of his skull. He turned, mouth lopsided, and tried to speak.

'Wha—' was all he managed before Gabriel cut his throat with the butterfly knife, then cradled him as he collapsed to the ground.

After removing the AK, Gabriel dragged the dead driver round the side of one of the Escalades and then rolled him between the axles. He patted down his pockets, but there was no key. Inside the G-Class then. It made sense. Who'd be foolish enough to steal a cartel boss's wheels from his own driver? Who indeed?

He opened the door and loaded the two long guns into the passenger compartment. It smelled of leather and Casildo's aftershave. He climbed inside and hit the central locking button. The fob lay in a cupholder in the centre console. It was a keyless ignition, so Gabriel simply thumbed the engine start button. From somewhere up ahead, muffled by armour-plating and what sounded like some state-of-the-art sound insulation, the engine woke with a muted growl. As he'd suspected, this was no ordinary factory motor.

The G-Class was blocked in by one of the Escalades. He put the transmission into reverse, looked over his shoulder and backed out of the tight scrum of black vehicles surrounding the Merc like a rugby scrum around the hooker. Or, given he was within spitting distance of the USA, globally speaking, a bunch of line-backers protecting the quarterback.

Once he was clear, he looked forwards again, snicking the buttery transmission into Drive. Only to see the SUV's clearly enraged owner exiting the front door of the bar, that gold-plated hand cannon raised in his fist and aimed directly at the windscreen.

Casildo's eyes burned like pools of dark fire. His mouth was working. Lip-reading was not among Gabriel's skillset. Not as a language asset, anyway. But Casildo was employing a very simple vocabulary. Gabriel had no trouble decoding it.

'You fuck! Steal my car? I'll kill you, motherfucker!'

Casildo loosed off three shots. Gabriel flinched involuntarily. The high-powered .50 slugs smacked into the glass with a sound like branches breaking. Each left a white crater, starred with radial cracks. None broke through. Off course they didn't. What would be the point if they did?

He was about to floor the accelerator, mashing Casildo back into the frontage of the bar, when he had a better idea. One that might get him safely out of the barrio. Out of the city altogether. He switched off the ignition.

Casildo was still roaring, but he'd realised that he was just wasting his limited stock of ammunition and stopped shooting. Gabriel drew his Smith & Wesson Model 629. Then he opened the driver's side door. Casildo's eyes widened. He stood, legs apart, Desert Eagle raised and gripped in both hands in the classic shooter's stance.

Gabriel moved sideways, leaving the protection of the

windscreen. Seeing his chance, Casildo fired twice. The two bullets hit the ground directly under the edge of the door and ricocheted away to smash into the bodywork of one of the Escalades with dramatic echoing bangs. If Gabriel had stepped down onto the concrete, he'd now be bleeding out from the ragged ends of his shins, where his feet used to be. But he'd held onto the grab-handle above the door-frame and hunched his legs up tight to his body, using the open door as a shield.

Now he popped up over the top of the door and fired at Casildo. The Smitty's muscular recoil sent his arm jerking upwards, slowing down his rate of fire. But Casildo knew enough about guns to see what he was up against. He was already turning to run back towards the club. Gabriel couldn't afford to let him get inside.

He dropped to the ground and fired from beneath the door. His first shot clipped Casildo's left calf, tearing a chunk of flesh free along with a portion of his suit trouser leg. Casildo went down, screaming and clutching his ruined lower leg.

But men like him didn't die without putting up more of a fight than that. He rolled onto his back and brought the Desert Eagle up. He fired two shots. Both went wide. Neither would have hit Gabriel, who'd rolled under the raised suspension and was already emerging on the passenger side of the G-Class.

Casildo swore loudly. Gabriel knew why. Three rounds into the windscreen, two under the door, two more just now. His pistol was empty. He had no time to swap out the magazine, even assuming he carried a spare. Gabriel ran up to him.

Casildo held his hands out. The left was smeared scarlet.

'Tell me what you want,' he grunted through bared teeth. 'You can have it. Money? Drugs? Diamonds? We can go to my compound right now before my men get back. You can take whatever you like. Even a chopper if you know how to fly one.'

'I want you,' Gabriel said. 'You're my passport out of here.'

'Sure, sure,' Casildo said, nodding. 'Get me in the Mercedes. I'll tell any of my men we meet to let us through.'

Gabriel shook his head.

'Too risky. You might give them a codeword then I'd be a dead man.'

Casildo groaned and clutched his bleeding leg wound again.

'Then what the hell do you mean, gringo?'

'Open your jacket. Let me see your shirt.'

'What?'

'Do it!'

Casildo spread the sides of his jacket wide, exposing his shirt-clad chest.

Gabriel tucked the Model 629 away and pulled out the nine. 'I'm sorry. It's nothing personal.'

'What? No! You can't!'

Gabriel contradicted him with a single squeeze of the trigger. The round entered Casildo's chest right over his heart. He slumped sideways.

Casildo was a heavyset man and it took Gabriel a minute to drag his corpse over to the Mercedes. Twice as long again to manoeuvre him into the passenger seat.

'Now, let's get you looking your best,' he said, tugging the suit jacket so that it covered the bloody flower on Casildo's white dress shirt.

He fastened the seat belt over Casildo's torso and tugged it tight, so the inertia reel mechanism locked it. There was nothing he could do about Casildo's lolling head. Or was there?

He had a feeling a cartel boss would have an interesting selection of hardware in the back of his personal transport. Gear that went well beyond the first-aid kit, emergency triangles and toolkits that Mercedes would have included as standard.

He was right. Behind the last row of seats, he found a black nylon holdall. The kind of bag in which a Special Forces soldier or maybe a counter-terrorism cop would keep their specialist kit. Inside he found a couple of pistols, spare ammunition, a bundle of black cable ties, a tactical knife, a hammer, and a long-bladed cross-head screwdriver, its tip encrusted with dried blood. He took the screwdriver and the hammer and went back up front again.

Sitting behind the passenger seat, Gabriel placed the tip of the screwdriver against the back of the headrest. It took several hammer blows but eventually the screwdriver penetrated the leather, entered the foam padding and emerged on the far side.

Gabriel pulled it back until the tip was flush with the diamond-stitched upholstery. He held Casildo's head tight against the rest with his left hand, pushed the screwdriver's handle until he felt the tip meet the back of Casildo's skull. He picked up the hammer again.

He hit the butt-end of the screwdriver's handle dead centre. The tip entered Casildo's skull with a sound like an egg breaking. It took a second blow to drive it all the way home until the handle met the rear of the headrest and refused to travel any further forward.

Gabriel let Casildo's head go. The body stayed upright, suspended from the screwdriver, locked into place with the seatbelt. The eyes were closed. But it didn't matter. He looked more alive than dead, and was now unlikely to offer any curious cartel guard a codeword.

He arranged Casildo's lifeless hands in his lap and restarted the engine.

Time to be off.

34

For the first time since arriving with Don in Comayaguela, Gabriel felt he had a measure of security.

He was sitting behind the wheel of an armoured SUV with a high-powered engine under the bonnet. He had two long guns, a 9mm pistol and a revolver. And, beside him, the best guarantor of a peaceful journey out of Comayaguela and into Tegucigalpa. Dead, admittedly, and held in place with a screwdriver through the back of his head. But he was still Luis-David Casildo. That had to count for something.

As he drove fast down Calle Ocho, he called Don.

'Where are you, boss?'

'The bar at the Marriott. Where are you?'

'On my way. Order me a martini, would you?'

'D'you still have that very specific list of instructions?'

'Nope. Just lots of gin and very, very cold.'

'I think we should be able to manage that.'

'Got to go.'

'Take care, Old Sport.'

Gabriel turned a corner into a wide avenue flanked by colonial buildings in wedding-cake stucco. The pinks, blues and greens all rendered in sickly shades of yellowish grey by the streetlamps that hadn't been shot out.

Coming the other way was a police car. Fixing his eyes on the road, Gabriel slowed to a more sedate speed than the sixty he'd been cruising at and flashed past the cruiser. In the rear-view mirror he saw it execute a screeching U-turn. Damn.

The rack of blue lights flashed out their urgent semaphore and the siren managed to penetrate, just, the G-Class's soundproofing and armour-plating.

He pulled over. Waited. Breathing easy, keeping his pulse down to a relaxed sixty five. The cop emerged from his car, gun already drawn. He pointed a long black torch like a billy-club up the road at the Mercedes and swaggered towards the driver's window. Gabriel placed the nine in his lap. Had he been north of the Mexican border, that kind of move was apt to get you killed. In this part of Central America it was likely to keep you alive.

Gabriel kept his gaze fixed on the windscreen. The craters smashed into the glass by Casildo's Action Express. 50 rounds looked a tad out of place, but there wasn't much he could do about them now. Did Autoglass have a franchisee in Honduras? On the whole, he thought not.

The cop rapped on the side window with the barrel of his pistol. Gabriel slowly turned his head and looked down into his doughy face. A luxuriant black moustache hid the cop's mouth. 'Open it,' he mouthed.

Gabriel buzzed down the window. Eyeballed the cop.

'What?'

No fear shown. He had every right to be on the road. Maybe a touch of dismissive, aristocratic hauteur. Not from his position of birth. From his role with the organisation headed by the corpse to his right.

'Your rear light is out, my friend. That's gonna cost you a hundred dollar fine.' He held out his left hand, palm uppermost, and grinned. 'Cash is fine.'

By way of answer, Gabriel sneered and looked down into the cop's greedy eyes.

'You see who's sitting next to me?'

The cop peered around Gabriel's head. His face blanched. He opened his mouth and stuttered out an apology.

'I'm sorry, man, OK? I had no idea this was Señor Casildo's car.' He frowned and scratched at his moustache. 'Hey, is he OK?'

'Just a touch of flu. He took some meds along with his vodka tonics. Now he's sleeping it off.'

The cop kept staring at Casildo. Gabriel softly curled his right hand around the pistol in his lap.

'You sure he's OK? Something happened to his face, I think. Looks all funny.'

'You want me to wake him up? Hey, boss!' he shouted into the corpse's face. 'I got this nosy cop wants to take your temperature.'

He leaned over and shook Casildo's shoulder for good measure.

He looked back at the cop, who was retreating, gun holstered now, a look of panic on his face.

'No problem. Just go. Get him home. I was never here, OK?'

He scuttled back to his cruiser and was pulling round the Merc seconds later, leaving the empty street to Gabriel once again.

Sometimes, he reflected, superior firepower was the way out of a tight situation. But others, a poker face and a willingness to tell the big lie worked just as well.

For several blocks he encountered nothing living bar a couple of scrawny urban foxes, standing dead-centre in the street, seemingly impervious to their imminent destruction beneath the wheels of the onrushing human vehicle. He tapped the horn button. Eyes lit like glassy green searchlights by the Merc's headlamps, they scampered off to the side of the road.

Up ahead, the bridge over the river back into Tegucigalpa beckoned, rising in a low but graceful arch over the turbid waters. The entrance to the bridge was lit brightly with a pair of tall streetlamps casting a pink glow over the approach.

Gabriel gunned the engine, already tasting the ice-cold martini Don was ordering for him.

35

Four armed men stepped out of the shadows and blocked Gabriel's route over the bridge.

He braked hard. Beside him, Casildo's corpse lurched forward. He slammed his hand into the face to keep it stuck to the screwdriver.

The cartel soldiers spread out in a line. Each held a squat submachinegun. Uzis, by the look of them. One stepped forward and patted the air for Gabriel to slow down.

He was out of options. He could slam it into reverse and try a different route, but he knew somehow that all he'd encounter would be more teams of gunmen at the other bridges. And who knew: he'd only encountered men armed with AKs and Uzis so far. Somewhere there might be a guy with an RPG. No amount of armour-plating would save him then.

He brought the Mercedes to a halt, put his foot on the brake to hold it still, and dropped the side window.

The lead soldier stepped forward and walked up to the driver's side, just like the cop had done. He peered up at Gabriel, then at Casildo.

'Who are you?' he asked Gabriel. 'Where's Sandro?'

'Sandro's dead. The gringa shot him. I work at the Chupacabra. Security. *My* boss told me to take *your* boss home.'

The gunman shook his head. 'No way. Get out the car. I'll take it from here.'

Gabriel stayed where he was. 'No chance! I got my orders just like you. He tells me "Take him home", I take him home.'

The gunman's brow furrowed with doubt. He'd know just how inadvisable it was to disobey orders from a superior. But was he really going to let a total stranger drive off with his boss, one of the most powerful men in Honduras? Then he peered closer at Casildo.

'What's wrong with him? Hey, boss! Boss!'

Gabriel turned to look at Casildo. A trickle of blood had emerged from his left nostril and was tracking down into his moustache. Shit! That blow to the face to keep his head impaled on the screwdriver must have pushed it through a bone and into a blood vessel.

'He caught a bullet from the gringa. It's why my guy told me to get him back to his compound.'

'But then you should be taking him to the ER, you dummy.'

The gunman climbed up onto the running board and stuck his head into the cab. He reached past Gabriel and shook Casildo's shoulder. The corpse shifted inside the seat belt and lurched over sideways, tearing the head free of its improvised pinion. Blood flooded from both nostrils and the mouth, which now lolled open.

'What the hell? He's d—'

The rest of the word died in his throat, blocked from emerging by the blade of the butterfly knife, which Gabriel had just thrust upwards into his neck. He pushed the bleeding body back out of the window and sent it crumpling to the ground. As the other three cartel men came running, Gabriel took his foot off the brake and mashed it down onto the accelerator.

The Mercedes leapt forwards, engine roaring. He hit the centre guy dead-on, flinging him back in an arc that ended when his broken-legged body hit the water. Behind him, the two remaining gunmen opened fire with their Uzis.

The few rounds that hit the rear of the car bounced harmlessly off the armour plating, sounding like stones thrown against a corrugated iron shack. Gabriel was readying himself to cross the bridge when he realised he needed to deal with the last two gunmen. Leaving them alive would only lessen the time he'd have to reach Don and then get out of Tegucigalpa.

He spun the wheel and took the Merc into a tight swerving circle, rear wheels screeching on the asphalt and filling the air with pungent blue rubber smoke. He levelled the Model 629 and as he closed with the left hand gunman, leaned out and shot him in the chest. The high-powered round blew a fist-sized hole straight through him, sending blood and tissue spraying out of his back in a sloppy red cone.

The last shooter had emptied his Uzi and was frantically trying to jam another magazine home when Gabriel ran him down, the wheels double-bumping over his body. He turned round so he was facing the bridge again and cruised up beside him. Over his screams as he tried to reach his broken legs, Gabriel shot him in the head, leaving another decapitated corpse behind him and a nasty job for the street-cleaners who'd be out in a couple of hours' time.

He hit the bridge at forty, the big SUV leaving the ground then slamming down again. With the corpse bouncing and lolling beside him, Gabriel reached the far side and powered down a straight, wide avenue lined with plane trees.

The Marriott loomed out of the dark, its red neon logo emerging from between two tall buildings like a beacon of civilisation in Tegucigalpa's urban jungle.

Tyres squealing on the gloss grey paint of the underground carpark, echoes bouncing off hard concrete walls, Gabriel drove the G-Class down to the second level, parking in a dark corner next to a fire door. His battered blue pickup sat a few spaces away surrounded by sleek Audis, Lexuses, Mercs and BMWs, a hillbilly invited to a suburban prom.

He took the roll of black plastic from the load space and used it to cover Casildo.

He blipped the fob to lock the doors and then strolled away to the stairwell.

He had a cold martini waiting for him.

36

The Marriott's bar was all but empty when Gabriel entered through the polished wood doors. Maybe at midnight it had still been playing host to foreign executives and whichever shady politicians or cops they needed to placate with bribes. But at just after four in the morning, it was him, Don and a very bored-looking bartender, currently sitting on a high stool at the end of the granite-topped bar, his face lit a ghostly blue by the screen of his phone.

Don sat in shadow at a small, circular table. A tall rubber plant provided cover. In front of him a tumbler containing half an inch of golden spirit. Opposite him, a glass jug sat at an angle, nestled into a mound of crushed ice, a pyramid of four green olives and a spray of wooden cocktail sticks beside it: the whole assembly resting in an oval stainless-steel dish. A waiting martini glass stood on a cocktail napkin: white with a scalloped red edge and the hotel's red 'M' monogram.

The old man looked tired. That was Gabriel's first thought as he took the seat across from his boss. He raised the jug from its icy berth and tipped half its viscous contents into the glass. He impaled three olives on a cocktail stick and dropped it in. Then raised the glass.

'Cheers!'

'Chin, chin.'

The drink was so cold it hurt, sending a shaft of pain spearing up into the bones of his skull just above and behind his nose. The alcohol hit his stomach and in that moment, Gabriel felt it might all, just, finish in a win for the old team.

'You all right, boss? You look done in,' he said, replacing the glass, now half-empty, on the napkin.

Don wiped a hand across his forehead. 'Honestly, I feel as rough as old boots. My doctors back in Jerusalem would be having kittens now if they could see me. When they said light exercise after four or five months, I think they might have been thinking of a short walk around a rose garden somewhere placid.'

'And not getting contacted by cartel soldiers armed to the teeth with automatic weapons.'

Don chuckled, then winced and raised a hand to his midriff.

'In one. Did you find Margot?'

Gabriel drained his glass and refilled it. Took another, more measured, sip.

'I did.'

'She's dead?'

'She is, but not by my hand. Seems she took out her frustration on a little girl from the barrio earlier in the evening,' Gabriel said. '*La niña* blew her brains out with a Colt .45 before I could do anything.'

Don sighed, and sipped his own drink.

'So that's that, then. We're done.'

He replaced the tumbler on the table with a clank from its cut-glass base.

'Not quite.'

'What do you mean?'

'Just before the girl shot her, Margot told me who gave her the order to kill us all. You won't believe it. Actually, maybe you will.'

Don placed his hands together beneath his chin, for all the

world as if he were praying for divine guidance to help him with the answer. His eyes narrowed. He frowned, so that they almost disappeared beneath wiry grey brows.

'Hm, mm-hmm. Are we talking domestic or international?' he asked, finally.

'Oh, domestic. Very much so.'

Don raised his head and looked at the ceiling, where several fans whirred, their blades brass-plated with French cane inserts.

'Domestic. Wait. You remember when we got the job of clearing up after that bloody awful PPM business. We met the home secretary, didn't we?'

'We did indeed.'

'You said at the time you thought there was something off about her. Oh Jesus, it's not her, is it? It's not Gemma Dowding?'

'The very same. Our glorious leader, the original architect of Pro Patria Mori, sent Kevin Bakker and a whole squad of mercenaries after you and me to protect her reputation. Eli got caught in the crossfire.'

Don drained his drink and pushed the tumbler away from him, his lips twisted with disgust.

'Forgive me this lapse into the language of the sergeants' mess, Old Sport, but what a fucking mess.'

'I'm going to take her down, boss.'

'Take her down the way you did with Barbara Sutherland, or...'

Gabriel shook his head. 'Like I did with Joe Tamerlane.'

There was no need to clarify. Both men knew that Gabriel Wolfe was the only man to have killed a British prime minister since a Liverpool merchant named John Bellingham murdered Spencer Perceval in 1812.

'That's going to bring you peace?'

A dangerous edge crept into Gabriel's voice as he answered. One he was unable to tamp down.

'I highly doubt it. Are you saying I shouldn't go ahead? Be satisfied that Margot McDonnell's gone and leave it at that?'

Gabriel's heartrate had escaped his conscious control and was spiralling upwards. He felt it as a storm tide ripping through his system, engendering murderous feelings not only towards Dowding but also the man sitting before him.

'Would it make a difference if I did?'

'No.'

Such a lot of meaning crammed into that two-letter word.

No, I no longer need your permission or heed your advice.

No, I'll do whatever it takes to avenge Eli's death.

No, it doesn't matter how important someone is. If they've done an evil act they will have to answer for it.

No. I will not stop.

'She has protection,' Don said.

Gabriel banged his fist on the table, making the glasses jump and the barman look up from his phone.

'I don't care! She can stick every man in the Regiment round her and I'll still find a way. And I don't mean some thousand-yard sniper shot, either,' Gabriel hissed out. 'When I kill her, she's going to know exactly who's ending her life and why. That's a promise I made to Eli and it's one I intend to keep.'

'Even if it's the last thing your ever do.'

Don wasn't asking a question, just stating a fact. But Gabriel answered him anyway.

'I don't care. In fact, maybe I'll rig some sort of posthumous infodump on the web. Show everybody the kind of people who've been running our country in recent years.'

'That would damage the UK's reputation around the world, Old Sport,' Don said gently, though there was steel beneath the velvet. 'Are you sure King and Country means nothing to you anymore?'

Gabriel leaned forwards across the table and spoke in a low, scraping voice, more of a growl than a murmur.

'Nothing means anything to me anymore, Boss. Nothing.' He stood, and drank the last of the martini straight from the jug. 'We have to go. I've got Señor Casildo's wheels downstairs, with him inside, and he's starting to smell.'

He tucked a fifty under the dish of slushy ice, nodded over at the barman who was regarding them with interest, and left, Don on his heels.

37

LONDON – 11:30 A.M.

Gemma Dowding inhaled sharply. Felt the suit jacket, which she'd moments earlier buttoned across her chest, resist the expansion of her ribcage. Pushing back. Like the bloody establishment.

They'd wanted her gone from the start. She could see that now. Maybe she'd always known it. Sir Rodney Speer with his oily good manners, looking down that patrician nose of his at her. Just some oik from a comprehensive school with ideas above her station.

Oh, they'd been perfectly happy when the serious crime figures took that sudden – and, to everyone but a few carefully chosen people, unexplained – dip. She'd been hailed as the most transformative home secretary since Sir Robert Peel had created the Metropolitan Police Force.

But now she'd overstepped the mark. Ironically, not because of the containment units. Just the matter of some money from a

Russian businessman. A *legitimate* Russian businessman, despite what the oleaginous Sir Rodney Speer believed.

Dmitri's record wasn't spotless, of course it wasn't. How could it be, for someone who'd survived communism, the fall of the Soviet Union and the rise of the crony capitalism that had taken its place?

They'd given her a deadline. They thought they controlled the narrative. They thought they controlled *her*. In that, she intended to disappoint them.

In her former career as a political journalist, she'd made a point of always filing her copy *ahead* of the deadline. She thought she might as well continue the tradition of being early to the party. One final trick up her immaculately tailored sleeve to throw the Old Fart brigade off their carefully calculated stride. Bastards.

Only half an hour earlier, she'd gathered her press secretary, her personal assistant and her political adviser together in the Yellow Drawing Room. They were the only people in the sprawling Downing Street operation she trusted. She'd explained what she was doing and what she needed from each of them. Ashen of face, damp of eye, trembling of lower lip, they had all nodded.

And now it was time.

She checked her tights were unladdered. Smoothed her skirt over her hips. Settled her lapels on her collar bones. Touched the pearls set in gold clasps on each ear-lobe.

She strode across the deep-red carpet covering the black and white tiles of the hallway. The domestic staff had been gathered and watched respectfully from each side of the lobby as the security man pulled the vast front door inwards. Sunlight streamed in, temporarily blinding her. She blinked, but the bluish-green after images floated around in her vision. No matter.

Two long strides across the freshly swept paving slabs. Her pace measured so she could step smartly off the kerb and onto the dark tarmac of the street. Five more strides to the peculiarly ugly wooden lectern. A twisted tower of Jenga blocks, dragged out by her press secretary ten minutes earlier, black cables snaking away beneath strips of silver duct tape.

A lump formed in her throat. She swallowed it down. No way was she going to sniff and whimper through her speech as one of her predecessors had done.

She stared out at the reporters, the photographers, the camera crews and imagined mowing them down with a machinegun. The image made her smile sardonically, despite her own resolution to maintain a stern visage throughout. It would lead one friendly newspaper to run with the headline, 'Smiling Gemma Leaves No 10'.

At the back of the press of journalists, she spotted the man whose dagger even now was protruding from her back. She placed the speech Sir Ian Greene had drafted for her on the lectern, out of sight of the waiting press-pack. Glanced at it, even though she'd read it so many times she had it off by heart.

Becoming prime minister was the peak of my political career, the summit of my ambition. I have been granted the greatest honour my party, my constituents and the Great British voting public could have bestowed on me. *What bullshit. It barely made grammatical sense, let alone constitutional.*

I have done my best to steer the country through tumultuous times, from global crises to domestic upheavals, and striven to give my all in service to the nation. *Makes me sound like some Victorian dowager duchess.*

But such demanding duties have taken a greater-than-expected toll on me, and my family. However ready I thought I was, it has become apparent to me in recent weeks that I was, perhaps, guilty of reaching further than my grasp would permit. *Are you serious? This is me saying I wasn't up to the job.*

Etc. etc. etc. Blah blah blah. Heavy heart…after much soul-searching…resigning to spend more time with my family. *Not. Going. To. Happen.*

She raised her gaze to the waiting media. Opened her mouth. And spoke. The pleasure she felt as she watched Sir Ian react to her opening sentences was primal. A thrill deep down in her belly that fizzled like a teenager about to have sex for the first time.

'Conspiracy. It's a nasty word. It speaks to our deepest fears. That there are people who move in the shadows. Controlling us. Managing us. Herding us, like sheep, towards whichever pen they have constructed for us.'

The flashes that clattered in front of her sounded like a flock of birds taking off. An incessant crashing clatter: white noise. But the assembled press corps remained utterly silent. A couple of them had their mouths hanging open. Sir Ian looked like a man who'd just been run through with the sword he'd been knighted with. An expression of horror had transformed his face from its normal, well-fed ruddiness to a sickly beige.

'You might think that someone like me, the prime minister, would be a *part* of any such conspiracy. One of those shady elites pulling your strings, deciding what you will be permitted to know, distracting you with social media and streaming video. All the while digging their claws deeper into the state and robbing its citizens of the power to decide their own fate.'

Sir Ian had his phone to his ear. He was – what would be the best word for it? Yes, she decided – *yammering* into it.

'But in that, my friends, you would be entirely wrong. The people I'm talking about think they're better than you. Better than *me*. To them, democracy is an annoyance. Oh, they let us play the game, but they don't tell us the rules. We get to vote, we get to believe we're in control. But the establishment have loaded the dice, marked the deck, tipped the playing field so far in their favour it's like a ski slope.'

Her heart, which had been fluttering in her chest like a trapped bird when she'd begun, was calm again. She was making history. Dmitri would be watching. She'd texted him herself. Maybe the liberal universities and the risk-averse corporations wouldn't be inviting her to address their staff or putting her on their boards. But there were plenty of others who would pay, and now even more handsomely, to hear her speak.

'I am no longer confident that I can lead this once-great

country. The forces ranged against me – against *us* – have seen to it that my hands are tied. Therefore I am choosing to resign while I still can. I wish my successor all the luck in the world. They're going to need it.'

And with that, as the digital cameras continued to seed the air with their insane chittering, and the bright electronic flashes turned her vision into a kaleidoscope, she turned on her heel and marched back inside.

There. Let Sir Ian Greene and the rest of his grey-suited, public-school-educated cronies suck on that.

38

TEGUCIGALPA

As Gabriel led Don over to the black Mercedes G-Class, he scanned the deserted floor of the car park. At the first sign of trouble, his pistol would be pressed into duty. This side of the river or that, it made no difference.

But they were alone.

Alone if one discounted the cartel boss's corpse stinking up the interior of his old wheels.

Don nodded towards the passenger side.

'In there, is he?'

'We need to dispose of the body. Somewhere it can be found.'

'Leaving his lieutenants to squabble over the top job?'

Gabriel offered Don a grim smile. 'If by squabbling you mean going at each other, daggers drawn, then yes. Either that or word will get out to their rivals, sparking a war.'

'They'll all be focused on the power struggle. Might be an

opportunity for the cousins to throw a few well-aimed punches of their own.'

'Do you know anyone at the DEA or ATF?'

Don shrugged. 'Not directly, but I know people who know people.'

'Make the call then.'

Don's call was short and rich in detailed information. There were no questions. Whoever he'd called obviously trusted him implicitly. Don simply said what he needed to say and ended the call. He turned to Gabriel.

'Wheels up, then?'

'I think so. Do you want to take my pickup or this monster?'

Don looked over his shoulder at Gabriel's battered Ford pickup.

'I think, on balance, an old man driving an old truck might be less conspicuous. Especially if questions are asked about your passenger.'

'Fair enough. So, follow me out of the city. We need to make a stop at the zoo. Hang back, though. If I get contacted, I'll deal with it on my own. Can't have you getting perforated again.'

Don nodded, rubbing his side.

'Reluctantly, I had to agree with Uri. My fighting days are behind me.'

Gabriel handed him the old Ford's keys. The fob was worn red leather with the blue and silver oval logo still attached, though most of the enamel had fallen out of the casting.

'Push the throttle halfway down when you start her, then ease off,' Gabriel said. 'She should catch straight away. Let her idle just for a minute or she'll cut out as soon as you put her in gear.'

'Sounds a bit temperamental.'

Gabriel shook his head. 'Just needs a little gentling to get going then she'll take you all the way to Texas if you want.'

Don grinned. 'I'll take your word for that. As long as she gets me to Santa Rosa, I'll be fine with that.'

The two men climbed into their respective vehicles, only one wrinkling his nose at the smell inside the cabin.

Although it was still dark at street level, the first glimmers of sun were lightening the sky, turning it from indigo to a deep, bruised purple fading to a soft blue at the horizon. Gabriel turned right out of the Marriott's above-ground parking lot and headed north.

* * *

The zoo's main entrance was protected by tall iron gates surmounted by elephants, but there was no padlock. They were just secured with a length of chain. Gabriel slid it out of the bars with a rattle and flung it aside. He pulled the gates wide and drove in, parking in a small tarmac circle by a children's playpark. The brightly coloured swings and climbing frames were at odds with the gruesome display he was about to erect.

He dragged Casildo's body out of the Mercedes and over to the play equipment. There, he settled it across a gaily painted red and black ladybird on a thick steel spring.

Blood poured from the head wound onto the ground and began trickling down the slight slope towards some grass. It smelled of iron and copper. The old, old smell of battle.

He Googled a media organisation and tapped the phone icon. A tired-sounding woman answered the call.

'*La Tribuna*, night desk.'

Gabriel adopted a rough-edged barrio accent.

'Luis-David Casildo was murdered tonight. The shooter was a Red River man. You'll find the body at the north gate of the zoo. The playpark. Send a photographer.'

'What?' She sounded wide awake now. 'This is true? Can you send me a picture?'

'No pictures. But it's true. Get there now or I'll call CNN with the story.'

'No! Don't do that. What's your name?'

'I tell you that I sign my own death warrant. But I work for the Zinguizapa cartel. That's all. Goodbye.'

Before returning to the Mercedes, he bent and took a heavy

gold signet ring from Casildo's right middle finger. Cartel bosses used them as seals, sometimes stamping their logo into a dead enemy's face. To lose one was a mark of weakness, of disgrace.

He turned. Don had pulled into the side of the road on the other side of the zoo gates. Gabriel climbed back into the Mercedes and reversed out of the parking lot. Then he simply pointed north. The meaning was clear. Home.

Once they were clear of the city, the road surface deteriorated rapidly from smooth concrete to patchy blacktop and then, when he turned onto National Route 41, loose grey gravel. What he wanted to do was floor the throttle and take the SUV up to its top speed. But his beloved old F100 ran out of steam at fifty and comfort at forty, so he maintained a sedate cruise during which he kept one eye on the rear-view mirror, watching for pursuing cartel vehicles.

After two hours of driving, he pulled off RN41 on the far side of a small town with a big name. San Francisco de la Paz. He slammed the door behind him, shutting in the smell.

Don pulled in behind him and climbed out, rubbing his back over his kidneys.

'Maybe I should have taken that bloody thing after all,' he complained.

'You could always get yourself a massage at Frida's when we get back.'

'According to you, Frida's is a brothel. I don't think I could take that level of excitement.'

Gabriel tipped his head on one side.

'It *is* a brothel. But they also offer very good massages. You only have to take your shirt off.'

Don harrumphed. 'Another couple of hours in that thing, and I'm fairly certain I'll be taking you up on the suggestion. So,' he lifted his chin at the G-Class, 'are you going to dump it?'

Gabriel nodded. 'I don't want to leave a trail that will lead them to Santa Rosa. They'd torture everyone there to find out who killed their boss.'

'Better do a thorough job, then.'

'I intend to.'

'How do you propose to destroy it? It's armoured, by the looks of it.'

'Very. But those tuning outfits are all about protecting the occupants from *external* attacks.'

Don nodded. 'Ah. I see. Well, if you don't mind, I'm just going to have a rest and see if my kidneys will still speak to me.'

The old man walked stiffly away and perched on a smooth-topped grey boulder. He pulled out a handkerchief and mopped his forehead. For a moment, Gabriel felt a prick of worry. But there was work to be done. Don was just tired and bruised. Plus he was convalescing after a near-fatal shooting. He'd be fine.

The sun was coming up, turning each tree into a source of green-tinged light. The road ran straight in either direction for a dozen kilometres. He saw no plumes of dust. If anyone *did* come past and decided to slow down for a look, they'd be met with the business end of his AK. If they appeared dangerous, the meeting would conclude with a burst of its 7.62mm ammunition.

Back behind the wheel again, he reversed across the road and signalled for Don to stand well back. Then he accelerated hard across the road towards the barbed-wire fence separating it from the forest. The wire screeched along the SUV's bodywork and two wooden fenceposts popped free of the earth's grasp to bang harmlessly off the rear windows.

Dragging the wreckage of the fence, Gabriel drove for two hundred and fifty metres into the forest until he reached a small clearing. He parked on the far side, climbed out and opened the rear passenger-side door. He lifted the sniper rifle clear, leaving the AK.

Across from the G-Class, a rock outcrop of the same grey stone Don was sitting on rose from the brown leaf litter of the forest floor. Maybe thirty metres away from the SUV. Not ideal for what he had planned. But it would still provide shelter.

At its peak, the outcrop divided in two, offering a cramped but usable cradle in which he could shoot across and down at the G-

Class. He had a clear shot into the rear of the passenger compartment.

He worked the bolt to chamber a round and sighted on the rear seat. Squeezed off a shot. Felt the recoil in his shoulder, an old, familiar sensation. Foam padding puffed out like back-spatter from a flesh wound as the bullet tore through the seat. But it didn't find its target. The G-Class sat there, a malevolent black presence among all the greenery.

He adjusted his aim, and fired again. No joy. He resighted and tried a third time. And this time, he found his mark. The tuners had shielded the sides and underneath of the petrol tank with thick steel plate. But not its upper surface. After all, who shoots at their own fuel tank? And from inside their own vehicle? An unnecessary expense, and a level of redundancy that would exceed any security expert's calculations. And therefore to be avoided.

The red-hot bullet tore through the relatively thin steel on the tank's upper surface. And in a split-second, the rifle's percussive crack was drowned out by a roar that sounded like a high-explosive 155mm howitzer shell.

Already ducking behind the rock, Gabriel felt the blast-wave singe the top of his head. The boom echoed through the forest, rolling away and bouncing off the distant hills like thunder. The fireball boiled upwards, rolling around itself, tangerine, lemon-yellow and a deep blood-red, wreathed in coiling clouds of oily black smoke.

Gabriel shouldered the rifle and scrambled down off the outcrop. It was still early for people to be about and he doubted any cops out here in the boonies would be rolling down RN41, but the mushroom cloud might draw the wrong kind of attention.

39

SANTA ROSA

Gabriel and Don rolled into Santa Rosa mid-afternoon. Here, the gunfights and violence that had marred the streets of Comayaguela throughout the night might never have happened.

Chickens and goats wandered along the dusty street. A mule brayed in its tiny paddock, exposing long yellow teeth. A gaggle of children, some barely able to walk but being guided by older girls, themselves no more than four or five, played in someone's back yard.

And as they passed each side street, they caught glimpses of the ocean, its wind-ruffled surface throwing out silvery splinters of sunlight. Don inhaled deeply.

'Smell reminds me of the coast where you used to live.' He slapped his leg. 'Damn! Sorry, Old Sport. An old man's insensitivity.'

'It's fine, boss. But I think the water here smells softer than the

North Sea. Like she might actually welcome you in if you wanted to swim.'

'And not turn your balls into plum stones?'

Gabriel smiled wryly. 'Something like that.'

'Jesus, I'm shattered. How do you keep going?'

'More of my little white helpers.'

'You want to be careful with those. I've seen more than one soldier end up seeing the psych team with addiction problems.'

Gabriel turned down the side street that would take them to the beachfront track and his house.

'Not sure I have that gene. I mean, I've got plenty of other problems up here,' he added, tapping the side of his head, 'but I think I can handle the odd speed bump.'

'Fair enough. I'll keep my nose out of your business.'

Gabriel suddenly felt ashamed. He'd dragged Don halfway round the world searching for him. Then got him involved in a murderous night-hunt with some of the most dangerous people on the planet. And finally forced him to drive across Honduras in an antique bone-shaker of a farmer's pickup truck, all while recovering from being shot by a machinegun.

He pulled up outside his place.

'I'm sorry, Boss. You didn't need that from me. I am being careful. And I'll kick them now. Something tells me my cage-fighting days are over anyway,' he said. 'Let's both get some sleep and then we can talk some more about what happens next.'

Don wandered down to his landlady's two-storey house. His stumbling gait gave him the look of a man who'd spent the day working his way down a bottle of guaro.

Gabriel went inside, carrying the rifle and assorted handguns in a rolled-up square of tarpaulin he took out of the load bay. Once he'd stashed them somewhere safe, he went through into his bedroom and lay down. He felt he'd sleep better if he got undressed, but even contemplating unlacing his boots doubled his fatigue.

'*Let me do it for you, darling,*' Eli said.

Her voice was low and sweet. It seemed to come from everywhere, all at once.

He knew she wasn't real, but it was still her. He smiled as she lifted one leg onto her lap and began pulling the laces free. The tears that inched their way down his cheeks, wetting the side of his neck didn't stop the smile, and in this way he fell asleep.

Casildo slapped Eli aside. He pulled out the gold Desert Eagle and shot her through the stomach. He swivelled his head round to glare at Gabriel, revealing the screwdriver's black pimpled-rubber handle protruding from the back of his skull.

'You're gonna die in my country, *Hijo de puta*,' he grated out through clenched teeth.

Blood streamed out through the needle-thin gaps between teeth made from the same glittering metal as his pistol. Then he opened his mouth wide, and, as his eyes rolled back in their sockets, a scarlet tide washed down over his chin, his chest, his corpulent belly and onto the bedclothes where Eli sprawled, her belly soaked red with her own blood.

Gabriel screamed and sat bolt upright in bed. His shirt, his trousers, the sheet were soaked in rank, fear-smelling sweat. His heart was pounding and he felt nausea roiling in his gut.

He staggered out of the back door into blindingly bright morning sunlight and threw up beneath the palm tree that leaned drunkenly over his neglected vegetable patch.

He lurched down to the surf and sank down to his knees in the warm, shallow water and howled his grief at the pelicans floating offshore and regarding this crazed human with their grotesquely elongated heads cocked to one side.

Eventually he regained enough composure to push himself upright and go back inside. He stripped off his clothes and kicked them into a corner. The hot water in Santa Rosa was intermittent at best but he didn't mind the lukewarm showers the situation forced him to take.

He pulled on fresh clothes: a crumpled grey shirt, cut-off jeans and a pair of flip-flops. He checked the time and frowned. Waiting for the digits on his phone to make sense. He understood.

He'd slept from mid-afternoon the previous day until 8:00 a.m. the following morning.

His stomach growled. He realised he was very hungry. Speed always did that. Shut down that part of his system while shifting the rest into overdrive. Coming down always left him with a headache and a pressing need for carbohydrates.

The chipped white enamel box he kept bread in yielded a brick-hard crust that might be useful as a weapon, but which would yield its nutrition grudgingly if at all. He tossed it out the back door. Food for whichever scavenger found it first. A lone orange sat in a simple unfired clay bowl on a shelf. He bit into the thick green skin, tasting the bitter orange oil, and peeled it. It was gone in three bites, tart juice running down his chin, which he wiped away with the back of his hand.

Maybe he could buy some breakfast from Señora Cruz, Don's temporary landlady.

He found them sitting together in her immaculate yard beneath the shade of a Coca-Cola beach umbrella. A pot of coffee sat on the table between them along with a bowl of mangos, bananas and papayas, a basket of fresh bread rolls and a pot of Nutella.

'Good morning, Gabriel,' she said, smiling. 'Would you like some breakfast?'

He pulled out a chair. 'How much for non-residents?'

She pulled a face. 'You are a friend of Señor Webster? No charge for you today! Here. Eat. I will make some fresh coffee.'

Gabriel broke open one of the rolls, slathered the warm interior with Nutella and took a bite. The chocolate and hazelnut spread melted immediately in his mouth, flooding it with sweetness, and the corners of his jaw twinged as his saliva glands let go in response.

With the lady of the house gone, Gabriel switched back to English.

'Morning, Boss. Sleep OK? How are the wounds?'

'Much better, thanks. Berta caught me coming out of the shower and when she saw the scars she practically fainted. Once

I'd explained I wasn't about to die in her guest room, she took on nursing duties. Insisted I sleep in her bed.'

Gabriel raised his eyebrows.

'We swapped,' Don said firmly. 'I protested but the *señora* is not a woman to be trifled with. In the end, I accepted defeat against superior forces. Slept like a baby. She brought me tea in bed and then laid this on.'

'And when you say she "caught" you coming out of the shower…'

Don shrugged. But was that a hint of a grin Gabriel caught before Don hastily rearranged his features?

'She was bringing more towels.'

Gabriel decided that Berta wasn't the only person with whom it was inadvisable to argue.

'Once we're done here, I thought we could go back to mine to make a plan.'

'Ah, yes. That small matter of assassinating a sitting prime minister.'

Further conversation on the topic was forestalled by the arrival of Berta with a fresh pot of steaming coffee.

'We'll talk about it later,' Don said with a tight smile, before widening it into something Gabriel felt was more genuine for his landlady.

'*Gracias, Berta. Eres un angel,*' Don said in perfect, if English-accented, Spanish.

She held a fanned hand to her chest.

'Oh, Mister Webster. You are a,' she hesitated, tutted, looked up at the cloudless sky, '*O, cómo se dice* – a gentle man.'

Honours even, and cordial relations bolstered, she sat between the two men and made sure both were happy with their coffee, their rolls, their fruit, and the position of their chairs in relation to the sun.

While the conversation meandered across various small-town topics, from the price of fresh chickens to the health of one's neighbours, Gabriel and Don were conducting a wordless conversation of their own through minute gestures and eye movements. Essentially, it boiled down to, *We need to get going as soon as possible.*

After finishing their meal and thanking Berta, who seemed quite unable to believe either man could possibly be either full or intending to leave, they managed to extricate themselves from the warm bosom of her hospitality and escape back to Gabriel's house.

Where they found Pera waiting on the doorstep, her face streaked with tears.

40

Gabriel took Pera in his arms as she stood then staggered into him.

'What's wrong? What's happened?'

She lifted her tear-streaked face. Dark circles around her eyes told him she'd endured a sleepless night.

'They took him, Gabe. They took Santiago. Oh my God, it was awful. Now they say they will kill him unless, unless...'

She stuttered to a stop and wailed, a heartrending sound that chilled Gabriel to his marrow. He'd heard that sound before. Mothers grieving for their sons, either killed in battle or taken by insurgents.

'Let's get you inside,' he said, steering her by the elbow through the door, Don bringing up the rear.

He led her into the sitting room and guided her to his least uncomfortable armchair.

'I'll make some tea,' Don said, striding toward the kitchen.

'Who took him, Pera? And what do they want?'

She clenched her fists together between her skirted knees. Unable to make eye contact with him. The general answer he already knew. In the league table of crime in Honduras, kidnapping ran extortion a close second. Though given kidnapping was always followed by a ransom demand, it was really just a variation on the roadside stop.

He cast his mind back to the four men who'd attempted to rob him on the way back from Bonito. The one who'd escaped. And all became clear. What Pera said next confirmed his fears.

'This man, a gangster, came to see me at work. He said he works for a man called El Rey.'

'The King.'

'Yes. So, they've taken my Santiago. The gangster said someone killed four of The King's men,' she said, staring down at her fingers, which were now twisting and picking at the frayed hem of her skirt. 'He saw it happen. He knew it was an Englishman from his voice. Now The King wants your head in exchange for Santiago.' She wailed. 'Oh, Gabe, he send me something. Look.'

She rummaged in a pocket of her skirt and brought out a small bundle wrapped in a scrap of brown cloth. Darker spots had broken through here and there. Gabriel readied himself. It would be either an ear or a finger. A memory caught him by surprise. A young woman, kidnapped along with her mother by Chechen terrorists. They'd sent her ear to her father, in a matchbox.

'Pera, there's no need,' he said, gently.

But she shook her head violently. 'Here!'

She pulled the last fold of cloth free; the corner adhered to the contents. On its own, the finger looked so small. Smooth, like a child's, though Santiago was fourteen. He swallowed. What could he possibly say?

'We know he's alive. That's a good thing. It would have hurt. A lot. But they don't want to kill him. It's me they want. I'll go.'

Now, at last, Pera did turn to look into his eyes. Hers were a deep brown, very round, and still beautiful despite the dark bags beneath. She grabbed his hands, eyes wild.

'I need you to save my boy, Gabe. The police won't do anything. El Rey probably pays their wages. But ...'

She hesitated. He knew what she was thinking. She had a

mother's primal urge to protect her child. Yet by asking Gabriel to rescue Santiago she'd be asking him to risk his own life.

Gabriel shook his head. The tide of anger that washed back and forth through him overspilled its usual channel and surged out. What was wrong with people? They robbed, and raped and murdered and when he tried to stop them, it just drove them to further obscene excesses.

'Don't worry, Pera. They *want* to kill me,' he said, in a low voice. 'But they won't.'

Don appeared with three cups of tea and set them down on the floor.

'Drink this, my dear,' he said. 'Gabriel's right. He and I will bring Santiago back to you alive.'

Gabriel whipped his head round.

'It's not your fight, Boss.'

'I think you'd better let me be the judge of which fights are mine, Old Sport,' he said, not unkindly, but with a warning note in his voice. 'Since Christine died, and the Department went to shit, well, I've been looking for a purpose. A little like you. Seeing as Kevin Bakker didn't extinguish the flame, I think I'd rather like to spend my remaining years doing whatever the hell I like. I'm through with bureaucracy. Through with meetings, paperwork and bloody *budgets!*'

This last word he spat out with such venom, Gabriel had a vision of Don machinegunning a roomful of Treasury accountants.

Gabriel nodded.

'You see, Pera?' he said. 'Don and I'll bring Santiago back and he'll be playing football on the beach with his friends again before you know it.'

He added a smile he wasn't feeling and felt gratified when her own mouth curved upwards a little.

'You can really do this? You are,' she hesitated, 'I mean, you are strong and fit but, Don,' she glanced at the older man then switched to Spanish, 'well, he is an old man, isn't he?'

Something about the way she dropped her voice and blushed

as she said these words must have communicated itself to Don. He raised his wiry grey eyebrows.

'*Viejo?* I am old, that's true. But I'm also tough. And I'm a decent shot with a long gun.'

'But that is the trouble, isn't it?' Pera protested. 'These men, they have guns. Lots of them. I know what you do in Tegucigalpa, Gabe. Remember, I have patched you up enough times. But you can't win by punching and kicking men who have machineguns.'

Gabriel looked at her. How much should he tell her? As little as possible.

'Don't worry. Don and I will find a way. Now, did he say where he was holding Santiago or how he wanted to make the exchange?'

She gave Gabriel a scrap of paper. He unfolded it to find the gang boss had written down a one-line instruction. *Bring the body here by noon on Friday or the boy dies.* El Rey had given directions to his compound in the hills southwest of Bonito. A poor decision, Gabriel thought. It bespoke over-confidence. He thought he could use that. They had a location. Now they needed a plan.

Reluctantly, Pera allowed Gabriel to take her back to her house. She had to work in any case. When she'd first told him how she made her living, he'd entertained fantasies of heroically rescuing her and the other girls who worked at Frida's in Bonito. But one night, when he'd drunkenly raised the subject, Pera had angrily shut him down.

Who was he to say how she should or shouldn't support her son? What did he know of life in Honduras, anyway? Some rich white man hiding from his own troubles, looking to forget them by solving everybody else's problems?

He'd never raised it again. Although when the man who fought as Wrecking Ball had raped her, he'd bided his time before settling that score at least. And he kept a watching brief out for the girls. Listening carefully whenever Pera talked about work, alert for any clue that someone hadn't been content merely paying for sex and had acted out some violent fantasy.

He left her, promising again to bring Santiago back safe and sound. Apart from a missing finger.

* * *

Gabriel and Don had two hours before the gangsters killed Santiago. Back at his own place, he found Don leaning on the rail, looking out at the Caribbean. The water was impossibly beautiful at this time of day. A shade of blue-green Gabriel had never seen anywhere else in the world. Like gemstones overlaid with peacock tailfeathers.

Don turned as Gabriel's feet creaked on the warped planks of the deck.

'Better brush up on your stealth moves, Old Sport,' he said wryly.

'You're serious about coming along?'

Don nodded. 'I meant what I said to Esperanza. I may not be up to hand-to-hand combat anymore, but if I can live out my days delivering some justice where it's needed, well, it sounds a hell of a lot more fun than playing golf or learning the ukulele.'

'You could get killed.'

'True. But then, I could have stayed in Israel and bought an apartment. Had a stroke on my balcony. I'd be dead then, too.'

'Not from a bullet.'

Don shrugged. 'It comes to the same thing in the end, though, doesn't it, Old Sport? Now, are we going to stand around discussing philosophy, or did you want to spend a few minutes concocting a battleplan?'

It felt good, bantering with the Boss. Like old times. Gabriel smiled. The expression felt alien on his lips, as though someone was manipulating his face in unfamiliar ways. Had he really not smiled since Eli had died?

'Well, given what we know about proper planning and preparation—'

' – preventing piss-poor performance.' Don was smiling, too.

'I think we should. Let's go inside.'

They sat at the kitchen table. Gabriel fetched two cold Cokes from the fridge. Knocked the caps off on the edge of the sink and handed one to Don.

'Cheers!'

'Chin, chin.'

Don took a swig of the Coke then set his bottle down carefully.

'Something else Pera said I do happen to agree with, though. They'll be armed to the teeth with Kalashnikovs and God knows what else. We have a high-tech sniper rifle, but with only a couple of rounds, and the AK you liberated from the cartel in Tegucigalpa. Plus sidearms. Is that going to be enough?'

Gabriel took a swig of his own drink then got to his feet.

'Can you give me some space, please,' he said.

Once Don had moved back, Gabriel pushed the table against the wall then rolled up the threadbare native rug in cream and brick-red that covered the centre of the floor. Beneath it, an iron ring was set into a recessed plate in one of the floorboards. A trapdoor.

He heaved on the ring and lifted the trapdoor up and over, resting it against the cooker to reveal a dark staircase.

'Come and see,' he said to Don, as he descended the stairs, flicking on a switch as he went and flooding the tiny basement with yellow light.

Don followed him down, sliding his palm along the wooden handrail.

'Well, well,' he said when they'd both reached the bottom. 'And there was me thinking you'd left your old life behind.'

Gabriel surveyed the shelves, the wooden bench and the corners of the earth-floored cube, walled by unpainted cinder blocks. The plan was yet to come. But he'd already done his preparation.

After arriving in Honduras and finding somewhere remote to live, Gabriel had woken up one morning, his head pounding with the latest in a long and increasingly painful line of hangovers, with a realisation.

The fact that he was alive meant that, however assiduously he'd faked his own death, the people who'd come for him, Don and Eli, might not have given up. After all, he'd not given them a body.

He needed to be ready.

Reasoning that any country, but particularly one notorious for its levels of gun violence, would have a ready market for black market firearms, he'd gone shopping one day in Tegucigalpa.

The dealer he'd eventually tracked down had been more than happy to supply the first few items Gabriel asked for. Pistols, assault rifles, shotguns and submachineguns were his stock in trade. His eyes had widened as Gabriel reeled off his list, then narrowed with each precise requirement Gabriel gave him. At some point, he realised that the gringo he was negotiating with had the kind of background that would make any kind of double-dealing a very poor move indeed.

Only at the end of Gabriel's shopping list had he paused.

'Those are very specialist items, sir,' he'd said, the respect unfeigned for once. 'Very hard to come by. Very expensive.'

Gabriel popped the catch on the scuffed and stained woven shopping bag dangling from his left hand and spread the opening wide. He held it out for the arms dealer to inspect. The man had nodded, smiled broadly, revealing gold dental work.

'I have a friend in the army. Give me a week.'

With his acquisitions stashed in the cellar the previous owner of the house had dug into the soft earth beneath the house and reinforced with the cinder blocks and sturdy planking, Gabriel had felt safer, and relaxed into his grief. Now events had caught up with him again, but not in the way he'd expected.

Gabriel folded his arms and watched as his former CO inspected the armoury. Don took one of the weapons off its hooks and put it to his shoulder.

'I think we can safely say this counts as "proper preparation",' he said with a smile.

Gabriel nodded. He hoped the kidnappers were enjoying their week so far. It was about to get much, much worse.

41

Gabriel checked his watch. It was 11:00 a.m. Ideally, he'd have staged the rescue at night — 3:30 a.m. by choice — but the deadline made that impossible. Plus, attacking during the day might give them a small advantage. If El Rey's men were out hijacking, extorting or whatever he'd set them to, there'd be fewer at home guarding the house.

Beside him, in the F100's passenger seat, dressed, as Gabriel was, in jungle camouflage, Don cradled a brand-new Russian-made rifle. An ORSIS T-5000, chambered in .338 Lapua Magnum.

According to the dealer, it was part of a consignment from Cuba destined for the Honduran military. Somewhere along the journey from Havana to Tegucigalpa, part of the shipment had vanished, both from the manifest and the container.

He'd parked on a ridge overlooking the kidnapper's house. Thickly wooded, with lush undergrowth of soft-leaved plants and scrub. The man had obviously not thought he'd ever come under attack from snipers.

While Don sat on a fallen tree, Gabriel turned the truck round and backed up to a tall, yellow-flowered shrub, its blossoms giving off the smell of honey.

Together they lay blankets and rugs in the Ford's load bay, creating a comfortable sniper nest from which Don could operate. Once Don was lying down, Gabriel began covering the truck and his old CO with branches cut from the ferns, shrubs and palms that abounded on the hillside. He concluded the camouflage process by slipping a piece cut from a pair of tights over the scope and retaining it with an elastic band.

When he was finished he walked off twenty metres then turned. Even at this distance, and knowing the truck was there, it was impossible to make out a single straight line. The battle-scarred bodywork with its flat paint finally came into its own. Even where it *was* visible, there was not a square millimetre of chrome or even bright metal to throw out a reflection and give Don's position away.

When he'd acquired the ORSIS, Gabriel had zeroed the sights at 500 metres. A third of the effective firing range for the rifle in its .338 variant, but as Don had said earlier, 'I told Pera I was a decent shot, and that's true. But I was never in your league, let alone a proper shooter's. Five hundred's fine by me.'

With Don ensconced in his hide, an olive-green steel case of 200 shells beside him, Gabriel set off down the hill, towards '*El Presidente*', the modestly named house and compound owned by one César Rey.

His plan was simple. Create a diversion. Stage a covert infiltration. Find and rescue Santiago. Exfil with covering fire from Don. To that end he'd brought two additional items of clothing with him that he'd use once he and Santiago were on their way out. White baseball caps to distinguish them as friendlies.

Keeping under cover of the trees that covered the hillside, it took Gabriel seven minutes to reach the road that led to *El Presidente*. He crossed the road then tracked at an angle to the main house until he picked up a dried-out riverbed littered with smooth pink and grey pebbles the size of baseballs. Scrubby plants and spindly trees snaked from its southern bank to the edge of the compound.

Eight minutes later, equipment banging on his back, he reached the end of the cover. The last hundred metres was exposed. High overhead, the sun blazed down.

Gabriel raised the binos to his eyes. The backs of his hands were coated with the same greenish, brown camouflage paint as his face. It smelled greasy, but it was a chemical scent, rather than the putrid stench of rotting food from the stuff he'd smeared on his cheeks in Comayaguela.

The gates were tall, topped with razor wire and security cameras. Extending out left and right, and presumably continuing all the way round the house, was a high wall. Brick or cinder block but plastered with the same white stucco he saw everywhere in Honduras.

The copings were terracotta barrel tiles. No more wire, though. That made things easier. Rey obviously thought his reputation was enough to deter any serious attackers. From what Gabriel had been able to glean, he had no cartel connections. He was just a big fish in a small pond.

But eventually, every big fish met a creature with longer, sharper teeth. Just ask Luis-David Casildo.

Gabriel lifted the heavier of the two weapons he'd brought with him off his back. Like Don's ORSIS, the heavy, tube-shaped weapon was made in Russia. But whereas the T-5000 was a state-of-the-art rifle, the RPG-7 was considerably simpler, and positively venerable.

From a kneeling position, he rested the unit on his shoulder and aimed at the gates.

He squeezed the trigger. The launcher jerked, and with a roar and a hiss as the motor ignited, the rocket sped off towards its target trailing a plume of white smoke. *El Presidente* was about to be impeached.

With the stink of the rocket exhaust invading his nostrils, Gabriel ducked down and waited.

A few seconds later the rocket-propelled grenade hit the gates.

The explosion shattered the silence, the rolling boom echoing off the hills where Don lay in his hide. Above the fireball, one of the gates spiralled upwards, long tangled strands of razor wire glinting in the sunlight as they lashed in the wake of the steel grid.

As men came running, some firing wildly, he made his way around to the rear of the compound. It was now unguarded, as more men assembled at the gateway and locked their trigger fingers down on their AKs.

From the camouflaged daysack slung across his front, Gabriel retrieved a length of nylon rope tied to a grappling hook. He swung it back and forth a couple of times then sent it looping up and over the wall. It landed inside with a dull clonk. He took in the slack then tugged until the hook caught on the far side of the coping tiles. It wasn't ideal: he'd have preferred something that was an integral part of the wall, but beggars couldn't be choosers.

As he started climbing he heard a voice shouting commands. Deep, carrying real authority. Rey? Or his second in command?

'Tony, Chico, Patch, you stay here and guard the gate. The rest of you, spread out. Find those fuckers and bring them in.'

Good luck with that, Gabriel thought as he reached the top of the wall and slid over the smooth surface of the sun-warmed barrel tiles and dropped silently to the far side. It took four tries before he could dislodge the grappling hook, which he caught deftly as it fell back towards his head. He coiled the rope and stuffed it with the hook behind a huge terracotta plant pot housing a barrel-shaped cactus bristling with two-inch spines like sharpened matchsticks.

Crouching in the lee of the wall, he surveyed the buildings. The main house was a large, two-storey building. Gleaming white stucco, ground-floor windows barred with ornamental ironwork. A small grove of orange trees cast more shadow on the left side of the house as he looked at it. A swimming pool complete with white plastic loungers occupied most of the yard to the rear. He closed his eyes and listened. No dogs. Another point in his favour.

How did people reach their swimming pools? From a rear door that led out from either a wet room or a changing room. It seemed the best way to get inside.

In a crouching run, silenced pistol in his right hand, he crossed the gap between the wall and the back of the house. Sure enough, a door faced the pool, shaded by a dark-leaved climbing plant studded with bright-orange, conical blossoms twining through a wooden trellis.

Picking the lock took ten seconds. He slipped inside and closed it silently behind him. People were shouting. He heard a woman screaming and a man shouting at her to calm down. He supposed having your home attacked by RPGs would do that to a person. She had nothing to fear from him, though. Not unless she drew down on him.

He had to find where they were holding Santiago. Chances were he'd not be on the upper floor. That would be bedrooms, surely. For Rey and his family, if he had any, plus maybe a couple of his most trusted men. No, captives would be kept either downstairs or in a basement.

He emerged from the small, tiled changing room into a large square hallway. Immediately he had to duck back into the shadows as a man ran across the centre of the space carrying an assault rifle, yanking the charging lever back as he went.

In the silence that followed, Gabriel saw what he was looking for. Beneath the elegant curving staircase, a door. He crossed to it and tried the handle. It opened immediately. No lock-picking required. He slipped inside and closed it behind him. The stone staircase descending in a curve was lit with bare bulbs every five or six metres.

He pulled out a tactical knife from its nylon sheath and transferred the silenced pistol to his left hand. He needed to keep the noise to a minimum now he was in the belly of the beast.

The distraction caused by the RPG wouldn't last for ever and then someone would make the connection. They weren't under attack at all; a different play was being executed. He'd agreed a second phase with Don. When Rey's men stopped shooting, Don would begin. Not shooting to kill. Not yet. But hitting vehicles, the roof, anything that would make a fine noise when slammed with a round from the T-5000.

Gabriel rounded a curve in the underground corridor, pistol up, knife held out in front, then stopped dead.

A man in a black ballcap, stone-washed jeans and a brown leather bomber jacket sat in a hard chair, tipped back so its front legs were off the ground. He was maintaining his pose by jamming his boots against the opposite wall. He held an AK across his lap. Just beyond the guard was a door. And behind that door, presumably, was Santiago. Gabriel breathed shallowly as he assessed the threat.

The peak of the cap was pulled down low over the guard's eyes. He was reading, or perhaps more accurately, looking at, a pornographic magazine. Breathing slowly, Gabriel took aim. This far underground, a silenced pistol round wouldn't penetrate to the ground floor. And he doubted anyone would notice even if it did, given that Don would, by now, be sending .338 Lapua Magnum rounds slamming into his chosen targets and receiving wild bursts from AKs and Uzis in return.

Gabriel's index finger was curled around the trigger when the guard let out a deep, reverberating snore. The magazine slid from his lap. Neither his own nasal eruption nor the slap as the magazine hit the concrete woke him. That effect was caused by the knife blade that Gabriel punched into his throat a second later.

The man spasmed in the chair like a game fish trying to throw a hook, but it was too little, too late. He died, eyes wide, with Gabriel's hand over his mouth and his lifeblood flowing out around the knife and soaking the front of his jacket.

Gabriel patted him down. Found the keys in the right hand pocket of the bomber jacket. He yanked them clear and started trying them in the lock of the cell door.

The second key worked and he pulled the door wide. Cowering in the far corner of the tiny room, which stank of damp plaster and piss, Santiago looked fearfully towards him.

'Please, no!' he cried out. 'Don't kill me.'

Gabriel realised that with his camo paint and full tactical gear he was unrecognisable.

'Santi, it's me,' he said. 'I've come to get you out. Are you OK to go? How's your hand?'

Santiago held up his left hand. It was wrapped in a filthy bandage, stained red.

'They cut my finger off. It hurts like hell.'

'I know. We'll get you fixed up properly. I promise. Come on, we need to go.'

Santiago nodded and got to his feet. Gabriel was pleased to see they'd left him in his shoes. The grubby Nike trainers would be silent on the house's hard floors. So much the better.

They left the tiny cell. Gabriel turned right, stepping round the guard's corpse. 'This way,' he murmured. 'Keep close behind me, OK? If anyone starts shooting, hit the floor. I'll deal with it.'

'Give me your pistol,' Santiago said. 'I know how to shoot. You can use the assault rifle.'

He had a point. Gabriel had brought an M4 carbine as well as the RPG-7. But he shook his head. He didn't want Santiago going down that route. Once a young man killed, he crossed a line he could never recross.

It had happened to Gabriel and he had never regretted it until Eli's murder.

Now he wanted to protect Santiago from a life that would end in death and grief.

42

Boots clumped on the stairs at the far end of the passageway. Two men. Voices raised. They'd come for Santiago. Gabriel spun round.

'Back inside your cell,' he urged the boy. 'Help me with the guard.'

They dragged the body inside the cell. Gabriel ripped the leather bomber jacket free and took the man's ball cap.

When the two men arrived, Gabriel was leaning back against the wall, head down, cap pulled low over his face, the magazine spread across his lap. His heart was racing as he brought his breathing under control. The passage was too narrow for men to walk two abreast so the lead man was shielding his partner. He stood so close Gabriel could smell his sweat.

'Hey, asshole, didn't you hear the shooting? We're under attack.'

Gabriel said nothing.

'Hey, get up, Marti. The boss says we have to move the kid.' He leaned down over Gabriel and lifted the peak of his cap with a finger. His eyes widened. 'Who—'

His final words were left unsaid as Gabriel shot him through the pages of the magazine. The silenced 9mm round blew a hole through the centrefold girl, setting the paper on fire before entering his chest.

Gabriel let him fall on top of him – extra protection – and shot the other man through the head before he'd even realised what was happening.

He rolled the body off his lap and fetched Santiago from the cell.

'OK, this time we go and we don't stop. I've got someone waiting to get us out of here but we need to move fast.'

Santiago nodded. Then he bent and picked up the second guard's AK-47. The look he gave Gabriel, determination mixed with teenaged surliness, persuaded him that there was no way he was going to persuade the boy to drop it.

'Keep tight in behind me. Once we're out front, shoot bursts left and right,' Gabriel said. 'Don't worry about hitting anything. Just keep firing. When you run out of ammunition, point it at people's faces.'

Santiago nodded grimly.

'Let's go,' he said tersely.

Gabriel pulled the two white ballcaps out of a pocket and handed one to Santiago.

'Put this on.'

Gabriel pulled open the front door. The yard was empty. Fifty metres ahead, the gateway beckoned, its gates lying blackened and twisted halfway between the pillars and the house itself.

Two AK-wielding men were standing behind the wall to the left and right of the gate, peering out into the scrubland beyond. But that was it. Either Rey didn't have that many men at his disposal or Gabriel had been right and the rest were out and about, shaking down the locals for their hard-earned cash.

He sprinted towards them, M4 at his hip. Gabriel heard Santiago's AK chattering from behind him. The gate guards turned at the noise and, wide-mouthed, raised their weapons. He dropped the man to his right with a burst of fire that almost cut him in half. The man to his left screamed as a round took him in the throat. But not one of Gabriel's. Whether Gabriel wanted it or not, Santiago had just crossed the line.

He had no more time to think about it. They needed to be gone. The extraction was underway.

Through the gate and out into the flat expanse of ground between the Rey compound and the riverbed. More automatic fire. He turned and fired a short burst. He'd have no time to swap out the magazine when it emptied.

Heads down, he and Santiago crossed the scrub at a run. The riverbed with its protective screen of thornbushes was just a few more metres away. A single shot rang out. For a moment Gabriel thought it was Don, taking out another gangster.

Then Santiago's scream penetrated his thoughts. He skidded to a halt and spun round. White-faced, Santiago was clutching his right leg. Blood streamed from between his fingers. The bullet had entered his calf.

'Stay down,' he said.

In the gateway, a single figure stood, aiming a long gun directly at them. Gabriel brought the M4 up to his shoulder and began firing single shots back towards the shooter. He was exposed. The shooter had the high wall to hide behind. Then the firing pin dropped on an empty breech.

The shooter waited another few seconds, then emerged from his cover a hundred metres distant. Slender, dressed all in black, he had a swagger to his gait that sat oddly with the long gun now raised once more to his shoulder and pointing directly at Gabriel. Sunlight glinted off gold at his neck and the sunglasses masking his eyes.

Was this Rey himself. Out in front, defending his property?

Gabriel threw himself to the ground beside Santiago.

'We need to get into the riverbed,' he said. 'Can you crawl?'

'I don't know, man. My leg. They shot me.'

'I know. I know. Hang on.'

Gabriel rolled onto his back and pulled the belt out of his trousers. He slithered round and looped it around Santiago's calf then slid it higher before cinching it tight just below his knee.

Santiago howled. Gabriel ignored it. Howling was fine. Silence would have worried him more. With the tourniquet in place, the bleeding slowed to a trickle.

'Come on,' Gabriel said, 'we've got to move or we're going to die here.'

Half-crawling, half-dragging Santiago, he began inching painfully across the stony ground towards the shelter of the riverbed. Another rifle round spanged off a rock to his right sending stone chips flying off. A needle-pointed sliver caught him across the cheek. He wiped the blood away and felt a flap of skin slide disgustingly beneath his fingers.

Where the hell was Don? If ever a man needed covering fire, it was now.

The riverbed was just a few metres away now. Grunting with effort, Santiago hauled himself over the lip of the bank and slithered down the gritty slope into the rocky bottom, emitting a yell of pure agony as a rock caught against the gunshot wound in his leg.

The shooter sent another round ricocheting off a rock to Gabriel's right. Then another to his left. Was he *playing* with him? He needed to neutralise him. No way would he be able to get Santiago back to the truck with one leg out of action.

But a pistol against a high-powered rifle? Because he had no time to reload. Those were shitty odds.

He swivelled round and crawled on his stomach towards a twisted old thornbush. Another rifle round whined overhead, the report catching up with it a split second later. They said you never heard the round that killed you. The thought did not offer comfort.

Then a hissing filled the air. It came from Don's direction. Gabriel glanced up. Couldn't see anything. Ahead a small canister bounced on the hardpan. It detonated and suddenly the air was full of grey smoke. Yes! Among the 'toys' Don had selected from Gabriel's subterranean armoury was an M40 grenade launcher. No HE shells; the arms dealer had explained there was a shortage. But he'd offered smoke instead.

He got to his feet and sprinted wide to his right hoping to come up behind or at least to the side of the shooter. In the light breeze, the smoke was hanging low over the ground, drifting towards the hills in a sluggish cloud. Pistol up, Gabriel walked into it at a point where he estimated he could catch the shooter from behind.

He pulled his neckerchief round his neck up over his nose and mouth. The acrid smoke made him want to cough. He swallowed hard, fighting the urge down. No point in visual cover if you gave your position away with sound.

Then, disaster. The breeze picked up from a gentle zephyr that barely stirred the leaves on the trees to a stiff wind that could rip palm-leaved roofs off houses. He'd experienced it for himself several times. Something to do with the interaction between sea currents, coastal topography and the hills. They even had a name for it in this part of Honduras. *La Furia* – The Fury.

The smoke-cloud dissipated in seconds. Gabriel had miscalculated. The shooter was nowhere in sight. Then he spoke from behind Gabriel.

'Drop your weapon!'

It was easy to disarm someone prodding you in the back with a gun barrel. Duck, twist, roll – elbow, grab, twist – yank, fire, kill. All done in two or three seconds. But Rey was standing too far back for Gabriel to try a Krav Maga move.

He let the pistol fall from his hand. Rey hadn't shot him, so he wanted him alive. At some point on the journey back to the house, he could use his knife then go back for Santiago.

Boots scuffed on the gritty earth and then his right leg gave way as Rey kicked him hard behind the knee. He toppled sideways then spun round and got to his feet again.

He got his first look at his captor. Standing a good ten feet away.

Pulled back snugly against his right shoulder, in a manner any firearms instructor would have approved of, was the stock of an all-black, long-barrelled rifle. A .30-06 Blaser R8, he noticed. No scope, just iron sights. But Rey obviously knew how to use it, unlike the guy on overwatch whose escape had led to the situation in which Gabriel now found himself.

'I hope you said your prayers this morning,' Rey said, his mouth distorted by the stock pushing against his cheek. He closed his right eye and sighted down the long black barrel. 'Goodbye, gringo.'

With the visual acuity that affects those about to die, Gabriel actually saw Rey's finger tighten on the trigger. So this was it. To be shot down on some undistinguished patch of scrub outside a gangster's estate, having failed to free one of the few people he cared about in the world. Behind Rey, Eli, Smudge and Britta wavered in the heat haze. Their voices joined in a whisper.

'It's time, Gabriel.'

But it wasn't. In that moment, as the universe offered him the chance to be reunited with those he had loved and lost, he fought back.

No. It isn't. I'm sorry. I don't want to. I want to live.

Gabriel looked into Rey's eyes. Was it too late to try to hypnotise him? To bring Master Zhao's training into play one last time?

'You don't want to do this,' he began, striving to recapture the precise sequence of tones and coordinated eye movements that would rob even the most determined killer of their reason.

It felt wrong. Clumsy. He began to try again.

Rey's finger tightened on the trigger.

43

Gabriel flinched as the spray of blood blew back into his face.

In front of him, Rey died as the top of his skull spun away, trailing blood and brain tissue behind it.

Though the Blaser dropped to the ground from lifeless hands, the corpse remained on its feet for three seconds. Blood fountained up from the arteries supplying the brain for several beats of the dying heart.

The wind caught the scarlet jets and blew them towards Gabriel, soaking his jacket and plastering his hair and beard to his skin. Then the corpse toppled sideways, landing in a crumpled heap on its side, one leg folded beneath the other to form the number '4'.

Gabriel ran over to where Santiago was crawling steadily away down the riverbed towards the forest. He bent and slung the boy's arm over his shoulder.

'Come on. Let's get you back to the truck.'

Climbing up through the trees took two more hours. Santiago fought on, despite the obvious pain he was in. Not one word of protest escaped his lips, though he maintained a steady stream of colourful Honduran expressions Gabriel filed away for future use.

Finally they emerged into the tiny clearing where he'd left Don in the truck. It was so artfully concealed that at first Santiago exclaimed, 'Where is it?'

Gabriel pointed to the mass of torn branches and creepers.

'Boss, it's us!'

Emerging like a Green Man from old English folklore, leaves in his hair, his head and chest swathed in more vegetation, Don clambered out of the load-bay.

'Sorry about the lack of covering fire back there,' he said. 'Bloody gun jammed. Russian rubbish. Had to field-strip it. Did the smoke grenade work?'

'More or less. Help me with Santiago. He took a bullet to the leg.'

They manoeuvred Santiago into the back of the truck, lying him on the bedding and propping his leg up on a box of ammunition.

'I'll stay with the boy,' Don said, climbing in beside him. 'Drive carefully, that's all I ask.

Gabriel shook his head.

'You need to be behind the wheel. Get him back to Santa Rosa. In fact, no. Take him to Bonita. They have a decent doctor there who can treat the gunshot wound. I've got to finish things down there.'

'What on earth do you mean?'

'You shot the boss. I need to mop up. If we leave anyone alive it'll only spark a tit-for-tat war. I can't allow that.'

Don grunted. Whether in approval or its opposite Gabriel couldn't tell. Either way, ten minutes later, once they'd cleared the truck of the undergrowth, he was rolling away, waving out of the window.

Resupplied with ammunition, Gabriel headed back down the hill. On the way to the house, he stopped at Rey's corpse. Flies rose in a dark cloud, buzzing loudly and swarming around Gabriel's head.

He squatted beside the body, took Casildo's signet ring from his pocket and dipped it in the blood. Using a careful rocking motion to avoid smearing the transferred image, he applied it to the back of Rey's right hand. When he lifted the ring clear, it left a perfect impression. A complex design of three capital letters: L, D, C encompassed by a larger Z.

Anyone brave enough to investigate would draw the conclusion he wanted them to. This was a Zinguizapa cartel hit. Reasons unknown. And only a fool would want to find out. He walked on.

The compound stank of gunsmoke and blood. Thousands of flies had congregated. The busy handmaidens of slaughter were always first to the corpses, before medics, stretcher bearers or civilian looters.

Bodies lay everywhere. Most killed by precise shots to the head. Don had been busier than he'd let on. Typical of the old man. Did the job and that was enough.

One body emitted a groan. A man with florid bandido moustache and beard. He'd taken a shot to the chest and was bleeding steadily into the dust.

Gabriel delivered a coup de grâce with his pistol. Stamped the cartel sigil onto his hand. He found nobody else alive. When he'd finished, eleven bodies bore the Zinguizapa mark.

He needed a ride back to Santa Rosa. Something anonymous. Nothing obvious that could be traced back to César Rey.

The group's vehicles were clustered together on the east side of the house, directly opposite the swimming pool. A couple of white pickups, an SUV, and a Ford Mustang in a shouty green that screamed 'gangbanger'. No. None of them would do. He walked round the corner, hoping maybe someone drove a beaten-up old Chevy or a boring little hatchback.

Nobody had lowered themselves to that level of vehicular Plain Jane. But just as he was about to give up and start looking for the keys to one of the trucks, he saw a knobbly crescent of black rubber peeking from beneath a worn and faded green tarpaulin.

He went over and dragged the cover off. A trail bike. Nothing fancy. Just a 125cc scrambler that might once have been white but was now covered in the tawny dust that blew around everywhere in this part of the country.

No plates. The VIN had been crudely obliterated with an angle-grinder by the look of it. He nodded with satisfaction. For him, at least, crime did pay.

He took out his knife and bent over the ignition to start hotwiring the ignition. The move saved his life. Automatic fire erupted from a position off to his right. With a bang and a whine from the ricochet, a bullet smacked into the wall above him. Its trajectory would have taken it straight through his head if he hadn't crouched beside the tank at that precise moment.

Pistol out, he scuttled for cover around the corner of the house. He had just enough time to see a leather-jacketed gang member advancing with a light machine held in front of him, its ammo belt dangling over his left arm.

He strained to hear the shooter running, but the whole compound was eerily still. *La Furia* had stopped blowing as suddenly as it had started and the only sound was the buzzing of the flies and the keening of a buzzard high overhead.

Behind him, a plastic bucket riddled with bullet holes lay on its side beside a much-used yard brush, its stiff bristles worn away into a slope. He poked the broom handle into the bucket and popped it out around the corner of the wall.

Another burst shattered the silence. The bucket fragmented into sharp-edged shards of plastic that spun away into the dirt. He cursed himself for leaving all the long guns in the truck with Don. Now all he had to take on a machinegun-equipped shooter was a nine.

He crawled along the wall until he reached a door. Reached up and tried the handle. It was locked. No time for niceties. He put his elbow through the glass panel above the lock and was inside seconds later. He reached the foot of the stairs. Now he did hear a sound. The shooter was running for the wide-open front door, shouting curses.

'*Eres hombre muerto, hijo de puta!*'

Gabriel shook his head. People had told him he was a dead man before.

One by one, he tried the doors that lined the hallway. Each led to a bedroom, one of which had two bunkbeds. For gang members, he assumed, not children.

The last door he tried opened into a richly furnished master bedroom. A vast wooden four-poster bed hung with brightly coloured woven curtains in the native style. Indian women sold them at country markets or even roadside stands for ten or twenty dollars a piece, more for the really intricate designs.

Tall mahogany wardrobes in the highly ornamented Spanish colonial style lined the walls. At the foot of the bed sat a more rustic blanket chest, its iron-bound planks streaked with rust from the nails holding it together. Acting purely out of intuition, Gabriel lifted the heavy arched lid.

Perhaps in more conventional Honduran households, such a chest would hold spare sheets, blankets and quilts. In the Rey *menage* it was a repository of serious firepower. A black Colt M4 plus spare magazines and a box of ammunition. A Mossberg 500 Hushpower pump-action shotgun and a box of shells. And a dozen hand grenades. American M67s still in their original US Army packing.

He grabbed the Mossberg and stuffed a handful of shells into a pocket. He pulled the pump back and checked the breech. A shell was already present. He tried loading another, but the feed tube was full. He'd expected nothing less. Hardly much point keeping an unloaded shotgun close at hand if you were expecting a full-on attack from a rival gang or the police.

Downstairs, the last remaining member of the Rey gang was striding around, making no effort to conceal himself. He was still yelling.

To Gabriel it sounded as though he'd lost his mind. He could imagine that to go from being one of the undisputed masters of a little corner of Honduras to the sole survivor of a blitz attack might take some getting used to.

Tough.

He opened the window and climbed out onto the ledge. It was wide enough to stand on. From there, with the Mossberg slung over his head on its webbing strap, he hauled himself up onto the roof and slithered around until he was lying on his belly, looking down over the gutter.

The breeze sucked the thin curtains out of the window, just as he'd planned. They fluttered and flapped like flags. From inside, the implication would be as clear as a broad-head arrow painted in blood on the wall. *He went thataway.*

Now he waited. He listened as the gunman clumped along the hall, swearing furiously, opening and then slamming each of the bedroom doors Gabriel had already checked.

After what felt like hours, the gunman entered the master bedroom. He uttered another curse and crossed to the window. Gabriel counted his steps. Reached five. Leaned further over and readied himself, legs spread wide on the warm barrel tiles, feet turned out and flat against the humped terracotta.

When the gunman poked his head out of the window, he did what any homeowner would do if they were looking for the intruder who'd invaded their sanctuary. He looked down.

Without hesitation, Gabriel squeezed the Mossberg's trigger.

The corpse fell back inside the bedroom and what was left of the head fell in pieces to the ground twenty feet below to darken the dusty compound.

Gabriel shuffled back and got to his feet. Shouldering the Mossberg, he re-entered the bedroom, avoiding the headless corpse and the lake of blood seeping into the gaps between the floorboards.

The Cesar Rey organisation was finished. He applied the final Zinguizapa blood-transfer to the back of the corpse's hand and left. On the way, he collected the M4 and the crate of M67s. As he left, he tossed a grenade into each of the bedrooms and ran down the stairs. With the upper storey disintegrating in a series of loud bangs, he repeated the process on the ground floor.

He sprinted out of the front door just as the first of the ground floor grenades detonated towards the back of the house. Smoke blew out past him carrying fine fragments of wood and plaster.

With the house burning behind him, he hotwired the bike and slewed it round, throwing up a rooster-tail of grit and dust, the shotgun and the M4 bouncing on his back. He twisted the throttle grip and accelerated out through the ruined gateway and onto the scrub-studded hard pan.

A low boom roared out from the house. In the surviving mirror he watched the fireball roll upwards through the shattered roof. It seemed Señor Rey had more than just a few M67s stored at *El Presidente*.

Three miles out from Santa Rosa he took a detour off the highway and headed up a narrow, red-grit road just wide enough for a single vehicle. The bike skittered and jumped over the rutted and potholed surface and he had to stand on the foot pegs to avoid being either thrown off or suffering permanent damage to his kidneys.

After five minutes, he emerged onto a sloping gravel road that led to old mine workings. Two hundred metres further on, the road ended in a smashed-up section of asphalt. A rusted backhoe that might once have been painted a sunny orange was canted over, its left-hand wheels dangling above a gravel pit filled with water.

Gabriel dismounted and aimed the front wheel at the precipice. Clutch lever held in, he kicked the gear lever down for first and then opened the throttle wide. With the little engine screaming, he held the bike vertical and simultaneously released the clutch lever and his grip on the handlebars. With a roar, it shot forward, sailing out over the water and plummeting for a count of three before splashing into the blue-green pool and disappearing.

Changing his mind about the long guns, Gabriel unshouldered them both and, one after the other, sent them spinning out over the water. Unencumbered now, apart from the nine, which he'd already tucked into the back of his waistband, he began the walk home.

The realisation of what he'd done hit him like a hollow point, filling his soul with black splinters of depression that lodged in his bones, his muscles, his soft tissues. He'd become a liability to the people he thought of as his friends and neighbours.

Attributing the destruction of *El Presidente* to the Zinguizapa cartel would act as a deterrent to anybody thinking of taking over from César Rey. But realistically, Gabriel was just a magnet for trouble. Santiago was safe, but at what cost? He'd lost a finger and sustained a gunshot wound. That was no way for a young man to make the transition into adulthood.

'You joined the Paras, though didn't you, boss?' Smudge said from beside him. *'Plenty of shooting when you were Santiago's age.'*

'That was my choice,' Gabriel said, aware, and not caring, that once again he was holding a conversation with the dead. 'I forced it on Santiago.'

As he walked, with Smudge, now silent, beside him, sadness stole up on Gabriel like a coyote tracking a wounded deer. Because he knew.

Santa Rosa was his home no longer.

It was time to leave.

44

LONDON – 10:00 A.M.

Gemma Dowding's ascent to the pinnacle of British politics had been rapid. Even so, the speed of her descent caught her by surprise.

One moment she had the run of 10 Downing Street, and Chequers, the Buckinghamshire country house where British prime ministers could let their hair down at the weekends. The next, she was forced back on her own resources as the men she'd so gleefully offended while in office took their revenge.

She'd not sold her house in the Yorkshire Dales town at the heart of her parliamentary seat. She retreated there now. On arriving, she called Dmitri Rublev. The man whose astronomical wealth had, first, propelled her into the top job and then, on its discovery, shoved her off the pinnacle without a parachute.

'Dmitri, I'm in trouble.'

'So I see,' he said, the tobacco in one of those revolting Russian cigarettes he still insisted on smoking crackling as he drew on it close to the phone. 'That was quite the exit speech. Did they not offer you a more dignified route out?'

'Of course they bloody did! Be a good girl, toe the line, admit I wasn't up to it and they'd let me retire to a life of anonymity and good works. No harm, no foul.'

'Why can I imagine how that particular conversation went down?'

She heard the humour in his voice.

'You know something, Dmitri? You and me, we're actually very similar. You came from nothing. Son of two mill workers in Siberia. You worked your way up through the ranks of the army and then the KGB. When the time was right, you made your move. Now you're one of the richest men in the world.' She took a breath. 'I may not have your money, but I fought and clawed my way out of the path society expected of me. I succeeded on ambition, talent—'

' – and utter ruthlessness. We could have used someone with your...vision...in my department. I was always very impressed with your little experiment in crime prevention. Stalin would have been proud, although he would probably have called it,' he inhaled and then sighed out what surely had to be a lungful of that pungent Russian tobacco smoke, 'reduction in recidivist elements. Something like that, anyway. Those old Communists were so fond of their euphemisms.'

'Look, Dmitri, all due respect, but I didn't call you to discuss the history of the Soviet Union. I need a job. I've lost all my income bar the pittance they give MPs and it looks like I'll lose my seat at the next general election.'

'A job. Well, as I recall, you were all set to cash in on the American lecture circuit. Don't tell me your impromptu speech outside your former home turned off the banks and the Ivy League universities?'

Pain darted up the inside of her left thumb. She looked down. She'd just pulled a strip of skin away, leaving a raw red triangle at its base. Blood was seeping along the groove between the flesh and the nail. She sucked at it, wrinkling her nose at the salty, coppery tang that flooded her mouth.

'I thought you might have something for me at one of your companies. Or maybe you could introduce me to some of your friends. I have high-level experience.'

She heard him light another cigarette. The distinctive metallic click of the lid of his brass Zippo lighter the only sound on the line.

'Gemma, you have to understand something. The circles in which I operate? How can I put this diplomatically? Well, *everybody* has high-level experience,' he said, almost wistfully. 'A couple of years at Number Ten Downing Street? Maybe in England that sounds impressive. But you have to remember, every world stateswoman and man wants a slice of the action.'

'You owe me, Dmitri!' she hissed, feeling a worm of anxiety wriggling in her belly and not enjoying the sensation. 'The government contracts I sent your way. The deals I helped you finesse with my contacts. The peerage, for God's sake! You can't just abandon me now.'

'You're right, my dear Gemma,' he said. 'And I have no intention of abandoning you, as you rather melodramatically put it. Even though I have been informed that I am no longer welcome in Britain. But these things take time. Leave it with me. I'll make some enquiries.'

'Don't—'

'Some *discreet* enquiries. I must go. Sasha is playing in a polo match. I have to drive him.'

She stared at the black screen of her phone. Fought back an overpowering urge to hurl it at the wall. Dmitri was just like the others. Another man who'd lied and cheated his way to the top, bribing and corrupting as he went, using people the way he'd used her. And now, safe in his ivory castle, he'd pulled up the golden drawbridge. Well, not this time. Maybe she had one more card to play.

'No!' she shouted. 'Help me now or I let Wolfe know who funded the mission that ended up with his wife dead. From what I know about him, he's not a man to forget something like that. Maybe you'll end up driving to your son's funeral instead of a polo match.'

Silence. Then, as her ears adjusted, the sound of her backer, and the man she'd once, foolishly, believed to be a friend, breathing steadily through his nose: in-out-in-out. She pictured blue-grey cigarette smoke seeping from his nostrils: a sleeping dragon, awakened.

Then: 'Leave it with me.'

With Dmitri gone, she opened a browser and went to the BBC News site. And gasped. The fifth item on the page was brief, but it sent a chill down her spine that settled – a cold, hard mass of fear – in her stomach.

The body of a British woman has been found in the Honduran capital of Tegucigalpa. She has been identified as Margot McDonnell, a former civil servant. Ms McDonnell had been shot through the head. Police Commander Ramon Chavez said, 'We are treating Ms McDonnell's death as suspicious.'

'No shit!' Gemma exclaimed to her empty kitchen.

45

SANTA ROSA – ONE WEEK LATER

The doctor in Bonito had treated Santiago's amputation, and his gunshot wound, cleaning it, suturing the torn muscle and skin, and prescribing a course of antibiotics. Luckily for him, the round had been a full metal jacket. Not only that but it had passed cleanly, if a bullet wound could ever be said to be clean, through the muscles of his calf without hitting either the tibia or the fibula.

Santiago needed a crutch to get around, but his adventure had had an unexpected side benefit. He'd become an object of admiration among the boys in Santa Rosa, and fascination among the girls. One in particular, Christabel, had become his steady girlfriend and the pair could be seen strolling along the beach together, he limping, she with her arm supportively around his waist.

Gabriel had paid his medical bill and asked the doctor to keep an eye on Santiago's recovery, leaving more money to cover any future treatment or rehab from a physiotherapist if he judged it necessary.

Gabriel was sitting with Pera on her veranda, looking out at the sea. He swirled the ice and lime slices around his glass of guaro and Coke. Dolphins, regular visitors to this part of the coast, were sporting in the waves, using them exactly as human surfers would. Riding the breakers in, cutting left and right, even jumping clear, chattering and whistling excitedly before swimming back out to catch their next ride to shore.

In another version of his existence, he could imagine he'd found paradise. Built a life here. Raised his children. Grown vegetables. Caught fish for supper. Barbecued. And then, in the fullness of time, hopefully be the first to die, leaving Eli a grieving widow, but at least with a life full of good memories. And her children to comfort her in her old age.

He sighed deeply.

'Oh, Gabe, that came from the heart,' Pera said, turning in her wicker chair to look at him with her soft brown eyes. 'What's the matter. Were you thinking of Eli?'

'It's so beautiful here,' he said, swallowing down the lump in his throat. 'I can see why you love it.'

'Then why not stay? Grow to love it, too.'

He turned away, watching the dolphins ride the waves, clicking their pleasure.

'What makes you think I'm not staying?'

'Come on, Gabe. Do you think I am blind? In my line of work, you get very good at reading people,' she said. 'Your body is here, but your mind has already left. Where are you going?'

He sipped his drink.

'I don't know. But the person who had Eli killed is still alive and I need to find them.'

'You mean kill them, don't you? Why don't you say it? When they took Santiago, I wanted to get a gun and kill all of them.'

'Listen, Pera, about that. I covered my tracks pretty well. I don't think anybody would know it was me and Don. And I tried to leave it so others would be too frightened to take over,' he said, thinking back to the bloody Zinguizapa imprints with which he'd marked the corpses. 'But there's still a risk someone might come looking for me again. It's partly why I have to go. But why don't you and Santiago come too? Or at least leave the country? I could set you up in the USA. I have contacts, I could pay for everything.'

Pera set her drink down on the deck boards, bleached almost white by the sun and scoured smooth by the wind-blown sand. She left her own chair to come and kneel in front of Gabriel. Took his unresisting hands in hers.

'Gabe, that is a sweet offer. And I know it comes from a place of kindness. You are a truly good man. One of the best men I have ever met. From that first time we met in the queue for lunch, do you remember?'

Gabriel nodded. How could he forget?

'You were so kind to me that day.'

'But look around you.' She freed her right hand from his grip to sweep it out in an arc, twisting so she could encompass the sparkling Caribbean. '*This* is my home. I love it here. I know what everybody says about Honduras. The guidebooks, the tourist websites. But here? In Santa Rosa? Life is good. We don't have much money but we get along. People look out for each other. Neighbours, friends. It's a community. I couldn't leave this even if you bought us an apartment in Manhattan!' She grinned. 'Joking! I know that's not what you meant.'

Gabriel didn't say that if she'd asked him to, he could have. *Would* have, without a second thought.

'Would you at least let me give you enough money to set up that food truck you're always talking about? You could leave Frida's.'

She frowned.

'You still don't approve of what I do? We spoke about this before, you remember?'

'No! Of course I don't disapprove,' he protested, though he had to grudgingly admit that she was just as good at reading people as she'd claimed. 'It's just, I know you would be great as your own boss.'

'Hmm,' she said, putting a finger to the point of her chin and then grinning. 'Well, it *is* my dream. But it would be an investment, yes? Not a gift. You'd be a partner.'

He smiled. 'Whatever you say.'

Don wandered in from the house, yawning.

'Hello, you two. A man could get used to this life, you know. I may have to make a siesta part of my daily routine.'

Pera got up. 'You want some tea, Don?'

'That would be lovely, my dear lady.'

With the veranda to himself and Gabriel, Don took the chair Pera had vacated.

'I was just speaking to Uri. He'll be here in an hour.'

Gabriel started. 'What?'

'He flew in on an El-Al commercial flight, but the Israelis are doing some pilot training with the Guatemalans over the border and they borrowed a chopper. He's flying up now.'

'Why?'

'I'll let him explain the details, but basically, we've had a stroke of luck.'

'What do you mean?'

Don pulled out his phone, fiddled with it for a couple of seconds, then turned it round towards Gabriel.

'Watch.'

In a glitchy but still perfectly watchable video, Gemma Dowding came out of the famous black door of 10 Downing Street and approached a wooden lectern. Gabriel stared, open-mouthed, as she resigned, using the occasion to launch into a bizarre rant about some shadowy conspiracy and how she was going because they made it impossible for her to govern anymore.

'Blimey! She's gone full "deep state" on us.'

Don grunted. 'Huh. "Conspiracy." Bit rich coming from her.'

'This changes everything,' Gabriel said. 'She'll be much easier to get to.'

'She'll still have round-the-clock protection, remember. Perk of the job, or a mill-stone, depending on how you look at it.'

'Maybe. But what does that amount to? A couple of Special Branch guys with nines under their suit jackets?'

'More or less. But you'd have to go through them to get to her. Are you comfortable with that?'

'They know what they sign up for when they take the assignment. To defend her against her enemies. That might mean taking one for the asset. Well, I'm her enemy.'

Don raised his eyebrows. 'You're a cool one, I'll give you that.'

'And you're not?' From nowhere, Gabriel's temper boiled over. Suddenly he was in no mood to discuss the morality of shooting Dowding's bodyguards to get to her. 'Remind me why you're sitting on Pera's veranda while she makes English-bloody-Breakfast for you? Because I'm pretty sure you didn't come to Honduras for a holiday. You and Uri tracked me down because you wanted whoever had you attacked in Jerusalem and Eli killed, dead. Well, we know who. And she just made herself an easier target.'

Pera arrived with two mugs of tea. Worry creased her forehead. But she said nothing directly. Just handed each man a mug and disappeared back inside, saying, 'I have to go out for some groceries.'

But the look she'd bestowed on Gabriel was as eloquent as it needed to be. *Don't shout at him. He is old and he is your good friend. You should have more respect.*

She was right, of course she was.

'I'm sorry, Boss. I didn't mean to shout at you. It's just, I thought maybe this was all going to fade. Eli's death, everything. I was losing my anger. I'd even started to think I could get over it and just live out my days here. Then you arrived and that shit went down with César Rey and now it looks like we have a chance to avenge her.'

Don smiled and sipped his tea.

'Ah, that's good. Maybe I could give the Hondurans afternoon tea in exchange for the siesta. A fair trade, wouldn't you say?'

'Is that your way of saying I'm forgiven?'

'Listen, Old Sport. I was fortunate with Christine. We had many, many good years together. Really good years. No children, which would have been nice, but we had the best of each other nonetheless,' Don said, smiling. 'And when she did go, it was swift and painless. I wish with all my heart that you and Eli could have had the same. You were destined to. More in fact, since she was carrying your child. We will see this bloody business through to its end and then, maybe you can take stock. Reconnect with Tara. God knows she'll be pleased to hear you're not dead.'

As Don had spoken of his long marriage to Christine, Gabriel hung his head. Tears were flowing again. He let them. What else was there to do? In Honduras, despite the macho culture among its menfolk, crying was not seen as shameful. Men would weep at a poor football result, the death of a favourite dog, or even at a sad song performed in a bar.

It was true, every word. Don and Christine had had decades together as man and wife. He and Eli had managed less than a month. The rage he felt, tamped down over the last seven days by the action over at *El Presidente* and then the aftermath, roared up into incandescent flames once again.

He envisaged a firefight. Special Branch officers on one side, him on the other, the stink of gunsmoke and burning brass stinging his nostrils. Bloodlust tinting his vision red, the percussive rattle of small arms fire, bullets criss-crossing the air searching out targets to dismantle in fragments of bone and ragged scraps of flesh, all subsumed in the pink mist of vaporised blood.

And there, standing amid her soldiers, the woman at the centre of it all. The architect of the conspiracy that had led to the deaths, not just of murderers and rapists, but a human rights lawyer and his baby daughter, and, ultimately, Eli and Gabriel's own unborn child.

He refocused his eyes. Beside him, Don sat, sipping his tea, apparently content to watch the dolphins. As if he had retired to the Honduran coast to enjoy nature rather than journeyed there to drag Gabriel back into action.

They were still sitting there when the distant *whop-whop* of an incoming helo broke the monotonous regularity of the waves breaking on the beach. Coming in from the sea, a dark-blue chopper with a yellow tailfin grew larger as it flew straight towards them. It passed overhead and the note of its engine changed as the pilot slowed it down and then hovered, looking for a spot to land.

Gabriel thought they'd probably pick the cleared rectangle of scrubby grass where the village kids played football. He rose from his chair.

'Looks like Uri's here. Come on. We can go and meet him.'

Don winced as he pushed himself up from the low wicker chair and placed his right hand over a spot low in his ribcage on the left side.

Gabriel hoped the pounding he'd taken from Bakker's machinegun hadn't left him permanently damaged. Gabriel himself had his fair share of scars from gunshot wounds, not to mention the stabbings, slashings and, on one memorable occasion deep in the bowels of the Iranian Ministry of Intelligence and Security, a six-inch nail through the back of his hand.

But he was younger, fitter. Yes they still hurt from time to time, giving off random twinges or electrical zaps at odd times of the night, but they didn't bother him.

No, for Gabriel, the wounds he thought might never heal lay in places bullets could never reach.

46

The helo, a Honduran navy Bell UH-1, was setting down as Gabriel and Don arrived. The palm trees surrounding the grassy field were lashing under the blades' downdraft. Red dust swirled high into the air, vortices that rolled around themselves as they curled upwards. Gabriel flinched as grit blew into his eyes, turned away and caught a flash of bright sunlight directly on his face.

The world lurched sideways.

The hard snap of the blades chopping the air. The smell of dust in his nostrils. The smell of burnt aviation fuel from the helo's exhausts. The sight of armed guards in the open door. Panic ambushed him. His heart started pounding. Palms slick with sweat. Vision clouding, darkening, spiralling with sparks. Terror of imminent death. Gunfire. Men screaming, falling, shooting, fighting, dying. It was happening again and he was powerless to stop it.

He fell to his knees, eyes squeezed shut, arms over his head. Where was his rifle? He needed a weapon. The Taliban were coming. Their AKs chattered insanely loud in the whitewashed village street, empty brass shell casings plinking everywhere as they rebounded off the plastered walls to spin into the dust.

A hand on his shoulder. They'd found him. He felt the machete blade on the back of his neck. The hairs erected as they sensed the incoming blow. He whimpered. Unable to fight back, to resist. Death was here for him. He heard Eli's voice calling him. *'Gabe. It's time. It's time. Don't leave me here alone any longer. Please don't—'*

'Nooo!'

He screamed and fell sideways, curling into a foetal position, arms cradling his head, knees drawn up to his chest. Barely able to draw breath into his iron-bound chest.

The hand on his shoulder was now rubbing his back.

'Gabriel. Gabriel. It's OK. Look at me. Look at me, bro! You're going to be OK.'

A man's voice. Not Taliban. He was speaking English. But that accent. Half East European, half somewhere rich with the smells and colours of the Middle East. Cooking spices, olives, thyme and bay leaves, garlic, hummus, rich red wine, grilled lamb, puffed flatbreads. A rich, deep voice of a middle-aged Israeli security officer. Of Uri Ziff.

He creaked his eyelids open. Let Uri draw his folded arms down away from his face.

'Gabriel, bro. You were having a flashback, that's all. Come on, let's get you up.'

Uri drew him upwards, onto his feet, his face just inches from Gabriel's. He saw no fear or ridicule, no worry or naked curiosity. Just the concern of one brother for another. Beyond Uri, in the helo, one of the guards was staring, frankly, straight at him. But even he looked concerned rather than amused.

Then Gabriel realised Uri hadn't come alone. Standing beside him, a khaki holdall dangling from her right hand, was a woman in her mid-thirties. Sandy hair cut short, watchful eyes in a heart-shaped face.

'Nurit,' she said, holding out her hand and smiling.

He took it. Warm, dry to the touch. Steel behind the soft palm. Any woman – or man, for that matter – who Uri chose to accompany him on a mission would be as tough as they came. He wondered whether she'd known Eli before she transferred from Mossad to the Department.

'Gabriel. I'm sorry about…that.' He pointed to the ground. 'It's, I thought it was cured, but—'

'PTSD,' she said, with a brisk nod. 'My brother Avihai suffers from it. He and his patrol were caught in an ambush. Everybody but Avi died. I understand. It's not a problem.'

'No,' Uri said, firmly. 'It isn't. What is a problem is the woman who planned and executed an attack on Israeli soil that very nearly robbed me of one of my dearest friends, not to mention our prime minister. And then another in Scotland that … well, we know what happened there. Nurit is one of my most experienced field agents. She'll be helping you in the final stage of the operation.'

Gabriel nodded. He'd been about to argue, to say that he worked best on his own, but then stopped. Had he ever really worked best on his own? He'd run ops with Britta Falskog, with Eli, of course, with the boys back in the Regiment. Only a madman or a fool would turn down help from Mossad.

He nodded at Nurit. 'Thank you.'

She shrugged. 'Let's get it done first. Then you can thank me.'

He led them back to his house, stopping first to leave a thank-you note for Pera on her kitchen table, complete with a PS.

Maybe think about putting together a business plan. Partner.

* * *

The quartet of current and former intelligence operatives sat around Gabriel's rough-hewn wooden kitchen table. Coffee made, it was Uri who spoke first.

'Dowding is currently living on the outskirts of Halifax in West Yorkshire.'

Nurit produced a map from the holdall and spread it out on the table. She stabbed a finger down onto a red X.

'This is the house. It's detached, set in one-point-eight acres of land. Woodland to the east and west, a main road, the A58 along the southern border, open countryside for five miles across the valley to the north.'

'What's the security like?' Gabriel asked.

'Two armed police on the property at all times. Special Branch. Three shifts, changing at 7:00 a.m., 3:00 p.m. and 11:00 p.m. One man accompanies her wherever she goes. Her car is a silver Jaguar XJ. Armoured.'

'We think a sniper shot might be the best option,' Uri said, looking first at Don and then at Gabriel. 'She makes a regular weekly trip into Halifax. We've identified a number of suitable—'

'No,' Gabriel said quietly. 'We're not doing this long-range. I'm going to be there with her. I'm going to tell her why it's happening.'

Uri shook his head. 'It's too risky. My way is—'

'We're not doing it your way,' Gabriel said, leaning towards Uri. Keeping his voice level. 'We do it my way or not at all.'

He leaned back and held Uri's gaze. Seconds ticked by. Finally, Uri broke.

'I assume you have a plan, if you want to disregard mine? We had everything worked out, by the way. A location for the shooter, exfiltration, extraction. It would be a clean getaway.'

'No.'

'No? No, what?'

'No, I don't have a plan.'

Uri flapped his lips in exasperation.

'Look, Gabriel. This is serious. We are planning the assassination of a former prime minister. You can't just go and knock on her front door and blow her head off when she answers it.'

'Why not?'

Uri's eyes flashbulbed. Nurit merely looked amused.

'Why not? You'll be killed! Even assuming you can get through the Special Branch men before they shoot you, they'll have an armed response team after you in minutes. They'll gun you down.'

'I doubt that. Since her evil little conspiracy was taken down by a friend of mine, the British police have tended to arrest people rather than shoot them.'

News stories floated in front of him contradicting his assertion. A Brazilian student visiting the UK. A black rapper. He swallowed hard. 'Tended' was doing a lot of heavy lifting in the sentence he'd just uttered.

'If I may?' Don interjected. 'Like Nurit, Gabriel's a sound operator in the field. I've seen what he's capable of, as have you, Uri. A certain Iranian nuclear facility that no longer poses a threat to Israel? He also possesses excellent tactical skills, and if he wants to run things with more room for, what shall we call it, improvisation? Well, it's how he was trained. You can blame me for that.'

'It's true, Uri,' Gabriel said. '"Question your orders." We had that drilled into us from day one. The complete opposite of the green army. Why? Because if we knew *why* we were doing something, we could figure out a new way to achieve the objective if the original plan proved unworkable.'

'"No plan survives first contact with the enemy." Von Moltke,' Uri said.

'I prefer "Everyone has a plan until they get punched in the mouth." Mike Tyson,' Nurit said dryly.

Over the ensuing laughter, Uri patted the air for silence.

'OK, OK. We do it Gabriel's way. I assume you at least have a plan for getting back into the UK without alerting the authorities?'

'I have some false identities and the documentation to go with them.'

'From your days at the Department? You can't be sure they won't be red-flagged.'

Gabriel opened his mouth then closed it again. Uri was right.

'We could get ourselves smuggled in, then. Swim ashore from a RIB. I know the Suffolk coast pretty well.'

Uri nodded. 'You could do that, of course. But I have an easier way. If, that is, you think help from the Deputy Director of

Mossad leaves enough room for,' Uri made air quotes, 'improvisation.'

Gabriel nodded. 'Point taken. What did you have in mind?'

'Israeli passports. Nurit already has hers. We can produce yours at the embassy in Tegucigalpa. All I need is a digital photograph of you.'

Gabriel ran his fingers through his beard. 'Yes. That could work. And I have an idea.'

The rest of the meeting was spent discussing access to weapons once Gabriel and Nurit were inside the UK, and possible approaches to getting Gabriel close enough to Gemma Dowding and then out again.

At three, it broke up. Uri and Nurit drove back to Tegucigalpa with Don.

Gabriel went to find Pera.

He found her tending the little patch of vegetables – beans, squash, tomatoes – at the back of her house. She looked up as he arrived and smiled. But he saw the sadness there.

'How are they doing?' he asked, pointing at the tomatoes.

'They need a few more days before picking. Just as long as The Fury doesn't come, they'll be fine.'

'Listen, Pera, I'm leaving in the morning. And I don't think I'll be coming back.'

She came closer, held him by the arms, stared intensely into his eyes.

'Don't say that! You can't be sure. And what about my food truck? We'll be business partners. I'll need your help.'

He smiled. Brought her into an embrace. Felt her wiry arms tight around his chest.

'You'll be brilliant. I've tasted your cooking, remember.' He held her at arms' length. 'It's been great here, you know? Your friendship, well, it helped me over the worst of it after Eli died. I couldn't have coped without you and Santiago. I hope you know that.'

Tears streaked Pera's brown cheeks. 'Oh, Gabe, I'm going to miss you. Santiago, too. You're the nearest he's ever had to a dad.'

Gabriel had to swallow hard at that. The lump in his throat expanded to the size of a golf ball and was physically painful.

Something told him that the life he'd, briefly, enjoyed here in Santa Rosa was the closest he'd ever get to domestic bliss.

And now it was over.

47

LONDON – TWO DAYS LATER

His holdall slung over his shoulder, Gabriel waited in line, one traveller among hundreds, snaking their way inch by tortuous inch towards the row of immigration desks in the arrivals hall.

In front of him, a young couple bickered as they struggled to control their three children, none older than five he guessed. The woman had a baby strapped to her chest in an olive-green cotton sling, its long trailing straps knotted in the small of her back.

The infant regarded him over its mother's shoulder, blue eyes wide with curiosity. The eyelashes were long and curved. An upturned button nose, a little crusty with dried mucus. Had it been the one making all the noise on the long flight from LAX to Heathrow? It didn't matter. Gabriel had put noise-cancelling earplugs in and slept for most of the journey.

The baby kept clenching and flexing its left hand, digging its tiny nails into the frayed webbing holding its sling against its mother's body.

Gabriel was unable to tear his gaze away. Finally, not knowing what else to do, he smiled, raising a hand and twiddling his fingers in a wave. The baby tipped its head on one side, staring, entranced by the movement in front of its face. A string of transparent goo dripped from its lower lip. And then it smiled back at him. Pink gums, with, what, a white crescent of a tooth coming through?

The baby gurgled and its mother looked round. Initially her expression was suspicious, lips pursed, forehead creased, ready to warn off a predator or just an over-eager stranger.

'He's cute,' Gabriel said. 'Is he teething?'

'She's a she, actually,' she said, with a smile. 'Bit of a nightmare, to be honest. I hope she didn't ruin your flight.'

He shook his head. 'Not at all. I hope she wasn't in too much discomfort.'

The woman sighed. She had dark circles under her eyes.

'Let's just say I'll be glad when we're home.'

She looked down at his left hand, and the wedding ring he still wore.

'Lacey seems to like you. Do you have children of your own?'

He shook his head. 'We...it didn't happen for us.'

She looked confused. He felt guilty, using the past tense like that. But in the moment, he couldn't think of an answer that wouldn't lead to a question he knew he'd have no way of answering. And he realised, he would have to get used to answering that question, or a myriad of painful variations, for the rest of his life.

'I'm sorry,' she said.

The queue moved off, and she turned away from him. His phone buzzed and he took it out. A text from Uri.

Meet Nurit at 9:00 a.m. tomorrow. Caffé San Marco, Columbia Road, E2.

. . .

After another two hours in the queue, he stood in front of a tired-looking immigration officer in her glassed-in booth. Behind her and slightly to the left stood a man in his fifties. Silver hair and matching beard and moustache. Piercing blue eyes behind black-framed glasses. A watchful expression streets away from the blank stares of the men and women staffing the cubicles.

Gabriel wasn't sure which branch of the security services he belonged to. MI5, perhaps. Or the Met's counter terrorism command. Or another agency, deliberately kept quiet by the government, out of sight of the social media commentators, academic 'experts' and freelance journalists who thought they had a handle of the entire security apparatus just because they had Google and a few contacts inside Whitehall.

Was he looking for Gabriel? Had Gemma Dowding put out an alert? It didn't matter. Gabriel Wolfe, even if she suspected he wasn't dead, was a ghost. In his place, Eyal Abarbanel, a Sephardic Jew of Spanish and Portuguese extraction – Uri's idea, given Gabriel's features and colouring – who had been born in Israel after his parents immigrated from Madrid in the 1960s.

He handed her his passport, offered a brief smile, half-friendly, half-weary. A smile that said, *I'm tired, you're overworked, but I know you have a job to do so let's get on with it.*

She scrutinised the navy blue document. First the front cover, with the olive boughs and seven-branched menorah, plus the gold-blocked words, in Hebrew and English: STATE OF ISRAEL and PASSPORT. She opened it and turned to the photo ID page.

Gabriel's stomach twitched. It was natural. He doubted whether even the most hardened of spies, travelling on a genuine passport, could stand in front of an immigration officer and not experience just a *frisson* of nerves.

She looked from the ID page to Gabriel and back again. Then focused on his face again. His palms were sweating. He kept his right hand loosely clasped on the shoulder strap of his holdall, the left dangling by his side.

'Welcome to the UK, Mr Abarbanel. What is the purpose of your visit today?'

'Work,' he said. 'I'm a musician.'

She glanced at his hair. One of Pera's friends worked in a hairdressing salon in Bonito. Before he'd left Honduras, he spent four hours in her chair while she washed and cut his hair, before bleaching it and styling it into a slick, androgynous look. They'd debated what to do about his grizzled beard, in the end opting to bleach it, too, though trimming it down to a neat goatee.

'Oh yes? Are you in a band?'

He shook his head, keep the movement easy, relaxed. No stiff-necked jerk that would give away his anxiety to the hawk-eyed man behind her desk, who was now paying extra attention to Gabriel and his interaction with the immigration officer.

'Session musician. I'm playing on a new album. Have you heard of Adele?'

She beamed. 'Really? Awesome!'

He smiled back at her. He had no weapon. And even if he did, if she hit a panic button or summoned over the overwatch guy, it was game over. No way could he shoot his way out of a crowded airport, even if he wanted to. A horrific vision of the little baby – what was her name, Lacy? – hit by gunfire made him flinch involuntarily.

'Is everything OK?' the immigration officer asked.

'Reflux. Airline food, you know?'

'Yeah, tell me about it.' She took one final look into his face, then stamped the passport and handed it back to him. 'Enjoy your stay in the UK, Mr Abarbanel. Tell Adele I love her!'

'You got it,' he said, with a wink.

He walked past her, his booted feet on British soil once again. Now he just had to collect his luggage, which was a single battered silver Samsonite, and take the train into Central London. Breathing easier than he had for three hours, he turned right and headed for baggage reclaim.

As he turned to take the stairs, he glanced back at the silver-haired security guy. But he had lost interest and was strolling further down the line of booths, hands in pockets.

His case was the last to clatter off the conveyor belt onto the carousel. He dragged it behind him towards the exit, one chipped wheel rattling in a rhythmic tattoo on the glossy floor tiles. He looked up at the direction signs and, dodging a woman pushing a trolley laden with matching Louis Vuitton cases piled three or four high, headed for the trains.

A woman called out to him. 'Gabriel!'

He glanced round, then cursed himself for his stupidity. A young woman was standing ten feet away, hand inside her jacket. A muscular hand descended onto his right shoulder, fingers clamping into the soft flesh between neck and shoulder like an iron claw. Something hard dug painfully into his ribs. The silver-haired security guy had come up on Gabriel's blindside. He leaned close and murmured into Gabriel's ear.

'Easy way, you come with us for a little car ride. Hard way, we yell "armed police" and shoot you down right here. My spare nine finds its way onto your corpse and you're tomorrow's front pages and the day after's fish-and-chip wrapper.'

Gabriel let his shoulders slump, dropped into a defeated posture. Yes, he could take the guy's pistol off him and kill both him and the young woman no doubt gripping her own pistol tightly inside her neatly tailored suit jacket. But they wouldn't be working alone. And the collateral damage was too much to think about.

The young woman approached.

'Hands behind your back.' She zipped his wrists with plastic cable ties. *Definitely not police*, he thought. 'Let's go.'

The impression that he had fallen into the clutches of one of the more discreet branches of the British security apparatus was reinforced when he was gently but firmly steered into the back seat of an all-black Range Rover with tinted glass all the way round. Strictly illegal in the UK, where the police liked to be able to see who was driving a vehicle through the side windows. Obviously these guys had the kind of Get Out of Jail Free card that Gabriel and his fellow Department operatives had enjoyed the use of during their service.

With the young woman beside him and the silver-haired guy at the wheel, they moved off.

'Who are you guys?' he asked. 'I'm guessing not Five. Definitely not police, if you were really willing to shoot me on the spot back there. I'm going to go out on a limb and say some kind of back-channel outfit. A bit like the one I used to belong to. I'm guessing you know about the Department, right?'

Neither of the other two people in the car made a sound. They were well trained, he'd give them that.

They slowed for the roundabout that fed traffic onto the M4 motorway. From the slip road it was a short drive east into Central London and then, what? Interrogation? *Enhanced* interrogation? If they *did* know about his past, they'd know that he was very unlikely to break under torture. Or were they not interested in anything he might have to tell them? Plan B was to gun him down as a terror suspect. Was Plan A to murder him and dump his body in the Thames? Make it look like a suicide?

He needed to kill them both and get out of the Range Rover before it was too late.

The driver signalled left and took the exit. They joined the M4 heading west. *Away* from London.

This was bad.

This was very bad.

48

Gabriel's fear jacked up.

Not going into London meant either they were heading for some secret facility out in the countryside or they were going to deal with him out in the boonies and dump his corpse in a flooded gravel pit or ancient woodland. Maybe dangling at the end of a rope from a tree, somewhere it wouldn't be discovered for a couple of weeks.

He turned to the young woman, who now cradled a Glock 19 in her lap, the business end pointing at Gabriel's belly.

'Where are you taking me?'

Silence.

'Are you working for Gemma Dowding?'

Silence.

'Is that thing even loaded?'

Silence.

Gabriel smiled at her. 'That was a neat trick in Arrivals. Calling out my name, I mean. Did you ever see *The Great Escape*? The Gestapo pulled a similar move when Steve McQueen was getting on the bus. Said "Good luck!" in English and the fool answered, "Thank you".'

'Idiot. That was Gordon Jackson,' the driver said.

Gabriel smiled. Even from this angle he could see the man's jaw muscles bunch as he clenched his teeth.

'He *can* talk! So, come on. Where are you taking me? I hope you've got good security. Now there aren't any passengers to get in the way, I'm pretty sure I can take you and your pretty little sidekick here. Even with my hands tied behind my back. What's the plan, anyway? You going to torture me or just kill me and make it look like suicide?'

Every word was calculated to rile them. Especially the jibe at the young agent, who, Gabriel was sure, was bridling now at being thought a mere accessory.

'Brave talk,' she said. 'But we don't need to fake anything, do we? You very helpfully committed suicide already. As far as the outside world's concerned, you're already dead. As for Eyal Abarbanel, something tells me he only exists on a time-limited Mossad database entry. Once they know you've been burned they'll just erase you a little bit early.'

They were confident. Careless. Now they were out of London and on their way to their destination, they felt they could afford to be. And now they'd revealed their hand, as well. He was to be executed and his remains disposed of.

A horn sounded from behind the Range Rover. Three sharp, angry blasts. Gabriel swivelled in his seat, ignoring the cable ties biting into the thin skin on the insides of his wrists. A motorcyclist was weaving from side to side not twenty feet from the Range Rover's back bumper. Black leathers, black helmet, black visor.

'Idiot,' the driver said. 'Get back or I'll make you.'

He hit the brakes for a second, throwing Gabriel forwards against his seat belt. The distance between the bike and the Range Rover collapsed to ten feet before the bike dropped back, blasting its horn again and giving the driver the middle finger.

'Enemy?' the female agent asked.

'Arsehole, more like.'

Gabriel saw the rider toe the gear lever down and rip open the throttle. Exhaust screaming, the bike, all-black like its owner, swung right and overtook the Range Rover. As it drew level with the front, it slowed to match the Range Rover's speed. Beside Gabriel, the female agent was holding her pistol up, her left hand poised over the button to drop the side window.

The rider looked over, tapped the side of his helmet, then pulled away, shaking his head. His body language was clear. But he had one last trick up his sleeve. Clearing the front of the Range Rover, he leaned back, opened the throttle wide and pulled a huge wheelie, racing off with the front wheel spinning in mid-air, left hand trailing, middle finger upraised.

'You, too, prick,' the driver said.

The bike disappeared round a long, sweeping left-hand bend. The female agent peered ahead between the front seats.

'Slow down anyway. Give him a chance to get away from us. If he's still there we'll have to do something.'

'Whatever.'

The driver shrugged and slowed the Range Rover to forty-five for a minute or two. But then, as they exited another S-bend, he hit the brakes hard, bringing the big black SUV to a stop. Three hundred yards further on, the bike lay on its side, facing into the woods that bordered the road. The rider was on his back, arms and legs outflung. Not moving.

'Ha!' the driver said. 'What did I tell you. Go out and clear the road.'

'What if he needs an ambulance?'

'Our orders are clear. Deal with Wolfe, not act as paramedics to some dipshit biker with an ego bigger than his brains.'

'Why can't you go? That bike looks heavy.'

The driver swung round in his seat.

'Three reasons. One, I've got more years in than you. Two, I literally outrank you. And three, my sacroiliac joint's been giving me gyp since that little jaunt in Kosovo. So do me a favour and shift your arse, OK? We haven't got all day.'

'Fine. But you're buying the drinks tonight.'

He chuckled, deep in his chest. They were following a series of well-worn moves. Like an old married couple. Gabriel kept his eyes on the body splayed in the road. At best the rider had knocked himself unconscious, probably taking the final bend too fast. At worst, he'd be ending up on a mortuary slab somewhere, just another statistic.

The female agent climbed out of the car, holstering the Glock. She looked back in at Gabriel.

'Don't even think about it,' she said, glaring at him. 'Only two of his excuses were real.'

She slammed the door. The deep thunk reminded him of the SUV he'd stolen from Luis-David Casildo. Armoured, almost certainly.

'I'd listen to her, if I were you,' the driver said, without turning round. 'I know all about you and your Oriental voodoo. If I hear so much as a peep out of you, I'll do you right here. Are we clear?'

Gabriel didn't bother to respond. Why give his captor the satisfaction? He leaned back, trying to find a comfortable position for his cable-tied wrists.

What happened next took him by surprise. The man's arm swung round. He was so much faster than his heavy build would suggest. The movement was blurry. He'd punched Gabriel in the thigh.

But when the driver withdrew his fist, Gabriel caught a flash of shiny metal, streaked scarlet. Blood welled up, soaking his jeans. He'd been stabbed. The pain wasn't too bad. The blade had gone in directly over the scar from a bullet wound he'd sustained in Mozambique fighting a militia group called The Rock and Roll Boys. Most of the sensory nerves in that part of his leg were deactivated, never to regrow.

Grimacing nonetheless – the blow wasn't completely without impact – Gabriel locked eyes with the driver, who was grinning at him as he wiped the blade clean on a pristine white handkerchief.

'You're going to regret that.'

The driver laughed. 'Says the man currently tied up in *my*

Range Rover, with his blood leaking all over the leather upholstery thanks to *my* knife. OK, big shot, do your worst.' He tipped his head on one side. 'No? Not going to give me some bullshit Special Forces move? I thought not. You lot are all the same. Fine when you outnumber the enemy and you've got all the weapons. But then you're just shooting fish in a barrel. One on one? Nope. It's all revealed as the bullshit it really is.'

But Gabriel wasn't listening any longer. He was watching the scene playing out through the Range Rover's windscreen.

The female agent had reached the fallen rider. She prodded him with her toe. The supine rider was unresponsive. Gabriel's second option was looking more and more likely. She bent and grabbed him under the armpits and started hauling him off the road, swinging from side to side in an ungainly struggle with the deadweight.

While he watched her drag the body into some ferns at the side of the road, Gabriel clenched his teeth and twisted his wrists against each other, and the plastic cable ties. The pain overwhelmed the dull ache from his leg, which was still bleeding, though not badly. Obviously, the guy in the driver's seat knew a lot about causing damage to human bodies.

He felt the skin on his right wrist split first of all. A gleaming white wire of agony that encircled his arm and had him grunting with the effort of staying silent.

'Leg hurting you, is it?' the driver asked, his voice dripping with sarcasm. 'Don't worry, that's nothing compared to what's waiting for you.'

Ahead, the female agent dropped the rider into the ferns. Gabriel saw one black-leather arm flop down into the prehistoric-looking foliage. She stood and walked across the road towards the bike.

The skin on Gabriel's left wrist tore next, adding its own lancing agony to the burning in his other arm. His hands and wrists were slick with his own blood and he worked it between them, straining harder to weaken the bonds of the cable-ties.

People thought plastic was more efficient than steel or rope for immobilising captives. People were wrong. He began twisting his hands against each other, taking the strain on the bones of his arms. Master Zhao's voice came to him through the white-hot fire consuming his mind. '*Use the mantra against pain, Gabriel.*'

From somewhere deep down, words formed themselves into a coherent sequence he'd used many times before.

Pain passes like clouds on a windy day...

He looped the words into a Mobius strip – a twisted infinity symbol that cycled endlessly through his pain-speared brain – and carried on working his bloody wrists against the sharp-edged plastic.

The male agent gasped. Something strange was happening in the middle distance.

Halfway towards the bike, the female agent appeared to be having some kind of seizure. Her arms flew out to the sides and she shimmied her hips once, twice, three times. Then her head jerked back, blood spraying into the air, and in slow motion she collapsed onto the tarmac. It looked as though someone had detonated a bomb in her skull.

The biker appeared from the ferns. Clearly not dead, unless Gabriel was hallucinating from the pain of his wrists sawing against the cable ties. Something about the gait was off, though. It wasn't a man at all, but a woman. And she was raising a silenced pistol, aiming directly at the windscreen. The gun bucked in her hand and three white craters starred the glass, the impacts as loud as fireworks inside the cabin.

Swearing, the driver fought to get his own sidearm free of his shoulder holster. The rider was closer now, firing regularly, smashing more white-edged craters in the Range Rover's bullet-proof glass.

Figuring that his need to keep quiet had just disappeared, Gabriel let out a scream as he gave a final vicious twist to the cable ties. Something gave and they slipped by a few inches. Not enough to release him but that wasn't his plan.

The driver had his gun out now and was figuring out his

options. Get out and engage in a one-on-one firefight or sit tight. He'd forgotten the most obvious option. Barrel straight ahead, taking out the biker with his front bumper.

Gabriel lifted his hips and slid his screaming wrists under his backside, feeling the skin slip on the bloody upholstery. He brought his knees up to his chest and slipped his heels inside the loop of his arms. Working his wrists back and forth and drew them over his ankles, his shins and then, finally, with a relief so profound it brought tears to his eyes, his knees.

He was free.

Up front, the driver had obviously made his decision. Pistol in his left hand he reached for the door handle. He was going to open it a crack and start shooting through the gap. Not a bad strategy considering he was protected by a couple of tons of armour plating and bulletproof glass.

The biker fired once more then had to pause to reload. She was dead. Yelling in triumph, the driver pulled the handle and kicked the door wide open.

Gabriel lunged forward and looped his bloody hands over the padded headrest and down to encircle the man's unprotected throat. He yanked back, dragging the cable ties deep into the soft fold of flesh with its tracery of veins, arteries and the cartilage-ribbed windpipe. Emitting a harsh gurgle, the man flailed in his seat as Gabriel leaned back into the choke-hold, adrenaline neutralising the agony from his lacerated flesh.

With a massive bang, the pistol went off, sending a bullet crashing into the leather headlining. Four more shots followed, deafening Gabriel and filling the cabin with acrid blue smoke. The arm dropped. The pistol clattered off the wood-veneered central console into the passenger footwell. The gurgling faded to a wet hiss. Then stopped altogether. He flopped forward, dragging Gabriel with him.

The biker wrenched the door open. She produced a knife and slit the cable ties.

Gasping with the pain Gabriel sat back. She placed the suppressor against the man's chest and shot him dead, through the heart. It was a professional's move for sure. Never assuming an unmoving body, even one with a bloody trough sawn into its neck by cable ties, was dead. Making sure.

The assassin reached up and unsnapped the plastic catch of her helmet's chinstrap.

49

Gabriel nodded at his rescuer.

'I thought we were meeting tomorrow,' he said.

Nurit rolled her eyes.

'You'd have been dead if I'd stuck to Uri's plan.' She looked down at his wrists and winced. 'That looks bad. We need to get you patched up.'

'I'm fine. Get the bike off the road first. And the body. Then we need to go.'

She nodded and ran back to the motorcycle. Once she'd wheeled it off the road and into the trees she ran back to the corpse of the female agent and dragged it into the ferns where she'd been dumped herself.

She sprinted back to the Range Rover and between them they shoved the dead driver into the passenger seat so Nurit could take the wheel. A few hundred metres ahead she pulled off the tarmac onto a track that led into the woods. She followed it until she reached a small clearing littered with the spiky, crunchy shells of beechnuts.

She killed the engine.

'Wait here. I need to get rid of him,' she said, nodding at the dead driver slumped in the passenger seat.

Back in the car, after covering the body with vegetation, she put the dead man's pistol on the dashboard. 'We can use that. He had a spare mag on him. Now show me where you're hurt.'

He held up his wrists. Dark blood flowed over the ragged edges of the lacerations.

'It's superficial, but it's still bad. You did that yourself?'

'I had to. They were going to kill me.'

'I've got a first-aid kit on the bike. Can you wait here?'

He nodded.

'Just don't take too long, OK?'

Nurit left him in the Range Rover and ran back towards the bike, staying amongst the trees. He held his arms up above his head to slow the bleeding. Now the pain from the stab-wound in his leg made itself known. He closed his eyes and breathed deeply and slowly, finding the mantra against pain again. He repeated it out loud to himself until he fell into a half-sleep.

The bike engine woke him. He picked up the dry crunch of Nurit's running footsteps as she arrived back with the first aid kit.

She climbed in beside him.

'I think it might need more than some antiseptic and a plaster,' he said as he took in the zipped black nylon pouch in her hand. 'Please tell me that's not just something you picked up from Boots.'

Nurit favoured him with a wry smile.

'Mossad standard field-issue. We'll be fine.'

She unzipped the pouch and laid it on the seat between them. In its left-hand side, threaded under black elastic loops were three morphine injectors. Beside them, other clear plastic vials with labels printed in Hebrew. On the facing side, sutures, gleaming stainless steel artery forceps, needle-nosed bullet extractors, a pair of red-handled trauma shears and a packet of QuikClot sponges. Plus assorted field dressings and two tourniquets.

Nurit went for one of the morphine injectors. Gabriel put out a hand, dripping blood onto her own wrist.

'No. No morphine. It's not that bad.'

'You sure? I need to put some stitches in your wrists.' She glanced at the blood-soaked patch on the front of his thigh. 'Stab wound?'

'It's not deep. He was just showing me who was boss.'

'It's going to hurt, Gabriel.'

'I need to be sharp.'

She sighed. 'OK, then. Let's do this. Wrists first.'

Twenty minutes later, during which time Gabriel had remained fully conscious, Nurit taped the final dressing in place over his thigh. His mind was overwhelmed with pain but he knew that would clear far quicker than the mushy-brained side effects of the morphine. He pulled his trousers back up and belted them.

Nurit looked at him critically.

'Your clothes are ruined.'

'Sadly, all my blending-in outfits were in my suitcase. This is all I have till I can get to a shop.'

'Better if I do it. You'd draw too much attention. You look like someone tried to feed you into a wood chipper.'

'Got some paper?'

She produced a black notebook and a ball-point pen. Gabriel scribbled down his sizes.

She glanced at the list. 'Get under cover. I'll drive to the nearest town. I think it's Windsor. I'll get some supplies, too. Food, water. Regular painkillers?'

'If you wouldn't mind.'

She grinned. 'You Brits and your ironic humour. No, I "wouldn't mind". Hang tight. I'll be back as soon as I can.'

Gabriel scanned the starred and cratered windscreen, the bullet-punctured roof lining and the bloody upholstery.

'Park it somewhere discreet. This thing looks worse than I do.'

He clambered out, swearing as he caught his left wrist on the edge of the door frame. Behind him, Nurit started the Range Rover and pulled away, its armour-burdened weight smashing the fragile beechnut cases to powder beneath its wide tyres.

He walked deeper into the woods, finally finding a hide he

liked the look of: an old oak with a fork in its fat, gnarled trunk. Gingerly, lest his stitches pull out, he climbed into the deep V of the fork and settled in to wait.

Nurit would have done a good job of hiding the corpses. And it would be a while before they started to smell, too. He reckoned they had a few hours minimum before anyone might chance upon them.

He closed his eyes and tried to sharpen his hearing, scanning across high and low frequencies, trying to pick out anything abnormal. But all he heard were birds singing and, from somewhere over to his left, the soft, chirruping babble of a stream. A breeze picked up, rustling through the oak's dense canopy. He inhaled deeply, filling his nostrils with the mulchy, sappy smell of an English woodland in full summer costume.

Could he risk relaxing? Just for a few minutes? He really needed to think. Clearly Dowding was smarter than he'd given her credit for. And still able to muster some darkest-of-the-dark black ops people to pick him up at Heathrow, despite his disguise and false passport. Maybe she'd even had the road closed: it would explain the lack of traffic.

'Where's she going to hide? That's the question.'

Smudge had climbed up and was squatting beside him on a thick branch that jagged out and then down, resting its gnarled elbow on the ground.

'Could be her place in Yorkshire. But if she knows you're coming, maybe she's in the wind.'

Smudge's South London tones made Gabriel smile. It felt good to have the old crew around him.

'Uri'll help me find her,' Gabriel said. 'Doesn't matter where she runs to, he's not going to give up until she's dead. And neither am I.'

Smudge held up his hands. 'I never said you were, boss. Just, you're still leaking claret and maybe a couple of days' R&R'll help get you match fit again.' His eyes widened. 'Sshh! You hear that? Someone's coming. You better find cover.'

Gabriel tried to straighten, couldn't. His body was wedged

into the fork of the oak's massive branches. He braced against them and pushed. He watched, horrified, as his hands sank into the rough, fissured bark, which regrew like creeping mould, locking his fingers in place. Thick tendrils of ivy twined around his ankles, shins, knees, constricting the blood supply and flattening his legs against the tree's own limbs.

He watched, powerless as Gemma Dowding strode into the clearing, a double-barrelled shotgun at her hip.

'I'll get her, boss, don't worry,' Smudge said then slid away, dropping to the ground without a sound.

Dowding's first blast took Smudge high in the chest. The shot blew a hole right through his torso. Forehead creased in puzzlement, Smudge looked down and poked his entire right hand into the gaping cavity.

She fired again. His head burst, releasing a swarm of black flies that buzzed upwards angrily, surrounding Gabriel and flying into his nose, his eyes, his mouth.

Dowding looked up at Gabriel and grinned crookedly. Her lower jaw dropped away from its hinges and he screamed as her long, wet, pink tongue flopped down to lie against her chest. She broke the shotgun and pushed two blood-red cartridges home.

Britta rushed towards her, only to receive both barrels full in the face. Her skull exploded and then, as if an unseen viewer had paused a video, the red, grey and white cloud of tissue fragments hung, motionless, in the air.

Dowding looked past Britta's dying body, up at Gabriel.

'You can't stay up there for ever, Gabriel. And I'll be waiting for you when you come down.'

He strained the muscles in his neck to grind his head round on his spine. Just far enough to lock eyes with Eli, who'd appeared in the centre of the clearing.

'Run,' he hissed out. 'Before it's too late.'

She smiled sadly at him. 'It's already too late, my darling. Forget Dowding. Just for a couple of days. Come and see me. I miss you.'

'Say goodbye to your lady-love, Gabriel,' Dowding crowed at

him from the foot of the tree, one leg resting on a moss-covered root that rose out of the leaf litter like the back of a sea serpent.

He screamed out a desperate, 'No!' but it was too late. Dowding fired upwards, hitting Eli in the abdomen.

Gabriel jerked awake, almost falling from the fork in the trunk as his convulsive jerk robbed him of his balance. His forehead sheened with sweat he lay back, eyes closed and steadied his breathing. For a second his nostrils filled with the smells of lemon and sandalwood, then it was gone.

Dream-Eli was right. It wouldn't be long before Dowding figured out that her hit team had screwed up. They'd have missed a call-in, or a text. Some pre-arranged signal to let her know the job was done. She'd disappear while she followed a new line on her flowchart.

Is the target dead?
No.
Is the team still active?
No.
Brief new team.

The next time, he'd be ready. And this time, he'd make sure he took at least one of them alive. Use whatever methods he needed to extract their boss's location from them. Until then, he could vanish himself. Scalpay was a good two days' travel. And he had the perfect way to reach the island without tripping any of Dowding's early warning systems.

50

HALIFAX

When she needed to think, Gemma Dowding always headed for the same place. Set in acres of rolling, hilly parkland, Shibden Hall was more impressive than Chequers, the grace and favour residence she'd just lost. She preferred its rugged architecture and the soaring hills beyond its landscaped grounds to the manicured Buckinghamshire countryside.

Holidaymakers, local families with young children, history buffs, fans of a BBC drama series: all flocked here to soak up the atmosphere, walk along the lakeshore or traipse around the interior, oohing and aahing as each new room revealed its treasures.

She'd dyed her hair a fiery shade of red, and wore a black baseball cap pulled low over her eyes, themselves shielded by oversized Jackie O sunglasses. In black and navy running gear, topped off with a nylon windcheater, she was about as unrecognisable as it was possible to get.

As she cast an eye over her fellow trippers, she reflected that people were far less interested in what ex-politicians were up to than their advisers and security personnel officers claimed. Their interests were more…boring. Getting to the front of the boat-hire queue. Dragging their kids off the swings so they could go inside. Feeding bread to the ducks. Any one of these simple activities loomed far larger than the doings of a disgraced ex-prime minister.

In some ways, it gave her comfort. Knowing that her newfound anonymity was more effective than an invisibility cloak. But part of her still grieved for the world of privilege they had forced her to give up. She wanted to grab an old couple just meandering down the steep grassy slope beside her and yell into their startled faces: 'I used to have dinner with the President of the USA!'

Instead she turned her head away and ignored their friendly greeting as they passed her.

Her anonymity also allowed her to dispense with the Special Branch escort. He'd protested, somewhat half-heartedly, she thought, that his orders were to keep her in sight at all times. To which she'd responded that he could take a hike to the other end of the park then and watch her through binoculars if he was that worried.

Alone, shielded from the gaze of any curious passers-by by the long bill of her cap, she looked at the screen of her phone for the hundredth time.

No messages.

It should have been done by now.

There should have been a two-word text emblazoned across that shiny black rectangle of glass.

Pack headless.

It had been Orrin's idea. Orrin was the man Dmitri had assigned to the task of finally eliminating Gabriel Wolfe. He'd grinned as he suggested it, no doubt pleased with his wit. He'd even started to explain it before she'd shut him down with a sharp rebuke. 'I get it. Wolves live in packs. Headless equals dead. Just get it done and let me know when you have.'

Only he hadn't, had he? That was the only meaning she could ascribe to the absence of a text. If they'd lost Wolfe, they'd have let her know. Given her an updated plan.

She'd told Orrin to be careful. That Wolfe was no ordinary target. And Orrin had just smiled. Patted her on the shoulder, even; an unearned familiarity for which she'd had to fight down a sudden violent urge to slap him.

'Relax. I've met his type before. They think they're superheroes because they know how to kill a man with their bare hands or blow up a truck with a box of fireworks. *They're* the ones who're complacent. I'll bring you his ears to prove it.'

And now, presumably, he was lying dead somewhere. In a compactor at a scrapyard, probably, or dissolving in a vat of acid on some abandoned industrial estate.

She clamped her lips and strode on. Her destination, a distant grove of trees, their upper branches swaying in the wind that was taking the edge off the day's heat.

'You're here for me, aren't you, Gabriel?' she murmured. 'And now you know I was expecting you. What's your next move?'

She reached a trio of silver birches, mature enough that the smooth white bark of their trunks was split and corrugated. Sat with her back to one of them.

What would Wolfe do next? Where would he go, knowing she had eyes on him?

'Where would *you* go, if you were him?' she asked a blackbird as it hopped closer, pinning her with its yellow-rimmed gaze. 'You've got nothing left here.'

The bird cocked its head to the right, its egg-yolk beak catching the sun.

'I've got *one* thing left.'

She started. Unsure whether Wolfe had spoken, or the bird had, or she'd just drifted into a micro-nap. Since taking on the job she'd spent her whole life aiming for, she'd learned to snatch as little as a minute's sleep between appointments.

The bird was right, though. Wolfe would need to stay under the radar. But in the whole of the British Isles, there was one place that still meant something to him.

The place where he'd left his wife.

Was it really that simple? Was he going to head north for a bolthole where he could regroup and plan his next move?

Foolish boy.

51

The burble of the Range Rover's engine shook Gabriel out of a half-sleep.

Nurit was back with a rucksack containing clothes, supplies and, to his surprise, a set of cordless hair clippers.

'What are they for?' he asked her once he'd changed into the outfit she'd bought for him from an army surplus store in Reading.

'You're a bit too recognisable with that hair. Cutting it's easier than dying it brown again. Go and sit on that log over there. I charged them in the library.'

He complied, head hanging down, watching as clumps of white-blonde hair tumbled from the clippers to land at his feet. While Nurit worked, buzzing his blonde hair down to his scalp, he scuffed the evidence into the leaf litter. Maybe it would end up softening a bird's nest somewhere the following spring.

The goatee followed. He rubbed at his stubbled chin and top lip.

'How do I look?'

She wrinkled her nose.

'Like a neo-Nazi, but it can't be helped. I got you something, though. It might help.'

From the depths of the rucksack she pulled out a bubblegum-pink plastic bag, on the outside of which was the slogan, *Ella's Hair: Change Your Look!*

Inside was a reddish-brown wig. He pulled it out and flipped it onto his head. Nurit tugged and tweaked, jerking Gabriel's head this way and that, until she was satisfied.

'Come and see.'

The man staring back at Gabriel from the Range Rover's wing mirror was still recognisably him. But from the back, or at a distance, the disguise might fool someone looking for a blonde, Israeli session musician. It wasn't much, though. Not when Gemma Dowding had who-knew-what kind of killers for hire after him.

As if reading his mind, Nurit produced a pair of Ray-Bans, some tortoiseshell-framed glasses with plain lenses and a grey cotton bucket hat.

'More options. That's if you're still set on going solo?'

'I am. And thanks.'

'Uri's not happy. I spoke to him while I was shopping.'

'Did he order you to stay with me?'

She smiled. 'No.'

'Then he's not that unhappy. Taking her out on British soil poses all kinds of problems I'm sure he'd rather not have to deal with. This way, even if I'm caught, or killed, it's just a rogue British security operative with a grudge. No diplomatic incident, no high-level shitstorm—'

' – and no posting to the admin department for the rest of my career.'

'Exactly.'

'So what now? Where are you going to look for her?'

Gabriel didn't answer at once. He pictured a windswept island in the Outer Hebrides. Terns, shearwaters and guillemots wheeling over the surf. A grassed-over grave whose location only he knew.

'I'm not. She wants me dead. She knows I want *her* dead. And she knows I won't stop until one of us gets their way.' He stared off into the woods. 'I'm going to wait for her to come to me.'

'Where?'

'The place I left Eli.'

'How do you know she'll come?'

'She's a clever woman. She'll work it out. I'm going to wait there until she arrives. It could take a day, it could take a week. Or a year. But she'll turn up. I know she will.'

Nurit frowned. 'It doesn't sound like much of a plan. What if she brings more mercs with her?'

'She's tried that twice already. It didn't work either time. Like I said, she's a clever woman. And she's a politician. She won't waste resources giving a failed strategy a third chance. She'll try to talk me out of it. Offer me a deal. Money, power, freedom.'

Nurit shrugged.

'What do I tell Uri?'

'Tell him to keep an eye on the classifieds in the Jerusalem Post.'

'That's it?'

'That's it.'

Gabriel refused Nurit's offer of a lift to the motorway. She must have half-expected this; the rucksack she'd bought was stuffed with everything a man might need to survive on his wits for days. She handed him a bundle of cash and squeezed her hand around his to fold his fingers down over the shiny plastic notes.

'Avenge her, Gabriel. And stay safe.'

Then she kissed him quickly on the cheek, left, right, left, and was swinging her right leg over the bike's saddle seconds later.

He watched her go, consulted the mapping app on the phone she'd bought him, and began walking north.

* * *

Riding his thumb, it took Gabriel three days to reach the Outer Hebrides. As Terry Fox, a persona he'd adopted more than once when undercover, he'd caught his final ride with a truck delivering fish food to a salmon farm in Stornoway.

'Cheers, Terry,' the driver said, offering his hard, dry hand to shake. 'Enjoy the birdwatching. You've come an awful long way so I hope you won't be disappointed.'

Gabriel climbed down from the cab, shouldered his daysack and struck off, heading south. It was a thirty-five-mile walk from Stornaway to Tarbert, the nearest town to Scalpay. He could have chosen a more direct route from Skye, and avoided an arduous tab, but this served his needs better.

At nine that evening, he arrived, footsore, on the outskirts of the town. The ferries didn't start running until the following morning. He ate a sandwich and an apple, finished his bottle of water and settled down in his sleeping bag in a wind-scooped hollow among the heather.

After a dreamless sleep, he awoke to the cries of seabirds. He packed up, erased all trace of his occupancy of the heather nest and walked into Tarbert. A cafe was open and he ordered a coffee and a full Scottish breakfast, including square lorne sausage and the fried potato pancakes called tattie scones.

'Is it a holiday you're here for?' the waitress asked him as she brought the bill.

He smiled up at her. 'Birdwatching.'

'Well you'll have a wonderful time, then. I heard someone from the mainland logged a Golden Eagle last week.'

'Fingers crossed, then, eh?'

She smiled. Pretty. 'Aye. Fingers crossed.'

She took his money. He left another note on the table and left while she was at the till.

52

SCALPAY

Avoiding the bridge and its security cameras, Gabriel paid a local fisherman to take him across from Tarbert to Scalpay, the busy outboard motor putting paid to conversation for the short journey. The arrangement suited them both, the fisherman clearly someone who preferred his own company and for whom only the offer of two hundred pounds had tempted him.

Ashore again on the beach where he'd found Eli hiding beneath a ruined wooden boat, Gabriel walked inland immediately. He had to fight down the waves of nausea and anxiety competing in his breast for breathing space.

Over to his left, the abandoned house where they'd held out against Kevin Bakker's team of mercenaries still stood. Ravaged by heavy machinegun fire and the blowback from Claymore anti-personnel mines, it was surrounded by a cordon of iron stakes, tied to which were wind-torn streamers of red-and-white incident tape. He walked closer. The snapping tape was printed with a repeated message: DANGER! – UNEXPLODED ORDNANCE – DO NOT ENTER. For good measure, they'd hammered red-and-white signs into the ground. Each bore a skull-and-cross-bones motif and a single word. MINES!

He was sure the clean-up team would have emptied Bakker's subterranean armoury of anything that might conceivably explode, but the warning would keep the curious at bay. Even those most eager to demonstrate how edgy they were on social media would draw the line at getting blown to pieces for a few likes.

Passing the house on its southern side, he made his way to the shallow gully where he'd buried Eli.

A football-sized rock marked the spot. He'd scratched nothing into its grey-white sides. Made no obvious markings that might alert a birdwatcher to the significance of the site. But, on his hands and knees, leaning so close he could smell a faint metallic tang from the crust of lichens, he half-closed his eyes and let the blobs of yellow coalesce into a single initial. After burying Eli, he'd used the point of a knife to delicately cut away some of the lichen, leaving a disjointed E only he would recognise.

The turf he'd transferred and laboriously woven into the existing grass at the grave's edges had taken strongly. Wild flowers poked their pink and white blooms through it on tiny yet robust stalks, the better to keep themselves out of the wind while still attracting pollinating insects. As he knelt there, a gold and black hoverfly darted in from his right side and alighted, briefly, on the yellow centre of a daisy before zipping off again.

'Hi, Eli,' he said, rocking back on his heels. 'It's nearly over. I think she's coming for me here. It's the only move for her that makes any sense. Unless she wants to live the rest of her life looking over her shoulder.'

He looked around, hoping her ghost would appear to him here. In the most appropriate moment. At the most precious place to him of all. But he was alone. He inhaled deeply. Maybe she'd appear to him as a scent in the air, then. But all he could detect was the salt and iodine smell of the beached heaps of kelp, brought to him on the warm southerly breeze.

As a fighting man, Gabriel had been trained by a succession of instructors to develop, enhance and maintain the highest levels of situational awareness. From the simple drill of his days in basic training – *'presence of the abnormal, absence of the normal'* – to advanced techniques never publicised in the glossy PR documentaries or TV adaptations of Special Forces veterans' memoirs.

But here, at his wife's grave, he forgot it all. An error that was about to cost him dearly.

The scuff of boot on rock was audible enough. But Gabriel didn't hear it. Or if he did, his brain refused or was unable to process it into useable intel.

Then the visitor spoke, and her voice penetrated the fog of grief.

'I knew you'd come.'

He got to his feet and turned round.

'Hello, Gemma.'

'Hello, Gabriel.'

She had her hands thrust deep into the pockets of a windcheater. The right pocket looked lumpy. Like she had her fist balled up in there. She looked tense, eye muscles taut, mouth a grim line.

He shifted his stance, just a little. Right foot ahead of left. Torso twisting in the same direction, Not much. Just enough. His pistol was in his daysack. He needed to get to it. But he'd not been expecting her to contact him so quickly.

She must have been waiting for him in the house. Safe inside the cordon. A black widow spider in her lair. He'd lost his edge. Lost it a while back. In Honduras. Relied on anger and grief and helplessness, and a death wish in the face of it to get him through.

He spread his hands wide. 'Come to offer me a deal, or to kill me?'

'Would you take a deal?'

He shook his head. 'You know I wouldn't.'

'I know,' she said, pulling her right hand free. And with it, a subcompact pistol.

A Glock G43X. Nice little weapon. Easy to conceal, nothing to snag on a pocket on its way out. Perfect for a novice shooter. And, at this sort of range, as deadly as it needed to be.

She held it out in front of her, both hands wrapped round the butt in a clumsy grip no firearms instructor would ever sanction. The pistol, though, was steady and the look in her eyes said everything.

No time to think. To bargain. To try and hypnotise her.

This was a woman with everything to lose and the will to do anything to prevent that happening. No way could he reach the pistol in the daysack.

Only time to act.

He glanced above her head and to the right, registered the minute movement in her eyes as she followed his gaze involuntarily. He twisted left and lunged at her, covering the eight feet of air between them in half a second.

53

Muzzle-flashes. Flat bangs as she fires, one, two, three...

She's emptying the magazine in panic, her finger spasming on the trigger. He hears one bullet whine past his left ear. Close enough to feel the red-hot metal.

She's missed with every shot. Not really surprising. He met a contractor once, back in the sandbox. Got ambushed by a jihadi and emptied an entire magazine from point black range, missed every time. Would've died except the sniper on overwatch took his man out with an *un*-panicked shot to the head.

Click...click...click.

A firing pin descending on an empty chamber.

As he rears up to strike at her throat, the black barrel swings round. A desperate move. But a lucky one. The metal catches him above the eye, opens a cut. Vision, red.

He reels back. Disorientated. His heel catches in the turf and he goes over, toppling onto his back. His head smashes against Eli's grave marker. Black curtains swing shut over his vision. In the narrowing gap he sees Dowding running.

Men are shouting. Not panicking. Not yet.

'Contact!'

'I need ammo!'

'Medic! MEDIC!'

'Ammo!'

'Wolfe, with me!'

He's up. Running. Rifle held up. Spitting bullets at the unseen enemy. Jesus, it's loud. Thundercracks of heavy weapons firing. The lightning of muzzle flashes. Smoke drifting across the battlefield.

Hard to tell friend from foe.

There's Smudge, half-hidden by a ruined Humvee. RPG-scarred, blackened and burnt. He's pinned down, burning through mag after mag after mag, bloody teeth bared in a ferocious warrior's grin.

Ahead, he sees her. Heading away from the fighting. He fires from the hip. A short burst. Misses. He gives chase but this ground is treacherous. Where did the desert go? This is all green. Who has grass in the sandbox?

Another burst, another, then he's out. Pats his pockets. No more mags. Discards his rifle. A soldierly sin, but it's dragging him down. Anyway, he wants Dowding to feel it when the time comes. To know why she has to die. Because of *her*. Eli. The IDF girl.

He was going to ask her out. Once the fighting was over, obviously. She's pretty, but more than that, smart. Funny. Holds her own in the drinking games. She drank Daisy under the table that first night at Camp Bastion. God, how they laughed.

He stumbles, then regains his footing. The sky's lightening. The tawny umbrella they've been living under for weeks is splitting along its seams, letting sunshine and a sapphire blue sky shine through. Wisps of white cloud, seabirds crying above the noise of the sea.

The sea: he can smell it as he runs after her. That shushing rhythm as the waves climb up the beach before retreating, only to try again and again, reminding him of family holidays when Dad could get time off work and they'd fly to Bangkok and on to an island, or occasionally back to England, setting out a tartan blanket and a windbreak at Broadstairs or Bournemouth. Ice creams, donkey rides, paper flags on cocktail sticks poked into the top of sandcastles.

He shakes his head. This is all wrong. He's not there. Not in the suck, either.

The shouts of his comrades are losing definition, pitch-sliding upwards, no words just drawn-out cries. Seabirds? Here? No. Not here, here isn't the sandbox. Here is…

…is…

…is Scalpay. Shit! That was a bad one. He looks around. He's on a hill. He recognises it. It's the same one where Kevin Bakker hit the clacker on the Claymore he had strapped to his chest. Blew himself in half.

Mossy ground, grey rocks studding the green-grey grass like the knobs of spines poking through wizened flesh. A couple of low-growing trees, their spindly branches smeared sideways by the wind, whipping in its grasp now, straight down all the way from the Arctic.

There's no way off the island without a boat. And he didn't see anyone on the Tarbert side. Maybe she was going to call for extraction once she'd ambushed him.

He crests the hill and there, not five hundred yards away, he spots her. Not running, but staggering, hand clutching her side. No bullet-wound, just a stitch. Politico-training probably doesn't involve a huge amount of PT.

Gritting his teeth he races down the slope after her, the gradient increasing steeply so that he ends up running in seven-league boots, each step more of a leap as he tries to spot his landings to avoid the lumpy boulders ready to break a leg on contact.

'Gemma!' he screams out.

She turns, stumbles, windmills her arms out then spins round as her left ankle folds over.

Miraculously, she's still holding the dinky little subcompact. She raises it and for a split-second he's staring down the barrel, closing the distance between them and wondering whether she found time to reload. But there's no time to take evasive action so he ducks and keeps running.

Her trigger finger crooks, and the knuckle whitens.

He flinches, but the gun's still empty.

And then he reaches her, snatches the pistol out of her hand and spins it away, towards a trio of boulders, hears its metallic crack as it bounces and lands among them with a soft thump.

Her chest is heaving. Her eyes, wide.

'Don't,' she says. 'Please. I'll do anything you say. Confess. Hold a press conference. Just, don't kill me. I don't deserve to die. Everything I did, I did for my country.'

He looks at her for a long time, then. But the face he's seeing isn't Gemma Dowding's. It's Eli's. Her greeny-grey eyes. Sensuous lips, cocked in a half-smile.

'Come with me,' he says. 'I'm tired.'

He takes her in his arms and leads her to one of the low-growing trees, and eases her down with him to sit, like lovers, his back against the trunk, her leaning back against him.

54

Pleased with his morning's work so far, Iain MacAulay crests the low hill, on his way to check on the small but growing colony of Manx Shearwaters on the south side of the island. Nobody but him on Scalpay today, it seems. It's how he likes it. His wife calls him a misanthrope and he always replies in the same way.

'I don't *hate* people, darling. I just prefer the company of birds.'

His job, as a warden employed by a large nature charity, allows him the freedom to do what he wants. When he isn't monitoring the birds, he writes poetry, mostly on the same subject: the natural beauty he finds everywhere he goes on Scalpay and the other islands that form his 'beat'.

As he begins his descent towards the colony's roosting site, he stops.

What on Earth? On the flat ground between him and the shearwaters, a couple have picked that very place to stop for a cuddle.

He feels suddenly embarrassed to be confronted with such an open display of affection and hangs back, watching. If they've noticed him, they give no sign. Feeling guilty, even as he does it, he slips into the cover of a tall standing stone, left over, so goes the local legend, by the Vikings. And he watches.

The man sits with his back to the tree's arthritic trunk. The woman reclines against him, nestled between his outspread legs. He's draped his right arm across her chest, the elbow crooked so he can cup her left shoulder.

With his poet's eye, Iain appraises them carefully, noting posture, eye contact, a thousand tiny details.

And yes, in some ways, their pose does resemble the unselfconscious physical intimacy of two people in love.

But as he looks closer, other details reveal themselves to him.

Her head, turned to her right so she might catch sight of her lover's face, stands on corded neck muscles, the tendons straining beneath her pale skin.

Then there is his *left* arm. Surely a lover would use it to caress, not to brace his right, creating a fulcrum so he might exert greater force on her neck? Her head is prevented from returning to a more natural angle by his biceps, which press hard against her cheek.

Her chest is heaving in the approved manner. As if she is experiencing the breathlessness of first love. *First* love? Neither of them will see forty again. Then there is the wildness in her eyes, stark white around the irises, that suggests the cause of her heaving chest might be more physical than emotional. In *his* eyes, there is a look that suggests he has experienced, at least once in his life, the variety of pain that ages a man.

Her feet, shoeless, are backpedalling at the earth as if she is struggling to find enough purchase to push herself up and over him. He lifts his heels and brings them down inside the V of her legs, pinning them to the ground.

The woman looks vaguely familiar. Though the cap and the dirt on her face make it hard to discern her features. Her lips move.

The man seems to listen, then bends his head so that his mouth is a few centimetres from her right ear. He says something to her. A lover's entreaty to be his for ever? Or perhaps an earthier suggestion. In any case, it is delivered through taut lips and bared teeth.

There is something unsettling about the intensity of their embrace. A stifled passion that leaves Iain unsure whether to advance and ask whether everything is all right, or retreat, anxious not to trespass on the emotions of others.

He has never been a bold man. He averts his eyes, turns around and retreats. He can always check on the shearwaters later.

* * *

Her legs tense beneath Gabriel's, Gemma Dowding opens her mouth and croaks out a question.

'You wouldn't kill a woman, Gabriel. Would you?'

In her tone she is aiming, he supposes, for emotion. Some semblance of human feeling that might arouse pity in him. But in her cold grey eyes he sees nothing but a machine, calculating odds, assessing strategies.

Gabriel leans over her and whispers the last words she will ever hear, as the remaining seconds of her life, seven in all, tick by.

'Why not, Gemma? You did.'

Bracing his arms against each other, to tighten his grip, he looks away from her, towards the treeline. Long-winged birds, fulmars, maybe? Gannets? Anyway, they fill the air with their cries, too rough to be called song.

Against this noisy background, the dry snap is barely audible. Gabriel hears it. Of course he does. Feels it, too.

It is over. Gemma Dowding is dead. Eli is avenged.

He leans back, closes his eyes, searches in his mind for that calm, quiet place where he can find her.

* * *

That evening, over an early dinner with Helen, his wife of many years, a small glass of red as it's a Saturday, Iain tells her the story.

He gives voice to his puzzlement, even admitting to a nagging sense of doubt.

'Maybe I *should* have intervened, after all.'

She leans across the table and takes his hand in hers. Searches for a word or two to reassure him.

'I'm sure it was nothing, darling,' she says with a smile, her beautiful island accent lulling him as it always does. 'Love makes folk do strange things.'

He smiles at her wisdom. Sips his wine.

But the image, the way the man locked the woman's thrashing legs under his own, will stay with him for the rest of his life.

55

JERUSALEM

Uri Ziff sipped the strong coffee his wife had just placed in front of him, then turned, as he had been doing every day, to the classified section of the *Jerusalem Post*.

His eyes skittered over the small ads, ignoring the used cars, offers of babysitting, lonely hearts, requests for softball players, rooms to let, and prayers. Looking for the message from Gabriel. Not finding it.

He sighed. Another morning when he'd go into the office with that small burden of anxiety still lodged in his chest.

But then, tucked away in a corner, where all but the most diligent of searchers would miss it, he saw what he'd been looking for. And, as he read the short text, the tightness that had encircled his heart for the past few weeks eased, as if someone had cut him out of an overtight Kevlar vest.

Eli Schochat-Wolfe

Rest in peace, at last
1991-2023
G

That date. It was out by a year. Eli had died in 2022.

Uri nodded with quiet satisfaction. Eli couldn't rest while her murderer was at large. Now she could.

He rose from the table, kissed his wife, and went to work.

56

HONDURAS

Esperanza rolled up the gaily painted shutter – palm trees and a bright yellow sun alongside the words, 'Pera's Place'. The old VW Camper Van was fully restored now and she could drive it from home to the markets and local villages where she sold her street food.

She'd have a few minutes before the first of her customers arrived looking for a coffee and a taco, a slice of honey cake or some fried plantain. She was slicing avocados when someone knocked on the counter.

'Is it too early to get a chicken baleada?'

Her eyebrows shot up and with a grin as wide as the serving hatch she turned round to greet her business partner.

'Gabe! You're back.'

He smiled.

'Couldn't go into business without checking the merchandise, now could I?'

While Pera assembled his breakfast, Gabriel turned away and leaned his back against the van's side. White clouds scurried across the sky as if late for an appointment with the distant mountains. High above him a large black bird of prey soared, ascending on the thermals that acted like express elevators for the raptors who populated the county's airspace. This one was unmistakable: a condor, its vast black wings recognisably huge despite its altitude.

He sighed. He'd never get Eli back, he knew that. Never hold the child she would have borne them. But maybe he could find a way to make some sort of a life for himself. The last of his enemies was down. He could live out his days in Honduras, grow old with friends like Pera to share the odd beer with. Maybe teach Santiago how to play chess.

He'd called Tara on his way back to Honduras. Once she'd got over being mad at him for faking his own death, she'd cried. Then he had. Finally, they'd lapsed into laughter that, on his side at least, got so uncontrollable he drew the attention of a security guard at the airport – he'd forgotten which one – where he was waiting for a connecting flight.

She'd begged him to turn around and fly straight out to Hong Kong. He'd demurred. He was almost back in Honduras.

Pera interrupted his thoughts. She was holding out a cardboard plate on which rested probably the freshest chicken baleada in all of Honduras.

'Here you go, partner,' she said, beaming. 'I hope you like it.'

'I'm sure I will. How much?'

Pera's eyes widened comically. She pressed fanned fingers to her chest, over her heart. 'How *much*? No charge, that's how much!'

Taking his first bite, he realised just how hungry for real food he was, after several days living off airport and airline cuisine.

He finished his meal and arranged to meet Pera for dinner in Santa Rosa at the end of the day. Arriving back at his place, he parked the Ford and went inside. The day was already unseasonably warm, humid too, so he threw open the back doors and let a cooling breeze clear out the hot, stale air from the house.

He opened a beer, then looked at it and found he didn't want it. He tipped it down the sink and put some coffee on instead.

Later, after an evening with Pera where she excitedly told him how the business was doing – 'flourishing' was her word – he left her and returned to his own house.

Eyes closed, as he waited for sleep, he listened to the *shush* of the surf. If he was expecting other sounds, voices of the departed, for example, to add to the sound of the sea, he was to be disappointed.

All was quiet.

READ ON FOR AN EXTRACT FROM
PURITY KILLS...

...the story of Gabriel's sister.

1

1998 | A SMALL VILLAGE IN GUANGDONG PROVINCE, CHINA

The fish was a giant: Wei Mei had first seen it when her gang had been swimming in the river. An expanse of silver scales that flashed in the sun as it rolled over a few centimetres below the surface and dived for the bottom.

She planned to catch it and then sell it at the market. Think what she could do with the money someone would pay for it.

'You're twelve, Mei,' her best friend, Ping, had said when she'd shared her plan. 'You can't have a stall. The authorities won't permit it.'

'Who cares about the authorities? I'll do it anyway,' she said, folding her arms. 'By the time they find out, it'll be too late.'

Squatting by the edge of the slow-moving water, she pictured the fish snaking along the bottom looking for something tasty to eat.

'Come along, beast,' she murmured, eyes fixed on the softly rippling surface of the river. 'Come and get your dinner.'

So engrossed was she in the hunt that she failed to notice the older boy creeping up on her through the reeds and broad-leaved plants that thronged the bank.

Tan Hu was fifteen. A good head and shoulders taller than Mei and all of her friends except Beanpole. But Beanpole was too skinny to defend himself against the village bully.

Because that's what Tan Hu was. Actually, Wei Mei thought 'bully' wasn't strong enough to describe the kind of boy who would beat up little kids for fun. Throw sharp-edged stones at them when they were playing quietly in the dirt. Or steal their snacks right out of their hands and run off laughing as they cried.

Mei kept the line nice and taut against the current. Behind her, Tan Hu grinned as he manoeuvred into position. Keeping low, he slid a knife from a nylon sheath on his belt. As he watched her, he pressed the palm of his left hand against his groin, enjoying the hot, fluttering sensation it produced in the pit of his belly.

Mei blinked as a flash of sunlight bounced off the water. When she looked again, the tip of her fishing pole was dipping sharply.

With a cry of triumph – 'Got you!' – she jerked the rod up to set the hook in the beast's great bony-lipped mouth. Immediately the rod seemed to fight back, almost pulling free of her hands.

'Oh, no you don't!'

She heaved back and felt the fish resisting her, a surge of power like when you tried to lead a mule with a rope and it didn't feel like coming with you.

Straining every muscle, she levered the rod upright and was rewarded with a flash of silver as the fish broke the surface, rolling and thrashing in the dull green water.

She leaned backwards, and the combined strength of her arms, the bamboo pole and the heavy fishing line brought the beast curving and bucking towards the bank.

Leaning over and trying to avoid the gaping mouth with its double row of ugly, needle-pointed teeth, she stuck her thumb and fingers into its gill slits and clamped down hard. It was cold in there and slippery, but she squeezed tighter and readied herself to yank it out of the water.

She could already imagine what she'd shout at the weekly market.

'Come on, ladies and gents! Who wants this beautiful fish? One-hundred-and-fifty yuan and it's yours.'

She knew she'd have to haggle, but even a hundred would be a fortune.

Then another hand gripped the rod and pulled the giant fish closer. She whirled round, ready to thank whoever was helping her land the beast. And a cold tremor flashed through her.

Still holding the rod, Tan Hu swept his knife out in a wide arc and cut the line.

The fish folded itself double then disappeared back into the green-dark depths, showering the two children with water from its scimitar-like tail fin.

'What did you do that for, you idiot?' Mei shouted.

She punched Tan Hu in the face, drawing blood from his lower lip.

In response, he brought the knife up where she could see it.

'Do what I say or I'll cut you open like a fish belly,' he said. 'Take your clothes off.'

'No!'

He grinned; an oddly disjointed expression as if his lips had forgotten to tell his eyes something was funny.

'My friend here says you will.'

The knife was small, but the blade looked sharp. If she tried to take it off him, he'd probably stab her or give her a good cut. Mei wanted neither. Instead, she meekly said, 'OK, Hu.'

His eyes widened. 'Really?'

'Yes, really. Just turn around.'

'You'll run.'

'No I won't. Anyway, you can run faster than me, you know that,' she said, holding her hands wide. 'So what would be the point?'

He nodded. And, like the stupid brute he was, he did just that.

1

Mei launched herself at him, grabbed a handful of his thick, shaggy hair and pulled back hard. His head snapped back and he howled with pain. Then she dug her fingers into his throat, choking off the sound.

'Try that again and I'll come to your house at night and castrate you with your own knife. I mean it,' she muttered into his ear.

Then she shoved him, hard between the shoulder blades. With a cry, he pitched forwards into the swirling green water of the river they all called Little Mekong, even though the real one was way, way, *way* over to the west.

But as Tan Hu toppled in, Mei's foot slid in a patch of clay where the weeds had been torn away in the scuffle. She went in straight after him.

His head broke the surface a few seconds later. Ten metres downstream from where she was treading water.

'I'll kill you!' he screamed, spraying river water from his mouth.

'Try it!' Mei yelled back. 'Next time maybe I'll slit your belly open.'

He opened his mouth to shout something back but swallowed river water instead. Coughing, he went under again, only to reappear another twenty metres downstream, now facing in the direction of the current and striking out towards an overhanging tree branch.

Mei reached the bank easily: she was a strong swimmer. She hauled herself out and clambered to her feet, careful not to slide straight back in on the slippery red mud.

Laughing, she ran back the way she'd come, through bamboo and the pink-berried plants with long, sharp-pointed leaves that had earned them their nickname: Devil's Tongue.

Halfway back to the village she looked over her shoulder, just to check Tan Hu wasn't after her. Maybe he'd try it on again later, but she'd be ready for him this time. Probably she ought to take a knife from the kitchen just in case.

She looked forward again and crashed into Ping, who was running the other way.

Mei jarred her ribs as she tripped and fell onto the hard-packed red earth of the track. Ping stumbled, but stayed upright. Hurriedly, she pulled on Mei's wrists, dragging her to her feet.

'What is it?' Mei asked her friend as she rubbed her elbow. 'You look like a demon's chasing you.'

Ping's eyes were wide. 'There's a man at your house. He's got a gun! He was pointing it at your mum and shouting.'

Mei's heart was thumping in her chest. She'd forgotten all about the pain from the collision.

'What about? What was he shouting? Tell me!'

'You!'

'What do you mean, me?'

'He said she had to tell him where you were. He said he was taking you away. And he's wearing a suit!'

This was bad. Nobody from round here wore suits. The only people who had guns *and* suits were Party officials. Mei had seen them now and again when Mummy had taken her into Shenzhen. Mummy would delight in pointing them out.

'*See those two over there? They're Party. Secret police, most likely. If they don't like you, you just disappear. Turn up three weeks later in a ditch outside the city limits with a bullet in your brain.*'

At the time, Mei thought Mummy Rita was doing a poor job of frightening her. But one was actually here, in the village. And looking for her.

Mei took Ping by her narrow, bony shoulders.

'Listen, Ping. Listen to me really carefully,' she said. 'Go back to the village. Just act normal. If he asks you, say you haven't seen me.'

'Why? What are you going to do?'

'I'm going to get a better look at this guy without him seeing me.'

Ping's eyes widened.

'That's a really bad idea. What if he spots you?'

Mei grinned.

1

'He won't!'

With Ping gone, Mei turned off the track. She knew the woods round the village like her own skin. Every animal track, every fallen tree, every patch of boggy ground that would swallow you whole if you fell in.

She started working her way back to the village using every bit of her skill. She'd come out in a stand of bamboo just behind the house. Dense enough to hide in, but with enough light coming in between the thick green stems to spy on the house.

She wanted to get a good look at whoever was threatening her mum. Eventually he'd leave and then Mei would have a think about what to do afterwards. But, for now, she just needed to see him.

Reaching the house meant pushing through some dense patches of spiny shrubs. They had inch-long thorns hidden amongst gaudy orange flowers with black centres. It didn't seem fair that such pretty flowers concealed those evil little spikes.

By the time she reached the stand of bamboo, her arms, legs and face were scratched and bleeding. But that was fine. Scratches healed.

She peered through. At first she couldn't see either Mummy Rita or the Party man. Then she heard him. A deep, boomy voice riding over the top of Mummy's higher one.

'Where is she?'

'I told you already, Jian! I don't know. She's a naughty girl. Always running off. Never in school when she should be,' Mummy said, repeating the complaints she usually threw in Mei's direction. 'She spends every day by the river or in the forest. Why don't you look there?'

'Oh, I will. Maybe for now I'll just sit here. Bring me some jasmine tea.'

Mei frowned. Not at his rudeness. In her experience, men were usually rude to women. Party men, especially. But because Mummy Rita had called the man by his name. Jian.

That was weird. As far as Mei knew, the village headman was

the only Party official Mummy knew. And this wasn't him. And why did she sound cross with him and not frightened?

She decided it didn't matter. She'd ask Mummy later. What mattered was making sure the fat Party man with the gun didn't catch her.

And anyway, she had no idea what she might have done to attract the attention of the Party in the first place.

Sure, like Mummy said, she skipped school most days. But honestly, what was she going to do with all that stuff about fractions and minerals and the history of the People's Republic of China?

The stuff she really needed to know? How to fight off boys like Tan Hu? How to snap a chicken's neck? How to milk a goat or tell which berries in the forest were OK to eat? Those, she either knew already or could ask real people in the village, like the blacksmith or one of the farmers.

She took one last look at the man with his shiny silver gun and his slicked-back hair. *See you later, Mr Party Man!*

Something crackled in the dry grass behind her. Maybe a rat. Too loud for a mouse or one of the big purplish-black beetles that trundled around the place pushing balls of cow dung. She prepared to go.

The pincers that suddenly clamped on the back of her neck made her scream. A giant stag beetle had got her! She felt herself rising to a standing position without using her legs.

'Got you!' a man said from behind her.

With his fingers still digging into the soft flesh at the sides of her neck, the man marched Mei over to her house.

The fat man got to his feet, a broad smile on his face revealing flashing gold teeth. He put the gun away in a leather holster inside his suit jacket.

Mei was terrified. She started gabbling.

'Look, I don't know what I've done, OK? But I'm sorry. I love the Party. I love Chairman Mao. And all the ones in charge now. I know I've skipped school, but I can explain. Just, please don't hurt my mum. I'm a disobedient girl. I never do what she says, it drives her mad, she can't control me. I'm—'

The torrent of phrases, most of which had come originally from Mummy Rita's own lips, dried as the fat man burst out laughing.

'Wait! You think I'm with the *Party*?'

He laughed harder, only stopping when a fit of coughing seized him. Bending double, hands flat on his wide thighs, he shook his head until the coughing stopped.

He pulled a red handkerchief from a pocket and wiped his streaming eyes.

'You hear that?' he said to the man gripping Mei's neck, 'She thinks we're with the Party!'

'Fat chance,' the man said, chuckling deep in his chest.

The first man cleared his throat and sighed out a big breath.

'Listen, Mei, I'm about as far from being a Party man as you can ever imagine,' he said. 'You won't remember me, but I've known you since you were a baby. I'm here to take you back to Hong Kong.'

'What?'

Mei couldn't believe what he was saying. Hong Kong? Why? And if he wasn't a Party man, what was he?

'Hong Kong,' he said. 'A place of opportunity, still, despite the handover.'

Mei had no idea what he was talking about. What handover? But she did know there was no way she was going to Hong Kong with him. She wasn't going *anywhere* with him.

She slapped at the man's hands around her neck.

'Get off me.'

Mei watched the fat man signal something with his eyes over her head. The other man let go of her neck.

'Do you need to get some things before we leave?' the fat man asked.

'I need to pee. Your bully-boy frightened me,' she said.

Fat man laughed again. 'Fine. But don't even think of running off. We'll only catch you.'

Mei shrugged. 'Who said I was going to run? Hong Kong sounds fun. And I hate it here anyway.'

Mummy Rita reappeared just as she said this. Mei watched her face crumple. Her lips trembled as she handed the small china cup of tea to the man she'd called Jian. Mei felt guilt wash through her. But she couldn't explain she'd only said it to get the fat man to relax.

'Fine,' he said. 'But be quick. We've got a long journey ahead of us.'

Mei nodded. She walked off around the side of the house. As soon as she was out of sight, she ran. She ran as fast as she'd ever run in her life.

She found Ping playing down by the stream that fed the Little Mekong.

'Ping!' she hissed. 'I have to go.'

'What? Where?'

'Shenzhen. That guy's not from the Party. I don't who he is, and I don't care. But he's not taking me to Hong Kong.'

Ping's lower lip trembled.

'You're coming back, though, right? When they've gone, I mean.'

Mei smiled. 'Of course, silly.' She had an idea. 'Look, if you really, really need to find me, leave a message somewhere only we know about.'

'But where?' Ping asked, crying properly now.

Mei looked up. Where would be a good place for a secret message? Mummy always took her to the big city on the bus. Yes! That was it.

'The bus station,' she said. 'Where the bus from here pulls in. Queue number seven. There's a stand selling *People's Daily*. All decorated with red-and-yellow banners. The hammer and sickle.'

Ping smiled tearily, wiping her snotty nose with the back of her hand.

'I know it. We went to Shenzhen last year. Dad bought a copy off the sales lady.'

'Put your message inside an empty drinks can and squash it

flat,' Mei said, 'then leave it at the back of the stand. I'll check every week.'

Ping nodded, gave an almighty sniff, then turned and ran back towards the village. Just before she disappeared out of sight, she turned and raised a hand in a farewell wave.

* * *

Three months passed. As did Mei's thirteenth birthday. Every week for her first month in Shenzhen, she checked round the back of the *People's Daily* stand at the bus station.

But soon after arriving, she fell in with a group of street kids and found she enjoyed the life. Stealing food from stalls, and wallets from head-swivelling tourists. Running from the cops if a daring raid caused too much commotion. Sleeping on the top floor of an unused carpark, warm in the humid night air of high summer.

Little by little, her memories of the village faded as the thrills of city living took hold of her.

2

THREE YEARS LATER, SHENZHEN MEGACITY, CHINA

With her practised thief's eye, Wei Mei spots the three rich kids before Binyan does.

She picks out her mark. The one on the left, nearest the road. She can hit him, snag his wallet, chuck an apology over her shoulder – '*Sorry, mate, wasn't looking where I was going!*' – then escape through the traffic.

He won't follow. His threads look too new, too fancy, too damned expensive. No way he's going to risk a chase across nine lanes of traffic. He might fall down and get his wuvvly wittle blazer dirty and then what would Mummy and Daddy say?

She snorts. Who is she kidding? They'd probably buy him two more to replace it. His mates'll cluster round him, when any fool knows you leave the fallen man and go after the attacker.

Has Binyan even noticed? Probably not. He's probably daydreaming about setting his next fire. It's how he got his nickname.

Spark just about sums him up. Show a normal kid an empty

car or an abandoned building and they look for stuff they can sell on. Spark starts looking for matches.

Weirdo! But she likes him, just the same. They hang out together every day. Binyan calls her Juice.

'Because you've got the juice. You know, the rush, the swagger,' he exclaims, when she presses him for an explanation. 'The juice!'

But Mei knows better. She heard him once, talking to another member of their gang. 'Plum juice, man. It's my favourite.'

Her name means Beautiful Plum. Spark's in love with her. Or so he thinks. That's OK. He never tries anything. Good job, too, 'cause he'd have to learn to piss like a girl if he did.

She nudges him.

'I spy dinner,' she murmurs.

Spark nods. 'I got your back,' he mutters.

It's a tried and tested routine. She goes in for the kill, Spark lingers, ready to trip a pursuer or generally get in the way: whichever'll give Mei time to get away with the loot. Then they find somewhere quiet to divvy up the spoils.

The snazzily-dressed trio are about five metres away now. They've got that look. Not just the money. The confidence.

It comes from knowing they're protected. Not by bodyguards, nothing so obvious. Though she and Spark aren't averse to rolling the odd executive or tourist dogged by some shaven-headed goon with a bulge on his belt.

No. These kids have *protection*. The only kind that really matters. Their parents are high-ups in the Party. You fuck with them, the Party fucks you straight back. But, like, a thousand times worse.

Last year a girl – who they called Panda, on account of her striking black and white hairdo – pulled a knife on a Party kid and took his wallet.

'Total result,' she crowed later, round the fire on the top of an abandoned building as she showed them the genuine dollar bills the kid'd been carrying around.

Panda turned up dead three days after that. Slung onto a pile of stinking rubbish behind a cafe. Eyes crudely gouged out. Fingers removed. A Party pin hit so hard into the skin of her forehead it had lodged in the bone beneath. Her mouth stuffed with a crumpled sheet of glossy, coloured paper that, when they hooked it out, depicted a smiling Chairman Mao.

In blood-red writing, someone had added an unofficial slogan:

THIEVES NEVER LAUGH FOR LONG

Poor Panda. Mei had stretched out a hand and stroked her cheek. The dried blood gave her skin a sandpapery feel. They couldn't bury her. It wasn't their style, in any case. They just left her and moved on. You had to.

The Party kids are only a couple of metres away now.

Mei's heart is racing. It's mostly excitement. She's never been caught and doesn't intend to start now. Mostly excitement, sure. Maybe a little jag of fear running through the middle of it all like a guitar string vibrating.

'Ready?' she hisses.

'Ready,' Spark hisses back.

Mei takes a step to her left and then, as the Party kids draw level, stumbles sideways and gives the nearest one a hefty bump on the shoulder.

'Hey! What the fuck?'

He spins round. Shiny, well-fed face a mask of righteous indignation. *Where do they learn that expression?* she has time to wonder.

'Sorry, man,' she says holding him by the shoulder with her left hand, while her right snakes inside his Burberry bomber jacket. This style has the inside pocket on the right. 'I tripped. Are you all right? Did I hurt you?'

He sneers. Behind him, his two friends are watching with smirks on their faces.

'Yes, Ren,' one says sarcastically, 'did the street rat hurt you? Shall we call a private ambulance? Shall we get her friend here to fetch you a glass of water?'

2

'Piss off, Ching!' he snaps. He glares at Mei. 'Of course you didn't hurt me, you little street whore. Now fuck off.'

Which Mei is happy to do, his fat leather wallet nestling inside her own jacket. She and Spark are halfway across the road when a shout goes up.

'Hey! The little bitch stole my wallet!'

'Get her!' the one called Ching shouts.

Without turning her head, Mei shouts, 'Run!'

It's force of habit: Spark doesn't need telling. Together they dart through the traffic, zig-zagging between cars, motorbikes, vans and trucks.

Ignoring the parps and toots from the drivers' horns, Mei streaks for the pavement on the far side of Shennan Avenue, almost bumping into a drably-dressed woman fiddling with oversized sunglasses.

Mei's grinning. The Party kids won't dare chase them into the stinking, smoking traffic; once she and Spark are safe on the other side, they can dodge into an alley and make their way home via the back streets.

There's a loud bang. And a scream. A boy's scream.

Spark's scream.

She looks back, just for a second. Through a gap in the traffic she sees her friend lying in the road. Something's happened to his neck. His head's at completely the wrong angle.

Beyond him, she sees the three rich boys charging towards her. The leading boy, the one she rolled, actually leaps over Spark. His teeth are bared.

'Come here, whore!' he yells.

Tears streaming down her cheeks, Mei sprints away. Poor Spark. She hopes he's just injured. That some kind person will gather him up and take him to hospital.

Yes. That's what will happen. And once he's better, he'll discharge himself and come and find her. But for now, she needs to put some serious distance between her and the rich kids.

Mei reaches the safety of the pavement, although it's choked with people and keeping ahead of the rich kids is proving hard.

352

Now she can feel it. Fear. She doesn't want to end up like Panda.

She weaves through the oncoming shoppers like a snake, twisting and turning her body while keeping her balance as she races down the street. She's got a destination in mind. A place where she knows every square centimetre: every climbable fence, every blind alley, every elevated walkway, every nook, cranny and hidey-hole.

She reaches the side street that leads to the building site and – *Oh, thank you, thank you!* – it's almost deserted. Just a couple in drab, much-washed, old-people clothes gumming their way through coconut cakes they're eating out of a paper bag.

She skips round them and hurtles through the gates into the deserted site. The workers have all been redeployed to another city project. It's why she and Spark like to hang out here.

She risks a look over her shoulder.

Shit! The lead boy is only twenty metres away.

A lump of concrete the size of a mango whizzes past Wei Mei's head and bounces harmlessly off a corrugated-iron sheet with a loud clang.

'Come back here, bitch!' he screams after her. 'I order you!'

Yeah, like she'd follow *his* orders.

Mei runs on, deeper into the huge building site.

A fire is burning in a blue-painted oil drum. Three peasants from the countryside are gathered round it. They're passing a bottle from one brown hand to another.

They look over, mouths agape. Like they've never seen a sixteen-year-old girl fleeing three Party kids for her life before. Idiots!

Another lump of concrete flies past her head and strikes the oil drum with a boom like the world's most out-of-tune gong. She laughs. He might be rich, he might be protected, but he's got a shit right hand.

Mei streaks around a huge red-and-yellow crane and through the slit in the chain-link fencing she and Spark cut last month. This is the supply yard and it's the perfect place to lose them.

2

Huge piles of stone slabs, bricks and bamboo scaffolding poles everywhere.

She vaults a stack of wooden pallets and skids sharp-left down a narrow corridor between two temporary cabins the workers use.

Then her heart stops. One of the rich kids appears at the far end, turning the light to dark.

'Got you now, bitch,' he says with an evil smile.

Mei turns, intending to run back the other way. Then her hopes explode. Ching is standing at the other end. She's trapped.

3

They advance on her. Walking. More of that confidence they get spoon-fed from the moment they're born.

'I bet she's a virgin,' Ching calls out to his friend.

'Not for much longer!' he calls back.

Mei looks up. The cabins are about two and a half metres tall. Their sides are smooth.

She turns sideways onto the two boys, braces her back against one cabin and her left foot against the other. She's done this before, in the hills where she and Spark found a really cool cliff for practising being famous mountaineers.

With a grunt, she lifts her right foot off the ground and sticks it against the wall at her back.

Now she starts climbing. Push up, reposition left foot. Lift hands and stick the palms against the hot metal. Push up again. Reposition right foot.

The boys have reached the spot where she was standing a moment ago. The one called Ching stretches up a hand and manages to grab her dangling right sneaker. She jerks her knee up, pulling her foot free of his grasping hand, then kicks out and catches him a glancing blow across the face.

'Shit! You broke my cheekbone, bitch. You're going to pay for that,' he screams up at her.

What is he *talking* about? She's wearing knockoff Nike Air Jordans. How the fuck does he think she broke his bone with a squishy lump of foam?

He's jumping up, but she's safely out of range. Another couple of pushes and she's on the roof of the cabin.

She runs to the far side and looks over the edge. It's a big drop to the ground, but there's a pile of empty sacks about two metres out from the cabin. In the distance, she sees the peasants still round their oil drum. The rising heat makes their faces wobble. One looks over, smiles and waves. She sighs. How do they ever think they're going to survive in the city, acting like dumb cows?

The boys are shouting. Calling out. The usual names. Bitch. Whore. Cunt. Mei grins. They're down there and she's up here.

She backs up a few paces, gets into a sprinter's crouch, then hurtles towards the edge, leads with her right foot and leaps, arms outstretched, sailing over the gap, over the hard concrete strewn with cigarette butts and broken glass, and lands with a perfect roll on the pile of sacks.

She rolls to the edge and stands…and comes face-to-face with the third boy. Who she totally forgot about.

He's holding a stave of wood. He swings, but he telegraphs the move with an exaggerated backswing and Mei ducks as the club whistles towards her face.

The wood glances off the side of her head, spinning it round. Her vision darkens and tiny red fireworks pop around the edge of her vision. She staggers, but then is on her feet and running.

'Come back here, you!' he shouts.

Now she hears two more sets of running footsteps. The side of her face is warm. She puts up her hand and her palm comes away covered in blood. It's fine. She's had worse.

Hoping to throw them off by a metre or two, she tips her hips to the right, then suddenly jinks left, scooting round the back of a cute yellow dumper-truck, its scoop full of red sand.

But she's miscalculated.

She's boxed herself in between tight-packed pallets of bricks. She leaps towards the first stack and starts climbing. The toe of her Air Jordan misses the lip where one brick stands proud of its fellows and drags her fingertips painfully out of the crack she's wedged them into.

Searing pain shoots up her left arm, all the way from her fingers to her shoulder. She looks. Two nails have torn down to the quicks.

Then a hand grabs her right shoulder and spins her round. The incoming blow knocks her over, her head narrowly missing the edge of a column of bricks. A kick to her midsection drives the wind from her and she curls into a little ball.

'I've got her,' her attacker shouts. 'Here! I've got the little bitch.'

Groaning with the effort of pulling air into her bruised chest, Mei levers herself into a sitting position, but he kicks her arm out from under her.

'You're going nowhere, cockroach,' he says with a triumphant smile.

Sweat sheens his round face, which is the bright red of a ripe tomato like the ones Mummy Rita used to grow back in the village.

For a second, Mei wishes she'd never left. That she was back there now, wandering the hard-packed red-dirt roads, singing to herself, or helping one of the farmers drive oxen to a new paddy.

The two other boys arrive, out of breath. Panting. Their sleek haircuts are properly mussed up now and they've got smudges on their soap-washed faces. As for the clothes, Mei reckons Mummy and Daddy might have a few sharp words on *that* score.

'You stole Dalei's wallet,' the boy says.

She's identified him as the leader. That makes him the most dangerous. But also it makes the other two vulnerable. They'll look to him for a steer on how it's going to go down. And they get their courage from him, too. So he's the one she needs to deal with first.

'He can get more money. I can't,' Mei spits back, pushing herself away from them with her hands and heels.

He puts his hands on his hips.

'Do you know who we are?'

She thinks of the famous clowns from the State Circus. 'Are you Piggy, Ducks and Uncle Sam?'

He scowls. 'Ha, ha. Our fathers are members of the Shenzhen People's Governing Committee. They're very powerful. You picked the wrong boys, men, I mean, to tangle with.'

The one called Ren looks at his leader. 'Come on, Dalei, I thought we were going to fuck her. I'm as horny as a goat.'

That's when she pulls her knees up to her chest in a lightning-fast crunch, braces her hands against the gritty concrete beneath her and shoots her right leg out. Her heel connects square-on with the front of his expensive American denims. He emits a high-pitched squeal, like a pig when the village butcher draws his long, sharp blade across its throat.

He falls sideways and Mei rolls onto her belly and is on her feet in a second. There's nowhere to escape to, and she's had it with running, anyway.

The one called Dalei looks panicked. His eyes are wide and Mei sees the fear in them. Good. He's not used to his victims fighting back.

He swings wildly at her. She doesn't even have to duck, the blow is so poor. She just leans back a little as his fist passes harmlessly in front of her face. Then she lunges and gives him a faceful of clawed fingers, aiming for the eyes, but content to hit him anywhere on that expanse of fat, pork-fed flesh.

She catches him across the nose and one fingertip slips, disgustingly, inside, but the real damage happens when her index finger, tipped with a torn and dirty nail, scrapes across his eyeball. He screams and his hands fly to his face. Mei shoves him hard and he trips over his own feet and tumbles to the ground.

She turns and meets Ching's incoming fist which chops her across the neck: a vicious blow that sends a spear of agony lancing across her chest and making her feel sick.

Staggering, she lets herself stumble sideways as if she's hurt worse than she is. She crashes against the nearest pallet of bricks, but the sound is mostly where she shoves them with her right hip. She straightens and swings her right hand across in a fast, tight arc.

When she connects with the side of Ching's head, he emits a short, grunting groan. His eyes roll up in their sockets. Mei drops the sharp-cornered brick to the ground. Blood is coursing down his face from the wound to his temple. He is still on his feet.

He groans again; an odd, disconnected sound as if it's coming out of his body and not his mouth. Then he falls sideways, slamming into the pile of bricks before coming to rest on the ground. A pool of dark-red blood the colour of ripe plums spreads out beneath his head.

A hand grabs her ankle. She looks down. Dalei, is it? The one whose eye is closed and weeping a slimy mixture streaked with red. He's trying to pull himself to his feet using her leg as a support.

'I'll kill you, you little whore,' he croaks.

'Not today,' she says.

She stamps hard on his other hand and hears a crackle like dry twigs snapping.

Yowling like an alley-cat, he lets go of her ankle. Mei turns to see Ren, still rolling around, both hands clutching his private parts. Funny. She'd have thought he'd be feeling better by now. But time slows down when you're fighting. She thinks about braining him with a brick, then shakes her head. They've learned their lesson.

She's about to go, then smiles. Taps her forehead. *Silly me!*

Bending, she relieves the other two boys of their wallets and sprints away from them. She stops briefly at the group of peasants round the improvised brazier. Hands them one of the wallets.

'Here. No need to go to work today,' she says with a grin, then runs off back towards the street.

She fails to notice the new arrival among the group, a woman dressed in a dowdy blue smock and loose matching pants. Perhaps because the adrenaline is messing with her perception. Or maybe just because the woman seems so utterly insignificant, even among a boring group of country bumpkins.

NEWSLETTER

Join my no-spam newsletter for new book news, competitions, offers and more…

Follow Andy Maslen

Bookbub has a New release Alert. You can check out the latest book deals and get news of every new book I publish by following me here.

BingeBooks has regular author chats plus lists, reviews and personalised newsletters. Follow me here.

Website www.andymaslen.com.
Email andy@andymaslen.com.
Facebook group, The Wolfe Pack.

© 2023 Sunfish Ltd

Published by Tyton Press, an imprint of Sunfish Ltd, PO Box 2107, Salisbury SP2 2BW.

The right of Andy Maslen to be identified as the author of this work has been asserted by him in accordance with the Copyright, Designs and Patents Act 1988.

Cover illustration copyright © Nick Castle

Author photograph © Kin Ho

Edited by Nicola Lovick

❀ Created with Vellum

ACKNOWLEDGMENTS

I want to thank you for buying this book. I hope you enjoyed it.

As an author is only part of the team of people who make a book the best it can be, this is my chance to thank the people on *my* team.

For his insightful first read and suggestions, my first reader and sternest critic, Simon Alphonso.

For their brilliant copy-editing and proofreading Nicola Lovick and Liz Ward.

For his super-cool cover, my designer, Nick Castle.

The members of my Facebook Group, The Wolfe Pack, who are an incredibly supportive and also helpful bunch of people. Thank you to them, also.

And for being an inspiration and source of love and laughter, and making it all worthwhile, my family: Jo, Rory and Jacob.

The responsibility for any and all mistakes in this book remains mine.

Andy Maslen
Salisbury, 2023

ABOUT THE AUTHOR

Photo © 2020 Kin Ho

Andy Maslen was born in Nottingham, England. After leaving university with a degree in psychology, he worked in business for thirty years as a copywriter. In his spare time, he plays the guitar. He lives in Wiltshire.